T0176281

Titles by Shayla Black

The Devoted Lovers Novels

DEVOTED TO PLEASURE

DEVOTED TO LOVE

The Wicked Lovers Novels

WICKED TIES

DECADENT

DELICIOUS

SURRENDER TO ME

BELONG TO ME

MINE TO HOLD

OURS TO LOVE

WICKED ALL NIGHT
(novella)

THEIRS TO CHERISH

HIS TO TAKE

WICKED FOR YOU

FALLING IN DEEPER

HOLDING ON TIGHTER

The Perfect Gentlemen Novels
(with Lexi Blake)

SCANDAL NEVER SLEEPS

SEDUCTION IN SESSION

BIG EASY TEMPTATION

Anthologies

FOUR PLAY
(with Maya Banks)

HOT IN HANDCUFFS
(with Sylvia Day and Shiloh Walker)

WICKED AND DANGEROUS
(with Rhyannon Byrd)

Specials

HER FANTASY MEN

The Sexy Capers Series

BOUND AND DETERMINED

STRIP SEARCH

ARRESTING DESIRE
(novella)

DEVOTED to LOVE

SHAYLA BLACK

JOVE
NEW YORK

A JOVE BOOK
Published by Berkley
An imprint of Penguin Random House LLC
1745 Broadway, New York, NY 10019

Copyright © 2019 by Shelley Bradley, LLC
Penguin Random House supports copyright. Copyright fuels creativity, encourages
diverse voices, promotes free speech, and creates a vibrant culture. Thank you for buying
an authorized edition of this book and for complying with copyright laws by not
reproducing, scanning, or distributing any part of it in any form without permission.
You are supporting writers and allowing Penguin Random House to continue to
publish books for every reader.

A JOVE BOOK, BERKLEY, and the BERKLEY & B colophon
are registered trademarks of Penguin Random House LLC.

Library of Congress Cataloging-in-Publication Data

Names: Black, Shayla, author.
Title: Devoted to love / Shayla Black.
Description: First Edition. | New York : Berkley, 2019. |
Series: A Devoted Lovers novel ; 2
Identifiers: LCCN 2018059572 | ISBN 9780399587382 (paperback) |
ISBN 9780399587399 (ebook)
Subjects: | BISAC: FICTION / Romance / Contemporary. |
FICTION / Romance / Suspense. |
FICTION / Romance / General. | GSAFD: Romantic suspense fiction.
Classification: LCC PS3602.L325245 D489 2019 | DDC 813/.6—dc23
LC record available at https://lccn.loc.gov/2018059572

First Edition: July 2019

Printed in the United States of America
1   3   5   7   9   10   8   6   4   2

Cover photo by Claudio Marinesco
Cover design by Judith Murello
Book design by Kristen del Rosario

To my constant helpers, the duo who's with me every day,
cheering me on and making sure I'm not alone
as I write ever closer to The End.

Floyd and Fiona, you're the best felines an author could ask for.
Thanks for the hours of moral support
cleverly disguised as naps in my office chair,
for never forgetting to remind me when it's meal time—
or rather, five o'clock—
and for prompting me to take breaks now and then
by lounging on my keyboard.

Love you two fur babies!
My writing would be less joyful without you . . .

CHAPTER 1

his has to be one of the most unusual weddings ever," Josiah Grant
murmured in his boss's ear as his stare passed over the small, hodgepodge crowd gathered for the ceremony.

Was that Jennifer Lawrence on the opposite side of the aisle, one
row back?

Logan Edgington, part owner of EM Security, cast a cautious gaze
around the room, too. "You got that right. My wife says the bride is
wearing a dress by Monique Lhuillier—I guess she's some important
designer?—to get married in a barn."

"Hollywood types . . ." he joked.

Despite the TV show that had made her famous being recently can-
celed, Shealyn West was still a star—one Hollywood had proven reluctant to release from the limelight. No surprise; she was a beautiful
woman with a talent for playing roles convincingly. Josiah's teammate
and fellow operative, Cutter Bryant, had been a lucky son of a bitch the
day he'd drawn the assignment to protect the gorgeous blonde's body.

"Actually, I meant the guest list," Josiah went on as he spotted
James Franco across the room. "Special agents and paparazzi don't
mix. Throw in ranch hands rubbing elbows with movie stars while
half the guests are packing . . . I'm worried there might be trouble."

Logan nodded. "Hell, I'm half expecting it. And if you add in that big compound just outside town?"

"Enlightenment Fields." Josiah snorted. "Sounds like mumbo-jumbo bullshit and a snake-oil salesman had a baby. That place made the hair on the back of my neck stand up."

"Me, too. That's another reason I called you here at the last minute. I did some reading up on the group. Its leader, Adam Coleman, supposedly trained with some guru in India a few years back, then returned to the States and started gathering followers. He teaches them about 'spiritual evolution' through surrendering the ego."

"If that's what it takes to be spiritually evolved, everyone who works at EM would be shit out of luck." Josiah couldn't see any of them giving up their self-respect, pride, or free will for any reason.

"Amen."

"As I drove in this morning, I saw the signs about conscious awakening, whatever that means. The guy sounds like a fruit loop."

"Fruit loops can be dangerous."

"Absolutely."

"Turns out Coleman and Enlightenment Fields own most of the land south of town for miles," Logan said quietly. "Maggie told me they've been trying to buy her grandparents' ranch for months. They've repeatedly refused the group's offers."

Josiah didn't blame them. The West family obviously loved their ranch. The pride of ownership showed in the homey place and the well-tended cattle. Besides, Shealyn's grandparents were older now and this had been home for decades. All their memories were here. Where else would they go?

"Understandable. Who's Maggie?" Since he'd only arrived this morning, he hadn't yet met everyone.

"Shealyn's younger sister."

She must be the beautiful blonde who'd been hustling Shealyn out the front door and into a big SUV when he'd arrived. As they'd passed one another, they had exchanged a long, lingering glance. She was so hot, she'd damn near burned his retinas.

"Yeah? What do you know about her?"

A grin quirked at Logan's lips. "What do you want to know?"

"Fucker." His boss was toying with him. "Is she single?"

"As far as I know."

Suddenly, he minded way less that he'd been ordered to attend this wedding to manage any possible threat. He had nothing against Cutter and his bride-to-be; he simply wasn't into matrimony. But some pretty female scenery would definitely make this last-minute trip more pleasant. "Excellent."

As Logan laughed, Josiah glanced at his watch, eager to lay eyes on the bride's sister again. "Wasn't this ceremony supposed to start ten minutes ago?"

"They're running a bit behind. The family was stunned and upset this morning to hear about their neighbor's murder."

Josiah had heard the whispers when he'd arrived. "An old man, right?"

Logan nodded. "Everyone is on edge. Apparently, he taught Shealyn and Maggie how to ride when they were kids. They considered him something of an uncle."

And from what Josiah had heard, the local police had no suspects. Someone had walked into the victim's house and pitchforked the seventy-year-old widower to the floor, leaving him to bleed out. No clues. No witnesses. No motive. No mercy.

So far, nothing about this town sat well with him.

Suddenly, the background music grew louder. Cutter entered the barn through a side door and trekked to the altar, looking both confident and proud. His older brother, Cage, followed, his expression solemn. Another guy Josiah didn't know trailed behind him. Someone nearby whispered that he was a high school pal of Cutter's.

The music changed again. Everyone turned and focused their attention on the back of the barn, decorated with white tulle, pale satin ribbons, and rustic-chic chandeliers. Discreetly placed space heaters kept the interior toasty, despite the January chill.

Carrying a bouquet of white daisies, a brunette appeared at the back of the room, her long hair arranged in beachy waves, her dark eyes sparkling. She somehow maintained a hint of innocence, despite the slight bulge of a baby belly under her flowing burgundy dress.

"That's Brea Bell, Cutter's next-door neighbor. She's like a little sister to him," Logan murmured.

"She's the girl One-Mile keeps getting in Cutter's face about?" At Logan's nod, Josiah asked, "*Did* Walker get her pregnant?"

Logan shrugged. He didn't know, but that expression said he was mighty interested in the answer. "I haven't pried . . . but that's my guess."

Holy shit. Pierce Walker, aka One-Mile, was a loner and an acerbic bastard. He and Cutter had been at each other's throats for months, and Josiah had known it had something to do with a woman. Brea's pregnancy would explain all that.

Thankfully, Walker wasn't at this wedding or shit would be going down.

As Brea made her way up the aisle, Maggie appeared behind her, golden hair upswept, eyes that looked neither blue nor green glittering, gray lace cupping breasts he'd love to get his hands and mouth on.

As he stared, Josiah flashed hot. He hadn't been imagining how gorgeous she was. If anything, she was more beautiful than he remembered.

Maggie floated past, casting him a sidelong glance. Their gazes connected for an instant. A strong zing zipped through his body before most of his blood jetted south.

The lust bug had bitten him hard.

A secretive smile flitted across her face as she focused forward and continued down the aisle. She wasn't immune, either. Good. If he played this right, tonight could be mighty interesting . . .

When Josiah caught sight of her backless dress and the exposed line of her spine, his jaw dropped and he rephrased his last statement. Tonight *would* be interesting. He was determined.

Seconds later, the music swelled once more. Everyone stood. The bride appeared at the back of the room. When the guests turned to her, they gave a collective gasp. No denying she looked absolutely radiant. Lace hugged her famous curves from the straps clinging to her slender shoulders to the womanly swells of her hips before giving way to the tulle skirt sprinkled with appliqué flowers. She glowed with happiness and looked at Cutter like he was a king. Bryant was a good guy, and if Shealyn made him happy . . . Well, Josiah wished them the best. This marriage gig worked out for some, and maybe Shealyn was actually the kind of woman who, despite being a celebrity, kept her promises. It happened for some lucky bastards.

Josiah refused to take his chances again.

The ceremony was brief but heartfelt. Together, they lit candles and said a few words to their closest family. Cutter's mom beamed when they handed her a rose. Shealyn's grandmother sobbed. Her mother looked so blessed and proud as she gripped the stem and kissed her daughter's cheek.

After that, the bride and groom had eyes only for each other, sharing promises of devotion and vows of love in front of their friends and family and in the presence of God. They kissed with abandon as people clapped. Someone let loose a whoop.

Then the newly married couple ran back down the aisle with clasped hands and shared laughter. Josiah hoped for their sake the good times lasted.

He focused on Maggie as she trailed behind her sister, her hand resting on Cage's arm. Josiah might have felt an urge to tear Cutter's older brother away from the pretty blonde he had every intention of propositioning tonight, but the guy wasn't paying a lick of attention to Maggie. Instead, he scanned the crowd for someone else, but came up seemingly empty and miserable.

"What's up with him?" Josiah gave a head bob at Cage.

"He hooked up with Karis, Heath's sister-in-law, at my brother's New Year's Eve party. Now, she won't return his calls. I guess Cage was hoping Karis would be here today, but she backed out of attending. She has a 'cold.'"

Another example of "love." Poor chump.

As soon as the wedding party exited the barn, the guests stood and made their way to the giant white tent pitched a few feet across the yard. Tables were set with pristine linens and accented with elegant splashes of gray and burgundy. Balloons rose all around the room. Flowers bloomed everywhere. Whoever had risen to the challenge of putting on a Hollywood-worthy wedding in the dead of winter in small-town Texas in just under four weeks had done a superhuman job.

The guests milled around, grabbing flutes of champagne from passing waiters and chatting as soft music floated in from speakers around the temporary structure. Josiah saw another handful of stars he recognized, including a few from Shealyn's former TV show, *Hot Southern Nights*. Someone introduced him to a music producer who would be working on Shealyn's upcoming album, as well as a TV executive determined to sign her to a new drama for the fall. The person he didn't see was Maggie. After a few discreet inquiries, he learned the whole wedding party had returned to the barn for pictures.

Impatiently, he paced. Stars and their bodyguards collected in one corner. All the operatives had spread around the perimeter of the room. His peers looked relaxed on the surface, but he knew their watchful, twitchy natures. He shared it. None of them was remotely chill.

A bustling forty-something woman he'd seen fluttering around the barn entered, scanning the room frantically.

"What's wrong?" he asked.

She zipped her stare to him and shoved a dark lock of hair from her face. "I'm Sarah, the wedding planner. We're having a little emergency. One of the bridesmaids is dizzy and needs some food and water now."

Maggie? That possibility worried Josiah. "I'll find both and bring them to you."

Sarah gave him a wilted nod. "Thank you. This wedding has been a whirlwind of insanity. Four weeks, and trying to plan everything during the holidays . . ."

Originally, Cutter and Shealyn had planned to elope to Vegas, but both families had been adamant that they wanted to attend the nuptials. Since Cutter insisted on hustling Shealyn to the altar as quickly as possible, this wedding had been rushed. All the tabloids were speculating that the bride was pregnant.

"You did great," he said in all sincerity. "Get back to the wedding party. I'll be right there."

"Yeah. Great. Thanks . . ." She sighed. "After tonight, I'm going to sleep for a month."

Then Sarah was gone.

Quickly, he barged to the front of the bartender's line with apologies and swiped a tall glass of water. Then he grabbed a plate and a napkin, filched some barbecued sliders and fruit from a nearby buffet table, and headed for the barn.

Inside the shaded space, everyone was clustered around Brea, who was seated in a chair, bent with her head between her knees. Josiah caught Maggie's concerned gaze and breathed an unexpected sigh of relief when the sexy blonde looked more than fine.

Cutter knelt beside Brea and murmured soft questions. Shealyn gently patted her back.

"I'm sorry," the pregnant woman said. "I'm still queasy some days, but if I go too long without food—"

"Don't apologize," Shealyn said. "You're growing a human being and it's hard work."

Suddenly, Sarah spotted him and darted over. "Thank you so much."

"I'm glad to help. What else can I do?"

Sarah smiled and shook her head. "We're fine. Maggie, can you—"

"On it." The gorgeous blonde glided toward them.

Josiah couldn't stop staring. He'd met women who looked attractive enough from a distance. Maggie was one of those rare gems who got more beautiful the closer she came. As he stole an eyeful of the delicate lace hugging her cleavage, his heart started to pound. She met his gaze, and he finally discerned the exact color of her eyes—a clear, bright turquoise. He couldn't blink his way out of an aroused trance. When she drew near and he caught a whiff of peaches and musk, a primal switch inside him flipped.

He had to have this woman tonight.

"Hi." He smiled her way. "I'm Josiah."

"Magnolia," she answered with a little blush, then held out her hand for the water glass.

He gave it over with his breath held because, damn, she was so fucking gorgeous. Maggie was a fine name, but this woman was a Magnolia—delicate, Southern, proud as a fresh bloom.

He stifled the urge to make his move in the middle of Brea's crisis. Instead, he followed her—ogling her naked back in that bang-up dress—toward Brea, who now sat up straight, her face ghostly pale.

"Did you tell the doctor at your last appointment that you're having trouble with your blood sugar?"

She gave a tired nod. "My glucose screening is next week."

Cutter's jaw firmed. "While I'm on my honeymoon? Bre-bee, you should have scheduled it while I could be with you—"

"I can't. My pregnancy is a little more than half over. This has to be done now."

"I'll take her," Cage volunteered.

"I don't need someone to hold my hand," Brea protested.

"You might need someone to keep One-Mile at bay."

That inconvenient reality shut her up. She pressed her lips together for a long moment. "He can't see me."

Cutter sighed. "It's not as if he doesn't know you're pregnant."

She slammed her eyes shut. When she opened them again, they were full of tears. "I don't want him to see me like this . . ."

Brea was working herself up when she was already overwrought. The grim expression both Cutter and Cage wore said they knew it, too. Time to change the subject.

"Hi, Brea. I'm Josiah Grant. I work with Cutter. I brought you something to nibble on if you can keep it down."

"And I've got water." Maggie crouched beside Brea and held out the glass.

Gratefully, the little brunette took them both and began cautiously consuming them. Five minutes later, her color returned, and the mood in the room lightened with relief.

Finally, Cutter helped her to her feet. Maggie took her empty plate and glass away while Sarah handed her a tube of lipstick. The pictures resumed.

In quick order, the photographer finished snapping wedding photos. The bridal party emerged from the barn and headed toward the tent. Cutter squeezed his wife's hand and sent her a look of thanks for her understanding, but her answering expression told him no thanks were necessary. She cared about Brea, too.

Maggie held back from the rest of the group, glancing over her shoulder his way. "So, you're one of Cutter's knight-in-shining-armor teammates, huh?"

She was flirting, and the slight Southern lilt to her voice turned him on, too.

He grinned. "Well, I ditched the armor a while back. Heavy, sweaty, high-maintenance. It got rusty . . . Not for me. But it's true that Cutter and I work together. You live here or are you in LA with your sister, making it big?"

"LA is fine, but Shealyn's loss of privacy isn't something I could deal with. Besides, my grandparents need me here to help with the ranch." She shrugged as if her staying behind was perfectly natural and made total sense.

Josiah wondered if she was actually content or wanted something more.

"You like it in Comfort?"

"I've lived here with my grandparents for most of my life. They raised me. I like it well enough, I suppose." She glanced toward Shealyn, who disappeared inside the tent. "I just wish those damn Enlightenment Fields people would leave Granna and Papa the hell alone."

He frowned. "They're harassing your family?"

"They come around once a week or so and try to persuade Papa to sign on the dotted line. Sometimes they offer more money. Sometimes they try to sell him on how great their agricultural commune will be for this isolated area of the map. Sometimes they give him fast-talking crap about his life coming to a close and his soul needing karma points or whatever they believe in. Lately, they've been a tad heavier-handed."

"Have they threatened him?"

"Not in so many words, but I definitely don't like their tone."

Scowling, Josiah narrowed his eyes. "Do they bother you?"

When she hesitated, it set off all his protective instincts. "Sometimes at the grocery store or while I'm running errands their followers try to talk to me about my grandparents blockading peace and prosperity in Kendall County. One literally begged me to talk them into selling. Even if I wanted to, I don't have that power. Papa is stubborn. Besides, if they sold out, I'd lose my home, too."

He disliked all that. But today was her sister's wedding day, and she shouldn't be worrying about bullies or having a roof over her head when they were celebrating. This shit was his department.

Josiah led her inside the tent. "That's not happening, and they're not worth your time. How about a dance later?"

She raised a pale brow. "Are you flirting with me, Mr. Grant?"

"It's Josiah, and yes, I am. If that's not clear, I'll be happy to try harder."

Maggie laughed, the sound light and melodic. Everything about her was so female, from the sweep of her arched brow, to the delicate bow of her lips, to the swell of her breasts and hips. *Damn* . . .

"I got the message." Then she leaned closer to whisper in his ear, "And I'm not going to stop you."

"So that's a yes to the dance?"

"Do you actually know how?" she challenged. "And I don't mean gluing your hands to my ass and rocking from side to side while you try to find the beat of the music."

"I know how. In fact, I know how to do a lot of things that may surprise you." He grinned.

Let her guess what he meant by that.

"Hmm. So what's your story?"

Josiah lifted his shoulder in a casual shrug. "Not much to say. I'd rather talk about you."

Because his story was typical and boring. Great parents, a couple of sisters, nice childhood . . . Nothing out of the ordinary.

"What do you want to know?"

"Right now?" He glanced around the room and saw that all was well if surreal. Shealyn was hugging the pretty boy from that vampire show everyone raved about. Cutter was shaking hands with a talk-show legend. "Let's start with what you'd like to drink."

There was that giggle that made him smile again. "What do you think I like?"

The way she often answered a question with another question was both frustrating and intriguing. "I think you're the sort of girl who likes things sweet and fruity, but you're not afraid to drink hard every once in a while."

She looked impressed. "You might be right. Why do I get the feeling you're not a mere light-beer drinker?"

He grimaced and shook his head. "Not even close. If I'm picking my poison, it's usually something with vodka. But I spent some time bartending in the past. Want me to pick for you?"

"Think you can?" she taunted.

"Absolutely. Hang tight."

Thankfully, the line to get drinks had died down and waitstaff were circulating the room, taking wine orders for the coming meal. Within minutes, he'd explained the drink to the bartender, who seemed oddly happy for a challenge. Then, with cups in hand, he returned to Maggie's side. She was chatting with Shealyn and some guy who starred in a family sitcom whose name Josiah had forgotten. He didn't like the way the actor leered at Maggie.

He sidled up to her possessively. "I've got your drink, baby."

She cast a grateful smile up to him. Good to know she'd wanted to be saved. "Thanks. What is it?"

With a laugh, he tipped his head to the bride and her famous friend. "Impatient?"

As Maggie tsked at him and took her drink from him, Josiah helped her to her feet, wrapped his arm around her waist, and led her away with a wave to settle into a quiet corner. "Take a sip. It's called Suck, Bang, and Blow."

"Is that what you're hoping will happen tonight?"

Josiah gave her a lopsided grin. "No expectations . . . but it wouldn't hurt my feelings."

"It might not hurt mine, either." She winked. "What's in this concoction?"

Holy shit. How long until he could get her alone? "So much booze. Gold tequila, two flavors of vodka, Jägermeister, peppermint liqueur, orange gin, cinnamon schnapps, cranberry juice, a lime, and some other shit you won't taste—"

"Right. Because the rest will put me on my ass."

He laughed. "Something like that. At least the glasses are small."

"So I might be able to walk out of here after one."

"Maybe," he teased. "Take a sip."

Her berry-painted lips pursed around the glass. Her eyes closed. She swallowed, then sighed in pleasure. His dick went hard.

"You like that?"

"Given how much alcohol is in this sucker, it should not taste that good. But it does."

Nice to know he'd guessed right.

She sucked down a few more sips, then the festivities got under way. Dinner was served. Toasts were made. There were laughs and tears. Shealyn's mother gave a heartfelt speech about how much her daughters meant to her. Josiah watched Maggie's guarded expression. They clearly had some history that wasn't all happiness and rainbows. The bride looked completely touched by her mother's words, but Maggie . . . She seemed unmoved.

Finally, Cutter and Shealyn cut their cake. Their first dance as husband and wife followed, and they kissed through most of it. Josiah tried to stay removed from the sentiment, but hell . . . Maybe he was getting older. He didn't believe he'd ever find lasting love, but the thought of having someone he could rely on, a woman he could cherish and protect every day for the rest of his life, didn't revile him the way it once had.

He sent a glance Maggie's way. Yeah, he'd just met her, so the odds of her being his lifelong one-and-only, if such a thing even existed, were slim to none. Maybe the wedding had gotten to him. Maybe he was feeling his solitary thirty-two years. Whatever the reason, he was going to shelve his cynical nature tonight, enjoy Maggie's company, and see if more than a one-night stand was in their cards.

Weirder things had happened, right?

God knew she tempted him. So much so that he felt compelled to figure her out.

What better time to get started than the present?

Now that the pomp of the reception was over and the party had commenced, he could start learning—and unraveling—Magnolia West.

He found her next to her sister and the groom, then reached his hand out to her. "How about that dance?"

Maggie was shocked to feel her hand tremble when she put her fingers in Josiah Grant's massive palm. He'd been more than nice to look at, and she'd already entertained more than one fantasy about how hot he might look out of that sharp charcoal-gray suit. But now that she was actually going to touch him, her brain felt in eminent danger of short-circuiting. How the devil would she manage if he actually kissed her? Peeled off her clothes? Thrust his hard cock—which should be large, given the size of his hands—inside her?

She'd combust on the spot.

"Sure," she managed to murmur while seeming somewhere between cool and detached. It was her signature move.

As they reached the dance floor, the party tune faded away, replaced by Ed Sheeran crooning that he'd love the woman in his arms until he was seventy. As Josiah pulled her close and began to sway to the slow beat, she peered up at him. Her lashes fluttered, along with her heart. She sucked in a breath. God, she had to stop being such a nervous idiot. He was a man. She was a woman. This would probably be nothing more than a fling she'd enjoy the hell out of.

But looking into his eyes, she wasn't so sure. They weren't blue or green or brown or even hazel. They were more unusual. They were a glinting gray with a thick fringe of lashes against tanned skin. That gaze, along with the buzz of his brown hair, made him look somewhere between exotic and dangerous. And he was staring right at her, looking entirely serious.

Mercy, what was it about this man?

He swallowed like maybe she got to him, too.

"So . . ." She searched for a conversational topic to cut her nerves.

"So . . ." He smirked in return.

"You actually can dance. I'm impressed."

He let loose a laugh. "See? I'm a lot of things, but a liar isn't one of them."

Josiah glided them around the floor effortlessly, turning her under his arm, reeling her in closer, then settling his hot fingertips in the middle of her bare back before he caressed his way down her spine and placed his palm close to her ass.

Lord, he felt good. Maggie tried not to imagine how his fingers would feel skimming her whole body with that soft, unhurried stroke. "Tell me . . . Were you in the service, like Cutter?"

Josiah shook his head. "CIA."

Wow. "That sounds dangerous."

"The mortality rate was higher than, say, for an accountant."

"Why do I get the feeling that's an understatement?"

He simply shrugged. Okay, he didn't want to talk about it. Or couldn't. She respected that.

"How long have you worked for EM Security?"

"About a year. I signed on because I wanted to learn from the best. Then a few months later, Caleb Edgington retired. Thankfully, his sons have proven anything but amateur. What about you?"

Since he'd done important things like save the world, he would laugh a million times at what she'd chosen to do with her life. At least he'd never guess. It wasn't as if a guy like him would ever read an Azalea North novel. In fact, no one had figured her secret out yet, not even her sister.

"I'm . . . on hold right now. Shealyn has this big life to lead, and now she's married. My grandparents are needing more help as they get older. Papa fell last week. Thankfully, he wasn't hurt, but Granna can't lift him. I barely can. And she can't remember to take her medicine half the time. They're little issues, at least right now. But they're going to require more care in the coming years."

"What about your mom? Can she help?"

Maggie bit back something pointless he wouldn't understand and she'd probably regret. "She lives in Costa Rica with her husband and my ten-year-old half brother. Up until the last few months, she really hasn't been in my life. We're, um . . . getting to know each other."

"You didn't grow up with her?"

She shook her head. "Long story."

Hopefully, he'd read between the lines. In her book, it was a closed subject. She still wasn't entirely sure how she felt about her mom. A few conversations didn't erase a whole childhood of resentment, but Maggie wasn't the sort to hold on to hate. And it wasn't as if her youth in Comfort had been terrible.

"What about your parents?" she said to fill what could become an awkward silence.

"Long story, as well."

In other words, he had secrets he'd rather keep, too. Fine by her.

The silence she'd been trying to avoid fell between them. Surprisingly, it wasn't awkward at all. But it was tight, full of awareness. She could feel herself yearning to be closer to him. But what blindsided her was his desire for her. It hung so thick in the air it was almost tangible. Like a blanket, it wrapped around her, warmed her from the January chill that blew in under the tent. It left her no doubt about what he thought or wanted.

The song ended. Neither one of them moved, they simply stared. Those wicked fingertips of his prowled their way up her bare back again, making her shiver, before gliding down in a barely there caress.

"Josiah?"

"How much longer do you have to stay at the reception?"

Half dazed, she scanned the room. Her sister was wrapped in her husband's arms on the opposite corner of the dance floor. Granna and Papa had already retired. Brea, bless her, had finally managed to calm her stomach enough to enjoy the festivities. The rest of the guests had either left or kicked off their shoes, started their third drink, and gotten ready to party.

"Not another minute. Are you planning to take me to bed?"

He cupped her cheek, looking like he wanted to kiss her. Instead, he backed away, teeth gritted in restraint—for now. She had a feeling that moderation wouldn't last.

Josiah took her hand. "Yes, I am."

CHAPTER 2

They were almost out the door. Almost . . . but those last few feet between them and the exit would prove to be a fucking pain in the ass.

First, Logan Edgington blocked their path and cast a discreet glance at their joined hands. "I need a word with you, Grant."

As much as Josiah wanted to tell his boss to fuck off until he got laid, that wasn't really an option.

"Sure." He turned to Maggie. "Can you give me a minute?"

"Absolutely. I'll go say goodbye to my sister. Since she and Cutter are driving to Dallas tonight to catch their flight to Maui tomorrow for their honeymoon, they're probably leaving soon."

"I'll find you in a few."

As she nodded and turned away, Logan watched her go. "You know what you're doing with her?"

"I'm familiar with the birds and the bees, Dad."

"Ha. I meant are you okay navigating around her recent breakup? I heard about it ten minutes ago."

She hadn't mentioned that. "How recent?"

"A couple of months back. They were supposed to get married, but . . ."

"Ten-four."

Josiah knew that drill. Shit didn't always work out. Maybe the residual pain Maggie felt from the split caused that hint of reserve she still wore like a shield. It got under his skin. All through the reception, he'd been trying to decide why her, why now, why was she tempting him to cross the line from friendly to personal? The only answer he could come up with was the woman herself. She flirted. She sent him long looks and lingering smiles. She'd even asked him point-blank for sex. But she held something of herself back, and he wanted it. He wanted her open to him. He wanted her gasping. No, begging. He wanted her pleading with him to fill her up in every way possible.

Yes, it was a stupid fantasy, but he was rolling with it, unless . . . "She and I are getting along just fine. Do you need me to stay here for any reason? Are you expecting trouble at this point?"

"I'm always braced for trouble. But now that the ceremony is over and only a handful of partiers remain, I don't see any reason you shouldn't get on with your evening. Just don't go far and keep your phone handy."

"You got it."

Logan nodded, dismissing him. Still, Josiah had some disquiet to get off his chest.

"Um, one more thing, boss. Maggie and I talked about the Enlightenment Fields folks coming around. They've been harassing her grandparents, trying to get them to sell. I'd like to stay an extra day or two, make sure they understand that no means no. That a problem?"

"Actually, I'd appreciate that. I've been trying to decide how we can help, but if you're willing to stick around and take care of the issue . . ."

"Consider it done."

Logan laughed. "I'm sure Maggie's fine form persuaded you to lend a hand . . . along with other parts of your body."

"It did." Why lie? If he helped her family at the same time he got lucky, it would be a win-win all around. "But I don't like bullies preying on anyone, especially the elderly. I'm happy to take care of these assholes."

With a clap on the shoulder, his boss nodded. "Good man. Be sure to watch your back."

"Always do."

"I'll see you back in Lafayette on Monday?"

"Or Tuesday." Josiah grinned.

With a laugh and a wave, they broke apart. He turned to find Maggie so he could finally get her alone. It didn't take long to spot her—and the young, handsome ranch hand up in her grill. Dressed in dusty jeans, a Western shirt, and a dark hat, he looked like a Cowboy Ken doll crashing the glamorous wedding. Her ex? Josiah hadn't seen him at the ceremony. When had he blown in?

Josiah sidled up behind Maggie and stood with his back to them both, pretending to scan his phone while shamelessly eavesdropping.

"Sawyer, don't do this, not tonight."

"Then when? I've waited for an explanation. And waited and waited . . ."

"What do you want me to explain? And why? It's not like you were in love with me."

"Maybe not, but—"

"If I didn't break your heart, your need for an explanation is about your ego. I'm sorry, but I'm not here to stroke it. We had some good times, but if I'm being honest, they should never have happened."

"You regret what we did? It meant nothing to you?"

"At the time, it meant something," she said softly. "I won't deny that. But you're my grandparents' foreman, the timing was terrible, and—"

"So I was just your rebound guy?" He shook his head. "You knew I liked you and you took advantage of my feelings so you could get your itch scratched."

Clearly, Sawyer wasn't the ex, but some guy Maggie dated after her engagement had fallen apart. And he was crying like a bitch that it was over.

"Seriously? What about the way you seduced me when I was unraveling?" she argued. "I was upset and confused, and you chose that moment to kiss me and tell me you wanted me. In some ways, you gave me an anchor when I needed one. And for that I was grateful. But—"

"You're insinuating *I* took advantage of *you*?" Sawyer growled.

That accusing tone made Josiah glance over his shoulder. The cowboy with the brown hat and the aw-shucks charm had definitely turned confrontational. His eyes narrowed with anger, pain, and something else Josiah didn't like.

Time to end this shit before it got out of hand.

He turned and slipped his arm around Maggie's waist, sending Sawyer a direct glare. "Do we have a problem?"

Beside him, she stiffened. But before she could say anything, the cowboy jumped in, casting a furious glare at Josiah's hand slung low on her hip. "This is between us. I'd appreciate it if you butted out."

"I'm with her tonight, so frankly I'd appreciate if *you* butted out."

Sawyer raised a dark brow and cast a stunned glower at Maggie. "Is he serious? Are you going to fu—"

"Don't you finish that sentence, Sawyer," Maggie insisted. "You and I are over, so who I spend time with and what I do now doesn't matter."

"We're *not* over, damn it. You're special, and I'm not giving up on us. Why are you?"

She winced and pursed her lips.

Josiah wanted to punch him for playing on her guilt. For now, he simply stepped forward, shielding Maggie behind him. "Listen, cowboy. In every language, no means no. The lady gave you her answer. Now you either fuck off or I'll help you to fuck off. Your choice."

Sawyer pushed his hat back on his head and tipped his chin up in challenge. "You think you're going to make me?"

"I'd rather not upset the lady, but if you won't respect her wishes, then yes."

He laughed. "I'll grind you into the dust."

Josiah loved proving that someone else's overconfidence was misplaced, especially when it came to fighting, but not here and now. "If you push me, I'll put my seven years with the CIA up against your experience wrangling mooing animals. And it won't be pretty."

The cowboy ground his teeth together, looking like he couldn't decide whether to shout in frustration or spit his vitriol, consequences be damned.

He did neither, turning to Maggie instead. "This isn't over."

Before Josiah could contradict him, Sawyer was gone. Cursing under his breath, he turned to Maggie. "You okay?"

She nodded, shielding her face with her hand. Was she frustrated? Embarrassed? Concerned? "I'm sorry you had to rescue me. I would have handled him eventually, but he . . ." She sighed. "He was a mistake."

"He came after your breakup?"

She sent him a sharp stare. "You heard about that?"

"A little."

"Davis, my fiancé . . . He was another mistake. I'd rather not talk about it, so I'm glad you know the basics. Can we forget tonight that Sawyer ever happened?"

Her past wasn't his concern, just her immediate future.

Josiah took her hand in his. "Lead the way."

With a nod, she grabbed a glass of champagne from a passing waiter. He passed on the bubbly and followed her toward the exit. A handful of steps and they'd be out of here. Then he'd finally know how it felt to have his lips on hers and what she looked like naked and needy.

Unfortunately, fate still wasn't on their side. A mountain with a beard, camo pants, and attitude stepped through the opening of the tent. He scanned the interior with a dark, intent gaze. One-Mile. *Shit.* Josiah had no doubt who the guy was looking for and he had little choice but to intervene.

"You shouldn't be here, Walker."

The big sniper sent him an annoyed glance, like one might a buzzing mosquito. "Fuck off."

Josiah gripped him by the arm. "Now isn't the time. Cutter doesn't need this tonight. He just got married."

"I don't give a shit about him." One-Mile scowled as he continued searching the area. "Where's—" Suddenly, his entire body stiffened. "Brea . . ."

A glance confirmed he'd spotted her. She saw him, too. Her dark eyes widened like a frightened doe cornered by a hungry bear. Then his gaze dropped a fraction. She wrapped her hands around her baby bump protectively.

One-Mile broke free of his hold and stomped toward her. "Brea!"

His voice boomed over the chatter and the music. Heads turned. It was clear One-Mile didn't give a shit. His sole focus was on the woman ten feet in front of him.

She shook her head. "Pierce . . ."

He tossed a chair out of his path and damn near hurdled a table to reach her. Brea backed away, but it was no use. He trapped her between a buffet table and his big body.

"I need to talk to you, little girl. It won't wait."

If Josiah had believed One-Mile capable of anything remotely like feelings he would have said the sniper's voice was thick with emotion. But this was Walker. The asshole. The snarling loner. Still, his big face looked . . . tormented. What was up with that?

"No. Not here. Go." Brea shook her head, looking around frantically for escape. "Please."

Josiah jumped to Brea's aid, heading straight for her so he could deliver One-Mile his second no-means-no speech of the night. Cutter joined him, his face without mercy.

They both reached her in seconds, flanking her small form and blocking One-Mile from coming any closer.

"You weren't invited, asshole," Cutter snarled. "She doesn't want to see you."

The sniper tore his gaze from the little brunette long enough to scowl at Cutter like scum on his shoes. "You're married, and Brea is mine. That's *my* baby she's carrying. So. Back. The. Fuck. Off."

"Hey, she said she doesn't want your company tonight, big guy," Josiah cajoled. "Turn around, get in your Jeep, and go back to Lafayette."

"Like hell." He settled his weighty stare on Brea. "I've waited weeks to see you. Talk to me."

Behind him, Josiah sensed Brea's indecision. She didn't want to make a scene, but for some reason she also didn't want to be alone with the man who'd gotten her pregnant.

"She doesn't have to talk to her rapist. Turn your ass around and leave."

"I didn't rape her," One-Mile growled between clenched teeth.

"Okay, you coerced her. We're splitting hairs over semantics. Either scenario still makes you scum."

Suddenly, Shealyn approached One-Mile. Her new husband tensed in worry when she fell under the giant's shadow, but she merely held out her hand. "Shealyn West. Well, Bryant now. Pierce, Brea is dealing with a lot. She will talk to you when she's ready. I know she wants to. She just needs a little more space and a bit more time to decide what to do."

He shook his head as he shook her hand. "What is there to decide? She's going to marry me."

Shealyn cocked her head, looking as if she was gearing up to be the voice of reason. "You can't force her—"

"It's okay. I'll talk to him." Brea's voice trembled. "We're drawing attention, and the last thing I want is for you to stop your reception for me. Go. Enjoy your honeymoon. I'll be fine."

Cutter looked reluctant. "I won't leave you when you need me."

"Yes." She took his hand and squeezed it. "You will. You and your wife have two amazing weeks in paradise at the most beautiful little bed-and-breakfast in Maui, ignoring the rest of the world, including me. I'll give Pierce ten minutes. Josiah and Logan are here, just in case." When Cutter still looked reluctant to throw her to the big bad wolf, she hugged him. "Really. I'll text you later."

Then, with a bracing breath, she squeezed her way between Josiah and Cutter to face One-Mile.

The sniper shoved his way forward and took her small fingers in one of his massive paws. Everyone held their breath, not knowing what to expect next. The last thing Josiah ever thought he'd see was One-Mile dropping to his knees and placing his free hand against Brea's swelling abdomen.

The small crowd froze, stunned silent. The big asshole didn't notice or care. He simply touched Brea with gentle reverence. Josiah would never have imagined the man capable of such tenderness if he hadn't seen it with his own two eyes.

"Come on," Shealyn murmured to Cutter as she tugged on the sleeve of his tuxedo jacket. "Let's give them some privacy and get started on our married life."

He let out a breath and finally nodded. "All right, sweetheart. Brea, call if you need anything at all."

Nodding absently, she fisted a trembling hand at her side, and Josiah thought she looked less like she was nervous and more like she had to restrain herself from touching One-Mile to urge him closer.

What was up between these two? Josiah wasn't sure, but one thing he had no doubt about? It was complicated.

After Maggie hugged her sister one final time, she urged him to give the estranged couple a little space. Josiah paced back a few feet. Logan loitered nearby as One-Mile guided Brea to a chair and crouched in front of her, his hands in hers. Despite the fact that he knelt on the floor, the big sniper was still taller than the pretty little preacher's daughter.

Josiah didn't really listen to gossip, but from what little he knew, he doubted they were going to solve their problems in the next ten minutes. Was Brea humoring the sniper? Did she understand that he killed for a living and wouldn't be set aside with a few Southern bless-your-heart catchphrases? One-Mile was all soldier. He drove forward until he met his objective. Right now, it appeared as if his mission was to put a ring on Brea's finger and get her back into his bed.

Their conversation was subdued. He rubbed her belly, stroked her face, brushed a thumb over her lip. She blushed and squirmed and whispered in return, tears running down her face. Then suddenly, she shook her head, rose, and darted out of the tent as if she were on fire.

One-Mile watched her go, standing slowly, his face full of resolution that didn't surprise Josiah in the least. Whatever was happening between them wasn't over—at least in the big sniper's mind.

"You've had your chat with Brea. Time for you to go," Logan said, his face hard.

Walker looked like he wanted to give chase, lash out—something. Instead, he kept his shit wired tight. "I'm leaving. For now."

Then he stalked out the door, fired up his Jeep, and skidded out of the dirt before hitting the paved road with a squeal.

Josiah felt kind of sorry for the guy. When love didn't work, it hurt like hell. Still, One-Mile should count himself lucky in some ways. Brea hadn't told him she loved him, then blindsided him with a totally different story on the very day he intended to make her his wife.

"Hey," Maggie murmured as she emptied her glass of champagne and left it on a nearby table. "You okay?"

"Totally." Maybe with all the drama over, he could shake this maudlin shit. Other people's relationships weren't his issue. What he and Magnolia West would have tonight was simple sex. And he intended to enjoy every minute of it. "Let's get out of here before some other crisis that's not our problem erupts."

She bit her lip, giving him the kind of seductive stare that churned his blood. "Then you'll finally kiss me?"

"You bet I will—and a whole lot more."

Maggie breathed a sigh of relief when Josiah took her hand and they finally made it out of the tent without further incident. Together, they dashed across the yard, toward the house. She was struck both by the stars twinkling in the cold, cloudless sky and the warmth the man beside her gave off with a simple touch.

Spending the night with him was impulsive and probably crazy. God knew she was good at throwing herself from the frying pan into the fire. But Josiah felt different. He wasn't anything like Sawyer, thank goodness. The moment she'd given in to her grandparents' foreman, she'd known it would come back to bite her. But she'd been proving a point to herself. If she could find pleasure in Sawyer's arms, then she couldn't possibly have feelings for Davis. Unfortunately, she'd let Sawyer prove that point to her more than once, and he'd gotten possessive just as she'd exited an unhealthy engagement. She hadn't been ready to even consider something exclusive or long-term with another man. She hadn't realized that Sawyer didn't suit her until the deed was done.

"Where are we going, baby?"

She wanted privacy, but she didn't want somewhere rife with the memories of her mistakes.

"I've got just the place." She squeezed his hand.

They slipped into the house. Maggie had no doubt Sawyer had probably watched them all the way to the door. As she locked it behind them, she shook off thoughts of him and focused on tonight. Most everyone else staying on the ranch had either retired or elected to bed down in the bunkhouse, so the coast should be clear now.

Creeping past her grandparents' bedroom, Maggie led Josiah up the stairs and veered right to Shealyn's childhood bedroom. It was bigger, more secluded, and blessedly empty tonight.

Once inside, she shut them away from the rest of the world, then turned on the bedside light. It gave off a subtle glow, illuminating the hushed room with a golden hue.

Josiah didn't give the place a second glance. He seemed to have eyes only for her. "You sure about this? It's been an eventful evening."

"Beyond, but yes. Unless you're not interested anymore?"

Maggie winced. She hated when her insecurity showed. Everyone in this town thought she was so self-assured and didn't have a care. She'd been Miss Kendall County three times. She'd been salutatorian of her class. She'd landed the lead in the school play as a senior. She'd been head cheerleader. Sure, high school had been fun and she hadn't minded being popular. She'd even recently landed a wealthy fiancé from somewhere way more cultured than here and could have married him. She might have lived a charmed lie of a life—like her whole life had seemed—at least from the outside looking in.

None of those people really knew anything about her.

She'd grown up without a mother because hers loved drugs more than her daughters. All that popularity had faded after graduation. Her fiancé? Gone. She'd ended the engagement without really knowing what she truly wanted or where she was even going. In fact, when Maggie boiled her existence down, what she really had were her grandparents, a sister too famous to bother with her problems, her budding career as an author, a stilted relationship with her mother . . . and a whole lot of confusion.

"Baby, I took one look at you and was determined to have you whenever and however I could. Come here."

The way he spoke to her, as if nothing and no one else mattered, made Maggie's insides flutter.

She wasn't seventeen anymore. She didn't have stars in her eyes. And she really wasn't looking for romance. But this man did something to her she had never experienced.

For some reason, she sensed this moment between them was right.

Without hesitation, she stepped into his arms and curled her hands around his neck. "It feels as if I've waited hours for you to kiss me."

"You have because I've waited those same hours, too." He caressed her face. "But before we do this, I need to know what you're looking for and whether you'll be okay if this doesn't last beyond tonight."

She buried her face in his neck, losing herself in the hot musk of his skin. The bronzed column was taut, delineated by muscles and veins. Everything about him was strong. Steady. He seemed like one of the good guys. She appreciated his calm and the way he tried to do the right thing, but under that he was wonderfully witty and sarcastic. She definitely liked his sense of play.

Somehow, she knew he wouldn't be like any man who had shared her sheets.

"I'm not looking for long-term," she assured. "My grandmother wanted me to marry Davis, and I tried to love him for her . . . but I just couldn't. One engagement was enough to last me quite a while, so if all we do tonight is make one another feel good, I'm fine with that. What about you?"

She hadn't even kissed him and she already suspected she wouldn't soon forget him. Still, the likelihood of Josiah being her Mr. Right—if such a thing even existed—was almost nil. Better to take what she could and move on.

"Yeah, I did the engagement thing once. Didn't work out. Never again. Just sex is fine with me."

Maggie wanted to ask about his ex-fiancée, but his voice and body language said that was a closed subject.

"Cool," she said instead, trying to sound casual.

"Cool," he echoed. "Now give me your mouth so I can start doing unspeakably dirty things to it, designed to give you all the pleasure you can handle."

"You don't have to ask me twice." She raised her face to his, her heart pounding, her belly tightening.

Josiah slipped a hand around her nape and bent to her. It seemed to take forever for him to come close. But as he drew nearer, she deciphered his masculine scent. Fresh-chopped wood, earthy moss, all man. He was a heady aphrodisiac as she breathed him, then let out a little moan.

He was there, luring her deeper under his spell, his hands calloused yet soft as his fingers tightened around her neck. He exhaled against her lips. The citrus and spice of their drinks lingered on his breath. Even his size made her feel petite and protected. Sure, he could hurt her. He'd probably learned a hundred ways how. But Maggie didn't believe for one second he ever would.

Arching closer, she tried to rush their kiss. She needed to feel him. Josiah hadn't really touched her yet, and already she ached. What would it feel like when he was inside her, possessing her, thrusting into her with all his strength and determination?

At the thought, a whimper escaped her throat. Their lips nearly touched. So close . . . His free hand at the small of her back pressed her body against his. The hard insistence of his erection dug into her flesh. Holy hell, he was massive and obviously ready to make her feel good. She was beyond eager. Why was he dragging out this kiss?

"Hurry."

"Hmm," he murmured as his lips brushed her cheek and glided toward her ear. "You're trembling."

She was. Maggie could hear it in her inhalations, feel it in the grip of her hands tightening on his shoulders as she tried to drag him closer. "You're tormenting me."

He chuckled in her ear, the sound a low rumble that did crazy things to her insides. "Yes, I am. I like that it's working."

As he nuzzled his stubbled cheek across her skin and dragged his lips down her jaw, she tensed, drew in an impatient breath, and found her thigh creeping up his hip. She invited him deeper. He caught her leg in his grip and pressed her closer, nudging her exactly where she needed his steely length.

"Kiss me already," she demanded.

"I'm getting there."

But he still wasn't in any hurry. His lips bypassed hers again, hovering just above her mouth, leaving her tingling and sensitive.

She tried to crush their lips together and get relief. But once again he was stronger and faster. Next thing Maggie knew, his lips were at her temple, skimming down her hairline. He inhaled her. The hand at her nape shifted up to graze her scalp. Then he grabbed her hair, closed his fist around the strands, and tugged. She shivered in need.

With a satisfied smile, he nipped her lobe, his teeth just sharp enough to snag her attention. Without a word, he forced her to acknowledge his growing mastery.

Never in her admittedly colorful love life had she ached for a man this badly. The fact that he hadn't even kissed her, that they were still fully clothed, and yet she was powerless against his seduction wasn't lost on Maggie. This man was going to utterly undo her. He would probably ruin her for months, maybe years. That should worry her. She should care. But right now, she didn't. She simply yearned to dive into the pleasure and drown. The consequences would come later.

"Josiah . . ."

"What is it, baby?"

His whisper was pure sex. Her nipples hardening, her fingernails digging into his skin, a keening cry falling from her lips. "Please . . ."

"That's the magic word. Oh, I'm going to love hearing you beg."

Maggie didn't have time to respond before he lifted her off her feet and carried her the last five steps to the bed. He followed her down, covering her body. As her back hit the mattress, he fitted his hips between her legs and dipped his head to her, finally slanting his lips over hers, capturing her in an instant.

She absorbed him with a gasp. He was everywhere, his hold unbreakable, his kiss unfightable. Not that she had any will to end it. Heavens no. All she could do was wrap her arms around him tighter, wriggle in silent plea for more, and kiss him with every fiber of her being.

The joining of their mouths seemed endless, timeless. Perfect. But she wanted him naked. She wanted to explore the strength he now used to hold her down. She wanted to map him with her fingertips and lips. She ached to know every inch of this man.

With a cry, Maggie tugged at his coat. He wrestled out of it without breaking their kiss. His shirt proved more difficult. First, because the row of his buttons lay between them. Second, because he seemed far more interested in divesting her of her panties. Still, he managed to seduce her mouth with a kiss that stole her sanity while working his hand up her thigh. Before she knew it, he'd lifted the skirt of her bridesmaid dress and fastened his fingers around the lace cupping her hips.

"With all the drama tonight, I missed out on cake," he muttered against her mouth. "I'm going to need something sweet on my tongue."

As his words registered, a wave of dizzying heat flared over her. "I can find you a piece. Or wrangle up some candy."

When she gave him a playful shove and made to rise from the bed, he pushed her back down. "Stay."

His voice was a growl. His word was a command. He yanked her panties off her body and flung them away, then flicked open the buttons on his dress shirt with sharp, sure movements. She swooned more.

"But you wanted something sweet," she teased. "I was going to help you."

He shucked his shirt and tossed it aside. "The only thing you need to do is spread your legs and let me eat your pussy."

On some level, Maggie knew she shouldn't like his demand. She believed in equality, equal pay for equal work, that a woman was every bit as smart as a man—and often smarter. But she felt her IQ temporarily slipping as she gaped at his massive shoulders and hard pectorals. His biceps looked bigger than her thighs, and he had abs for days.

Mercy . . .

Then Josiah gave her a wolfish smile, palmed his way up her thighs, and used his own legs to spread hers wider. Whatever intelligence she had deserted her then and curled up in the corner with a mental bowl of popcorn to watch the seduction unfold.

Using one hand, Josiah shoved the gray silk skirt around her waist. With the other, he spread her folds open and stared unabashedly. "Let's hear what you sound like when you orgasm, baby."

Maggie had a terrible suspicion it wouldn't take long before he found out. Already her breathing had accelerated, her clit ached, and her womb clenched. Somehow, she had to slow him down, find an opportunity to work her way under his reserve and undo him.

"Wait," she breathed. "Aren't you going to kiss me some more?"

"Of course I am."

But he wasn't looking at her mouth. Not at all. He was squarely focused on the slick, needy flesh between her legs, and his intimation was clear.

"Josiah, I—"

"You need to let me make you feel good, baby. Lie back." He grinned. "Bet you can't stay quiet . . ."

Her entire body tightened again.

Lord, she couldn't seem to stop herself from ceding her control to him, and Maggie struggled to cope. She was used to being the one to drive a man mad. She was usually the one who made them squirm and beg. No guy had ever turned the tables on her. She hated it. But god, deep down, she loved it even more.

"You're going to taste way better than cake," he murmured as he dipped his head.

Just like his kiss, he didn't come at her straight on. He teased, breathing on her sensitive flesh and making her shiver. He merely responded by holding her to the mattress and doing it again, then watching her shudder helplessly. As he glided his thumb across her hood, Josiah cataloged her responses and delighted in her gasp. He followed that by slowly pushing a finger inside her, encouraging her as she wriggled and tightened.

"I see you biting that lip. Don't hold back."

"You're trying to undo me."

Between her legs, his lips curled up. "There's no trying about it."

Maggie couldn't handle how right he was. Josiah Grant was going to learn every secret of her body in a single night, and there was nothing she could do to stop him.

He further proved his point when he breathed on her clit again as he slowly thumbed it while his finger inside her teased her most sensitive spots. She stiffened, tensed, writhed.

"C'mon," he cajoled. "I'm not going to stop teasing you until you make noise."

"But my grandparents are downstairs and—"

"You told your sister earlier they don't hear well anymore."

They didn't. She could probably scream the roof down and they would still swear the house was silent.

"Wedding guests are staying in rooms just down the hall."

"You care more about them than your orgasm? If you do, I'm doing something wrong and I'll be happy to try harder to wring pleasure from you."

If he did, he would melt her altogether.

"No." She shook her head. "You don't have to . . ."

"I think I do."

He took perverse pleasure in both her pleading and her predicament. Maggie didn't know how to respond. Some distant part of her wanted to rail at him to stop. The need jetting through her body and rushing blood to all her most sensitive places drowned that silly thought out.

As if to see whether she'd learned her lesson, Josiah torqued her up again, his breath falling hot over her needy bud as he swirled it under the pad of his left thumb and slowly fucked her with his right fingers.

This time, not even threat of death could have compelled Maggie to stay quiet. She let loose a shuddering, desperate cry.

"What a pretty sound," he said with satisfaction. "Let's see how you do once I've got my mouth on your pussy. And, baby? I promise you more feel-good rewards if you scream *my* name when you come."

CHAPTER 3

He'd definitely fucked up by not removing her dress first. Josiah would have liked to see Maggie's lush breasts sway and bob as he worked her to climax. But he couldn't regret much now. The night was still young, and he had his face right above her sweet, slick pussy.

Overall, life was good.

He liked the way she was already worked up, the soft blush spreading across her cheeks, the fact her feminine folds were swelling before he'd really touched her. Magnolia West was all woman, totally responsive. And unless he missed his guess, no man had put in the effort to learn her body so he could ply her with the perfect pleasure.

Josiah liked the notion of being the first.

But he'd have to keep his damn head above water. Every time goose bumps broke across her skin and his nostrils filled with her spicy female scent, he found it harder not to shuck his pants, climb on top of her, and thrust deep—everything else be damned.

Maggie grabbed fistfuls of the comforter and rolled her hips. The animal sounds of her desperation trilled in his ears, roared through his brain, yanked on his cock. Fuck, teasing her was tormenting him. Every moment he put her off and she begged a little more was a moment his self-control continued to unravel.

"I will. I'll scream for you. I'll cry out your name."

Maggie said that now, but she was a stubborn little thing. In fact, she was the kind of woman who would always provide a challenge; it was in her nature. That only whetted his appetite.

Over the years, he'd had both girlfriends and subs—more the latter than the former lately. His demanding job didn't leave a lot of room for relationships, and he hadn't missed them one bit. What he had missed, though, was actual human connection. He missed giving a shit about the woman he was fucking.

With Maggie, that didn't seem to be a problem. Caring about her was an odd change of pace.

Because he gave a shit, he didn't like her worrying about Enlightenment Fields. Or knowing that once he left Comfort, Sawyer would still be lurking, hoping to catch her in another weak moment. He especially didn't want to think that her soft mouth and velvety pussy wouldn't be his after tonight.

"Josiah . . ." Her little whine was like a lust injection straight to his bloodstream. Why didn't something—anything—about her not turn him on?

He thumbed her pouting clit again, then inhaled her. Jesus, he could stay hard to her scent for days.

When he'd nuzzled her neck, the hint of female and peaches had been a sweet turn-on. But between her legs? Her sweetness gave way to spice that was more vanilla–cinnamon sugar. More than woman. Josiah couldn't put his finger on what it was about her, but he inserted another finger inside her, eager to suck her needy bud and get her off.

"Give it to me, baby," he insisted thickly. "Give me everything."

She moaned and bobbed her head as her body undulated sensually beneath him. Then he nudged two fingers deeper into her sweltering depths and dropped his tongue to her clit.

The instant her flavor hit his tongue, she branded him. So sweet. He had to have more. He had to have his mouth on her when she found pleasure. He needed her right fucking now.

With his fingers swirling at her G-spot, he licked and laved her swelling button until her gasping, panting breaths filled the room, her body tensed, and her spine arched from the bed. She was seconds away, and he couldn't wait.

"That's it," he ground out, fascinated by the one-to-one relationship between his touch and the mewling roll of her hips.

"Josiah . . ."

"Hmm," he hummed against her engorged button. "Don't hold back, baby. Give me your fire. Your will. All of you."

She lurched off the mattress moments before she reached for him, one hand curled over the short-shorn hair on his skull. The other clawed at her thigh, and the sideshow of watching her dig her nails into her skin as she spread her legs desperately wider for him turned him the fuck on.

"Josiah . . ."

Her voice was higher, breathier, yet somehow louder. Around his fingers, her flesh tightened, clutching at his digits, rocking in search of satisfaction. *Yeah . . .*

"Come."

She nodded wildly, then her body went completely taut, and she let out a primal, throaty howl. Nothing had ever sounded so sweet to his ears. "Josiah!"

Maggie rode his face to the squirming, scorching, screaming climax's end. He worked every sensitive nerve until the tension left her body with an exhausted sigh of satisfaction.

He pressed a kiss to the inside of her thigh with a smile, drinking in the sight of her rapidly rising and falling chest, her flushed face, and her eyes closed in repletion.

In the silence, he shucked his pants, fished a condom from his pocket, and rolled it on. He crawled over her body, hovering, watching her.

If he were the sort of guy eager and capable of hanging on to a woman forever, he'd choose one like Magnolia. She was sweet enough to lure him, yielding enough to submit to him, uninhibited enough to scream for him, and sassy enough to keep him guessing.

Just as well she wasn't looking for happily ever after, either. They had tonight, and Josiah intended to fully enjoy it.

"How do you feel?" he asked smugly.

"Boneless. Content." She lifted lazy lids to him, her turquoise eyes glittering. "Ready to return the favor."

A minute ago, he might have been able to resist her mouth on him long enough to truly enjoy a blow job. But as soon as she looked at him, that was a big hell no. Every cell in his body geared up for one imperative and one imperative only.

Get inside Magnolia West.

"Another time, baby." He covered her and gathered her thighs in the crook of his arms. As if he'd done it a thousand times, the head of his cock easily and naturally found exactly the spot he wanted to invade.

"I—"

"Hold on." His rough thrust forward cut off whatever she'd been about to say and replaced it with a loud gasp that echoed in his ears and gave way to her long, low groan.

Josiah joined her as sensation rolled up his cock. Heat flared. She tightened on him. He swelled as fresh desire poured down his spine.

Shit. If he wasn't careful, this would be hard and fast and over too soon.

"Yes!" she cried out. "I don't know what you're doing to me, but dear god, please do it again."

Experimentally, he eased back, then slid in once more, this time deeper. She answered with another sharp inhalation. Her nails dug into his shoulders. She clung to him, thighs hugging him close.

"Good. I don't think I could stop fucking you right now for any reason. You feel amazing . . ."

There had been more to his speech, but he lost the thought as soon as she rolled her body beneath his, moving with the rhythm of his stroke while he shifted from one to the next, deep, slow, and bed-jarring.

What was it about this woman? Sure, she was pretty. But he'd fucked pretty women before. Hell, he hadn't even seen Maggie totally naked yet, and he was already so damn keyed up to stay inside her all night. The lacy bodice was covering the breasts he craved. But even without seeing her bare, he knew Maggie was . . . more. She was more interesting. She was kind. She was funny. She was an adorable, sexy-as-hell mess. She was dangerous to his equilibrium. She was a challenge he could get used to taming—or at least trying to.

Josiah slanted his lips over hers again and sank deep—tongue and cock. He'd been inside Maggie mere moments. Already, his blood ran scalding hot, turning to lava, pooling and bubbling, searing him with desire. He was unbearably hard, beyond sensitive, and on the edge of losing his control.

Holy shit, was it even possible to work Maggie out of his system in one night?

Thank god he had another day or two while he made a few things clear to Enlightenment Fields to sate himself with her.

Some guys thought he was bent because he got just as much pleasure out of getting a woman off as he did getting off himself. But no way would he leave Maggie less than utterly, sublimely satisfied. He wanted her smiling. He wanted her coming back for seconds. Hell, he wanted to wipe Sawyer, Davis, and any other man she'd given herself to entirely from her memory.

Refusing to wonder why, he distracted himself by clasping her tight and rolling to his back. Then he scooted to the middle of the mattress, positioning Maggie on top of him. "Ride me, baby. Show me how you like to be fucked."

She writhed on top of him, enveloping more of his dick. "Slow. Deep. Hard."

That answer was fucking perfect. "Hmm. What will it take for you to lose that dress?"

"There are two catches at my nape," she managed to get out between sawing breaths. "The bottom is held up by a zipper at the small of my back."

Josiah grunted. *Mission accepted.*

He pulled her down so she lay on top of him, breasts to his chest. In one maneuver, he worked at the fastenings at her neck and bent his knees so he could fuck her from below. They both groaned as he thrust up, Maggie when he scraped the sensitive nerves inside her pussy with each long stroke, and Josiah when the dress fell away from her shoulders to pool around her chest and revealed her velvety cleavage.

He continued to push his way inside her body as he attacked her zipper. The moment it came undone, he lifted her silken skirt. "Take the dress off. Pull it over your head and . . ."

He didn't have to tell Maggie twice. She tore it away and pitched it across the room, never breaking stride and never quite catching her breath.

Josiah knew the feeling. He took one look at her symmetrical, swaying, lush tits in his face and lost his damn mind.

She didn't need him to guide her in a rhythm. Maggie knew exactly what she wanted, and just like she'd said, she liked it long, slow, and deep. With every thrust, he submerged more of himself into her. Sweat beaded at his temples. He couldn't look at anything but her—her cloud of golden hair now tumbling around her torso, her undulating body, and the way she parted her legs to accommodate him. He especially loved watching his cock penetrate her.

As he filled her again, Maggie's head fell back. Her breaths quickened. He worked hard to keep his wits together. She didn't make that easy. Her every move was sensual, every reaction to him instant and perfect. He thrust; she tightened. He caressed; she moaned. He lost himself in her eyes; she fell into him in return.

Shit, he had to get her to climax now. His own was creeping up fast.

Gritting his teeth, he lifted up into her again, this time swirling his thumb over her hard, swollen clit. She was close, and his not-so-subtle push toward the pinnacle hardly went unnoticed. She gripped him tighter and chanted his name again.

"Kiss me," he breathed roughly.

Because that won't be at all like splashing oil on a raging blaze . . .

No, it totally would be, and he gave zero fucks.

Maggie didn't hesitate. She bent to him, softly layered her lips over his, and teased him with a kiss that was like a whisper. Like gossamer. It left him hungry.

Josiah demanded more, thrusting a hand in her hair and fastening his mouth to hers, nudging her lips wide and thrusting his tongue deep as he plowed into her body, shoving hard against sensitive spots that had her gasping and melting in his arms.

"You like that, baby?"

"Yes." She dug her fingers into his shoulders.

"You want more?"

"Please . . ."

He loved the way she panted. "If I give it to you, are you going to come?"

She nodded frantically. "I don't think I can stop it."

"Good. I want to watch you come apart."

She gyrated down on his dick with a whimper, as if protesting her inexorable need to feel more of him. "But I'm not ready for this to end."

"Oh, I'm going to fuck you again. You can bet on that. Now let go. Don't make me wait."

As if she had the reassurance she needed, Maggie went primal on him, working her way up and down his cock, which now screamed for relief. Roughly, he filled her again and again, gratified when he saw the color rising up her chest, flaring across her face. It doubled when she clamped down on his shaft so hard he could barely move.

"Baby. Oh, yeah. Oh, fuck . . ."

"Josiah!" Her answering cry nearly destroyed him.

Tugging his fist in her hair, he guided her lips over his own again and swallowed her next long, high-pitched wail.

Shit, he could feel her pulse around him, gripping, squeezing, milking him. No force on earth could stop him from giving in to the intrinsic animal need to merge with her, mark her, show her who she belonged to.

The thought spilled through his head, and he had only long enough to think a passing *whoa* before his climax erupted—volcanic and epic—stripping him of rational thought and hurtling him into dark, thick ecstasy. At the moment, Josiah didn't care if he ever found his way out. He simply groaned, a long, strangled sound that ripped from deep inside him, and let go of every shred of his control.

The orgasm seemed to go on forever. He wanted to believe it was because he hadn't gotten laid in a while. On some level, he knew he was bullshitting himself. His pleasure had nothing to do with deprivation and everything to do with Maggie.

As he recovered from climax, something more than the usual mellow filled him. Josiah rolled her to her back and delved into her stare for answers. Maybe he should pull out, put distance between them. But he didn't want to.

"Oh, my gosh." She was still trying to catch her breath when she pinned him with an intimate stare that reverberated down his spine. "Hi."

"Hi." He swallowed. Impossible not to notice that instead of slowing down, the longer he looked at her the more his heartbeat accelerated.

What was she doing to him?

"Wow. You probably hear that a lot, but . . . wow."

That made him grin. "Wow yourself. You were pretty amazing."

Her smile dimmed. "It's not me."

"Baby, it's not all me. Sex is usually a good time but that was really fucking intense."

"Because of you. My fiancé . . ." She shook her head. "Never mind. You don't want to hear my insecure BS."

"Was your fiancé the sort of a douche who tried to make you feel responsible for his shortcomings as a man?"

"No. I just didn't do it for him. He suggested that if I were less inhibited, sex might be better. But that was crap. And I just . . . couldn't."

"Not with him, maybe. With me? You weren't inhibited at all."

"I know." Her admission was so soft he barely heard it. "I'm surprised. It's not like I know you well."

"Maybe you feel more at ease with me."

"I wasn't self-conscious with you at all, but you make me nervous. I mean, you've been all over the world . . ."

Yeah, while working. Did she think the CIA had routinely sent him to places like the Côte d'Azur? Nice, France, would have been fantastic . . . and totally unrealistic. "Some places are really overrated."

Syria, Congo, Ukraine, and Venezuela all came to mind.

"But you've seen things, met people, obviously had a lot of sex."

No sense denying that, so Josiah didn't even try. "I don't think that has anything to do with it."

"You're wrong. I've barely set foot outside of Texas. Not that I really want to go anywhere else, but Comfort proper has about thirty-two hundred people. I feel like I've known the same thirty-two hundred people most of my life. There are fewer than seventy guys in this town who are roughly my age. I know them all. I've dated a number. I haven't been impressed by any. I didn't love my fiancé and . . . Oh, lord. We're supposed to be having fun, and I'm babbling." She pushed at his chest like she wanted to get free. "Sorry."

Regretfully, he withdrew from Maggie's body and disposed of the condom. She was still trying to find her way to her feet when he returned and urged her back down to the mattress.

Normally, he didn't hang around to hear whatever his lay of the moment had to say after sex. He wasn't looking for attachments, and subs, if he had sex with them, rarely had expectations beyond the moment. Maggie was different. He wanted to understand why she'd let this nonsense about her ex and her small-town life mess with her head.

"Don't apologize, baby." He caressed his way up and down her silky skin. "Tell me what you're thinking."

"It doesn't matter. Since things ended with Davis, I've been wondering what I'm doing and where I'm going. My sister and a lot of my friends are starting to get married, and I . . ." She sighed. "I'm not sure that's for me."

Josiah didn't press or pry. He understood. If she hadn't loved the guy, her broken engagement must not have been terribly traumatic. Lucky for her that she hadn't been the stupid sap ready to invest in forever, only to learn she'd been played. Josiah held that honor. But clearly, her breakup had left her unsettled.

"Because some tool told you that you needed to loosen up in bed?"

"No. I didn't really care what Davis thought. That was another clue. We simply didn't . . . connect. In fact, I don't connect with most people. I stayed in the relationship because I didn't want to disappoint everyone, especially Granna. I let the engagement drag on longer than I should . . . It's ancient history. What about you and your fiancée?"

"Ancient history, too."

"How ancient?"

"Three years ago." And that was all he wanted to say about that.

"Do you ever see her anymore?"

"No. It's definitely over."

"Do you miss her?"

"Hell no." Sometimes, he missed the illusion of a future and a family. In the rare moments when the world wasn't quite so crazy and work was a little slow, he reflected on his existence. Then, he sometimes wished for more meaning in his life. But hell, he had friends and family. He did his bit to save the world. It wasn't all bad.

Lately, though, he'd found himself wishing more often that he weren't quite so alone.

"I don't miss Davis, either. Why are we talking about this?"

Honestly, he couldn't remember. But he sensed she had a point.

Josiah pressed a kiss to her forehead. "You don't usually connect with people. I'm different, why?"

"I don't know. Maybe because we really only have tonight and I don't have to worry about what happens between us tomorrow."

"Or maybe you just haven't met anyone else who flipped your switch and you're selling yourself short. You're sassy and funny and easy to be with. You connect with your sister and grandparents, so clearly you're capable."

She bit her lip. "But I don't trust well, and I . . . don't have a good relationship with my mother."

"I noticed some distance between you two at the reception. Something happen?"

"Other than the fact she elected not to actually be a mother for most of my life?" She scoffed. "I can hear all the armchair psychologists now telling me I have attachment issues and that I just need to forgive my mom and work through my childhood trauma in order to have a happy, healthy adult relationship. News flash: My mom and I more or less worked it out a few months ago."

Josiah would guess less rather than more, but he didn't correct her. "How did that go?"

"Honestly, it wasn't the major catharsis I thought it would be. It seemed to do wonders for Shealyn but . . . nothing changed for me. I'm not mad at her anymore. And I know she's trying to make amends. It's just I don't feel . . . invested."

"Have you tried getting closer to other people since then?"

"No," she admitted. "But I don't think making peace with Mom makes anything any different for me."

"It'll most likely come," he assured her, because he really didn't know what else to say. And because having her naked and flushed underneath him wasn't doing great things to his logic.

"Maybe you're right." She shrugged. "Want a shower?"

"No. I want to fuck you again."

But he wanted more than that. He loved the idea of working her, coaxing her, finding the magic combination it would take to make her truly surrender herself.

A crooked smile slowly worked across her mouth. "I don't know. Maybe I should make you beg this time."

That wasn't how sex worked for him, but he wasn't going to argue, simply prove she had it all wrong.

For now, he chuckled and gathered her wrists in his grip, anchoring them to the mattress above her head. "Why don't you be a good girl and lie there while I suck on your nipples until you scream?"

Maggie's breath caught. Yeah, she liked it when he talked dirty. Josiah had noticed that the first time he'd worked his way between her legs, and he had no trouble exploiting her weakness.

"That sounds great, but don't be disappointed. I don't think my breasts work that way."

The fact her voice was already shaking told him she was woefully mistaken.

"Humor me." He tightened his fingers around her wrists. "Don't move your arms. Whatever happens, whatever I do, keep them right here."

"Why?" Her breath caught.

"Because I said so. Because I can make you feel so much better if you obey."

"I don't like that word." She wrinkled her nose. "Obedience definitely isn't my strong suit."

He laughed. "I won't make you eat your vegetables. Tonight, I'll only ask you to do things we'll both enjoy."

Maggie bobbed her head in consideration. "I'll try. But when is it my turn to make you feel good?"

"Baby, you already do."

Josiah couldn't wipe the smirk off his face as he lowered his head to her. God, he had the wonderland of her body spread out and all to himself, along with hours to learn it, pleasure it, master it. She would be tender tomorrow, maybe a little sore. But he'd make sure she considered every stinging, swollen ache worth her while.

He kissed her. That mouth of hers lured him. He couldn't not kiss her lips that had gone red and puffy from the previous melding of their mouths. She was too tempting to resist.

He went in slowly, sank deep, tasting her kiss with unhurried sweeps of his tongue. Maggie fired him up, defying description. How could she taste sweeter than before? What was that flavor of hers that kept him coming back for more? Every time he meant to pull away, he struck another rich vein of whatever addictive nectar she spilled. Then he found himself a prisoner until he drank all from her he could.

Under him, she sighed, softened, craned up to meet him. But she didn't move her arms. Not an inch. She kept them right where he demanded and let him overtake her body one kiss and one stroke at a time.

Josiah was dizzy, high, shaken when she finally whimpered and thrust her breasts up at him, bare nipples hard and stabbing the air. Tearing his mouth away, he panted and tried to regain his bearings. The sight of her lips, now dark and bruised, lured him back. But her breasts with those tips he had yet to sample beckoned him even more. Would she be the kind of woman he could drive to the brink of orgasm simply by teasing and tormenting them?

That possibility thrilled him.

Maggie gasped for breath as he stared at her. "I should be sated. I shouldn't want you this much."

She probably believed that. Maybe she'd never had a man devote every iota of his attention and desire to her. He'd fix that. What surprised him more was how readily she admitted her weakness for him. Knowing the usually reserved Maggie couldn't stop herself from aching for him was a heady fucking thrill.

"You shouldn't be sated. You should want me this much." He licked his way up her cleavage, ghosting his fingertips along the sides of her breasts in a touch so light, she'd probably wonder if she imagined it. "I'm going to make sure you want me even more. I'll work until you beg me to fuck you again."

Maggie whimpered. Her hips wriggled. Her spine twisted. She lifted herself to him—a silent offering. It was nice, but he wanted her to plead out loud, knowing damn well what he wanted from her and the damage he intended to inflict on her reserve.

"Josiah . . ."

He laved his way up one of her breasts, stopping just short of the peak, then delighting in her frustrated sigh. "Yes, baby?"

"I need . . ."

"What?"

"More."

He smiled against her skin as he dragged in her peachy-spicy scent. Not enough, not yet. But he'd fix that.

Inhaling the heady pheromones rising from her skin, Josiah bent to her nipple and wrapped his lips around it. She gasped. He nipped the tender tip with his teeth. She hissed. He engulfed her in his mouth and sucked hard. She gave him a shaky cry of need.

God, he couldn't keep his mouth off her after that.

He dragged his tongue along the bottom of her breast and inhaled there, where her scent was deep. He gently bit his way up the taut flesh until he reached the pinnacle. Then he sucked her in, drawing on her mercilessly, and abraded her nipple with his tongue until her legs parted restlessly and she let loose a long, strangling cry.

To prove he was equal opportunity, he did the same to her other mound, loving the way she keened and lifted to silently offer him more. The way those sweet tips hardened and darkened and stretched toward him provided another level of *hell, yeah*.

Back and forth, he worked her breasts with his hungry mouth, augmenting with his fingers. A pinch here, a tweak there. Maggie liked it rough. Her nipples were sensitive. He could do this for hours, and she would absolutely let him. They would both love it.

"These are going to be sore in the morning," he whispered.

"I don't care."

Every time she opened her mouth, he liked her better and better. Nipples were among his favorite toys, and if he could have her on his turf, with his equipment . . . the sensations he could unleash on these two beauties would blow her mind and excite the shit out of him.

"Josiah . . ." she moaned. "Do something . . ."

Ah, now they were getting somewhere. "I can keep plying your nipples and see just how sensitive I can make them or—"

"I need you inside me. I can't wait anymore," she panted out.

If he had more time with her, he would prove she could, in fact, wait. He would keep her suspended until she was desperate, nearly delusional. But they only had tonight . . . and her pleas didn't help his resolve at all. In truth, he wanted to fuck her so badly, he wasn't sure how much longer he could stand the depravation.

Reaching back into the pocket of his pants that were still strewn across the floor, he fished out another condom. Two left. That wasn't going to be enough to finish out the night. Maybe she had more? If not, he knew how to get creative.

"How about both?" he whispered against her ear. "Stand at the foot of the bed and bend until your palms are flat against the mattress."

"Are you always this bossy?"

"Yes. Do you always ask this many questions?"

She hesitated. "I guess I do."

Apparently, that fact had just occurred to her, and Josiah actually found her answer surprisingly cute. It didn't stop him from blindly needing to fuck her, just made her seem more real and human.

Maggie leapt off the bed as if the promise of feeling him inside her motivated her to be quick. When she positioned herself exactly where he wanted, in the way he'd requested, he hummed in approval. The straight, delicate line of her spine lured him, but it was the indentation of her waist that flared to the curve of her hips and led to her lush ass that had him salivating.

"You're beautiful, Magnolia." He stroked her back. "Do you prefer that to Maggie?"

"Everyone calls me Maggie."

"That wasn't what I asked. When you introduced yourself to me, you used your full name. It suits you. Is that your preference?"

"It is, but my friends and family aren't going to change their habits after all these years. Maybe you could call me Magnolia when you're inside me? I'd like that."

Josiah would, too. It would be their secret. Another way of connecting.

"Yes," he promised as he gripped her hips, aligned his crest with her opening, and pushed in slow and deep. "My pleasure, Magnolia."

CHAPTER 4

Sunlight splashed through her eyelids, summoning Maggie from sleep. The half-assed breeze from the lazy ceiling fan above tickled her skin. The pillow beneath her cradled her head softly, and some delicious whisper of happiness sat just outside the reach of her consciousness. A loopy smile lifted her lips, and she sighed. Screw opening her eyes. She could sleep a few more minutes . . .

"Wake up, gorgeous," a raspy male voice said in her ear as he spooned her, nudging her with yet another erection.

Memories came rushing back. Josiah. All the seemingly infinite touches. The four times he'd crashed inside her and aroused her until she'd climaxed with multiple screams. The firm yet tender way he'd held her when he had finally let her sleep.

Her smile widened as she lifted heavy lids and turned in his arms to face him. "Morning. Didn't you get enough last night?"

She asked the question smugly because she already knew the answer. He made it obvious when he shifted his weight, rolled her to her back, then maneuvered himself between her thighs and gave a teasing prod.

"Are you wishing I had?"

"No." But that didn't keep reality from intruding. "I wish we had more than a night together. What time do you have to leave? I need to help my grandmother and Sarah when the rental company comes to pick up the chairs, tables, and tent. But after that . . ."

"I'll help, too." He stroked the hair from her face, his expression going solemn. "I'm not staying and I'm not a relationship guy, but I'm also not going anywhere for a day or two. I intend to have a chat with the Enlightenment Fields folks until they understand that you're not selling to them. By the time I'm done, they will leave you and your family alone."

Her jaw dropped. "You'd do that?"

"Of course." He kissed her forehead.

She blinked. Why would he bother now that he'd gotten what he wanted? "Did someone ask you to? You're not obligated—"

"No, and I know I'm not. But I like you, Maggie. I want to take care of this for you so you and your grandparents can feel comfortable and safe in your home."

Wow. "Thank you."

He didn't have to do that. Or even care. Most people didn't. Hell, even half their community had welcomed Enlightenment Fields simply because they brought new blood to the county, along with a seemingly endless flow of cash.

"Of course."

"Hopefully, those folks will listen to you. They don't give a whit what I say. I'm a female. They don't listen to my papa, either. They've tried to paint him as ... not senile, exactly. But like his age makes him somehow less of a person."

Josiah frowned as if he didn't like the sound of that. "What can you tell me about this place? Know anything about their goals? Their beliefs?"

"The first time they came around, they left a pamphlet about themselves. I tossed it, but not before I'd skimmed it. It said something about building the farm of the future, using technology to create a greener, more earth-friendly harvest and meditation to create a happier culture. It sounded pretty harmless. Well, except the part where they mentioned devising innovative methods to be ready for the 'destructive forces soon destined to transform the planet.'"

He frowned. "You don't think they meant global warming on a massive scale?"

"It read like that. But some of the followers they've sent to insist we sell called it the 'collapse.' They talked about it as if it's an event, almost a cataclysm of biblical proportions. That worries me."

His expression morphed into a scowl. "Don't give it another thought. I have a way of making people see reason."

"I believe that." She curled her arms around him and held him tighter. "You certainly persuaded me repeatedly last night."

That made Josiah laugh. "You sore?"

"A little. But I'm more worried everyone will see I'm humming and glowing with pleasure."

"I think you look beautiful." He caressed his thumb across her cheek. "But I didn't persuade you to give me everything. Yet."

"What?"

"You held parts of yourself back from me."

Maggie raised a brow and scoffed. "I don't know what you're talking about. I gave myself to you."

Josiah caressed his way down her side, then cupped her ass in his big hand. "No. You gave me your body."

"That's what you wanted."

"When we walked into this bedroom, that's exactly what I wanted. And I enjoyed every minute of it. You were spontaneous and sexy as hell. You shared your pleasure perfectly. But there's something deeper I'm missing. I'm curious to know what's going on here." He tapped her temple. "And here." He pressed his finger to her heart.

Maggie wasn't surprised by that truth, just by how quickly he'd realized it. Anytime she was with anyone, the more intimate things felt, the more something inside curled up in a protective ball and hid behind walls to ward them off. The sudden turn of this conversation was a good example.

She pushed at his chest, rolled away, and leapt to her feet, grabbing for her sister's discarded bathrobe. "Like I said, I don't connect with

people. Sex is great. I'm glad we had it. I appreciate everything you're
doing for my family."

"But?" He wasn't pleased, and the sudden warning tone in his
voice said so.

Maggie ignored it. "But that was last night. Now I have to get
dressed and head outside to lend a hand. Help yourself to coffee in the
kitchen. I think Granna bought some bagels and cream cheese for
everyone. I'll . . . see you around."

She darted for the door, but Josiah was faster. "I'm not trying to
pry my way inside your psyche or heart. Hell, I don't even know why
I'm bringing this up. But I noticed the distance last night. It bugged
me. As a man . . ." He shook his head. "Fuck it, I should be honest. As a
Dom, it's not acceptable."

Wide-eyed, Maggie took a step back. "You're a Dom? Oh, I'm not
into that 'Yes, Sir. Thank you, Sir' kind of shit. I'm pretty much about
free will, and you bending me to yours runs counter to my wishes."

"Magnolia, why did you think I wanted to hear you beg so badly?"

"Don't call me that. You're not inside me right now."

"Give me three minutes." He slipped his palm between the lapels
of her robe and caressed her until he cupped her breast, thumbed her
nipple still sensitive from his touch, and awakened goose bumps all
over her skin.

She fought not to moan. "No."

"What did you think was happening last night when I ordered you
to put your palms flat on the bed and bend over so I could fuck you?"
Josiah raised a brow and caressed her taut bud again, his stroke slow
and mesmerizing. "You didn't seem to mind then."

She hadn't. In fact, she didn't remember ever wanting a man half as
much as him. That scared Maggie. If he stayed for even another day,
would she be able to stop wanting him before he unraveled her? She
had a sinking suspicion he was the kind of guy who would demand
way more of herself than she could ever give.

"I'm never going to open up more than I did last night, no matter how much you command it." She shrugged free from his touch. "So we should part ways here."

The words came out, but everything inside Maggie screamed in denial at the thought of never feeling Josiah's touch again.

She stifled it. They'd shared one night that ultimately didn't mean a thing. Granted, she'd never had a one-night stand. But neither of them was looking for tomorrow, and if she was already this mixed up after less than twelve hours with Josiah, she needed distance from him—fast.

"I don't think that's what you really want," he challenged, as if he could read her mind.

Maggie couldn't bring herself to say a word or even nod. Instead, she scowled, ridiculously on the verge of tears as she gave him a little shove and darted out the door. When she reached the sanctuary of her room, she was pleased to see the wedding guests who had spent the night had already stripped the sheets from the bed and cleared out. She slammed her bedroom door and locked it, stumbling into the shower as the first sob ripped from her chest.

That did not go as planned," Josiah muttered to himself as the slam of Maggie's bedroom door reverberated down the hall.

Yeah, he probably shouldn't have mentioned his kink. But that wasn't the real problem, just her excuse. He'd gotten too close, made demands of something other than her body too quickly. He wasn't even sure why he'd done it. He seriously wasn't a relationship guy. He didn't have any intention of staying more than another twenty-four hours at most.

Why had he pushed her for more?

Because he was ornery, and the Dom in him really didn't like the walls and no-go points he sensed between them.

Fuck it. Not his problem anymore. Maggie wanted it to be over? It was done. He'd drive out to Enlightenment Fields, say what he had to, let Logan know he'd done his duty, then get the hell out of Dodge. And if the thought of never seeing Maggie again, of never touching her exquisitely soft skin or drinking in her catching little moans, disturbed him . . . well, he'd get over it.

Hell, he'd gotten over a backstabbing fiancée he thought he'd love for eternity. Now, he barely thought about Whitney anymore. He'd get over Magnolia West, too.

With a sigh, he gathered his clothes, indulged in a quick shower in the all-pink bathroom. Lamenting the peony champagne body wash that had to be Shealyn's, he lathered up and got the hell out, making a mental note to throw on some masculine body spray before he returned to EM Security's offices and got ribbed by any of his fellow operatives.

Minutes later, he was dressed in last night's suit as he crossed the yard to his truck to look for the duffel he'd packed and his change of clean clothes.

Halfway to his destination, Sawyer caught sight of him and made a beeline, cutting him off while looking him up and down as if he were no better than shit on the bottom of his shoes. Josiah stifled a groan. Nothing good was going to happen.

"You spent the night with Maggie," Sawyer accused.

"That's none of your business." She may have kicked him to the curb, but he still felt compelled to protect her privacy. It was his, too, after all. Plus, he really didn't like this guy in his face.

"She's mine."

Sawyer's growl didn't scare him. "If you were to ask her, I think you'd get a different answer."

"She's confused."

Maybe, but not in the way this douche meant. "I just want something from my truck. Can you get out of my way?"

The ranch foreman merely planted his hands on his hips and stood his ground. "Can you just leave?"

Josiah sighed. "I do *not* want to fight you."

"Oh, because you're the big, bad CIA agent. Right."

"Former, and yes. That *is* right. Not that I owe you an explanation." He shook his head. "Look, I'm not staying on the ranch and I'm not taking Maggie with me. So you can stop snarling. Feel free to march upstairs and work out whatever's between you two."

Even as Josiah said the words, he knew that if Sawyer called his bluff and followed through, he'd do whatever it took to stop the fucker.

God, he didn't have his head screwed on straight.

Cursing, Josiah made to walk around Sawyer, but the foreman snagged his arm in a surprising grip. "You're just the new guy, you know. The flavor of the month. The fresh meat."

His sneer crawled up Josiah's back, but he refused to rise to the bait. "Whatever."

"I know because I was the flavor of the month, too. While Maggie was engaged to Davis, she was getting it from me. Right under his nose."

That sent Josiah's gaze zipping around in shock. Maggie had made it sound like Sawyer was the mistake she'd made *after* her engagement, not during.

"Didn't know that, huh?" Sawyer nodded. "Yeah, I was her favorite toy to help her forget about her boring fiancé."

Josiah tried not to let it matter. But he knew a thing or two about cheating brides-to-be. Sawyer's accusation did not sit well with him.

"And it was so hot between us, I was sure she'd let me keep fucking her after the wedding."

Josiah raised a brow. "And that was okay with you?"

"If Davis couldn't hold on to her, either before or after their vows, that wasn't my problem."

So adultery was irrelevant. Nice guy. "Well, apparently she changed her mind."

"No. Their engagement simply ended."

"Because Davis found out about you two?"

"I think he already knew, just like he knew he couldn't handle Maggie."

"And you can?"

Sawyer shrugged, but his smile was smug. "Oh, yeah. I know how to make her come."

Why are you patting yourself on the back for giving the girl an orgasm? It's not that tough, pal . . . Josiah swallowed down his quip. "Good for you."

"You couldn't get it done, I'll bet."

I did. Nine times. But who's counting? "Since you're so good at giving her pleasure, how many times has she let you touch her since her engagement ended?"

Sawyer puffed up. "Like I said, she's confused, and you're not helping. You need to go and leave her to me."

So the answer was a big zero. That made Josiah way happier than it should.

"Who Maggie spends her time with is her choice, and I'm not having this conversation with you. Get out of my way."

"Davis couldn't make her come," Sawyer blurted as if he hadn't spoken. "She confided that to me once. His inability to get her off was probably one reason she broke off their engagement."

Bullshit. Josiah didn't know Maggie well, but he knew she was more complicated than that. If all she wanted out of life was orgasms, he'd still be in bed with her, sharing more good times and tingles.

"So you shouldn't expect to last long," the other guy went on. "You'll look like a sap if you try. Davis did, especially when she gave him the heave-ho the morning of their wedding."

Josiah froze. The other man's words painted a vivid picture of an unsuspecting groom standing at the altar, ready to make the woman he loved his wife in front of God, family, and friends . . . and the bride never showing up. He didn't know Davis and hadn't liked anything he'd heard last night, but suddenly, he felt sorry for the sucker. And pissed at Maggie.

Just as well he was leaving.

"So you didn't know that, either?" Sawyer said acidly, obviously enjoying spilling Maggie's secrets.

"Why are you stirring shit, douchebag?" Honestly, Josiah would have beaten the hell out of Sawyer to shut him up if he weren't the kind of bitch who'd twist even a handshake into an assault charge. "You act like any of this matters to me. I never wanted to take your girl away, just borrow her for the night."

Finally, Sawyer shut up long enough for Josiah to shoulder his way past and dash to his truck.

"You're an asshole," the ranch hand called to his back.

Yeah, it wasn't the first time someone had hurled that accusation his way. It wouldn't be the last, either. He held up a hand and waved as he walked back to the house with his duffel. Why give the guy any more attention?

After a quick change of clothes, he headed to the kitchen for coffee. Maggie was there, brewing tea, wearing a pair of yoga pants and a too-tight T-shirt with her hair in a bun and buds shoved in her ears. She should not look so good to him. He should not still want her so badly that coming within five feet of her made him hard as hell. He should not get a single whiff of her sweet peaches scent and feel so goddamn desperate.

As if sensing him behind her, she turned. Pink flared across her cheeks. She plucked out her earbuds. "Breakfast? I'm making myself some if you're hungry."

It was probably dumb. He should get in his truck and head down to Enlightenment Fields to have that chat. But just like last night, Maggie's lure proved strong. Besides, he had to eat.

"I'd appreciate that. Mind if I make coffee?" He gestured to the single-cup coffeemaker.

"Help yourself. What do you want to eat?"

Josiah began to brew coffee. "What were you going to fix?"

"My sister says I have the palate of a five-year-old most mornings, so I was going to start my day as usual, with a bowl of Lucky Charms."

Josiah laughed—until he remembered that he was annoyed with her. She'd cheated on her fiancé and broken their engagement on their wedding day. At least according to Sawyer, who, admittedly, had reasons to lie. Then again, the truth didn't matter. He refused to get in any deeper with her.

"I don't think I've ever had a bowl of it," he found himself saying instead.

"What?" She blinked incredulously. "You've been deprived. We have to fix that right now."

"We do?" He cocked his head. "I thought we'd parted ways."

"That was before I knew your cereal education was so deficient. And clearly, I can't rely on anyone currently in your life to fix the catastrophe or they would have already done it."

This seemed like serious business to her. Against his will, Josiah was charmed.

He rubbed at the back of his neck, a smile lurking on his lips. "My last roommate was a personal trainer. His habit of eating a half-dozen egg whites for breakfast rubbed off on me."

"Which is why you have amazing abs . . . but that sounds like a protein bomb that would sit in your stomach like a boulder—after it bored the hell out of your taste buds on the way down."

"That hasn't been a problem for me." He took a sip of his blessedly hot black coffee.

"Only because you don't know any better. Wouldn't you rather start your day with fun marshmallow surprises? I mean, c'mon. Sit down and say nothing else until you've tasted the wonder that is Lucky Charms. And if you say anything crazy, like advocate kale as a side dish, I'm afraid we can't be civil anymore."

Who was *this* Maggie? Less than an hour ago, she'd been refusing to discuss the ways she'd held herself apart from him as a lover. She'd been rejecting any hint of the closeness they'd shared last night, along with any suggestion she might have enjoyed his Dominance. Now, she was playful, borderline flirting again.

Was her humor brought on by nerves? A glib distraction to put more distance between them?

Despite all the reasons it was stupid and impractical, Josiah refused to allow that.

"All right. I'll try some of your teeth-rotting, carb-heavy cereal *if* you agree to try some egg whites, too."

Maggie wrinkled her nose and bit her lip. "They sound repulsively healthy."

"Hey, I'm not the one who brought up kale."

"Okay, I'll give you that." She sighed. "I'll try the egg whites. Do I get bacon, too?"

"You think fried pork is a good sidekick to one of nature's most perfect foods?"

"Hell, yeah. It's tastier."

He laughed again. Damn, he didn't want to find her adorable. A cheating, dodging liar shouldn't be.

"How about a banana instead?" He spotted a bunch hanging from a fruit basket on the counter. It was higher in sugar than he usually indulged in, but clearly for Maggie that would be a step in the healthy direction.

She cocked her head as if his question required deep consideration. "Are you insinuating I need to lose weight?"

"No." She might be on the curvaceous side, but he liked women that way. And he liked Maggie's form more than most. Obviously, he must. He couldn't seem to stay away.

Maybe he was intrigued because this felt like a negotiation. No, getting her to try egg whites wasn't like coaxing her into a spanking or cuffs. But she was obviously enjoying their banter, their chemistry. And she might say she didn't want his Dominance, but last night she'd loved it every time he'd ordered her to perform some act or get into a position designed to ramp up her pleasure.

Who cared? He lived six and a half hours away. He wasn't in the market for a girlfriend, much less one who'd dumped her fiancé on their wedding day. Speculating about her natural submission was a stupid train of thought. He should jump off now, get down the road, and get on with his life.

But that meant he'd have to leave Maggie. He'd have to stop staring at her fine ass in those tight, stretchy pants. Walk away before he figured out why she'd seemed intent on rejecting him when he had only wanted to help her. Get closer.

Nope.

It would be smarter to walk away . . . but apparently his dick had eradicated his common sense.

"If I don't need to lose weight, why bring up the egg whites?" she challenged.

"I thought if I tried something you like, maybe you'd be willing to try something I enjoy." Yes, he was fishing for her reaction.

Maggie's smile fell. "You're not talking about food anymore, are you?"

"Smart woman."

"We've had this conversation." She grabbed a couple of bowls from the cabinet and a bright cardboard box from the pantry before swinging by the fridge for milk. She set everything on the table, not looking his way. "We decided that was a bad idea."

"No. You did that. I disagreed, if you recall."

She waved a hand in the air. "Semantics. I'm right."

Something inside Josiah demanded that he prove to Maggie just how wrong she was.

How? You can't force her to accept you or your Dominance in her life.

The voice of reason in his head needed to shut the fuck up.

"Eat your cereal," he commanded her with a low, stern tone usually reserved for the dungeon or the bedroom.

"Don't go all caveman. I'm going to."

Maggie bristled while she poured herself a bowl of processed corn and sugar . . . but her nipples hardened, too. Josiah couldn't flatten the smug smile curling his lips. She liked the fact he was a caveman. "Excellent."

"Aren't you going to try them? You promised."

He grabbed the box and shook some cereal into his dish, following up with a splash of milk.

As he watched the processed shit bob and float, she laughed. "Bon appétit."

Nothing about this looked like a culinary experience, but he always kept his promises, come hell or high water.

Josiah dipped his spoon into the cereal, shoveled it into his mouth, and chewed.

"Well?" she prodded between her own ravenous bites.

"It's . . ." He looked for a polite way to tell her it tasted like too-sweet cardboard. "Different than what I'm used to."

Maggie burst out laughing. "Oh, my gosh, you should see your face."

"That obvious?"

"That you hate it? Um, yeah."

"Sorry. If I'm going to indulge in something not-so-healthy, I'm a salt guy."

She rolled her eyes. "I should have guessed you're defective. If you don't like a good pie . . ."

"Now, I didn't say that." He shot her a simmering stare across the table.

It only took her a moment to grasp his unspoken meaning. Then she kicked him none too gently. "We're eating breakfast, perv!"

"I'd rather be eating your pussy." Why lie?

"You already did that last night."

Her embarrassed whisper and rosy blush amused him.

"I haven't heard a good reason not to do it again."

She shook her head. "I still think that's a bad idea."

"I still disagree." He tried another bite of the cereal but grimaced when he bit down on a marshmallow so sweet it hurt his teeth. After choking the spoonful down, he pushed the bowl away and rose.

"That's it? You're done?"

"Yep." He rustled around the kitchen until he found some non-stick cooking spray and a pan, then retrieved the eggs from the fridge.

Maggie just watched. "You only took two bites."

"That was one bite more than I needed to make up my mind. Now it's my turn. You promised to try my egg whites."

She sighed. "All right. But I'm eating the rest of your cereal first. I can't let all these delicious marshmallows go to waste."

Josiah started cracking shells against the edge of the pan, then separating the whites from the yolks. "Whatever you can swallow down in the next three minutes. Then I'm going to feed you real food."

That made Maggie dive for her processed treat even faster. She'd just about managed to consume his whole bowl when he slid steaming egg whites onto clean plates and grabbed a banana from the bunch.

He set both plates down in front of him. "Come here, Maggie."

Her eyes narrowed. "Why?"

If he had any intention of staying with her, the first thing Josiah would do was earn her trust so she wouldn't feel the need to question him. But he wasn't and he couldn't expect miracles overnight—even if he wanted them.

"I'm going to feed you." He sat and patted his thigh.

"And . . . you want me to sit on your lap for this?"

"Yes."

"We covered the fact I don't follow orders."

"So you said. I just don't think you understand how good it will feel to take them from me." He leaned in, got ruthless. "You promised to try the eggs. They're right here, getting cold. All you have to do is sit on my thigh and let me feed you."

"You're serious, aren't you?"

"Have I given you any reason to think I'm not?"

"No, but you didn't say I had to sit on your lap and take the fork from your hand when I agreed to this."

"You didn't ask."

She scowled. "That's underhanded."

He shrugged. "If you want to think that, go for it. That doesn't change the promise you made."

"Why are you pushing me?"

Good question. Because some stupid part of him wasn't ready to walk away. Because being with her felt so natural.

"I just want to talk to you."

With a sigh, she rose, circled the table, then plopped in his lap. "If my grandparents walk in, you get to explain this was all your doing and I'm simply your helpless victim."

Josiah doubted Maggie had been helpless for more than ten minutes put together in her whole life. But then he couldn't think about much else, not when she wriggled her lush ass against him, ostensibly to get comfortable.

"Sure. And in case that shimmying all over my lap is to verify I'm hard, I'll save you the trouble and me the agony, and I'll admit I am now. Bite?" He lifted his fork.

With a little flush, she stopped moving over his erection and opened her mouth. There was something decidedly sexual about setting the eggs on Maggie's tongue and watching her eat from his hand.

After she chewed and swallowed, he studied her for a reaction. "Well?"

"I'm sure it's very healthy."

"It is," he said, amused. "Is that your way of saying it's bland?"

"Pretty much."

When she tried to hop off his lap, he curled an arm around her and held tight, then reached for two shakers in the middle of the table. "Try salt and pepper. Did you cheat on Davis with Sawyer?"

That brought her stare whipping around to him. Maggie blinked like she was searching for an answer, but he already had it. She looked

DEVOTED TO LOVE   67

too guilty to be innocent and was obviously trying to avoid admitting the truth.

"Who told you that?" As soon as the words were out, she shook her head. "Sawyer did. Always stirring the pot . . ."

"Why did you do it?"

She shrugged. "Like I said, I didn't love Davis. I felt trapped. I think some part of me hoped Davis would find out and end things."

"Why not end it yourself?"

"And disappoint my grandmother who's sacrificed everything to make me happy? She'd handpicked him for me. One of her sorority sisters' grandson. Harvard Law. Wealthy family. Bright future." She shrugged, suddenly not meeting his gaze. "I couldn't do it."

When he looked at it from that perspective, he could see why she would feel as if her allegiance wasn't to the man who'd swept into her life a few months prior but to the woman who had raised her. But that didn't answer one question. "Why didn't you tell him how you felt instead of fucking around behind his back?"

"Why do you care?"

He sighed and admitted the unavoidable. "Because I want to understand you."

"It's not that hard."

Josiah sent her a censuring glance. "Don't lie and tell me you're not complicated."

"Okay, you're right. Shealyn pointed out a long time ago that I totally am."

At least they didn't have to argue about that. "So answer the question."

She bristled. "I don't owe you an explanation."

"You don't. But there's no reason we can't talk, be friends."

Maggie cocked her head. "You want to know why I didn't blurt out how I felt? I tried. It wouldn't have done any good. He was as trapped as I was. His mom and dad died when he was a baby, so, like me, his grandparents raised him. They held the purse strings to his trust fund, too. They wanted him married. Personally, I suspected he was gay and knew they wouldn't approve. He tried to be different for them, but . . ."

"You're saying he didn't love you?"

"Not even a little. I think he was too conflicted to love anyone, even himself."

"Why did you wait until the morning of the wedding to call it off?"

"Of course Sawyer told you that, too," she groaned. "In retrospect, Davis and I were playing an elaborate game of chicken. I flinched first. If it helps, he called me a few days later to thank me for having the courage to do what we both knew needed to be done. His grandparents hate me, but he's relieved. And we're both happier now."

Josiah scanned Maggie's expression. Nothing but calm truth lay there. Maybe he shouldn't be surprised by how forthcoming she'd been. She was merely sharing fact. And why wouldn't she? She had no reason to lie to him.

But her information changed a lot of things. Everything, really. Josiah couldn't be angry with her anymore. Which led him right back to wanting her all over again.

"Thanks for telling me." He pressed a kiss to her soft lips, gratified when she closed her eyes and gave him a little sigh and a buss in return.

"Sure. Thanks for making it not painful. I appreciate you not being totally judgey."

Actually, he had been, and Josiah wanted to kick his own ass. He shouldn't have judged before he heard the whole story. But he'd let his own baggage—not his brain—form his opinion. "Want more egg whites?"

"No. They're all yours." She hopped off his lap. "I really have to go help Granna with the cleanup after last night. Are you, um . . . heading back to Louisiana today?"

"I'm going to talk to Enlightenment Fields first," he hedged, knowing he should leave town before he dug himself deeper into her. "Then . . . we'll see."

"Don't leave without saying goodbye, huh?" At the prospect of his departure, she looked sad.

"I won't."

In fact, as much as Maggie intrigued him, Josiah wasn't sure how he'd say goodbye at all.

CHAPTER 5

The farther Josiah's truck rolled up the dusty lane toward Enlightenment Fields, the stronger his foreboding grew. When he reached the hodgepodge collection of wooden structures, he rolled to a stop behind a greenhouse. To his right stood a storage shed. Beside that sat a trio of well-used ATVs, some watchful muscle types sporting wicked ink and AR-15s, along with people carting forty-pound bags of soil on their shoulders. A few pregnant women milled around, passing out bottled water.

Josiah put his truck in park and killed the engine. Every single person stopped and turned their attention his way. Their stares held wariness. Their expressions teemed with suspicion.

He grabbed his phone from the console and texted Logan. If you don't hear from me in fifteen minutes, I'm at Enlightenment Fields and I need help.

What's going on? Logan returned in seconds.

Nothing. Yet. Came to chat. Stay tuned.

10-4.

Not that Logan could help from hundreds of miles away, but at least someone knew where he was. As a precautionary measure, it would have to do for now.

Josiah exited the truck and pocketed his keys. All the hair on his body stood on end. Fuck, he shouldn't have come alone. He knew from experience shit could go south fast.

To his surprise, the person who came to greet him wasn't a slab of beef carrying a semiautomatic rifle but a young woman in a white lacy dress splashed with pink flowers. "Hi, stranger. Are you lost? Or seeking your enlightened truth?"

"Neither. I'd like to speak to Adam Coleman."

"He's not available." She cocked her head and gave him a smile. "Maybe I can help you. I'm Mercy."

When she held out her hand, Josiah gave it a quick shake.

Mercy must turn male heads everywhere. Light honey-brown hair brushed her shoulders. Mossy green eyes sparkled. Her puffy lips beckoned a man to kiss her. And she had a mighty perky pair of tits. He pegged her somewhere around twenty-two, but she had a seemingly gentle quality and an unworldly air that begged corrupting. Until he looked into her eyes. The confidence in her stare told him she was used to men tripping all over themselves to talk to her and she fully expected them not to have a lot of control over their words once they started.

"Nice to meet you. Josiah."

"Welcome. Lemonade?"

She no more than said the word when one of the other women, this one barely beyond her teenage years and at least seven months pregnant, stepped forward with a cup filled with the sweet-tart liquid, condensation rolling down the plastic cup. She sent him a questioning glance but didn't speak.

"Thanks for your hospitality, but no. I'm only staying long enough to have a word with Mr. Coleman."

Mercy waved the woman away and pasted on a coy smile, then curled her fingers around his arm. "Unfortunately, he's very busy with Enlightenment Fields business. I'm his daughter." She smiled. "What do you need? I'm sure I can help. And you'll find me far more agreeable to talk to."

Because she thought she could lead him around by the dick and play him?

Josiah didn't know whether she was bored, vain, or horny. He didn't much care, either. On the other hand, something told him if he straight-up admitted why he'd come, this conversation could quickly become a confrontation. He was both outmanned and outgunned.

"I'm new to town. I heard about y'all from some of the locals. Maybe you can tell me what you're about?"

A smile brightened her face as she tightened her grip on him. "Absolutely. My favorite thing to do. I'd be happy to give you a tour and tell you about our mission." She pressed the side of her breast to his biceps. "Josiah."

He forced himself to smile down at her. This act must work on most guys. It set his teeth on edge. "Thanks, pretty lady."

"My pleasure." She preened.

Vain, it was. And maybe horny, too, since she refused to give him an inch of space.

"Adam started Enlightenment Fields nearly fifteen years ago. Back then, he could envision the promised land of his dreams. He tried a few places but kept looking for the perfect utopia to gather the followers who shared his vision. So he set about to find it. You see, we embrace a future filled with peace and simpler times, where people live off the land, care about their neighbors and community, and all work toward a common prosperity. Adam doesn't consider himself our leader, but our spiritual guide. Together, we meditate, sing, hold hands, and enjoy the bounty of our harvests."

Josiah's bullshit meter was wailing like a siren, but he forced a smile. "Folks said y'all run a farming commune."

"To sustain ourselves, yes. But we're so much more. We're a family."

Josiah nodded. If it was such a happy, joyful, all-for-one-and-one-for-all kind of place, why wasn't anyone smiling? And why did Brutus One and Brutus Two need semiautomatic rifles?

"Really?" He injected totally false interest into his voice.

"That's our philosophy. And I would know. When Adam bought this land I was one of the first settlers at his side." She smiled proudly.

"Well, you *are* his daughter."

"Only in spirit, not blood. I *choose* him as my sire."

So, a fanatic. Good to know . . .

"We've been slowly expanding since, not only in acreage but in believers. Nearly every day someone new comes to us to help relieve their worldly burdens and join our flock. We lift the cares from their shoulders and help them find the uncomplicated existence they've been craving."

Right . . . What she really meant was they took people who were lost and confused, lured them into the fold, fleeced them of their worldly possessions, then turned them into virtual slaves to work the crops. That wasn't a new story. But her too-chipper attitude and the weird vibes rattled Josiah. What else was going on here? What was their endgame?

"Interesting. How many people live on the ranch now?"

"Nearly five hundred. Maybe you'd like to stay and add one more to our flock?"

Oh, fuck no. "On my way into town, I saw a sign about conscious awakening. What does that mean? Is that one of Adam's philosophies?"

"Absolutely. Why don't we start the tour and I'll explain?"

He glanced at his watch. He'd probably used five minutes of the fifteen he'd told Logan to wait. "If it won't take too long. A friend is expecting me soon, and I don't want to disappoint."

Mercy pinned her smile a little more firmly in place as she led him past a few dozen laboring followers. "That's one of our first philosophies, that life shouldn't be rushed. You should spend every day soaking in your existence, not piling appointments into your calendar. At sunset, you should begin contemplating how you can make tomorrow more untroubled by the outside world."

Translation: You don't need friends or family or anyone who might toss you a lifeline, just us.

"Anyone ever leave?" Was that what the assault-rifle twins tried to prevent?

"Some do. Their minds are too closed to adjust to our way of life. The sins and the rush-rush-rush of the outside world lure them back, so we let those on a more self-oriented path go. Most of us, though—"

"Wait. Self-oriented? Do you mean . . . selfish?" Is that how these kooks pitched leaving them?

"If you like." She shrugged. "We wish those people well and tell them we'll welcome them back with open arms if they're ever able or willing to shed the skin of their outside existence and embrace the collective."

She painted a picture of free will, but he'd bet that dissenters or anyone second-guessing their message were either punished or shown the door and told they could participate only if they consented to becoming a mindless drone. "I see."

"Well, that would make you very enlightened. I don't expect you to truly understand yet. Most people don't right away. Most have to be here for weeks, sometimes months, before they truly comprehend the joy in self-sacrifice for our communal journey."

When they strolled past the big, gun-toting guards, he glanced at them out of the corner of his eye. Those two hadn't taken their eyes off him since he stepped out of his truck. Josiah had no doubt they'd had training—police, military. Something. They looked way too comfortable handling guns most of the general public would never touch to be amateurs.

"Everyone definitely looks content," he lied. "So why the armed guards?"

"Oh, not to keep people from leaving, if that's what you think. The new deputy in town is misguided and we've had a few run-ins. He doesn't seem to understand that everyone here has chosen to call this place home of their own free will. Eli and Samuel"—she pointed to the guys with rifles—"are here strictly to protect the Chosen. That's what we call those who have elected to embrace Adam's teachings and a brighter future. Some of the townsfolk don't understand our mission or they disapprove of the fact that we're not centered on their version of God."

"Do y'all believe in God here?"

She shrugged. "We're not against faith. But the Chosen have embraced the fact that the God of Christianity gave people free will. And with that free will, they've been both wise and humble enough to put their faith in Adam to lead them in a spiritual awakening so they can truly appreciate life."

And he did this by making them plow fields in the middle of nowhere all day? Yes, and listen to a shyster of a windbag and his creepy "daughter."

As they approached a large house, Mercy gripped his arm harder. When they reached the yard, music played, a song he'd never heard. Upbeat. Gratingly cheerful. He frowned as a woman with a haunting voice sang about rousing the spirit and surrendering the will to a higher cause. Enlightenment Fields had their own brainwashing tunes?

"You're listening?" She looked pleased by that possibility.

"I can't help it. It's . . . catchy."

"Thank you." She beamed. "I wrote and recorded it myself."

So Mercy was minister of propaganda. "I'm impressed."

She laughed. "I'd say you're good for my ego, but we discourage focusing on appearance or accomplishment for the sake of pride. It really is all about the collective here, and these songs buoy the Chosen. Sometimes I'm writing or recording long past exhaustion, but their desire for musical inspiration keeps me going."

"Hmm. I would never have thought of work in that way."

"As something good for everyone? Definitely. What do you do now?" she asked, leading him up to the porch.

Let's see how you respond if you think I'm flat broke. "Currently, I'm unemployed. I came through town to visit an old friend, but . . ."

"You're worried he or she will be unwelcoming?"

"You could say that."

"Too busy? Judgmental?"

He shrugged. "Maybe both."

"We're not like that here. Someone always has time for you. We never judge. You're here because you've been struggling. We like to take fractured people with imperfect lives and give them a communal love so glorious they have to pinch themselves to be sure the beauty is real."

Holy shit, this tripe is getting deep. "That sounds amazing."

She smiled and pushed her way into the house. Josiah followed, every sense on alert. He had no idea what he was heading into, but his instincts told him to stay sharp.

"Here we are. Home sweet home. I live and work here, along with a handful of staff."

Inside, the place was modest and lived-in. Every window was wide open, despite the January chill. A cozy brown sofa and a couple of big, mismatched recliners took up space around a massive fireplace. A few beanbags and lots of pillows were scattered across a braided rug. He saw no TV, no radio. In fact, looking around, he didn't see a computer or many electronic devices at all.

The nearby U-shaped kitchen was nothing fancy. Big covered pots simmered on every burner of the stove. Odd, given how early in the day it was. An unfamiliar scent wafted from the kitchen, earthy but laced with hints of both sweetness and tang. It wasn't a scent he'd ever smelled. Even more unusual, various plants took up most of the counter space. From a distance, he didn't recognize them, though several he would have sworn looked strikingly like cannabis. The others . . . not sure. He was no plant expert.

"Nice."

"Oh, it's not fancy. But Adam will gather some of his Chosen here at night and open his spirit, share what's in his heart. Everyone wants to have their name called."

"How does he share with his followers?" Josiah had suspicions, and none of them were G-rated.

"Through meditation, song, or heartfelt embraces. Sometimes we all hold hands and bare our feelings to one another. It's really illuminating. And freeing."

That description gave him hives. He'd bet money they called people who had something to give the sect . . . or something to hide. Then Coleman, Mercy, or one of their cohorts likely worked the target over, shrouding their manipulation in some free-love bullshit designed to make them believe that if they didn't sacrifice their worldly goods or independence for the collective good, they were somehow wrong, misguided, or defective.

God, he hated bullying, and in his mind, this was just another form of it.

"That sounds inspirational."

"It is," she assured him. "Where, in this day and age, can you find people who want to hear about your human experience so in-depth? These days, even so-called families don't communicate about their inner selves. They work outside the home, leave the raising of their children to relative strangers, and spend their evenings connecting with their electronic devices. Is it any wonder we have a society that's empty of meaning?"

He nodded as if truly considering her point. Yes, some families were dysfunctional. Parents did have to work to support their children, which meant realities like daycare and after-school sitters. They were tired at the end of a day and often did seek escape. But he also knew that many loved their spouses and offspring unconditionally. All of his married peers? Josiah wished his relationship with Whitney had turned out half as good as theirs, that she hadn't committed to him if her heart hadn't really been involved. They'd have recently celebrated their third wedding anniversary, maybe even had a child by now.

None of that shit mattered. It hadn't worked, and he needed to focus on Mercy. She was the kind of predator who would home in on any weakness she could spot and exploit it.

"I see what you're saying," he said finally.

"Excellent. Are you sure you don't want lemonade while we sit and talk?"

"Positive. I can't stay." He glanced at his watch. Four minutes before he had to check in with Logan.

"You're welcome back anytime." She sent him a soft smile and a flutter of her lashes.

Did she use her body as another means of coercion? Would she sleep with potential Chosen to persuade them to join?

"Thank you. I, um . . . really was curious to know what y'all were about."

She smiled and sidled closer. "Still intrigued?"

"Maybe a little." He forced a smile.

"I hope you'll be back. I'd love to see you again."

Josiah didn't feel the same. He couldn't wait to get the fuck gone.

He'd come to warn Enlightenment Fields away from the Wests and their ranch, but instinct told him that would only piss off these fanatics. Maggie and her grandparents would end up paying the price. Stepping carefully, seeing what they were up against, figuring out the best way to deliver the message so they wouldn't lash out made sense right now.

"I just might. Before I go, could I use your restroom?" That would give him some privacy to text Logan.

Instantly, she got nervous. "Ah . . . well. You'll have to give me a minute to clean up."

"No need, Mercy. I'm not expecting anything fancy." *I just want to figure out what you're hiding* . . . "Functional suits me fine. Simply point me in the right direction."

The woman arranged her mouth into something almost resembling a smile. "Um . . . well, okay. This way."

She led him down a short hallway. One door on his right stood ajar. Mercy closed it as she passed but not before he saw stacks of crates filling the room. Same thing with another door on her left. Wall-to-wall, floor-to-ceiling. What the hell were they stockpiling here? Whatever it was, she didn't want him to know about it.

"Here you are." She leaned into the little bathroom, kicked the cabinet under the sink closed, then flipped on a light before racing to draw the shower curtain. "Don't mind all my plants. I like to grow them. I have a really green thumb, and the light in here is just right for these sensitive babies."

Josiah stepped past her and inside the small space. Holy shit, it was like a jungle. Mirrors covered the walls. A little fan oscillated the breeze around the room from the bathroom counter. A humidifier sat between the sink and the toilet. The bathroom was a makeshift greenhouse?

"No problem," he insisted, eager to shut the door and figure out why jumpy little Mercy seemed so intent on hiding her growing greenery. "I won't disturb them. I just appreciate it, ma'am."

"No need for formality here." She brushed against him before she slipped out of the room. "Call me Mercy."

He gave her a nod, then shut the door, very nearly in her face. Clearly, she didn't want to leave him unsupervised in any corner of this house. But he had to connect with Logan now or the cavalry might show up before he figured out what the fuck was going on.

His phone buzzed in his pocket, a text from Logan. **All okay?**

I'm fine. This place isn't. I'll call when I leave. Gone in 10.

Ring me then.

He closed Messenger, then launched his camera. He didn't know shit about plants, but he could find someone who did. Maybe gardening was Mercy's hobby and this would amount to nothing more sinister than her being protective of fragile vegetation. But he'd bet every dime he had the explanation wasn't that simple.

Easing aside the shower curtain, Josiah snapped a few pictures of her "babies" getting sun. The green ones were definitely cannabis plants. So the sect of "conscious awakening" was into pot, huh? Hanging from racks attached to the ceiling were herbs of some sort with tiny purple blooms and open-bottom pots. Under the cabinets, he found mushrooms with brown caps growing in the damp shade. Hallucinogenic, maybe?

Mercy was definitely doing more than indulging her green thumb here. His guess? She was boiling down the elements she grew and brewing one hell of a trip.

Josiah snapped pictures of everything, focusing tight on all the plant species so they could be ID'd. Then he flushed the empty toilet, washed his hands, and emerged from the bathroom with forced cheer.

He was a little surprised Mercy wasn't waiting, come-hither smile in place.

"Where were you? You left the mixture untended and the plants lying around." Mercy sounded very unhappy with whomever she was berating.

"I-I was short on glycerin, and I didn't see any in the pantry, so I had to run to the storehouse and—"

"Never leave the kitchen untended," she snapped at the other woman.

"Yes, Mercy. I'm sorry. I won't do it again." The woman sounded terrified.

Mercy huffed. "Have you had breakfast?"

"No."

"After you're done here, take a bottle from the refrigerator and go to your room. Meditate until I come for you."

"But—"

"Don't argue. Strife poisons our collective spirit. Adam knows what's best for us all. This is his will."

"My baby—"

"Not another word." The hard edge in Mercy's tone said she didn't give two shits what happened to this woman or her child.

"Yes, Mercy." The woman's voice was so timid, Josiah could barely hear her.

Shutting the bathroom door with an audible click and stepping down the hall loudly, Josiah emerged into the open living and kitchen space, giving the counters a discreet glance. Colanders lined the sink. Several funnels rested nearby, along with smaller strainers, pieces of cheesecloth, and various jars.

They had to be making something shady.

Josiah smiled. "Thank you for the restroom. I should get on the road."

Mercy didn't spare the other woman another glance. Instead, she rushed over, all smiles again, encircling his arm. "You really don't have a few minutes for the rest of your tour?"

"I don't. I'm sorry I ran out of time." He sent her an apologetic glance.

"Well . . ." She tried to cover her displeasure with a smile. "Another time, maybe?"

"Maybe."

"Hopefully soon. I'll walk you to your truck."

Josiah wished she'd get away from him. "That would be great."

"We're having a welcome party for some new Chosen on Tuesday night. I'd love for you to join us, so you can really see the spirit of our community."

"If I'm still in town, I'll definitely consider it." On the twelfth of never as hell was freezing over.

She led him out the front door of the house. "I hope to see you."

He gave her a noncommittal nod. "So . . . what was your friend making in the kitchen? Soap? It smelled interesting."

"Oh, that?" She shook her head. "Just a homemade broth that's always wonderful to serve, but especially when the weather is nippy."

A mushroom and cannabis mystery broth? With glycerin, an ingredient common in soap? Bullshit.

This whole place was buckets full of wrong. He needed to get the fuck out, call Logan, and reassess another way to keep Maggie and her grandparents safe.

"I get that." He nodded as they crossed the yard and headed back toward the others toiling.

"Who are you visiting in town?"

Damn, he should have anticipated this question. Unfortunately, he didn't know anyone except Maggie and her grandparents. But he did know the name of their murdered neighbor . . .

"I'm on my way to the Haney ranch. I've always been close to Ben. I'm hoping he could help me find work."

Mercy flinched. It was a tiny moment, the merest pinch of her mouth, before she covered it with a sticky-sweet concern. "Oh, dear. You don't know?"

"Know what?"

"Mr. Haney had an unfortunate . . . accident."

She classified being pinned to the floor by a pitchfork and left to bleed to death a mishap?

"Oh?"

Mercy cleared her throat. "I'm afraid he died on Friday. I'm so sorry."

Josiah pretended shock. "What? I had no idea. I don't . . . understand. How?"

"I don't know the details. We don't talk much to the townsfolk since they don't understand us. I just know what the headline in the local paper said."

Instinct told him she knew exactly what had happened to the old man. Josiah had no proof, but everything about her reactions seemed somewhere between forced and rehearsed.

"I-I don't know what to say," he mumbled.

"I'm sure this is a shock. Josiah, there's no one at the Haney ranch to visit. It's probably blocked from visitors until the police finish their investigation . . ." She shook her head. "Such a tragedy. You're welcome to stay here. We can even talk through your grief."

Not on your life.

"It's just so terrible," he muttered, hoping she chalked his non-answer up to shock.

"You and Mr. Haney aren't related, are you? I didn't think he had any family left."

Josiah heard faint alarm in her tone, as if that possibility disturbed her.

He dodged the question. "I need to go. I have to make some phone calls and—"

"You really are welcome to stay. I'll personally take care of you."

How, by getting on her back and spreading her legs? The way she behaved, that seemed the most likely scenario. They were talking about a dead man, and she seemed awfully eager to crowd his personal space and press her breasts against him.

"That's kind of you. I just . . . I need some time alone. This is a huge shock. Wow . . ."

As they strolled past the workers toiling and neared his truck, Mercy released his arm. "I understand. I'm here if you want help or spiritual release."

Josiah tried not to laugh. Spiritual release? Did she mean shouting *Oh, god* as she came?

Instead, he squeezed her hand. "I appreciate it. I may take you up on that."

"I hope you do." She rose up on her tiptoes and brushed a kiss across his cheek.

"Can I call you to let you know?"

With a faint smile, she shook her head. "At Enlightenment Fields, we believe technology leads us away from our chosen community. We have a single phone in Adam's office so we can reach the outside world in case of emergency, but no one here has their own cell or any other personal communication method. We've all chosen to commune with nature and one another. For the most part, we have no need for anyone else."

This place got creepier and creepier . . .

"Sometimes I wish I could just toss my phone in the trash," he lied. "It beeps and dings and—"

"Ruins your calm and focus, right? We understand."

Josiah gave one last glance around the commune. Along one building in the distance he saw a rack of plastic fifty-five-gallon barrels marked DRINKING WATER. There had to be a hundred stacked on top of each other across multiple racks. A buddy of his in Minnesota was a prepper, and this shit looked right up his alley . . . Along the side of the greenhouse—he now wondered what they grew in there—were bags of seeds marked SURVIVAL GARDEN. Something else his pal would love.

Near the field, Eli and Samuel, the rifle-toting goons, had been replaced with two more remarkably like their ilk, long on watchfulness, short on communications skills, and quick with the trigger.

Really, what the fuck was going on around here?

"You're curious?" Mercy observed.

"How can I not be? Your way of life is very different."

"Than the outside world, yes. But that's the point. Everything out there seeks to use you up, drain your energy, block your journey of inner understanding, and leave you empty. I'm sure to most it seems odd here at first, but people soon understand that civilization out there is corrupt. Here, it's safe and comforting. It's home."

He nodded as if she'd given him lots of food for thought. "Thanks for your hospitality."

"I'm glad you stopped by, Josiah. My door is always open. I hope I see you Tuesday."

She stepped back, and he was glad to finally get some breathing room. He hopped in his truck and gunned the engine as his phone buzzed again. As he backed away from the commune and rattled down the dirt road, he saw a message from Logan.

Get out okay?

He didn't text back, just grabbed the device and dialed his boss.

"Yes, but holy shit. You were right about this place. Everything here is off."

"Goddamn it." Logan sighed. "Tell me what you know."

"Where are you?"

"Still on the road back to Lafayette. I pulled over to grab some breakfast. Getting back on the road now. Spill it."

Josiah did, not leaving out a damn thing. "I've got pictures of all the plants. But I'm telling you, they're brewing something over there that's not remotely legal. You and Tara still have contacts in the FBI?"

"Yeah. So does Sean Mackenzie, Callie's husband. We'll make a few phone calls, figure out who might be interested in your findings. Sounds like we'll need a botanist, too."

"As soon as I get back to the Wests' ranch, I'll send you all the photos."

"Good. What are you going to do about Maggie?" Logan hesitated.

"I don't know yet." But Josiah didn't like her being so near this place.

"You two weren't quiet last night . . ."

"We didn't mean to keep you up." But he wasn't apologizing for it.

"I'm used to it. It's like camping with Hunter and Kata. Or Tyler and Delaney. Or Kimber and Deke." Logan groaned. "And there's nothing more awful than listening to your sister getting frisky."

Josiah tried not to let it, but the image of his sisters and their husbands doing the nasty bombarded his brain . . . He winced. "Ugh. I hate you for putting that in my head. I need bleach."

Logan howled. "Now I don't have to suffer alone."

"Yeah, laugh it up . . . As for Maggie, I'm worried. I have zero proof, but I think Enlightenment Fields had something to do with Haney's death. I don't know why they'd want him dead but—"

"I've been doing a little investigating, so I can tell you exactly why. Apparently these fruit loops have been buying parcels of land southeast of Comfort, west of I-10, mostly uninhabited. But they'd like all the stretches east of town. They already own the sections that butt up against Comfort. Haney refused to sell his spread, but since he had no family . . . I guess it will be on the market now."

"Isn't that a coincidence?" Josiah quipped. "Mercy was quick to ask if I was Haney's kin."

Because if he had been, he would have stood to inherit it, and that would mean more obstacles to acquisition for them.

"I'll bet. Want to guess who owns the land sandwiched between Haney's and the commune?"

Josiah's blood ran cold. "Maggie's grandparents?"

"Bingo."

Holy motherfucking shit. "That definitely concerns me."

"It should."

"Look, I know I had an assignment starting Thursday, but—"

"Taking care of Maggie and her grandparents doesn't pay the bills, and guarding the senator on his trip to New Orleans does."

"Then I'll take vacation and do this on my own time. But I can't leave the Wests to suffer the same fate as Haney."

"As it happens, I promised Cutter that we would keep Shealyn's family safe while they're gone. I'd be letting him down if I didn't tell you to stay and take care of them."

Relief poured through Josiah. "Thanks."

"No problem. The senator is an asshole, anyway. I'll let him spend some time with One-Mile. And his absence from town will get him off of Brea's back. Two birds, one stone."

"Good thinking. I'll go back to Maggie and . . ." *Tell her what?* "Figure out what to do next."

Whatever happened, since Magnolia West was involved, it was bound to be complicated. But bottom line, he was moving in until this situation was resolved—whether she liked it or not.

How he'd keep his hands off her and other parts of him from becoming too attached would be a whole different question.

CHAPTER 6

When Josiah's truck pulled into the yard, Maggie felt more giddy and relieved than she should.

"You sweet on him?" Granna asked as she raised her hand to her brow, shielding her face from the sun as he parked.

Josiah exited his vehicle. She held her breath as he scanned the yard. His gaze screeched to a stop when he spotted her. Maggie swallowed down something that felt suspiciously like her heart.

What the devil? She didn't connect with people. Coupling up was definitely beyond her emotional capability. But from the second she'd set eyes on Josiah, it was as if some invisible string attached them. She'd thought she had snipped that tie this morning. She'd sent him on his way, after all.

Then you stupidly flirted with him about cereal. Face it, you're more than a little interested.

She was. And now, some subversive part of her wanted him to stay at least a little longer, see what might happen between them.

"He's all right," she told her grandmother.

Granna laughed. "From you, that's almost a declaration of love. And he seems really eager to talk to you, Maggie girl."

It looked that way. Those long legs of his, the ones he had used to spread her thighs wider and propel himself deeper inside her last night, ate the distance between them now. His gaze never wavered from her.

Lord, was she really trembling?

"I'll go see what he wants."

"You do that. I'll wrap up with the rental company now that everything is loaded."

Once Granna turned away to deal with the driver, Maggie headed across the yard toward Josiah, stuffing her hands in the back pockets of her jeans. If she didn't, she'd be more than tempted to touch him again. The truth was, everything about him flipped her switch. Even when she didn't want to want him, she did.

"Hey." She greeted him as they neared, steps slowing.

"Maggie." He studied her as if he could look inside her.

"How'd it go?"

He hesitated. Trepidation tightened her chest.

"We should talk," he said finally. "About a lot of things."

Did he mean the two of them? Normally, "romantic" conversations made her shudder and run. A lot of drama for something not meant to last. Why bother? But she wanted to enjoy the time she shared with Josiah. That mattered, probably more than it should. Some part of her even fantasized about sharing more than a fling.

Silly and impossible.

"All right. Papa went to see what he could find out about Ben Haney's death, so we can use his study."

"Let's go." He wrapped his arm around her waist and guided her toward the house. "The yard looks almost bare without the big white tent."

"Doesn't it? I'd kind of gotten used to the ranch looking like a circus."

He nodded, but there wasn't an ounce of levity in his expression. Something was definitely wrong.

After they entered the house, they each grabbed a bottle of water from the fridge. Nerves bunched her stomach as Josiah hustled her into the study and behind closed doors. The moment they were alone, quiet resonated. The room was so silent she could hear him breathe. The air pinged.

They sat facing each other in the guest chairs flanking her grand-father's desk. She sensed his nerves. Yeah, this wasn't going to be pretty.

"Just tell me," she insisted. "Enlightenment Fields isn't going to leave us alone, are they?"

"I didn't even broach that with them."

"What? The point of your visit—"

"Was to warn them away, I know. But Maggie, if I had, it would have painted a target on your back." He grabbed her hand. "I got a 'tour' of the place. Been out there since they moved in?"

She shook her head. "That strange girl Mercy came over when they first moved to the area and invited us to visit, but I didn't like her vibe right away. Everything about her said, 'Beware. Cult!'"

"Your instincts were right. I'm pretty sure they're doing some-thing illegal and sinister over there. It's not a place I should have vis-ited without a SWAT team and a boatload of heavily armed agents, so I got the hell out."

Maggie was disappointed, but she understood. He was wary. Hell, she had been, too, from the moment she'd met Mercy. Glimpses of Adam Coleman around town were few and far between, but there was something about the slick stranger that gave her the heebies.

"Makes sense," she murmured. "Thank you for trying. We'll just—"

"I want you to listen to me, Maggie. You and your grandparents shouldn't be here until this shit is resolved. Can y'all go somewhere for a few weeks?"

"What do you mean? Go where? Who will stay and tend the ranch?"

"The hands?" He certainly didn't trust Sawyer.

"It's not that simple. We can't just leave. This is my grandparents' home and livelihood."

"You have to. I suspect Enlightenment Fields killed Ben Haney. It's a gut feeling. I don't have proof, but if that's the case, you have a lot of reasons to be worried about your grandparents." Then his fingers wrapped around her wrist, branding her with his insistent heat. "And I have a lot of reasons to be worried about you."

Maggie froze. She didn't have to ask why he was worried; she knew. With Haney's death, his land would soon be up for sale. The cult would snap it up. Once they did, she and her grandparents would be virtually surrounded. Then what was the likelihood they'd accept Granna and Papa's refusal to sell?

"I see your point."

"Good. So let's talk about getting the three of you somewhere else while I stay behind to clean this mess up. Hopefully, the FBI will join me, and we'll figure out exactly what's going on and how to take these people down."

"I'm not leaving."

Josiah's voice turned stern. "You are. You have to."

She shook her head. "My grandparents will refuse to leave if I go, too. They'll insist one of the family stay behind to look over the spread. They've always been that way, but they've gotten more stubborn as they've gotten older. So either they stay behind—which I can't let happen—or I do."

He hung his head and shook it. His frustration spilled in the air. "Damn it, Maggie. I need you to understand—"

"I do. You're worried I'll be a target. Believe me, I'm afraid, too. I've never wanted to be a hero, just . . ." What had she wanted from life? Maggie still wasn't sure. It was easy to say what she didn't want: her sister's fame or her childhood pals' moves to the big cities and their high-powered careers. The thought of a husband and kids made her a little uneasy and squeamish, too. "Just do my thing."

"If I talked to your grandparents—explained—surely they'd see reason. I can't believe they'd ever want to risk your safety."

"No, but they refuse to bow to Enlightenment Fields. In their minds, as long as they stay strong, there's no problem. Since you have no proof they killed Haney, to them running away would be a show of weakness. If we're going to convince them to leave, we'll have to convince them it's a vacation, not a flight to sanctuary."

"So fucking stubborn . . ."

"Oh, you have *no* idea. Papa will get a notion in his head and *no one* can talk him out of it. Believe me, we've all tried."

He sighed. "Okay. We'll convince them to go on vacation. Where would they want to go?"

Good question. "They're homebodies, but they've said more than once that they'd like to see where Shealyn lives now. They've never been to California."

"Let me see what I can do about getting them on a plane to LA tomorrow. I know it's your sister's honeymoon, but can you contact her—"

"If I tell her what's going on, she'll cut her honeymoon short and return. I can't let her do that. She and Cutter need this time together. Clearly, their hope that Shealyn's career would end with *Hot Southern Nights* isn't realistic."

"Not even close. So don't tell her. Maybe just say that your grandparents would like to visit and stay at her place?"

Shealyn might guess that something was fishy. At the very least, her older sister would wonder why Granna and Papa were choosing to visit when she couldn't be there to show them around, but Maggie didn't see what other choices she had. "I'll try."

Josiah nodded. "If you can do that, I'll get you out of here ten minutes after they're gone. Someplace safe. I have a lot of friends in Louisiana. Hell, Cutter's boss wants you safe—"

"I have to stay here," she insisted, shaking her head. "My grandparents will call the phone on the ranch. If I don't answer, they'll get on a plane and come home."

"I'll forward the home phone to your cell."

"And when they ask me to go out and check on a certain head of cattle or run an errand into town for them or ask Sawyer to join me for a discussion about feeding schedules, then what? They *will* check in. Every day."

Josiah gritted his teeth. "You're not safe here, Maggie."

Didn't he think she knew that? "My grandparents took me in when I was two. I was a handful as a toddler, and to hear them say it, nothing has changed. I *owe* them. If not for them, I would have ended up on the streets with my mother when her drug addiction was at its worst. God knows what would have happened to me. This ranch means more to them than almost anything. It's been in my grandfather's family for four generations. Since my mother isn't moving here from Costa Rica, I'm supposed to be the sixth. They're counting on leaving it to me. My grandfather will die a crushed man if he loses this place."

"I'll bet he'd rather lose the land than lose you."

"If the FBI helps, surely they won't let anything happen to me."

"I can't guarantee they'll actually come, Maggie. I'll be here but—"

"Then I'll be safe."

He reared back. "You trust me with your safety? You believe I'll keep you out of harm's way?"

Josiah sounded surprised. Maybe the notion should surprise her, too. But he obviously took his role as a protector seriously. He'd made it his livelihood, for goodness' sake. He worked for badass people and had badass friends. She was tougher than she looked. Even if the FBI didn't come, Maggie had to believe they could keep the ranch from falling into the cult's hands.

"I have no doubt."

He hesitated a moment, cursed under his breath, then gripped her hand and tugged. She flew out of her chair and sprawled onto his lap. Their chests collided. He wrapped his arms around her, fingers circling her nape.

"Damn it, woman," he breathed. "Every time I swear I'm going to stop thinking about you, you make that impossible."

Maggie didn't have time to react. He bent and fused their lips to-

gether. The instant their lips touched, her body pinged from head to
toe. Suddenly, she was on fire. And she didn't hate it one bit.

As his tongue invaded, he arranged her so she straddled his lap.
Maggie couldn't help but respond. She pressed her sex to his erection.
More tingles erupted. Her womb clenched. She groaned into his kiss.

Lord, the friction between them generated a pleasure that un-
wound her . . .

Josiah tore his mouth free, panting. "You are a stubborn woman."

She'd heard that before. "I have to keep my grandparents and this
land safe. So you're stuck with me."

His sigh told her that he wasn't happy, but he knew he didn't have
a choice. He could hardly kick her off her own land. "Fine. But there
are rules. The first is that when I tell you to do something, you fucking do it."

"We've already had this argument. I believe I mentioned that I
don't follow orders well."

"I don't mean in bed, though we're going to talk about that, too.
But if Enlightenment Fields comes onto your land, I'm going to tell
you how to keep yourself safe. And you're going to listen."

Maggie wasn't going to argue; the fact was this was his area of expertise. "All right."

"Can you fire a gun?"

"Of course." She'd grown up hunting with her grandfather . . .
though he'd been unable to get out to bag white-tailed deer, antelope,
or javelina in probably ten years. "But I might be rusty."

Josiah nodded. "We'll fix that. I want to be prepared, just in case."

As much as she didn't want to think about that eventuality, Maggie
had to. If Enlightenment Fields really had killed Ben Haney, then
they were far more dangerous than she'd assumed. She had to be ready
for the worst.

"You're right."

"Anyone around town likely to be in our corner? Other ranchers?"

She shook her head. "Enlightenment Fields already bought out a lot of them. Many were older folks who never thought they'd get a dime for their spreads, so when these out-of-towners came and offered market value for land no one had shown interest in for decades, they sold fast. That's how the cult amassed so much space in the county so quickly."

"Law enforcement? Mercy mentioned a new deputy who didn't seem terribly fond of them."

"Kane Preston has been here about two years. Ex-military. Said he was looking for wide-open spaces and fewer people, so he landed in Comfort. He seems all right, but it's hard to say for sure. He keeps to himself. Sheriff Wayne is all right. He's kept the county safe for decades. He knows the area well since he was born and raised in these parts. He wants what's best for Kendall County . . . but he's getting older and he's counting the days until his retirement."

"Anyone against us?"

She nodded. "A few. Willa Mae at the Super S."

"Another ranch?"

"Grocery store. She was damn near bankrupt before Enlightenment Fields moved in."

"They grow their own food."

"Some, sure. But not all. They don't make their own bread. They only recently started milking and slaughtering their own cattle. They've got a few chickens, but not enough to keep the operation in eggs. Willa Mae is happy to augment their food supply. But she won't be useful to their cause. She's eighty-five if she's a day."

Josiah nodded absently. "Are you sure about staying? Things could get dangerous."

Logic told her staying to fight for a parcel of land was about the stupidest choice she could make. But if she didn't, Papa would . . . and he might not survive. "Yes."

"Then let's get started." As they rose, he grabbed her arm and drew her near again. "I don't know what's going to happen, but I'll do everything I can to protect you."

"I know."

"But I can't promise to keep my hands off you . . . Magnolia."

Hearing his husky whisper wrap around her name made Maggie shiver and melt. "What makes you think I intend to keep my hands off *you*?"

Three hours later, he'd figured out a shitload of details and cleared an equal amount of red tape. Logan had contacted the FBI, who said they'd get back to him. He'd also found someone to identify the three plants in Mercy's bathroom. What Josiah had suspected was cannabis was a particularly strong strain known as Bruce Banner. The brown-capped mushrooms were in fact a psychoactive variety known as psilocybin, and their use for mind alteration dated all the way back to cave drawings. The last plant with the unfamiliar purple flowers was *Salvia divinorum*, something in the mint family that also possessed hallucinogenic properties.

"So you think Enlightenment Fields is 'opening minds' by boiling these three ingredients together and . . . what? Getting their followers to ingest it?" Logan asked.

"It's possible. When a woman working in the kitchen displeased her, Mercy told her to grab a bottle, go to her room, and 'meditate.' The woman balked because she's pregnant. I'm wondering if that bottle was full of whatever they're brewing . . ."

"If so and Mercy made a pregnant woman take a trip, that's messed up."

"Totally." Josiah pressed his lips together, not liking anything he was hearing. "Hey, thanks for finding a way to transport Maggie's grandparents to California."

"Like I said, Xander, Javier, and London were flying to LA anyway. The guys have meetings, and London is going to take Dulce on her first trip to Disneyland before the new baby comes. It was nothing to add two more passengers to their private jet. Once they land, I'll arrange a car to pick up the Wests and get them to Shealyn's place. We'll just make sure they're conveniently unable to come home until everything gets resolved."

"Then we'll have to work fast."

If her grandparents were as stubborn as Maggie said, he wasn't sure how long he could keep them away. At the very least, Cutter and Shealyn would return from their honeymoon, and if the elder Wests were still conveniently away, they would start asking questions. Cutter was smart; he'd figure it out. And Josiah doubted the guy would be able to keep his beautiful bride in the dark for long. As soon as Shealyn knew, shit would hit the fan.

"Yep. Unless and until we get official support from Uncle Sam, I'm going to send Zyron and Trees your way. They'll be doing research for upcoming assignments, but they can take phone calls and work out tactical plans from anywhere."

Any support that would help keep Maggie safe Josiah welcomed. "Excellent. While I'm waiting for them to arrive, I'm going to pay Deputy Preston a visit. Since Mercy didn't like him, I'll see what he knows and what kind of ally he might be."

"Perfect. If there's a local paper, check that out, too. See if they've investigated the group. And check the tax records."

"Yep. On my list. If Coleman has violated IRS code . . . Well, it's not a glamorous way to take him down, but that would definitely land him in jail."

"Absolutely. What are you planning to do about Tuesday night? Mercy's invitation might be exactly the in we need for a recon mission."

As much as Josiah didn't like it, Logan was right. He needed to get inside that compound, see if they were growing more of the same crops, figure out what other sinister shit might be going on. For that, he might have to get closer to Mercy, gain her trust, and hope she would give him some clue about Enlightenment Fields' plans. Because not knowing worried him. The enemy would be easier to fight if he had any fucking idea what their objective was and how they planned to go about it.

"Yeah. I'll see what I can discern. How soon will we know whether the FBI will engage?"

"I wish I could tell you. Everyone Tara talked to played it close to the vest, so we're not sure if these fanatics were even on the feds' radar. Sean called his contacts and got a similar song and dance. If they're already looking at Enlightenment Fields, my guess is they'll respond swiftly and tell us to back off. If not . . . we may not get help until the eleventh hour. Hard to know which right now."

That was not good news. "These fanatics are trouble. I can feel it."

"I'm there with you. Get Maggie's grandparents on that plane tomorrow and keep looking for answers. Check in at least once a day. If I don't hear from someone over there regularly, Hunter, Joaquin, and I will be on your doorstep with a whole lot of 'oh, fuck.' Are we clear?"

"Crystal."

They rang off, and Josiah exited the bedroom he'd shared with Maggie the previous night and went in search of her. The sun would be setting in a couple of hours, and he hoped like hell she'd been able to convince her grandparents to go to California.

In the kitchen, he found her fixing sloppy joes and chatting with her grandmother.

"You're going to have a great adventure, Granna. Trust me, everything here will be fine."

The older woman shook her head, her white hair so well sprayed it didn't budge from its coiffure. "This trip is so sudden. We thought we'd stay here and recover from the wedding, get the house and the barn back in order . . ."

"I can do all that," Maggie argued. "You keep wanting me to show you how responsible I've become, that I can handle the ranch if something were to happen to you and Papa. Then let me prove I can do it. You two haven't taken a vacation in years. Now's the time to do it. Josiah's friends will fly you on their private plane. You'll have Shealyn's amazing place all to yourself. And I've seen it. Trust me, you'll love it."

"I don't know . . ."

"If not now, then when? The timing couldn't be more perfect. There's not much going on around here now. I'll have Sawyer if something comes up around the ranch. Josiah is staying for a few days . . ."

"Ah." Granna smiled. "And you want to be alone with him. Why didn't you say so?"

"I was trying."

Her grandmother pried apart some hamburger buns, slathered butter on them, then set them facedown on the griddle. "I'm sorry about Davis, Maggie girl."

She hesitated, and Josiah eased a step back, just out of the room to give them some privacy. But if he turned and walked away now, they'd hear him on the squeaky wooden floors.

"I know, Granna. And I felt like I let you down. I just couldn't love him."

The older woman sighed. "Clarisse called me last week. She apologized to me and wanted me to convey that to you. Apparently Davis came out to his family. You were right."

"I hope they accepted him and that he's okay."

"They were surprised—"

"I don't know why. It might not have been obvious at a glance, but anyone who spent much time with him should have been able to figure it out."

"Maybe they didn't want to. Anyway, they're all doing their best to be supportive now. Davis introduced them to a young man he's dating, someone named Martin. Apparently, he's much happier."

"I'm glad for him."

Her grandmother shot her a glance full of both love and sadness. "Oh, honey. I know you are. You have such a big heart, even if you don't think so. I want you to be happy, too. I want you to find a good man like your sister did."

Maggie scoffed. "As beautiful as Shealyn is, there's no way she was destined to spend her life alone."

"You're beautiful, too. Don't you know that?"

To his surprise, Maggie squirmed and shrugged. "But she's really sweet, too. We all know I have . . . What does Papa call it? 'A crusty outer shell.' It's fine. I'm happy alone."

"Magnolia Rose," Granna chided. "Don't you lie to me. And don't you think that's how you're going to end up. You're not unlovable. Don't let your mama's choice to bring you here make you think you are. She didn't bring you here because she didn't care about you. She brought you here because she did. She was sick and—"

"I know. Just like I know I was better off here than on the streets with her. It sucks that she has no idea who my father is. It would have been nice if he'd cared enough to want to meet me . . ."

"Maybe she never told him you existed." Granna's expression softened. "Your mama doesn't remember much about that time in her life."

"She told me a lot of those years are hazy." Maggie gave a brave nod, but her face held something . . . It was heavier than wistfulness, more profound than sadness. "It's fine."

She was lying. She wanted someone to love her and was one hundred percent sure she would never find her One.

Josiah held himself back from crashing their conversation, taking Maggie in his arms, and assuring her she was beautiful, intriguing, funny—all the things that made a man fall. But what the hell did he know about love personally? High school aside, his one significant foray into romance had been full of deception, betrayal, and bullshit. And maybe he'd just seen too much of the bad in the world to believe in lasting goodness.

He should stay the hell away from Magnolia. But he had no idea where he was going to find the will.

The ladies went back to cooking, and he waited a few moments before seeming to step into the hall and enter the kitchen. "I'm going to head out and grab some things in town since I'm staying for a few days. Anyone need anything?"

Maggie's grandmother bustled around the room to check her kitchen supplies, then disappeared into the pantry around the corner. Maggie herself sent him a questioning stare.

"I won't be long. Where can I find the deputy?"

"No telling, but I'd start just off exit 523 on I-10 eastbound. He likes to run a speed trap out there. Profitable for the town. If not, try the Cypress Creek Inn. He usually likes a late lunch, and this is about the right time."

"Thanks." It was surprisingly hard not to touch Maggie. Instead, he just nodded.

After the older West woman handed him a short grocery list, Josiah was jostling down the dirt road in his truck. Since he had to drive through town, he found the deputy at the restaurant, washing down the last of a grilled chicken breast and broccoli.

"Deputy Preston?" Josiah held out his hand.

"Yep." The guy, who looked around thirty and in exceptional shape, shook it. "Who the hell are you?"

"It's complicated. Have a minute?"

The deputy wiped at his neat dark mustache, then glanced at his watch. "About four, then I'm back on duty."

"I'll talk quick. Mind if I have a seat?"

"As long as you're not here to plead your case about a speeding ticket Sheriff Wayne wrote you . . ." The guy gestured to the chair beside him, obviously wishing Josiah would get to the point.

"No. Name's Josiah Grant. I work for a group of freelance security operatives out of Louisiana."

"You're a ways from home." The deputy turned to him with a curious stare. "You one of those badasses who came with the wedding party?"

"Cutter is a colleague, yes."

His expression turned slightly less suspicious but no less bored. "Were you an Agency man? You have that air."

Preston clearly wasn't obtuse if he'd guessed Josiah's CIA past. "Back in the day."

"So what do you want? To see how we keep order in a small town?"

Preston also had a chip on his shoulder . . . "I want to talk to you about Enlightenment Fields."

The deputy sat up straighter. "Yeah?"

"I went there to check it out today as a favor to Shealyn's husband. I met Mercy."

"A looker, isn't she?"

"Hmm." And probably a damn fine recruiting tool. "She mentioned you weren't a fan of the group."

"Are you?"

"Considering they're bullying Shealyn and Maggie's grandparents to sell their spread and I'm pretty sure they're up to something illegal, no."

Now he had the deputy's attention. "You know something I don't?"

"We'll come back to that. Got any leads on Ben Haney's killer? Maybe evidence that his murder was committed by someone belonging to the sect?"

"You know I can't comment on an active investigation. Besides, it's too early to have forensics back. I guess you hotshots who worked CIA aren't used to waiting in line for results."

Josiah sidestepped his barb. "Check for possible links between Haney and Enlightenment Fields. I'm not here for long and I'd like to make sure the Wests stay safe—"

"That's my job, and I'm capable of doing it. No one asked you to stick your nose into Comfort's business."

"You know, we're ultimately on the same side. I'm trying to establish how dangerous Enlightenment Fields might be. If they killed Haney for his land, the Wests are likely next."

The deputy mulled his words, his mouth flattening in a grim line. "Point taken. Between us?"

"Absolutely."

"We dusted the crime scene for prints and found it clean, except those belonging to the victim and his housekeeper, who had been there earlier in the day. She had a verifiable alibi for that night, so she's not the culprit."

"Any sign of forced entry?"

"None. But out here, that's not a surprise. A lot of the old-timers, especially those who live in the country, never lock their homes. Nor did we find any extra hairs or fibers at the scene. Whoever killed Ben knew exactly what they were doing." Preston hesitated. "But I found a fresh set of tire tracks in the yard that didn't belong. The vic drove a Ford F-250. So did his housekeeper. Tire size on a vehicle like that is two seventy-five. The size of tires that made these tracks are one ninety-five or thereabouts. They belong on a much smaller vehicle, probably a sedan of some sort. That might not seem like much of a clue to a city boy like you, but out here the number of people who drive something that small is finite. It's just not practical for most."

"Suspects? Who in town drives a car that small?"

"Only a few folks. The Weaver boy who came back from the big city and opened the liquor store a few years back. Mrs. Silverman, who manages the Dollar General. Trudy Hines, who owns the Kountry Kurl. And Magnolia West, to name a few."

There was no way Maggie had anything to do with Ben Haney's murder. She'd probably put on a brave face to hide her grief during her sister's wedding, but she was hardly the kind of woman who would swat a fly, much less pitchfork a grown man. But Deputy Preston was the sort who would only hear logic. "Maggie was tied up with her sister's wedding on Friday night. Houseful of people. Someone would have seen her leave."

The deputy shrugged. "She wasn't actually a suspect. None of those people are, in fact."

"What about Mercy?"

"Interesting question . . ." A gleam lit up the deputy's eyes.

"I doubt she could have killed him alone. She has the will to carry out something like this. But the strength? She's a small thing. You've seen the crime scene. What are your thoughts?"

Preston nodded. "You might be on to something. But I never said Haney's killer acted alone."

"Footprints?"

"Not inside. Outside the house, someone took the time to rake the dirt in the front yard, someone who knew I'd be investigating and that I've been nicknamed Scout for a reason."

Someone smart, Josiah conceded. "For shits and giggles, if Mercy had the will but not the strength to carry out Haney's murder to grab his land, who would she have brought with her as the muscle?"

"Probably a guy named Newt. He's a little slow up here"—Preston pointed to his head—"and pretty big everywhere else. He worships Mercy. I'm pretty sure he would do anything for her, even commit murder."

Josiah made a mental note to track the guy down on Tuesday night. Because there was no question he had to go back to Enlightenment Fields and dig up whatever clues he could.

"Does Newt have a smallish car?"

"No, but I've seen Mercy driving around town in a flashy red Mercedes that probably shares the same tire size as the killer's vehicle." Speculation lit up the deputy's face. He wasn't admitting that Mercy was his prime suspect, but he was definitely thinking it. "Analyzing the soil from her tires wouldn't tell us anything now. First, West Texas dust is the same no matter which dirt road you travel."

"And if she was the mastermind, she was smart enough to have washed the car since then."

"Exactly. As far as we can tell, nothing was taken from Haney's place. Whoever did this came there with murder on his—or her—mind."

"I suppose if you tried to serve a search warrant to Enlightenment Fields, you'd need to take the National Guard with you to do it."

"At least. I don't have any evidence, but I suspect they have some high-powered weapons in that place."

"AR-15s. I've seen them."

Preston's dark brow rose. "What else can you tell me?"

"Nothing yet, but Mercy invited me back on Tuesday night. I let her think I'm a prospect, a wandering soul who'd been looking to Ben Haney for answers to help me straighten out my messed-up life."

"And now that your savior is gone, whatever will you do?" the deputy asked, tongue-in-cheek. "Certainly, you need someone else to give you guidance."

"You got it. Here's my card." Josiah pulled one from his pocket. "If you can think of other things you want me to ferret out while I'm inside, I'll do my best to snoop."

Kane Preston snapped it up. "Why are you helping me?"

"The sooner we figure out if Enlightenment Fields is the kind of group who would kill over land, the sooner I can be sure the Wests are safe." Josiah tapped his finger on the table, then stood. "I'll be in touch."

CHAPTER 7

Josiah returned from town with everything Granna had requested. While Maggie helped her grandparents with last-minute packing, he checked the perimeter of the property, inside and out, almost compulsively tightening door handles everywhere. At the back of the house, he added a sturdier lock. He augmented the double doors in the dining room, which overlooked the patio, with a sliding deadbolt. He padlocked each of the side gates flanking the backyard. When she found him securing all the downstairs windows, she scowled and followed him.

"What the devil are you doing? You might be used to the big city, but out here, people rarely lock their doors. Nothing happens in Comfort."

"You mean other than your neighbor's horrific murder two days ago?"

With all the business of the wedding, she'd pushed her grief about losing the sweet Mr. Haney aside and focused on making Shealyn's big day the happiest possible. Now that her sister was gone and her grandparents were leaving, she couldn't help but think about the victim and the community he'd left behind.

"Do you really think anyone from Enlightenment Fields would break into the house to kill me, especially so soon after Haney's death? Wouldn't that be suspicious?"

Josiah latched the last of the windows on the bottom floor, then headed for the stairs, sparing her a glance over his shoulders. "I'm not taking any chances."

"I get that, but locks won't hold someone back forever who wants to do my family harm. You're only going to be my bodyguard for a few days. Then what? I'm going to have to take control of our safety. Tell me what I can do."

"I'm going to try my damnedest to make sure it doesn't come to that," he said, not even looking her way as he ducked into the guest bedroom.

Was he serious? "Since this is my house and my life, I deserve to know how to fix this situation."

"Right now, the less you know the better." He moved to the next window, latching it with an economy of motion.

Maggie resisted the urge to stomp her foot—barely. "Stop being macho. I can handle the truth."

"I'm not being macho. I'm being protective."

"It's the same thing. How will me staying in the dark help anything? If our culty neighbors are guilty, shouldn't I be on the lookout or trying to help you gather clues or—"

"No. You should act the way you always have and let me do my job."

Josiah spared her the briefest glance as he turned and sidestepped his way past her in the door frame, almost as if he were being cautious not to touch her.

What the hell?

"You want me to act the way I always have?" she challenged.

"That's what I said."

Oh, he had no idea what he was asking for . . .

Maggie followed him down the hall to her bedroom. As soon as he walked in the door, he stopped short. Behind him, she wondered what he thought of her personal space.

A few years back, she had redecorated it, painting over the yellow walls she'd had as a kid, muting them all to gray except one. That, she'd covered with a big wallpaper mural of a pink rose. The flower splashed across the bottom right corner just above her black padded headboard, its petals flaring out against the white background, all the way to the pale gray ceiling. She'd tossed a black-and-white geometric-patterned rug over the dark hardwood floors. A pristine white spread covered the bed. Bursts of color in every shade of pink surprised the eye all around the space.

"This is your room." It wasn't a question.

"Yeah." Why did his statement make her nervous? "How could you tell? Process of elimination?"

Josiah shook his head. "It looks like you."

"What do you mean?"

"It's bright. Unexpected. In your face."

Maggie frowned. Was that good or bad? Oh, hell. She shouldn't worry or wonder about his opinion. They'd had sex; they weren't starting a romance. Besides, it wasn't as if she could—or would—change who she was for any man.

"That *is* me," she quipped. "Take it or leave it."

Josiah stopped his visual tour of the room and turned to her. "Why do you do that?"

"Do what?"

"Get defensive whenever anyone sees the real you?"

It was something she did automatically, without conscious thought. And he'd noticed. That realization, along with the silence and the heavy weight of his stare, made her feel exposed, vulnerable. "We fucked last night. That's it. It's not like the answer matters to you. Dinner will be ready in thirty minutes."

When she turned to head for the safety of the kitchen downstairs, he snagged her by the elbow and pulled her closer. Josiah didn't force her to turn and face him, but she felt the heat of his chest against her back. His scent wrapped around her. Suddenly, her heart was galloping. She felt short of breath.

"And that right there," he murmured in her ear. "Whenever anyone tries to understand, you get prickly and push them away."

She forced herself to stay calm and find her emotional center before turning to him. "You suddenly looking for more than sex?"

"No."

"Me, either. So stay the hell out of my psyche."

Maggie jerked her arm free. To the visible eye, she didn't rush. But mentally, she made one hell of a beeline for the stairs.

Why *did* she push back whenever people—especially a man—wanted to get to know her? She had her suspicions, but really . . . This wasn't the most important item on her plate right now. She had a dead neighbor, a potential threat knocking at her door, and an interloper in her house. If he didn't want to share what he thought, knew, or plotted, well . . . she had her own crew.

After checking the casserole baking in the oven, Maggie pulled out her cell and hit Dixie Hill's number. Her former high school classmate worked as one of the local 911 dispatchers, but her building was adjacent to the police station. Sheriff Wayne's office was just down the hall. Dixie wasn't a particularly good friend. But the woman did love *any* chance to gossip. Maggie was in the mood to indulge her.

"Afternoon, Mags. What're you doing? Still cleaning up after the fancy Hollywood wedding y'all had yesterday? I sure would have liked to know what it looked like . . ."

Shealyn hadn't invited Dixie because she hadn't wanted to give the girl an opportunity to deliver her scoop to the tabloids. Even if no one had offered to pay her, Dixie would have handed over the juicy dirt. Cash wouldn't hurt, of course, but what Dixie really sought was recognition and validation.

Maggie didn't understand why the dispatcher couldn't simply find the good in herself.

"Hey, girl. What's going on?"

"Just getting ready to start the evening shift at the station. We missed you at Rhonda's birthday party last week."

Maggie hadn't gone. She wasn't close to Rhonda, either. For some reason, both women kept trying to include her in the female doings around town. Honestly, she couldn't care less. "Sorry. Everything with Shealyn's wedding was so busy . . ."

"I'll bet. Hey, I saw a stranger talking to Deputy Preston earlier today at the Cypress Creek Inn. Short brown hair, muscles on his muscles—a real hot number. I overheard him say he was one of Cutter's peers. What do you know about him?"

She had to be describing Josiah. If Dixie liked one thing even more than gossip, it was men. For some reason she didn't want to examine, Maggie felt decidedly reluctant to discuss the gorgeous hunk of man she'd spent last night with.

"Yeah. He's all right if you like a manwhore."

Dixie didn't. She'd gotten shafted—metaphorically and literally—by Curtis Garcia in the tenth grade. The next week, he'd moved on to Celine Moore, followed by someone else the week after. Since then, she seemed intent on finding a man who would fall madly, desperately in love with her and never fall out. Maggie couldn't picture that happening. Not because Dixie was unattractive or unworthy. But how did she expect someone else to love her if she wouldn't love herself?

"Oh," she groaned. "That sucks. He come on to you or something?"

Time to change the subject. "Hey, I know you're not supposed to say anything, but I'm scared and I could really use your excellent investigative nose. Ben Haney . . . What happened?"

For once, Dixie was silent.

"Hello?"

"I'm here. Honestly, Mags. It was really ugly. I'd rather not talk about it. We haven't had a murder in Comfort in forever, and this . . ."

"Gory?"

"The pictures looked awful. It wasn't like when Mrs. Adams got pissed at her husband for having a side thing with Gracie Lowe and shot him in the groin. Whoever killed Mr. Haney was really mad."

Maggie imagined the blood everywhere and grimaced.

Haney had lost his wife a few years back and his only son in Afghanistan a decade prior. He hadn't had anyone to look out for him since. He'd probably even thought he'd die alone—but not violently. When she thought about how terrified he must have been to see someone barge into his house with a pitchfork, she shuddered. The sweet old man must have suffered horrifically while the killer impaled and staked him to the ground, then let him bleed to death.

Maggie wished like hell she could have saved him. His family had always been so kind—his wife had baked her and Shealyn cookies, and Ben had often come out to the ranch to pick them up when he'd taken his boy, Todd, into town for ice cream. She felt as if she'd let the old man down.

"Dixie, anything you can tell me would help. Ben Haney was my nearest neighbor. My sister and most of her husband's badass peers are gone now. My grandparents have decided to take a vacation after the exhaustion of hosting Shealyn's wedding." Maggie gave Dixie that scoop, hoping the woman would reciprocate. "It won't be long before I'm at this ranch all alone for days. That didn't bother me until I realized there's a killer on the loose in Kendall County."

"Oh, honey . . . I didn't even think about that. I'm sorry. What do you want to know?"

"Please tell me they've identified the killer. Or at least have some idea who he is."

"I wish I could. So far we've got nothing. Sheriff Wayne doesn't seem too worried."

"Of course not. He's got Kane Preston to do his job for him."

"That, and . . . Let's face facts. Ben Haney wasn't young and he wasn't in good health. I think the sheriff feels as if someone merely hastened the Grim Reaper along."

Seriously? "The sheriff can't possibly know how much time Ben had left. And isn't it his job to protect and serve?"

"You mean with the forty-seven days he has left before he retires to his place at the lake so he can fish every day?" Dixie returned tartly.

She had a good point. "True. Can you tell me *anything* about the investigation?"

"Nothing. Kane has all the information under lock and key. Something is up. I've tried talking to him but . . ."

The deputy was way too smart to share the details with one of the town's best-known gossips. Maggie sighed. If she wanted something, she was going to have to go to the source.

"I understand. Thanks, anyway. If you hear something, will you let me know?"

"Will do. What are you up to tonight, Mags?"

"Getting my grandparents ready for their flight tomorrow." Then a little factoid Dixie had shared with her a few months back circled through her brain. "What days does Deputy Preston have off this week?"

"Let me see." On the other end of the phone, Dixie tapped on her computer. "Tomorrow and Tuesday. But he got off early tonight."

Maggie smiled. That was the first piece of good news she'd heard all day. "Thanks."

"What are you going to do?"

Whatever she had to in order to find out what Preston knew. "I don't know. Probably nothing. What can I do?"

Dixie snorted. "The day you don't have something up your sleeve is the day I become a virgin again."

Since that ship had sailed about ten years ago, Maggie rolled her eyes. But one thing she did know? The deputy was always looking for love—at least temporarily—and he often went to a bar in nearby Boerne to find it. Maybe if she bought him a couple of beers and got close to him, he'd be willing to talk.

"Well, good luck with that," Maggie quipped.

"Keep me posted, okay? When you make a move, I want all the juicy details."

Not a chance. "You'll be the first to know."

Not too long after they rang off, Josiah came downstairs. Her grandparents meandered into the kitchen, her stubborn papa trying to drag his suitcase across the house.

"Let me do that for you." Josiah reached for his luggage.

Papa snatched it back. "I'm getting on in years, but I'm not dead yet. If you want to be a help, boy, go see if Glenda needs any assistance with her suitcase."

Josiah looked like he was trying not to laugh. "Yes, sir."

As soon as he disappeared, Papa set down his bag with a sigh and peered at her with concern. "You sure about this? I hate to leave you so soon after the wedding . . . and Haney's murder. Your grandmother didn't say anything to you, but she's worried. Hell, I am, too."

"I'm sure. What happened to Mr. Haney was a terrible tragedy, but I can't imagine something like that would happen again in Comfort in the next few days." At least she hoped not. "Besides, I'll have Josiah here for a day or two. Deputy Preston isn't too far away. I'm sure I'll be fine."

Papa took her shoulder in a gentle grip. "We're going to call you every day. If there's a hint of trouble, girl, we'll come right home."

"Go. Have fun. Forget about this place. If there's a problem, I'll let you know. Otherwise, enjoy La La Land."

He snorted. "What's an old guy from small-town Texas going to do around all those pretty people and movie stars?"

"First, I'm sure Shealyn thought similar things when she first moved out there, and look how that turned out. Second, take Granna on the second honeymoon y'all never had. Enjoy not having any responsibilities for a while. If anything happens with the cattle, Sawyer and I will handle it. Stop worrying."

Papa rolled his eyes. "I'll try, but you know how that's going to go."

"I do." She smiled fondly.

He pressed a kiss to her forehead. "The first time I laid eyes on you, you were a wild, half-starved two-year-old with a temper. You've grown into an amazing woman, Maggie. I'm only hesitating because it's been in my blood to protect you since that day. I don't think I'll ever stop until they put me in the ground."

Tears pricked her eyes. That was her papa. If she could find a man like him, both gentle and protective, maybe she'd be willing to get hitched and have babies and all the stuff she'd been adamantly against her whole life. But who was she kidding? Men like him were from a bygone era. Guys now were from the Tinder generation, all about swiping right and hooking up. They tended to be as selfish as the day was long and they had the emotional range of a Skittle. Totally not worth the time and commitment.

"I know. And I appreciate you." She brought him in for a bear hug. "I love you so much."

He was the only man she'd ever said those words to and probably the only one she ever would.

"Love you, too, Maggie girl. Now, I've got to load up the car so we'll be ready in the morning."

"You realize you don't have to catch the plane until almost noon tomorrow."

"I do, but your grandmother doesn't get many opportunities to shop in San Antonio, so I promised her we'd squeeze a few hours in."

"So you're saying she wants a new purse."

"How did you guess?"

Maggie laughed. Her grandmother was one of the most practical women on the planet . . . until designer handbags were involved. Then? Granna turned into a squealing girl with no impulse control.

Just then her grandmother entered the room, Josiah in tow and carting her suitcases. Lord, she looked like she was prepared for the apocalypse, not two weeks in Los Angeles.

"Did you pack enough?" Maggie poked.

Granna waved the question away. "Oh, hush. I packed just enough."

Papa started to laugh, but after one glare from his wife, he lifted a fist to his mouth and covered the sound with a cough. Even Josiah resisted the urge to smile.

"Should I take everything to the car?" he asked.

After a quick conversation about logistics, they wandered outside, loaded up Granna's SUV, then came back in for a quiet dinner. While their meal settled, everyone sat on the sofa watching TV. Josiah answered a few texts, and Maggie found herself wondering who they were from. His boss? His family? Did he have a girl back home? A friend with benefits?

She wasn't sure she wanted to know.

About eight o'clock, her grandparents stood and stretched, declaring it their bedtime. Maggie took that as her cue to do the same. "It's been an eventful weekend. I think I'll turn in early, too."

She hugged her grandparents, who blew kisses and left the room. Once they were gone, she turned to Josiah with a preplanned speech perched on her tongue. She hated to do this; another night with him and all those orgasms would have been great but . . . more important matters called.

"You're welcome to bunk down in Shealyn's room, the guest room, or the bunkhouse. If you need extra blankets, I'll find you a few."

He cocked his head. "But I'm not welcome in bed with you?"

Maggie shrugged. "I'm tired, and we scratched that itch last night. You're only here for a few days, so what's the point? Besides, my grandparents will be up before five A.M. tomorrow morning. Why advertise that we've been having sex? G'night."

As she left the room and headed down the hall, Josiah hurried after her, stopping her with a deceptively soft grip on her elbow. "I'm not done talking about this. Something's wrong. Tell me."

If she did, he'd lose his temper and his mind. And while she appreciated that he'd stayed behind to make Cutter feel better, Maggie was the one who had to remain here after Josiah was gone. "I've already said all I'm going to tonight. Maybe I'll feel more like talking tomorrow."

She jerked her elbow free from his grip and climbed the stairs, knowing her hips swayed with every step . . . just like she knew he watched.

Fighting a smile, she let herself into her room and shut the door.

She turned off every light and fluffed her pillows under her covers so that if he peeked in, he'd think she was asleep. Hopefully, that would be enough to deter him if he was feeling frisky. Then she shut her bathroom door, dragged out her makeup, plugged in her curling wand, and dug through her closet to find her shortest skirt.

An hour later, Maggie looked every inch like a woman on the prowl. She killed the bathroom light, carried her boots as she slipped out and tiptoed across the patio's roof until she dropped down from the overhang, just outside the dining room. Through the windows in the adjacent room, she saw a flash of light that could only be the TV. So Josiah was still staring at the mindless box. Good. With any luck, she'd be long gone and back home from her mission, and he'd be none the wiser.

A faint slamming sound that didn't belong with the droning TV show had Josiah's head snapping up. If he wasn't mistaken, the noise had come from the carport, just outside the family room.

Creeping up from the sofa, he turned off the lamp beside him. As he prowled toward the window, a car's engine turned over and tires rolled over dirt. Suspicion brewed, and goddamn it, he wanted to be wrong. But when he peeked through the glass, Josiah just shook his head.

There was Maggie sneaking away from the house, driving slowly, no headlights to guide her.

Did she think he wouldn't see or hear her leaving?

Snorting, he leapt into his sneakers, yanked his truck keys from his pocket, and let himself out the side door, grateful that Maggie's grandfather had seen fit to give him a key to the house once he indicated he'd be staying a few days.

Josiah made his way through the dark and turned his engine over before shoving the vehicle into drive. As he turned off his automated headlights and pressed a heavy foot to the accelerator, he found himself less than a minute behind Maggie.

"Where are you going, girl?"

He intended to find out. And if his suspicions were anywhere close to reality—that she intended to stick her pretty nose in his investigation—the question wasn't whether he'd spank her but how hard.

Yeah, okay, she hadn't handed over her power or given him permission to top her, but the wild child clearly needed a firm hand. He probably shouldn't bother, but if she needed someone to keep her sexy ass out of trouble, he'd damn well do it. Clearly, no one else had or would.

He followed her in darkness down their dirt drive, then to a wider dirt road serving the people in this rural area of town. This finally led to the paved road a few miles away.

As soon as Maggie hit the blacktop, she flipped on her headlights. Since the road was utterly deserted—Comfort rolled up early each night—Josiah remained dark until they reached the edge of town. He hung back while she went through a yellow light. Then, as soon as she was out of sight and obviously headed to the freeway, Josiah activated his headlights and waited until the stoplight turned green again. Two minutes later, he was behind Maggie, watching her little Honda travel east on I-10.

He had about twenty minutes to wonder where she was going. When they reached Boerne, she pulled off at the far edge of town, then got on the frontage road heading west again. Had she changed her mind and decided to head home?

Josiah had his answer when she pulled into a parking lot. He read the neon sign and groaned. "Why the hell are you going to a bar at nine thirty on a Sunday night?"

She parked, then climbed out of the vehicle. He gaped at what she wasn't wearing while she obliviously scanned the lot, wrapping her arms around herself to ward off the January chill because she hadn't bothered with anything practical like a coat. An indecently tight white crop top cupped her breasts. In soft blue print across her boobs read the words COME AND GET IT. She'd paired that with a pink skirt so short, he feared a sudden gust of wind would reveal whatever she was—or wasn't—wearing underneath. Her studded, blinged-out, high-heeled denim cowboy boots reached the middle of her thighs and made her legs look a hundred miles long.

Suddenly, she spotted a big black Jeep and nodded resolutely, slamming her car door and heading across the parking lot, toward the door, with purpose.

Magnolia Rose was on the prowl?

"Fuck," Josiah muttered, gripping the steering wheel tight.

Who had she come to hook up with?

Shaking his head, he found a parking spot not far from Maggie's, shoved his truck into park, and tried to decide what to do next. He'd expected her to seduce him tonight, try her best to coax information from him about the Haney investigation between the sheets. He hadn't expected her to blow him off, drive to the nearest watering hole while wearing next to nothing, and . . . what? Josiah intended to find out.

He let her get inside and get comfortable—no sense not catching her red-handed—then he Googled the bar. Decent reviews, known for beer, chicken wings, and their constant sports on the big screens. For all that Maggie was a small-town girl, he wouldn't have pegged her for a woman who liked any of those things. Her room had revealed a more sophisticated, even romantic soul. This place just said country.

He surfed a little, looked to see if Maggie had updated her social media. She was silent, which told him she didn't want anyone to know what she was up to, least of all him.

As he pocketed his phone, he tapped his thumb on his steering wheel, then checked his watch. He'd promised himself he'd give her ten minutes. It had been seven. Close enough. He couldn't stand not knowing who she was sucking up to and if he had his hands all over her.

Yeah, he shouldn't care. But he did. He couldn't stand the thought that she'd dolled up and sneaked out under his nose to drive to the next town over and meet another guy. Were they already lovers? Or was she hoping to snag this guy's attention for the first time?

When Josiah had first joined the Agency, he'd worked with Steve, an older man whose wife was always getting into some scrape or another. She'd lose her car keys or buy a few extra bottles of wine a week, maybe stay out a bit too late with her girlfriends. She even got a tattoo for her fiftieth birthday without telling her husband. Steve always called Kathleen a minx. He'd said it fondly. He'd said it with a smile. Knowing what he did now, Josiah had little doubt the woman had provoked Steve because she'd known he would spank her ass red the moment they got home.

Maggie was a minx through and through—no question. Josiah didn't think for one moment she was lashing out because she would enjoy his punishment. If she did, that would be a happy coincidence. But regardless, he definitely intended to let her know he didn't find her behavior tonight remotely safe or acceptable.

Josiah exited his truck, grabbed a hoodie, and slammed the door. Part of him relished the thought of the moment she saw his face and realized she'd gotten away with nothing. The other part of him just wanted to yank her out of here, kiss her senseless, and not let her speak again until they'd fucked themselves raw.

Tugging the gray sweatshirt on, he did his best to cover his face with the hood before he headed through the door.

Inside, the place was loud. Luke Bryan was singing that it was his kind of night. No one was watching the Colts beat the Broncos on the big screens around the room. The place was surprisingly crowded, given that it was the last few hours of the weekend and most people would be working tomorrow. Some couples hung out at tables around the perimeter. A few single ladies positioned themselves under the neon signs near the door, advertising their availability. No one with a Y chromosome was paying a lick of attention to them.

They were all watching barely covered, hips-swaying Maggie.

She ignored every one of them—except Kane Preston. She directed all her attention and seductive focus on him. And he didn't look immune to her charms.

Goddamn it.

Was Maggie both fishing for information about Haney's murder and looking for a good time? Josiah snorted. Not on his watch.

He approached the pair slowly. Neither paid him a moment's notice. Preston sat on a bar stool, his arms slung low around Maggie, who stood in front of him. His palm rested too close to her ass for Josiah's liking as she smiled, batting her lashes and running a pink fingernail against the edge of his jaw before she leaned in and whispered something in his ear.

Kane merely shook his head and nuzzled her neck. He gave her a lazy grin, then murmured something in return. She tried not to let her irritation show. But when the deputy laughed outright, she huffed and stomped back, planting her hands on her hips.

"Deputy Preston, that's not very gentlemanly of you."

"Well, Maggie, you rubbing against me in a damn-near illegal skirt and trying to wheedle information about an active murder investigation isn't very ladylike of you." He grabbed her wrist and brought her between his spread legs before he grabbed her hips and stood. His body folded out against hers, and they touched from chest to toes. "What would you do if I actually wanted to kiss you? Accepted that unspoken offer and took you to bed?"

Fury pumped through Josiah. He really wanted the answer to that question, too. Would she actually leap from his arms to the deputy's barely twenty-four hours later?

Maggie swallowed and tried to jerk back. Preston held firm, giving no quarter.

"I said I wanted to talk."

The deputy raised a brow. "Among other things. And if all you wanted was conversation, you shouldn't have come dressed to fuck."

"I-I . . ." For once, it seemed Maggie didn't know what to say.

"Let's try this from a different angle. No matter what happens between us tonight, I'm not saying a damn word about the Haney murder. Now that we've got that out of the way, do you still want to share a few drinks, a few dances, a few laughs, and see what the night brings?" He caressed her arm. "I've noticed you around town, pretty thing. I've thought about asking you out. If you let me, I can make you feel good."

Silence stretched out, quickly becoming awkward. Josiah saw the indecision on her face. She bit her lip like she couldn't quite decide what to say.

He couldn't stand it anymore. For some reason beyond logic and the bounds of normal comprehension, he didn't want to hear her say yes to another man. Later, he'd give serious consideration to why and what the hell was wrong with him.

"I'm afraid that's not possible, Deputy. Maggie's pleasure is my department," Josiah insisted, easing back his hood.

She jerked her stare in his direction with a gasp, her eyes flaring wide. "You found me? Shit."

"Yep, and it's hitting the fan as we speak," he quipped.

Maggie turned back to the deputy. "I just met him last night, and what happened then doesn't matter now."

"Hmm . . . That true?" Preston volleyed the question his way.

"If Maggie needs to feel good, I'll take care of that. It won't be the first time." Josiah staked his claim.

"And if she wants information?"

"I'll lock that down, too," he promised.

Preston released Maggie with a shrug. "Well, there you go. You don't need me when you've got your Agency man. He'll take good care of you." The deputy chugged the last of his beer and set his empty mug on the bar. With a tip of his hat, he said, "I'll leave you two to

DEVOTED TO LOVE   121

enjoy your evening. And Maggie honey, next time I come out here looking for female companionship, don't follow me. I really didn't want to spend another night with my hand."

A moment later, he was gone, leaving Josiah cocooned with Maggie in uncomfortable silence surrounded by a room full of loud strangers. What happened next between them wasn't going to be pretty, Josiah knew. But he was damn well ready for the fight.

CHAPTER 8

Maggie let out a long breath and closed her eyes, mentally groping for her composure. Why the hell was Josiah here? How had he followed her without her knowing? And why, just looking at his stern expression and the promise of something darker in his eyes, was her body doing cartwheels and backflips?

"Why didn't you stay at the house?"

He raised a brow her way. "I could ask the same of you."

"You know damn well why I'm here."

"I do. Unfortunately for you, so did Preston. What did you think sneaking out here would accomplish, except to show me a fine pair of boots I intend to fuck you in in . . . oh, the next five minutes."

Was he serious? She was trying to figure out how to keep herself and her family safe after he went back to Louisiana, and he was fixated on her footwear? And sex. Can't forget that.

"Dream on. Now that you've ruined everything, I'm going home and going to bed—alone." She headed for the door, fully aware of Josiah two steps off her ass.

As she pushed her way out into the chilly January night, Maggie tried to slam the door between them. Josiah, the insufferable bastard, caught it with his palm, swung it wide, and stomped into the parking lot after her.

"Not until you and I have it out."

"I don't have to argue with you about *my* family and *my* safety. I have every right to try to prevent becoming a victim. Then you barged in here tonight and screwed up all my plans." She whirled for her car, digging angrily through her purse for her keys.

Josiah grabbed her arm and spun her around. "Here's a news flash: Whether I showed up or not, Kane Preston wasn't going to tell you shit. All I did was prevent him from giving you a case of sex hair and a sore pussy."

Her jaw dropped. "I wasn't going to have sex with him."

"You sure? I know what a woman willing to fuck another guy behind my back looks like." His expression hardened. "My fiancée made damn sure I knew."

Maggie blinked. His ex had cheated on him? Often and painfully, according to the mute rage in Josiah's expression. While she felt for him, his pain couldn't figure into her plans. They weren't committed to each other. But for some reason, he did matter, even when Maggie didn't want him to.

She softened a little. "I swear, I wasn't going to let him touch me."

"Did you really think he was going to get a good look at your tits—because it's obvious you're not wearing a bra—and spill all his secrets? You had to know he'd expect you to get naked with him for information."

Honestly, she'd been hoping she could buy Preston a beer or two, flirt and jiggle enough to entice him to whisper sweet murder investigation nothings in her ear, then be gone.

"That's wasn't my plan. And, for your information, I'm wearing a bralette." She crossed her arms self-consciously over her chest. "It provides coverage."

He grabbed her wrists and tugged her arms wide. "Uh-huh. And almost no support. So after you dazzled him with your rack, then what did you have in mind?"

"Conversation." But Maggie feared Josiah had interpreted the male mind far better than she, and now her answer sounded naive at best.

He scoffed. "You may have wanted the deputy for that. But too bad for you, baby. You got me instead."

"And an utter lack of information. Now I'll have to figure out some other way to learn what I need to know. I'm sorry about your ex. She sounds like a bitch, but I'm not her. So don't accuse me of her sins. And don't try to stop me from getting answers again." She jerked free and spun around to her car. "I'll see you back at the house."

"You want answers? Why don't you wave your tits in my face, and see if I'm more willing than Preston to cough up what I know," he called to her back.

She whirled to face him. "You're being a pig."

"I'm playing your game. And by the way, other than the killer, I'm the last person who can tell you squat. So how about it, baby? You willing to give me the same act you gave the deputy?"

"I hate you right now."

"Is that why your nipples are hard?"

"In case you haven't noticed, it's freaking cold out here." And not for anything would she admit he turned her on.

Josiah shot her a cynical smile. "Keep telling yourself that's the reason. Either way, you have two minutes to decide."

"I can either whore myself to you or stay clueless, is that it?"

He shrugged. "Your words, not mine."

"But that's the crux of it. Look, I was willing to *flirt* with him. But that's it."

"All right. Get in my truck and flirt with me. Let's see what happens."

"And how am I supposed to get my car home?"

The slow smile he shot her did crazy things to her heart. "Who said we were driving anywhere?"

Maggie paused. Her anger at his manipulation aside, her body definitely didn't hate his suggestion. If she had sex with him again, it would be so damn good. Even the memories of last night made her weak-kneed. And maybe he'd tell her everything he knew. Win-win.

And if she could make him feel the teeniest bit guilty for being a shit, even better.

Do you blame him for overreacting? The woman he planned to marry screwed around on him. He's got a gash in his heart, and you know plenty about those . . .

"So you're planning to nail me in the truck?"

"Pretty much."

"Despite what you think, I wouldn't have let Kane Preston have sex with me. Why should I let you?"

"Oh, I don't expect it. Just like you're planning to persuade me to tell you what I know, I'm hoping to coax you into spreading your legs for me." He ran the barest fingertip down her arm. She stopped breathing when goose bumps broke out across her body. A glance told Maggie he noticed, too. "I'm only asking for the same shot you gave him."

She swallowed. Last night, she hadn't been nervous with Josiah. It had been fun and light and easy . . . until the dizzying heat between them had gone to her head and overwhelmed her with pleasure. Since then, he'd rattled her. Being this close to him, she felt jumpy and unsure. She'd never not had the upper hand with a man. The experience was new and novel and scary as hell.

"You could be a gentleman and just tell me." Because she worried that if she let him touch her again, he would strip her armor, work his way under her skin, and dig deep into places more lasting.

"Where's the fun in that?"

His quip made her want to both wring his neck and melt. Every ball she fired at him, he lobbed back playfully—but with ruthless, teeth-grating efficiency.

"I'm not here for fun. Let's go home and talk about this like reasonable adults."

"Nope. Reasonable went out the window when you swished out here to pick up Preston. If you want answers, you and your indecent skirt get in my truck. We'll see what happens." He glanced at his watch. "You have sixty seconds to decide."

"You're forcing me?" she huffed, knowing it wasn't quite true.

"You're free to turn around and go home right now. You just won't get any information."

"You're a shit."

He shrugged. "We can stand here in the freezing cold and exchange barbs or you can make a decision. You gonna get into the truck with me or go home alone? Thirty seconds . . ."

Maggie held back a curse, not because she didn't want him in spite of all this bickering, but because she did. No one ever challenged her, and something about the way he toyed, manipulated, finessed, and cornered her turned her on. She clearly needed to have her head examined.

After he sated the pulsing ache between her legs she couldn't deny.

"Ten seconds."

God, if she said yes, he was going to be so smug. She freaking hated that . . . but not enough to say no.

"Five seconds. Four, three, two, on—"

"Fine," she bit out. "Your truck it is."

Josiah didn't even try to repress his smile as he dropped his hot palm to the bare small of her back. "This way."

So badly, she wanted to ask what he planned to do to her. But she knew her voice would shake as much as her body, and she'd be damned before she gave him even more power.

Pressing a thumb to his fob, he unlocked the truck with a beep and hustled her up to the bench seat, then sat beside her and shut the door. Immediately, the music spilling from the bar and the traffic noise disappeared, leaving only the sounds of their breathing. Maggie resisted the urge to wring her hands.

"So how's this going to work, hotshot? We just going to let whoever comes in and out of the parking lot see that we're getting busy? That's great for you, since you don't live around here. Not so good for me."

"My windows are tinted, and there's no light above us. No one will know."

"Unless the truck starts rocking."

He shrugged. "I can't stop people from guessing. I *can* stop you from risking yourself."

"How?" If he thought for one minute that he could actually prevent her from trying to find out the prime suspects in Deputy Preston's investigation, he was not only crazy, he was wrong.

"We'll get back to that. In the meantime . . ." Josiah reached over and encircled her ribs with strong hands, then lifted her onto his lap so she straddled him, her chest against his.

He was unmistakably hard.

Against her own will, she wriggled. The friction against her clit had her biting back a groan.

"I thought you were going to tempt me with your breasts, but this works, too." He slid his hands up her thighs and kept climbing. Once he cupped her ass, he dragged her closer.

Maggie almost melted. It would be so much easier to keep her head clear if her body weren't on fire. "You want me to ask you questions while I'm pressed against you like this? I wasn't this close to Kane."

"But you have my . . . attention, as you can clearly feel. Fire away." He pressed her against his shaft again. "We'll see how this plays out. Once we exit the truck, your opportunity to ask questions is over."

"That's not fair."

"Neither was you running down the road to seduce another man. So don't tell me my behavior is dirtier. What do you want to know?"

While Maggie gathered her thoughts, Josiah brushed a fingertip up her hip—and slipped under the elastic of her panties, veering dangerously close to her wet sex. She swatted at him. "Stop distracting me."

Not surprisingly, he didn't budge. "You think those pretty nipples in my face aren't distracting me?"

He leaned in and sucked one into his mouth. Through the fabric, she felt him draw on it, his teeth nip at it, his tongue lave it. She moaned. He intended to short-circuit her brain. If she wanted to learn anything, she had to find some way to ignore her hormones and get her shit together.

"Does Preston have any suspects?"

"That's a very direct question." He teased the hard tip of her breast in his mouth while pinching the other.

Did he expect her to play a cat-and-mouse game with her words, like the one he played with her body? "It's been forty-eight hours. Surely, he must have some suspicions about who killed Mr. Haney?"

"He does," Josiah muttered as he dragged his lips up her neck, toward her ear. "Same suspicion I do."

"Enlightenment Fields?" she managed to get out between heavy breaths.

"That encompasses a lot of people."

True. "Adam Coleman is a recluse. He never gets his hands dirty. It must be some of his followers. The first one that comes to mind is—" He bit a little harder at her nipple, and she gasped. "Oh. Mercy . . ."

"I don't have any," Josiah promised, suddenly sliding his slick thumb over her needy clit. "Try again."

She squirmed away from his touch. "No, I meant Mercy, that strange girl—"

"Isn't who I want to talk about when I"—he jostled her on his lap, then tugged her closer again, this time impaling her on a pair of his outstretched digits—"have my fingers inside you. I haven't forgotten what you sound like when you come. I want to hear that again."

Maggie exercised herculean effort to swallow a moan and block out the tingles soaring through her body. "Answer my question, and I'll give you whatever you want."

"Anything?"

Alarm bells went off in her head, and the distant, rational part of

Maggie's brain told her not to say yes. But between her need for information and her growing urge to climax, she couldn't find the vocabulary to say anything else.

"Anything."

"Yes, Mercy is our primary suspect, and we have absolutely no proof. Now that I've answered your question, lie across my lap, face down, ass where I can spank it."

As if he knew his words would pelt her with shock waves, he rooted his fingers deeper inside, finding the spot she couldn't resist, no way, nohow. He goaded her even more by lowering her T-shirt and bralette, then lavishing attention on her bare nipple before sucking it into the heat of his mouth.

"Josiah . . ." Maggie wasn't sure if she was protesting his command or begging for more of his touch.

Why could this man turn her upside down, inside out, and unravel her so completely?

"What, baby? Tell me . . ."

She gripped his shoulders, holding on for dear life. "You're supposed to tell me."

"I did. I answered the question you said you'd do anything to have the answer to."

"But I need more." Maggie couldn't help herself; she rocked her body on his big fingers.

"If you mean information, that's not what you negotiated. If you mean pleasure, well . . . as soon as you're done laying yourself across my lap, we can negotiate again."

But if she did that, she'd have to withdraw from his touch, and that wasn't something she was willing to give up, not when the stirrings of climax were burning deep and hot between her legs.

"I need you. The way you make me feel . . ." As she tightened on his digits, she bit at his lobe, breathed in his ear, kissed her way down his neck, gratified when his big body shuddered under her. "Please, Josiah."

"Baby . . ." He bent to her, eyes sliding shut.

She was getting to him, too.

Blindly, Maggie fused her mouth to his, losing herself in his taste, in the intimacy between them. Right now, no one else existed in this world. For two minutes, what could it hurt to be a woman enjoying the touch of a man? Couldn't the outside world wait for one hundred twenty itty-bitty seconds?

Maybe, but Josiah couldn't. After one last curl of his tongue against hers, he backed away, his heavy breathing the only indication she affected him.

"You're so fucking tempting and you kiss like a goddess, but none of that changes what happens next. You. Across my lap. Now."

When he withdrew his fingers and gave her a stubborn glare, she huffed. Sure, she could protest and resist, even slap him in the face and say no. But she was too damn curious . . . and turned on.

Maggie lowered herself over his thighs, the way he'd demanded, taking care to ensure that her cursedly short skirt covered the essentials. "You're going to spank me for bad behavior like I'm a little girl? You can't be serious."

She'd barely situated herself when he grabbed her wrists and immobilized them above her head, pinning her with his left hand and flipping her skirt up with his right. "Oh, I'm totally serious. Lacy panties like this are only good for seduction. You going to tell me again you had no plans to fuck Preston?"

Maggie bit back a snarky comment. He'd been burned, and that possibility would only bother him if either his ego was monstrous—which didn't seem like the case—or he cared.

Normally, the latter possibility would scare the hell out of her. In some ways it still did, but she couldn't deny it softened her, too. She wanted him to care.

Why? In what parallel universe was she actually interested in more than hooking up?

"I really wasn't going to let him touch me," she promised.

She didn't even know why that was true. Preston was attractive enough. They were both single. He lived in Comfort. He'd clearly been on the prowl. But somehow when she'd looked at him, she just couldn't.

Josiah's fingers around her wrists tightened a fraction. "I should give zero fucks about what and who you do."

But he gave many. The resignation in his voice told her that.

Against her will and better sense, her heart leapt with something that felt like thrill.

"Josiah . . ." Now she chanted his name for an entirely different reason. She ached for his hands on her, sensed that he craved this as much as she did. But it was more. Maggie wanted him to show her that what they did together mattered to him, in whatever way he needed to show her. "I'm telling the truth."

"Goddamn it, woman." His voice was rough, not with anger but with longing as he dragged her panties down, bracing the elastic of the waistband just under her jutting cheeks. As his palm cupped her backside, he swallowed audibly as his hot skin skimmed the curve. "Tell me I can spank you. Say it."

This probably made her crazy, but not only was she curious, every muscle in her body was both liquid and quivering with desire. "Spank me. I want you to."

"Thank fuck," he muttered a moment before he raised his hand.

She'd barely registered the *whoosh* before the distinct sound of a slap filled her ears. A jolt of shocking sensation followed. Pain at first. Fear, too. But then the sensations morphed. Her skin went warm. The tense muscles underneath heated. Fresh tingles brewed. Her body awakened.

Maggie held her breath, anticipating his next move.

He did it again, harder. The sound echoed louder. Her suffering and delicious anxiety climbed. Then heat rippled across her skin, fired her flesh. Her clit burned, almost turning nuclear with need. Maggie found herself mewling and lifting her ass to him for more.

"Like that, do you?"

It never occurred to her to lie. "Yes."

"Ever been spanked?" He rubbed her burning cheeks with his rough palm, withholding more stimulation until she answered.

"No."

"Does it make you wetter?"

He couldn't feel her on his thigh? "Yes."

Josiah shoved her panties between her knees and fitted his hand under her to cup her pussy. "Fuck, the heat you're putting off . . . It's killing me." Before she could say anything, he trailed a finger between her folds. "And you're drenched."

She nodded frantically as she wriggled and rooted around for his fingers.

He withdrew them. "No. I mean to give you five swats. You have three more to endure. And don't you dare come."

Was he freaking crazy? How the heck did he think she was supposed to control her body when he was methodically unwinding all her self-control?

Maggie couldn't find the words to ask, and he didn't wait for her reply before he lifted his hand in the air again, then sent it crashing back down across the fiery skin of her backside. She bit her lip to hold in a cry and rocked her hips, grinding against his thigh in search of relief.

"Oh, you're going to be a bad girl?" He tsked at her. "No, you get to suffer with me. You think it's a piece of cake to spank that pretty ass, to feel those soft, pert cheeks under my palms, and not be able to see how red they are? Not order you to spread your legs so I can see exactly how wet you're getting? Not fuck you? Suck it up, baby. Two to go."

How would she ever make it?

Her panting filled the cab of his truck, along with the scent of her arousal and the anticipation arcing between them, mutual and pinging electric. "Hurry."

"No. You've been leading Preston and a host of other suckers around by their dicks for years, I suspect. And you think you're going to do the same to me? Nope. I've finally found one way to make you listen to me. I always intended for you to enjoy every moment of your paddling, but knowing you love it? What a fucking turn-on. If anything, I'm going to drag it out."

Lord, why did that threat only arouse her more? "You're mean."

"I thought I was being awfully nice, bringing you so close to climax. You *are* close, aren't you?" He tested her again with his fingers.

Maggie gasped and clawed at his leather seats, swearing that at any minute she'd lose her mind. "Yes!"

"Hmm. Now there's the throaty little cry with that sweet begging note I love. Are you trying to excite the fuck out of me?"

Was there a right answer that would persuade him to put her out of her misery? "Not intentionally."

"Which makes your response even sweeter. Let's see how you like this, baby."

Before she could brace, Josiah shoved a finger deep into her. Then another. Then a third. His hands were huge, and she felt completely stretched around his digits. As if that sensation weren't provoking enough, he lifted his left hand from his grip on her wrists and landed it in the middle of her ass, sending fire screaming across both cheeks. Using his right, he toyed with sensitive spots that threatened to light her up like a fireworks spectacle.

She inched even closer to release, squirming to find that last bit of stimulation she needed to push her over the edge. Josiah pressed his left palm to the small of her back to halt her movements. Maggie groaned and whimpered in protest.

"I told you not to come."

"But . . ."

"I expect you to wait until I give you permission."

Permission? "Are you crazy?"

"Want to test me and find out?"

"No." She had no doubt he'd only dangle that orgasm a little further out of her reach.

"Good choice. One to go. Hold it together for me."

"Why?" No man got to control her pleasure. If she wanted to come and some man couldn't get the job done, she took matters into her own hands. But this was different. He could let her fly—if he wanted to. He simply didn't. Something about him having complete power over her body, especially when he wielded it so perfectly, aroused her to the brink of madness.

He caressed her cheeks, his palm almost seeming cool against the fire emanating from her backside. "Because I want you to give that orgasm to me. I want to see the ecstasy on your face."

Her aching sex clenched and pulsed at his words.

Some rational part of her brain gaped at both her reaction and her behavior. Sure, she'd fantasized once or twice about an alpha lover so masterful that he was able to command her—all while giving her sublime pleasure. She'd never believed such a man was real or that she'd find him. Josiah was proving her wrong. Even more deliciously terrifying, Maggie suspected that he was merely showing her a fraction of his capability.

"Want this last smack?"

"Yes," she gasped. Her heartbeat surged at the thought of it. Her skin ached with need of it. Her whole body shivered in desire for it.

Slowly, Josiah lifted his hand. Maggie held her breath, lifting to meet his downward stroke. When it came, it would be wicked and encompassing. It would be everything.

"Did you think you'd enjoy me spanking you this much?"

"Not at all."

His chuckle sounded smug.

If she weren't so aroused, she'd probably tell him to go to hell. But she couldn't now, not when he alone could give her this singular pleasure. Not when all she wanted to do was welcome him deeper.

"There's an art form to spanking," he went on. "It's a learned skill."

Clearly, he'd learned quite well, and Maggie hated to think of all the women he must have practiced on over the years. She pictured Josiah and a nimble, nameless beauty stretched across his lap, and something inside her couldn't stand it. Which made no sense. She wasn't possessive. She'd never been jealous. When she'd heard Sawyer brag to some of the ranch hands that he had another something on the side, she'd even cheered.

"No matter how good you are at it, some women still won't respond," he mused. "I've been wondering almost since I clapped eyes on you if you'd be the one to love it."

She was. That reality filled her with excitement and shame. The way he revved her up was like a forbidden thrill. She shouldn't like this so much . . . but she couldn't help herself. He confused her, aroused her. And in this moment, he owned her.

"Hurry. Please."

"You do understand who sets the pace, right?"

"Yes." Josiah obviously did. He'd made that clear, but . . . "I said please."

He laughed. "You are one interesting handful, baby. And in a minute or two, I'll get to call you Magnolia."

Before her hormone-soaked brain could work out his meaning, the whoosh she had been anticipating hissed through the air. She heard the crack of his palm on her ass a split second before the sting sparked across her skin, then flared underneath into a raging blaze.

Tingles leapt. Blood rushed. Her clit screamed. She gripped the edge of his seat with white fingers, her entire body tensing. She was *almost* there. So, so close . . .

Josiah caressed her cheeks, his slow rub adding a warm friction that both soothed and enflamed. "You did good."

"I'm dying."

He ripped her panties off, lifted her from across his lap, and sat her back to straddle his knees while he fished in his pocket. "Can't let that happen. I'll make it all better, baby."

The sight of him unzipping his jeans and rolling a condom down his length was both a relief and a turn-on. He did it with a well-practiced economy of motion in a minimal amount of time. Thank goodness.

Maggie almost wept when he lifted her up and over his erection.

"Guide me in." His voice sounded gruff, ringing with a hint of desperation.

She didn't hesitate. He was going to end this misery. Granted, it was enthralling, all-consuming, something totally new, but every sinew and cell needed him inside her.

"Good girl," he crooned as she aligned his crest with her opening, then he eased her down, pushing his way into her swollen sex. "Oh, shit. Magnolia, baby . . . This is going to be hard and fast and raw as fuck. Come whenever and as often as you can."

Before she could even weep with relief, he shoved down on her shoulders as he thrust his hips up and filled her in one rough stroke. The pleasure-pain was enough to send her over the edge with a high-pitched scream.

"One," he chanted with satisfaction.

When her body finally stopped shuddering and the euphoria began to dissipate, she regarded him with panting breaths, studying the gray glint of his eyes, which looked almost black with need in the dark. "You're counting my orgasms?"

He nodded and sent her a smoldering stare. "I gave you five swats. It seems only fair to give you an equal number of orgasms."

Was he out of his mind? "I don't think that's possible."

"I have a more can-do attitude about this. Let's give it a whirl," he suggested in a low murmur before he began to fill her with long, slow, hard strokes. The kind he knew undid her, damn him.

Within a half-dozen plunges inside her, the tingling flesh that hadn't been quite satisfied with the first climax soared again, boomeranging into number two.

Maggie gripped his shoulders, digging her nails into his skin when he kissed his way up her neck to whisper in her ear. "So fucking pretty when you come. I could watch you do that all night. Nothing turns me on more."

He loved that idea; his voice said so, just like it told her that he might want to give it a try. Already she felt dizzy, wrung out, and limp. He barely sounded winded or strained. What the hell was happening?

"I don't think I can climax again for a while."

"Sure you can. Mind over matter. I'll get your brain back into it . . . and prod the rest along."

Maggie could only guess what he meant, but he didn't leave her wondering. "Grind on my cock, baby. Don't bounce. Rub that sensitive area right behind your clit on me and . . . yeah. That's it. Good. Now, let's get three and four out of the way."

He sounded supremely confident, as if he weren't discussing anything more complicated than taking a breath. Then he settled his thumb over the stimulated nub between her legs and began rubbing slow, excruciating circles.

"Josiah!"

"Hmm . . . The way you tighten around me is perfect. What are you thinking about?"

"What you're doing to me. How you're doing it. And why. Is this some macho thing? Are you trying to prove you're better than Kane Preston in bed? Because you don't have to prove that. I believe you."

"Your thoughts aren't where they should be, baby. Want to know what I'm thinking about? I'm imagining you in nothing but those sexy-as-fuck boots, spread across my bed, nipples in the air, legs open for me. You toss your head back, flinging your hair across my sheets as I lift your legs over my shoulders. I'd spend half of forever feasting because I love going down on you. I would stare at you as you turn rosy and swell and your pleasure climbs until you . . ."

"What?" she gasped out.

But she knew. Orgasm was on the verge of overtaking her again.

His touch drove her mad, but his words added something else to the experience. A thrill, yes. But an intimacy. He knew her body. He'd demonstrated that repeatedly. He also knew her mind. He knew her fantasies. He spoke to them as if they were the only two people in the world.

"Why don't you show me, Magnolia? I know you want to . . ."

Did she ever. The ache she would have sworn her last climax had sated sparked back to life, growing and thickening as he'd manhandled her and whispered seductive words in her ear. Now as he dipped his head and lifted her nipple to his mouth, Josiah compelled her as if her body were his toy to play with as he wished. She had no power to stop him.

"I do," she keened.

"I know, baby. I know because I can't help wanting to make you take the pleasure. Give me number three. I need it now."

He'd barely finished the sentence when her resistance gave way to a deep clench of pulsing bliss that made her shout out in throaty agony. He shoved his way deeper, not only with his cock but with his presence. He kissed her and took more of her secrets. He prolonged her climax with his touch and opened her soul.

As she finally floated down from the sharpest, fastest pinnacle she could ever remember, Josiah groaned in her ear.

"That was so fucking gorgeous. I need number four pronto."

She was sweaty, limp, and near exhaustion, and he wanted another orgasm right now? "Can't. You've proved your point. You're better at sex than Preston. Hell, you're probably better at sex than anyone."

He laughed. "Glad to hear you think so. But I'm not inside you to prove that. I'm here because I can't seem to fucking help myself. Your body is so sweet, but your tongue is sassy and unpredictable. Tart. I usually like women obedient, but I'll be damned if you haven't proven to me that you're my fantasy on two legs. If you want me off you, baby, you're going to have to tell me no."

Maggie didn't see that happening. Every time this man put his hands on her, he unscrewed her common sense and destroyed her sense of self-preservation.

"Or you could just leave me alone." She teased him because, deep down, that was the last thing she wanted.

Josiah scoffed, then gripped her hips and braced his big feet on the floorboard. "Never. Going. To. Happen."

He punctuated every word of his vow with a rough, deep thrust. This time, he didn't stimulate her clit, as if he could magically read her body and knew she couldn't handle the direct touch again quite yet. He also seemed to understand that she was too wrung out to rock on his cock and ignite her own sweet spot. No, her climb to number four was all him—his determination to flip her switches and send her tumbling into ecstasy. It was all him understanding her body and ruthlessly using the knowledge to his advantage.

"Pinch your nipples," he demanded as he shoved inside her again. "Hard. Make it count. I love to see them swell."

Instead of resisting him, Maggie worked with Josiah. She might have resisted number four initially, but after less than two minutes of his devoted effort to awaken and arouse her again, she gritted her teeth, caught his rhythm, and fought to crest it.

The pleasure rose fast and strong, a gliding ascent. They were in this together. Of one mind. Of one spirit. Of one will. Instead of rubbing her independent streak wrong, Maggie clung tighter and gave herself over.

Quickly, she reached the stars and soared. Weightless, sublime euphoria wracked her body, punctuated only by her high-pitched wail and his thick, unswerving praise.

Maggie panted as she began to float down. Holy hell. What was happening to her? Sex had always been nice. A curiosity explored. An itch scratched. A pleasure experienced. It had never made her feel particularly fond of any man or—far more dangerous—close to him.

But when Maggie finally reached earth, she landed in Josiah's arms. He enclosed her in his embrace. Her soul followed, drifting gently into her body. Her heart fell next, but when it settled into her chest . . . the damn thing didn't feel wholly hers anymore.

"What are you doing to me?" Her voice shook.

Maybe she was in shock or simply exhausted. Whatever this was, she'd never felt it before. It caused tears to prickle her eyes. It caused the armor around her heart to melt.

He met her stare head on, suddenly somber, and unblinking. "I could ask you the same thing."

"I have no idea what's happening." But Maggie was afraid she did.

Josiah skated his palms up her back and brought her closer, soothing her, before he wound his fingers around her sweat-damp tresses and kissed her hungrily, possessively. That mysterious feeling turned up a notch and, weirdly, turned her on more.

She threw her arms around him, squeezing him with her thighs, gripping him with her sex. In that moment she never wanted to let him go. With his eyes, his touch, he gave her his raw heat, his covetous need. Feeling beautiful with a man wasn't new. Feeling treasured was, and it took her breath away.

"We'll get number five together," he murmured against her lips before he took them again.

Maggie didn't argue. His demand would have been impossible for another man. Josiah had already proven he was more than capable.

"You'll come with me?"

"Fuck, yes. I've been dying to." He held up his palms. "Give me your hands, Magnolia."

She pressed her palms against his, and he curled their fingers together, entwining their hands as effectively as their bodies.

They exchanged no more words. They both understood what the other needed.

She shifted up his hard shaft, poised on her knees, cradling his crest just inside her opening. When her breast brushed his mouth, he licked his way around her nipple, then gave it a soft bite. As she cried out, he rose beneath her.

Maggie lowered herself, meeting him halfway in a slow melding until she enveloped every inch of him. As their bodies joined completely, they groaned together. Tingles spilled between her legs. Fire ignited her bloodstream. Euphoria swam in her head.

He grabbed her hands tighter and kissed her fiercely. Maggie stroked him slowly again, and together they surged, then crashed. The mingled sounds of their pleasure filled the cab. Condensation covered the windows. Arousal hung thick in the air. Maggie hardly noticed anything beyond Josiah.

"Look at me," he demanded as he lifted her up, withdrawing and refusing to move again until she gave him exactly what he sought.

The moment Maggie met his stare, he thrust her down again, seating himself completely. She gasped, her head falling back. He wasn't any deeper inside her physically, but mentally? Emotionally? Somehow, they'd fused into one. He exerted his will to deepen their connection until Maggie couldn't deny that their joining no longer had anything to do with either of them making a point or mere pleasure.

With a nudge of his hips, he urged her to rise. Obediently, she did until he pulled back. But then he was no longer inside her, filling her, one with her. Denial—and panic—tore through her chest.

"Josiah?" She searched his face. "Please."

With an insistent growl, he plunged Maggie back down onto his thick shaft again, seeming to delve into her even deeper. She reveled as he filled her. They hung there, together. She balanced herself with nothing more than his grip on her fingers and his steadying stare on her face as she opened herself even more, welcoming him inside her deeper than any man had ever been.

Warning sirens and flashing lights went off somewhere in her head, but she ignored the distant calls. It was too late for self-preservation. All she saw, smelled, felt, and wanted was Josiah. God, he could *see* her. Not the her on the outside, but as he simultaneously penetrated her with his body and his gaze, he glimpsed her naked vulnerability, the woman she kept hidden underneath the sass and the bluster.

That both thrilled and terrified her.

Josiah simply smiled as sweat dampened his temples and ran in rivulets down his neck. His breath turned harsh. His face flushed. "God, you're beautiful."

Everything about the way he touched her aroused her. She mewled and tightened on him, falling even harder.

"That's it . . ." He picked up the pace of their thrusts.

Together, they were in sync. They were electric. They were perfect.

Josiah let go of her hands and clenched her hips once more, guiding her strokes into a faster rhythm. His fingers bit into her. "I want to own you in every fucking way I can."

The words came out in a forceful pant, as if he'd fought with himself and lost the battle.

Maggie swallowed. "Right now, I want to let you."

"Yes. Now give me number five." He clenched her flesh tighter, fingers pressing into her backside, still warm and throbbing from his spanking. And when she cried out with the sensations, he swallowed as if grappling for control. "No, never mind that. Give me all of you— your pleasure, your pain. Your soul."

His words seized her breath, along with the way he filled her. Together, they rocked and writhed, their tempos melding into a shared rhythm. She dug her fingers into his shoulders and pulled herself closer to him. He'd awakened her body so thoroughly, she buzzed. Her skin tingled. Her mind pinged. Her heart pounded. Every part of her was attuned to him alone.

"I already feel you there," she sobbed.

Fear mingled with gravity. Every moment, every touch linking them together, felt profound. With any other man, the minute the orgasm wore off, she moved on. With Josiah, she was praying he never left.

What had he done to her?

Then he captured her lips and dropped a hand between their bodies to kick-start her climax. Already well on the path to another cataclysmic jolt, it didn't take much until she gasped into his kiss, swiveled frantically for more of the dazzling sensations, then felt herself soaring straight toward the bliss only he could give her.

Josiah grabbed her hips, propelled his way inside her, and willed her with a growl. "Now."

With one word, Maggie crested into a pleasure so complete, she cried out for him until she ran out of air and voice. Josiah held her like she was his everything, locked his stare with hers, and yelled out his release. Watching him let go of his iron control, knowing *she* was the woman who'd gotten to him, flung her into another realm of ecstasy.

After their frantic mutual pleasure, exhaustion pulled her under. She could no longer hold herself up, so she slumped over, letting Josiah catch her. Normally, she'd never trust a man that much. But for the first time in her life, she was beginning to believe he might be there for her whenever she fell.

CHAPTER 9

Josiah stretched, languid and drowsy. Moments he'd spent with Maggie last night rolled in and out of his hazy thoughts. He hadn't been able to get enough of her, even after they'd returned to her grandparents' ranch and tumbled back into Shealyn's bed.

Seeking Maggie's warmth, he reached for her. When he felt her beside him, soft and sleeping and snuggled in blankets, his relief was instant and acute.

Rolling closer, he spooned her sweet body, gratified when she relaxed against him with a sigh. Because he couldn't stop himself, he kissed her bare shoulder—and barely resisted the need to press his aching cock inside her once more.

As they lay together in the morning silence broken only by birds chirping faintly in the distance, their breathing synced up. Slowly, sleep dissipated. His thoughts began to clear. Reality crowded in. And peace evaporated as one question pelted him over and over.

What the hell had he done last night?

After Whitney, he should have fucking learned how to lock down his heart and stick to just sex. Magnolia West was making that impossible.

Grimacing, Josiah rolled out of bed and donned his jeans. His gaze strayed back to Maggie, who restlessly grabbed her pillow as if she missed him and now sought warmth and comfort.

It would be so easy to slide back into bed with her . . . and even

easier to fall deeper under her spell. But he was here to stop Enlightenment Fields from taking her family's land. Period. He'd come here
to work on that.

No, he wasn't blaming Maggie or women in general for what had
gone wrong in his past. He wasn't bitter—well, not totally—and he
didn't believe that Maggie was as duplicitous as Whitney. He simply
didn't want another commitment. After his wedding had fallen apart,
he'd promised himself never again because he fucking hated being
vulnerable. Besides, Maggie would be just fine without him.

He yanked his shirt over his head, raked a hand through his hair,
and went in search of coffee. He'd just poured a cup when her grandfather walked in and greeted him with a nod.

"Morning." Josiah nodded in return.

The man usually didn't have much to say. Today, he reached for
the pot when Josiah set it down, not looking his way as he poured the
java. "Can you do me a favor?"

"Sure." Josiah sipped his brew. Undoubtedly, this was where the
old man would ask him to protect his granddaughter while he was out
of town, make sure that no one and nothing harmed her. He probably
had a speech rehearsed about how fragile Maggie was, how sheltered
her life had been, and how much she needed someone to look after her
in his absence.

"The next time you have sex with Maggie in a parking lot, would
you keep the volume down? Oh, and don't leave her car there overnight. People might notice."

He barely managed not to spit his coffee out. "Excuse me?"

The old man calmly added sugar to his cup and stirred. "I'm old,
boy. That means I'm not naive. I know Maggie has, ahem . . . looked for
love with guys she shouldn't. That probably includes you. I just hope
she doesn't rip your heart out like the last few. Sawyer is still moping.
But we live in a small town. Foggy windows in a rocking truck at the
bar down the road don't usually fly under the locals' radar. I had a
phone call about your shenanigans before you even left the parking

lot." He shrugged. "Thankfully, this friend won't spread gossip. Not that Maggie cares about her reputation, and I have no illusions about who she is. Shealyn has always been a good girl, but Magnolia ... She's got a wild hair, like her mother. I'm not sure any man will ever tame her. But if you give two shits about her, next time you won't plow her in semipublic and you won't leave her car in the lot all night, giving folks a reason to wag their damn chins."

Josiah groped for a reply. "Mr. West, I—"

"Don't try to convince me you've never touched Maggie. I hate liars, and I know what you two are doing upstairs. I see the way you look at her, like she's a present you haven't finished unwrapping."

Fuck. The old man might well complain to Cutter, who would bitch to Logan, who would definitely tell EM Security's co-owners, Hunter and Joaquin, who would collectively chew his ass out for being unprofessional and not keeping his pants zipped. And they would be right. Postwedding nookie was one thing, but now he was on a job. He also worried about whether this would put Maggie at odds with her grandparents. Josiah didn't at all like the thought that he might have heaped trouble on her.

"She's a beautiful woman, sir. She's interesting as hell. And . . ." Maybe he shouldn't tell her grandfather that she was hotter than any woman he'd ever fucked.

"Tying you up in knots, too? You poor bastard. Like I said, you're not the first to fall under her spell." The old man shook his head. "You won't be the last."

Did Maggie really run through men that quickly? "What about Davis?"

Maggie's grandfather waved that concern away. "He might be the only guy she dated who didn't get hurt. Then again, he's light in the loafers. Yes, I know that's not a PC term, but I'm too old to care. He came out shortly after the engagement ended. Supposedly, he's happier, so good for him. But Maggie is my problem and my responsibility. You seem like a decent enough guy. Unless you want your heart ripped out, I suggest you step back."

The old man was warning him away for his own good? "I can handle her."

But hadn't he been thinking just ten minutes ago that he should put distance between them?

"Pfft. Every guy thinks that. Can't tell you how many have sat in my office, looking all torn to bits because the girl doesn't get attached. Hell, she went to prom with one guy and left with another. She's as close to her sister as she ever will be to another human being. My wife and I have done our best to give her affection and a loving home . . . Mags has always kept herself a little removed. We even bought her a kitten to soothe her when she was four because she started having night terrors. She liked the cat. She played with the cat. She even cuddled the cat. When he had to be put down Maggie's senior year of high school, everyone cried but her. I love that girl to death, but I worry she's broken."

Josiah had wondered something similar, but he still felt the urge to defend her. "Maybe she just hasn't found the right guy."

"You keep thinking that. See where it gets you." Maggie's grandfather drained the rest of his cup and started to leave the room. "We'll be ready to leave for San Antonio to catch that plane in an hour."

Josiah stared after the old man. He wasn't surprised Maggie's grandfather had warned him away, just shocked at his rationale. Was she actually incapable of committing?

He was still contemplating that question when his phone buzzed in his pocket with a text from fellow operative Zyron.

Trees and I are about twenty minutes from the ranch. Need us to bring anything in?

I'm good. Just get here. A lot to fill you in on.

Roger that.

Josiah tucked his phone away and poured another cup of brew as

Maggie stumbled downstairs. He smelled her before he saw her because she reeked of sex and woman. His cock was already standing up before he turned.

When he caught sight of her, he almost dropped his mug.

She'd piled her long golden hair on top of her head in a messy bun, which left the graceful curve of her neck bare. Two love bites dotted her skin. The one on her shoulder he'd given her while they'd fucked in his truck. The other? How could he forget spreading her across the big bed upstairs and marking her skin because he'd sucked on her desperately just before unloading inside her?

As if the memories weren't enough to rattle him, Maggie wore only her infamous white lacy bralette—and holy shit, he could see the hazy hint of her areolas and her poking nipples—and a pair of tight black exercise pants.

"Morning. Coffee." She delivered the demand in a voice that sounded just shy of zombie.

Swallowing hard, he handed her a mug. "What the hell are you wearing? I can see your nipples."

She shrugged as she poured from the pot. "So? You've already seen them. And I think you liked them. Papa just wandered out to talk to Sawyer, and Granna is finishing up their packing. No one will see me but you."

"I have two co-workers arriving in a few minutes."

Maggie took a big gulp of the brew. "I'll put on something else then, if it makes you feel better. But it's not like I have three boobs or other body parts they've never seen."

No, she had two breasts, and right now, they were his. Well, they'd been his last night, and he wasn't willing to share.

On the other hand, if he was going to step back from her, why should he get any say in who saw any part of her body?

She took another sip and sidled up to him, her hand dropping to his cock. "So . . . we've got ten minutes. What should we do with them?"

At her firm stroke, Josiah resisted the urge to toss his head back in pleasure. Every time Maggie put her hands on him, she sparked his blaze. Damn her. He'd been over all the reasons he needed to put distance between them. Her grandfather had even added to the list. But right now, all he could think about was getting inside her again.

Gritting his teeth, he set her away . . . though he really didn't want to. "C'mon. Put some clothes on that don't show your tits."

She raised a tawny brow at him. "My breasts suddenly offend you? Does that have anything to do with the reason you got out of bed without waking me up properly?"

Properly? By fucking her?

Shit, if he'd been looking for something even semipermanent, Maggie would be perfect for him. She loved sex as much as he did.

"We couldn't spend all day in bed."

"No, but maybe an hour." She cocked her head. "Oh, I get it now. This is the part where you say we've shared laughs but, for whatever reason—I'll let you fill in the blank; it doesn't really matter—things have to end between us. It's all over your face." She released him and backed into a nearby chair, curling one leg beneath her and hugging her coffee mug like a security blanket. She didn't look at him, just stared into her brew as if he didn't exist. "Whatever. I was pretty much over it, too."

She was lying. Nothing in her expression or voice gave away her pain, but he sensed it. And he felt like a heel.

Goddamn it, he was trying to be a responsible adult, focus on the reason he'd stayed beyond Shealyn and Cutter's wedding. It hadn't been to sleep with Maggie. Well, not entirely. But right now, Josiah found himself wanting to comfort her.

"Baby, I'm supposed to be working. I won't be here much longer, and I don't think either one of us is looking to get tied up in a relationship when we live hours apart and—"

"You don't have to explain. Itch scratched. Moving on. It's fine."

No, it wasn't. In fact, something about her face told him that he couldn't have hurt her more if he'd gone out of his way to wound her. *Fuck.*

"I've got to go." She stood, steadfastly not looking his way. The mood in the room turned uncomfortable.

"Where?"

"To cover up." She stretched, arms above her head, rising on her tiptoes.

The sun slanted in through the window and turned her bralette completely transparent. Desire jolted him. Jesus, he couldn't stop wanting her. But what he felt now was more than simple lust. Of course he wanted inside her body. But he also found himself wanting to be even deeper so he could assure her that . . . what? She was beautiful? Maggie had been chased by too many men not to know it. That she was fascinating? Worthy? That he wanted her? All of those seemed so obvious.

Then what was it that kept her from truly allowing other people close?

"After all, I don't want to offend you." She rolled her eyes.

Josiah could just imagine those nipples in his mouth, his cock inside her, his lips covering hers. He could imagine himself beside her, sharing hopes and tomorrows with her and—

He stopped the train of thought there. After all, he had a million fucking reasons to shut this desire down.

None of them changed how much he ached to have and hold her again.

"See you around," she tossed out.

"Maggie, don't—"

"We have nothing left to say, hotshot."

Her dismissive tone made his teeth grate, and the last thing he wanted to do was pick a fight with her. So he chose another tactic. "You going with me to San Antonio?"

She shook her head. "I'll say goodbye to Granna and Papa here.

While you're gone, I'll convince Sawyer to take me out to the bar so I can pick up my car."

"I don't think you should be alone with Sawyer."

She turned and swayed toward the kitchen door, glancing at him over her shoulder. "I don't think that's any of your business."

Before Josiah could reply, she rounded the corner and disappeared. He started after her, but his phone buzzed again in his pocket.

We're here.

Fuck, his fellow operatives had terrible timing. With a sigh, he headed to the door.

When he yanked it open, he found two familiar faces. Zyron, whose nickname had developed because he was a dead ringer for Zac Efron, strolled up, those piercing blue eyes assessing everyone and everything. Trees climbed out from the driver's seat next, his warm brown hair glinting in the sun. He unfolded his big body to his towering height, rubbing his palms down long legs. Josiah wasn't short, but he couldn't imagine being six foot seven. Trees had to duck everywhere he went. The guy wasn't scrawny, either. And as usual, his expression was unreadable.

"Hey," Josiah called to them.

"Hey," Zyron shot back with a bob of his head. "How's it going?"

"Oh, you know. The usual. Murder, a crazy secretive sect, home-made hallucinogenic drugs . . ." *Woman turning me inside out.*

"Damn, that sounds like a good time. Don't you think?" Zyron clapped Trees on the shoulder.

"No. It sounds like a recipe for more people to get hurt."

People said Trees lacked a sense of humor. From what Josiah could see, they were right.

"I know, buddy. It's actually worrying the shit out of me."

"So what's next?" Zyron grabbed his duffel from the cab and headed to the house. "And what do you need us to do?"

As Trees snagged his bag and marched toward the front door, Josiah filled them in on Mr. Haney's murder, Mercy and her home-brewed concoction, and everything about Enlightenment Fields he knew. He didn't say a word about Maggie.

When Josiah was done, Zyron whistled as they all sat around the kitchen table. "That's a lot of deep shit."

"And it needs to stay on the down-low from Shealyn and Maggie's grandparents. They're already targets, so we've convinced them to leave town for the foreseeable future. A conveniently timed vacation to California."

"And with Shealyn on her honeymoon with Cutter, that keeps her safe. What about the sister?"

He sighed. "That stubborn woman refuses to go anywhere. So we'll have to keep her safe. I'm worried she's a target, too. I wouldn't put it past any one of 'the Chosen'—that's what they call themselves—not to use her to get to the Wests."

"In their shoes, I would." Zyron confirmed Josiah's worst fear.

Trees nodded. "Ditto."

"So if Maggie won't leave the ranch, we have to be sure she's never alone."

Josiah was grappling with the logistics of that when the woman in question strutted into the room. "Hey, y'all. You must be Josiah's co-workers. I'm Maggie."

Zyron and Trees both stood like good Southern gentlemen. As if in a trance, Josiah did, too. What the hell was she wearing? Or more precisely, what wasn't she wearing?

She'd replaced the transparent bralette with a pale blue . . . something he hesitated to call a shirt. It covered her breasts, sure. But it hugged them so tightly he'd have known their exact size and shape even if he'd never put them in his hands and mouth. The long, lean line of her torso was bare, in all its sun-kissed glory. The indentation of her small waist gave way to the flare of her hips, exaggerated by the tiny scrap of denim that clung to them and passed as shorts. She wore beat-up brown cowboy boots and a smile full of hospitality.

Josiah wanted to cover her with a blanket and carry her up to the bedroom, especially when he caught Trees staring at her with a rapt gaze and definite wood beneath his fly.

Shit.

"Hi." Zyron held out his hand and introduced himself. "Nice to meet you."

"Likewise." She turned to Trees, caught his expression, and fucking batted her lashes. "And you?"

"T-Trees. Well, real name's Forest, but . . ."

"You're tall as a tree, so everyone gave you that nickname?"

"Yes, ma'am."

Maggie shook her head, tendrils spilling from her messy bun brushing the delicate line of her neck. "I'm not 'ma'am.' That's my grandmother. You can call me Maggie. Or Mags." She slid a gaze in Josiah's direction. "Or by my given name, Magnolia. Josiah called me that for a while, but he won't be doing that anymore."

Son of a bitch. She was inviting Trees to use her full name? Did she imagine he'd be inside her when he said it, too? Josiah tried to look unfazed, but he was so *not* okay with that.

"That's a pretty name." Trees swallowed.

"Thanks." She sent the big guy a flirty smile.

Josiah watched mutely. She was goading him. He'd tried to cut her loose because it was better for them both. And here she was, tossing his nobility in his face. Clearly, she wanted to make him jealous and regret his decision.

It was working.

"Can I get y'all something to drink?" she offered, sashaying to the refrigerator and extracting a water bottle.

Everyone declined, but Trees did so with his eyes glued to her ass.

"So what happens now?" she asked them. "Josiah is taking my grandparents to the airport and . . ."

"I'll be staying here." Trees couldn't seem to blurt that fast enough.

Of course he'd volunteer. If anyone could figure out how to defend a ranch this size with limited resources, it was the hulk. And that was probably the instructions Hunter, Logan, and Joaquin had given him. But Josiah didn't like how eager Trees seemed. He would be alone with Maggie for at least three hours.

Josiah stifled a curse. Maggie had managed to unwind him in far, far less time. His tall counterpart had made no bones about the fact he was always looking for a pretty woman.

"Looks like I'm with you, buddy. And you're driving." Zyron bumped his shoulder. "On the way back, we can strategize. I'll tell you about some of my research. We'll do a drive-by of the enemy territory."

"Sure." But all Josiah could think about was Maggie and Trees alone.

"If you have time, Forest, maybe you could take me to retrieve my car?" Maggie sidled over to his fellow operative with a smile. "It's just down the road. If you'd like, we'll have a beer and a few laughs, too."

Josiah gritted his teeth. She was pushing his buttons, swinging her hips and batting her lashes—and begging him to take her over his knee. He should leave it alone, but he'd be damned if he let Trees touch her.

"I'll take you to get your car when I get back."

"You don't have to trouble yourself." She wrapped a hand around Trees's trunk of a biceps and gave Josiah a saccharine smile. "Forest looks more than capable of helping me out."

As Josiah bit back a retort he'd probably regret, Maggie's grandparents shuffled into the room, rolling more luggage behind them. Josiah made quick introductions and reminded them that Zyron and Trees had come at Cutter's behest to shore up security on the ranch.

Maggie's grandfather nodded, seemingly relieved.

"Well, we're ready." Mrs. West looked a tad reluctant to go. "We never had time for a first honeymoon, much less a second one, so this will be an adventure." She turned to Maggie. "You sure you don't want to go to LA instead? Maybe you'll get 'discovered' like your sister."

"And take away your time together? Heavens, no. I don't want that. I want to be famous even less. Go," Maggie said softly. "Have a good time. The boys and I will be fine."

"If you need anything—"

"We'll take care of her," Josiah promised, fighting everything inside him not to put his arm around her.

Why did he still want a woman he shouldn't? One so bad for his peace of mind?

"All right, then. We'll see you in a couple of weeks, Maggie." The older woman looked at her granddaughter fondly, as if she was going to miss the hellion very much.

Maggie dropped Trees's arm, along with her attitude. Her face flushed with emotion and her eyes welled as she hugged her grandmother tight. "I know we're not apart much, Granna, but I always miss you when we are."

Mrs. West cupped her cheek. "Call us, sweet girl."

She backed away quickly with a brisk nod, trying to compose herself. "I will."

Then her grandfather wrapped her in a big hug. Maggie reciprocated without hesitation. Josiah watched wordlessly.

Did Maggie get more attached to people than she wanted to admit? Than she wanted anyone to know?

With those questions burrowing into his brain, he shot Trees a warning glare, picked up the Wests' suitcases, and hauled them to their SUV. Moments later, they were heading to San Antonio.

The ride and the subsequent hours of shopping seemed to drag on forever. But thankfully the trip was uneventful. Maggie's grandparents seemed delighted to meet the Santiagos, despite their unconventional family. Then again, Javier and Xander's wife, London, was about the nicest, warmest woman he'd ever met. The pretty blonde had a contagious smile, as did their daughter, Dulce. When London dropped a hand to her swelling stomach and said they were going on a family trip that doubled as a babymoon, Mrs. West especially seemed to melt.

Josiah sent them off with a wave and well-wishes. When they hopped back in the truck, he turned to his pal. "Let's hurry. I want to get back to the ranch."

"So you can stake your claim on Maggie?" Zyron raised a brow.

"So . . . I guess I wasn't very subtle."

"You all but peed on her, dude. How serious is it?"

"I tried to break it off with her this morning, but . . ."

"The fever hasn't run its course."

"Hell no. If anything, it's burning hotter."

Zyron smiled cynically. "The bosses won't be happy. They've barely forgiven Cutter for fucking on the job, and only did eventually because all ended well and he married her."

Yeah, he knew. "If they find out what's been up between me and Maggie, my ass is grass, and they're the lawn mowers."

"I won't say a word, but . . . are the bosses' opinions really that important if you like this girl?"

"No, but Maggie isn't the marrying type." At least he didn't think so. "Neither am I. What about you and little Tess? The bosses still firm that she's off-limits?"

"Unless I want to quit, yes." He groaned. "She's a receptionist, for fuck's sake, not a fellow operator. I don't get it. But it doesn't really matter. She's gun-shy and too busy being a new mom. I'd sure like to meet the son of a bitch who got her pregnant and ran out so I could punch him in the face."

"I second that."

Quiet Tessa Gilbert was so sweet and shy and full of gumption to face all she had and still keep smiling. For a moment, he wished he could have been drawn to someone like her. She'd never walk out on their wedding or break his heart, like Whitney had. Like Maggie probably would, given half a chance. But no, he had to be drawn to the kind of woman who kept him hot and yanked his chain.

What a stupid bastard.

For the next forty minutes, Josiah drove down the highway. He felt antsy, like he itched. Gripping the wheel, he shifted in the seat and gazed out at the road. Nope, he was still uncomfortable. Squinting against the bright, cold January blue, he flipped down the visor, rolled his shoulders, and turned on the radio. Was the SUV fucking moving in slow motion? It felt as if they'd been on this road for three years, and he was still miles from Comfort.

A glance over the side of the freeway at the bar he'd confronted Maggie in last night told him her car was gone. So she'd sweet-talked Trees into taking her to pick up her vehicle. She hadn't listened. Had she flirted with him while she'd sidled into the bucket seat beside his for the cozy twenty-minute ride here?

Maybe, but wasn't that better than the two of them banging at the ranch?

Josiah swallowed down fury, turned up the radio, and tapped his thumb on the wheel. None of that distracted him. His thoughts whirled. Agitation prevailed. He changed the radio station.

"This girl really has your balls in a twist." Zyron slanted him a pitying stare.

How could he refute that? "Don't I fucking know it."

"What are you going to do?"

The smart thing to do would be to stand his ground, stop giving a shit what Maggie did. He especially needed to quit worrying what she might be doing with another man. He didn't need the distraction while he worked. He didn't need his bosses pissed off. He didn't need to get tangled up with another female who ultimately wouldn't commit. Hell, he didn't even want her to commit.

Then why was the fact that she probably never would crawling up his ass?

"No fucking clue."

"Do you want Trees and me to take over? You go back to Lafayette and—"

"I can't do that. Remember, Mercy is expecting me tomorrow night. If I don't show up, we'll never find out what's going on out there."

"Fair enough. Want my advice?"

Not really, but maybe Zy would have better ideas about how to get himself focused on the right things. After all, he'd completed a string of really successful assignments without Tessa Gilbert screwing up his thoughts. "Shoot."

"Roll with it. You fighting what's happening between you two is only wasting energy. I knew in five seconds that you and Maggie had something going on. She might have flirted with Trees for some girl reason that only a human being with a vagina can possibly understand or explain. But she's into you, man. That much I know."

Josiah didn't want to be relieved at his pal's words. "Maybe. With Maggie, it's hard to know. She's complicated."

Zyron laughed. "That's the attraction, isn't it?"

He sighed. "Why am I so stupid?"

That only made Zy laugh harder. "Look at it this way. What are your alternatives?"

Good question. Trying to quit Maggie was proving pretty fucking impossible. And no matter how logical it might be, the idea of never having her again was unacceptable.

"Shut up and find a decent song on the radio," he grumbled.

Zy finally stumbled on a classic rock station. AC/DC was a shit-load better than oldie moldies from the fifties and sixties. He tried to concentrate on the music and his fellow operative's words as they did a quick pass along the Enlightenment Fields property line. Josiah was surprised by how quiet and still the place was.

"I did some research on Adam Coleman. He's a weird bastard," Zyron murmured, casing the compound from the cab.

"I'm not surprised. Tell me."

"Coleman is originally from Santa Barbara. Wealthy family. A loner in high school, but really smart. Finished top five percent of his class. Went to Stanford, but dropped out. There were whispers about him being shuffled off to a mental hospital for a few months. The family passed it off as rehab, but his past social media posts were . . . interesting. Rants about world overpopulation, coming food shortages and droughts, calls for a purge of 'undesirables.' Crazy shit. Then he disappeared for a few years. Visa records indicated he went to India and made the rounds with a bunch of shamans and gurus. All his posts online were about his 'enlightenment.' Sadly, he started finding people who believed him."

"Like Mercy?"

"Yep. In her defense, she was born to dirt-poor farmers who beat the shit out of her, so it's no surprise she went looking for a 'savior.'"

And she had settled for Coleman? "What then?"

"Then . . . I'm not too sure. He moved out here, suspended all his personal online accounts, instead setting up a website and social media for Enlightenment Fields. Nothing in their come-on makes them sound too unhinged, but if you read between the lines, you still hear 'the sky is falling.' Apparently, it's this crazy cult's duty to act now. Oh, it sounds all organic crops, water purification, and seed preservation, but they're thinking more drastic."

"Son of a bitch." Josiah needed to process all of this, read up more, figure out how to use the knowledge to his advantage tomorrow when he faced them again.

"Be careful. I don't know what their homemade hallucinogens have to do with the collapse of the food chain but . . ."

"Nothing good. I'll watch my six."

They fell silent, and instead of focusing on Enlightenment Fields and ways to glean information while returning unscathed, Maggie crowded in instead. How fucking much longer until he saw her?

Twenty interminable minutes passed before they arrived at the ranch. Josiah barely took the time to glimpse her car in the driveway before he put the SUV in park and leapt out, darting for the house. If Trees was anywhere near her . . . If they were kissing or touching or fucking . . .

Suppressing a growl, he tore the front door open and clenched his fists as he prowled from one room to the other. Kitchen, office, upstairs bedrooms—all empty. What the hell?

"Maggie?" he called out.

Silence.

He darted through the house again, anxiety turning to fear. Shit. Never mind her having sex with Trees. What if she wasn't answering because something sinister had happened? What if Enlightenment Fields had paid them a visit in the past few hours? Trees would have done his best to protect her. He would have seen it as his mission and his purpose. But what if he ultimately hadn't been able to stop them? What if they'd taken Maggie and—

"Josiah?" she murmured from the back door. "Were you calling for me?"

He didn't stop and he didn't think. He raced across the room, long strides eating up the space between them, grabbed Maggie, and pulled her against him.

"What—"

He didn't let her finish her question. Instead, he covered her lips with his own and plunged deep, taking her mouth as if he could inhale and own her all in one breath. God, she tasted alive. Perfect. Like *his* woman. He cupped her nape, tangled his fingers in her hair, ate at her mouth, and breathed her in all at once.

After three fucking hours, how could he have missed her this much? And what the hell was he going to do about it?

CHAPTER 10

W ell, now I know why you've been so preoccupied," Trees drawled from behind her.

Maggie jerked out of Josiah's embrace guiltily and turned to Trees with an apology on her face. He'd been nothing but nice to her. Dutifully, he had taken her to retrieve her car. He'd thanked her profusely when she made him lunch. Trees wasn't much of a talker, and she hadn't felt like chattering. Of course, he'd stared, and she felt self-conscious wearing this silly next-to-nothing getup she'd tossed on to rile Josiah. But Trees hadn't touched her or made a pass. In fact, when she'd wandered outside after lunch to sit on the porch swing, he'd followed her with a blanket, wrapped her up to protect her from the chilly wind, and rocked with her in blessed silence. And when she'd sidled up to him for warmth, he'd done nothing but brought her closer to his body heat and given her a soft smile.

Flirting with him hadn't been at all interesting without Josiah giving her the jealous side-eye. And that wasn't fair to Trees.

"Thank you for keeping me company on the porch swing," she said softly, then turned to the others. "Did y'all eat any lunch? I have leftovers . . ."

Before Josiah and Zyron could answer, the home phone rang. Hardly anyone called it except stupid telemarketers anymore, and she would have ignored it, but the number display said the sheriff's station was calling.

Frowning, she grabbed the old olive green receiver, circa 1977, from the wall and lifted it to her ear. "Hello?"

"Oh, thank god you picked up." Dixie sounded out of breath. "I've been calling and texting your cell phone for almost an hour."

Alarm began brewing in her belly. "Why? What's wrong?"

"You haven't heard? Someone ran Mrs. McIntyre down in the street earlier this morning."

Maggie blinked and gripped the phone. She couldn't have heard that properly. "What do you mean, ran her down?"

"You know . . . Mags, they ran her over with their car. I was working when the dispatch call came in. Mr. Klein was coming home from Lowe's market when he saw a woman lying in the street. He called . . . but when Neil and the crew got out there with the ambulance, it was too late."

"She's . . ." Maggie's heart stopped. "Dead?"

"Yeah. They found that little schnauzer of hers circling her body. Harvey was wandering around with his leash flapping and no one to walk him home."

"You're saying it was a hit-and-run?"

"Yeah. The driver didn't stay at the scene or call for help. From what we can tell, they didn't even try to stop the car. It's like . . . they wanted her dead."

Dixie's words went into Maggie's ears but shock kept them from penetrating her brain. There hadn't been a single violent incident in the community for years, and now they'd had two murders in four days? Granna would be crushed. She and Mildred McIntyre had grown up together.

"Oh, my goodness . . . Any suspects?"

"None. And so far, no witnesses have come forward, either. Mrs. McIntyre wasn't far from home when the incident occurred, and you know she lived out in the boonies."

Maggie swallowed hard. "Thanks for letting me know. If you hear anything else . . ."

"I'll holler."

She murmured something else to Dixie—Maggie really didn't recall what—then hung up.

"Baby?" Josiah was right behind her, hands braced on her shoulders as if he intended to prop her up.

Closing her eyes, she welcomed his comforting touch. "Someone ran over my first-grade teacher with their car this morning while she was walking her dog. They plowed her down on purpose . . . and left her for dead."

Josiah's grip tightened. She opened her eyes to see him exchange worried glances with both Zyron and Trees. "Did she have any enemies?"

"How can anyone hate a woman who dedicated her life to teaching small children to read and gave her spare time to making care packages for soldiers? She sews the costumes for the holiday parade every year. She plants little flags in everyone's front yards for the Fourth of July. She's . . . a saint. I can't believe she's gone."

The news hit Maggie hard. A gentle soul suddenly and senselessly taken. It made no sense. None of this did. Was there a killer on the loose in Comfort? If someone wanted kind Mr. Haney and sweet-as-pie Mrs. McIntyre dead, who was next?

"And what do I tell my grandparents?" She blinked at him. No, Josiah didn't have the answers, but she felt so stunned and lost, and he was right beside her, looking so solid.

"Would your grandmother come home if she got the news?"

"Absolutely."

"Then you can't tell her," he said grimly. "Or will someone call them anyway?"

"Granna and Papa don't like cell phones. And no one but me knows how to reach the folks out at Shealyn's place. They aren't Internet savvy, either. They won't go online to read the local rag." She bit her lip. "But they'll be awfully put out with me that I didn't tell them."

"Better mad than dead."

"Amen," Zyron tossed in.

Trees simply nodded.

Logically, Maggie knew they were right. Emotionally, not telling the people who had protected her since she was two rattled her even more. She felt shaken and afraid.

"I always thought of Comfort as ... well, a comforting, safe place."

Josiah brought her closer. "Times change. So do circumstances."

She pulled from his embrace. "But why would anyone intention-ally take the life of an old woman who's harmed no one? None of the locals would have done that. If we had any strangers in town except y'all, the townsfolk would be all a-chatter about them. That only leaves ... Would Enlightenment Fields really kill Mrs. McIntyre? She didn't own her land, just rented the house."

"That's what I intend to find out tomorrow night."

Tuesday's sunset approached, and a terrible déjà vu curled through Josiah's veins as he pulled his truck to a stop behind the greenhouse at Enlightenment Fields once more. He spotted a small bus unloading people carrying suitcases and staring at the compound as if they'd found home. The new converts?

With honey-brown hair glinting in the waning sunlight, Mercy strolled in his direction, wearing a smile he'd almost call smug. "Hi there."

Josiah stepped out of his truck, assaulted by the grating cheer of one of Mercy's homemade hymns. His Sig in its shoulder holster un-der his baggy hoodie made him feel loads better. "Hi, Mercy."

Her smile widened. "I'm glad you came."

Said the spider to the fly.

He didn't want to be here. This place and these people gave him the creeps. He especially didn't want to be near this woman. If he didn't care so fucking much about Maggie, he'd be back at the ranch, trying to seduce her again. But it said a lot about his feelings that he'd rather keep her safe than get off.

She'd asked him not to come tonight. Actually, almost begged. Well, as close to pleading as Maggie got. She'd been upset since she'd gotten the call about Mrs. McIntyre's death. Fuck, he hated to leave her scared and hurting. Or alone. Yesterday evening, he'd remained close to her, intent on protecting her, reassuring her. He'd remained glued to her side while she watched a silly comedy on TV. Or tried to. But all her fidgeting told him she wasn't focused on the film.

Before too long, he found himself reaching for her hand. Soon, that hadn't felt close enough, so he'd pulled her onto his lap. But another ten minutes into the movie, and the lure of her lush backside against him had revved him past his control. He hadn't been able to stop himself from fisting her hair and guiding her lips to his. Maggie had welcomed him instantly with open arms and panting breaths.

Quickly, one kiss quickly morphed into many. When he had to fight the urge to undress her on the sofa, he'd stood, urged her legs around him, then trekked up the stairs with their mouths plastered together and their passion running hot. As they'd passed by the kitchen, he'd blown off Zy's silent disapproval and Trees's glower. Yes, he was stupid. But despite telling himself to take a giant step back from Maggie, Josiah found himself kicking the bedroom door closed, tumbling her onto her back, and tunneling as far inside her as he could.

What the hell was it about that woman?

"You said to stop by tonight if I wanted to know more about your mission and your teachings." He shrugged. "Here I am."

"Since Mr. Haney is gone, I'm surprised you're even still in town. But glad," Mercy added quickly. "Why don't you come with me? I'll fill you in and you can witness people finding their enlightened truth as they join the Chosen."

Josiah would rather have hanged himself with barbed wire, but he managed a smile. "Sure."

"Then we'll have dinner and talk as a group. You can see who we are for yourself and . . . we'll go from there."

As he followed Mercy, he saw a string of people headed toward a barn that had been converted into a makeshift church. They'd whitewashed the building and improvised a steeple. Along the side, they'd painted a symbol he remembered seeing the last time he'd visited. It was a circle with four lines outstretched at top, bottom, and each side. Smaller dashes sprung up from the round center in between the arms. A wholesome, farm-style font had been used to paint a sunny *EF* right in the middle.

"Your logo?" Josiah nodded at the artwork. "What does it mean?"

"It revolves around the sun, like we do. We need it to grow all our crops. The line up top points to the sky from which we get the air and rain necessary to flourish. The one below indicates the ground and the rich soil we require to feed our family and our future. The lines left and right indicate our head and heart, since the Chosen must fully devote both in order to make Enlightenment Fields flourish." She shrugged. "That's it. The people in Comfort make us out to be odd or even sinister because we're outsiders. They're very traditional, and the notion of community farming doesn't sit well with them. But we're doing nothing more than growing crops and working toward a collective future brighter for all mankind."

Maybe that was true—in her head. Josiah wasn't buying it.

There were dozens of ways he could play this, but Mercy wasn't stupid. If he acted as if he were, she would be suspicious.

"That all sounds great, and I agree mankind should always look for ways to improve the yield from the soil while still preserving its nutrients. But I saw a few things last time I was here that concerned me."

"The nectar of Rapture? That's what we call the recipe we were brewing in the kitchen. It started when our sire, Adam, began having trouble sleeping. I tried a few homemade ways to help him rest peacefully at night." Her smile turned self-deprecating. "That's not what I ended up making. In testing various blends, we discovered that some gave us unexpected effects. Several people reported deep meditative states or altered consciousness, almost like a Native American vision quest. They all swore they'd had a spiritual rapture that had opened their minds and hearts and allowed them to see deeper inside their mission with us. They asked for more." She shrugged. "I consulted the half-dozen doctors who have come to live with us, made sure we wouldn't be hurting or addicting anyone with long-term use. They all said the concoction was strictly herbal and perfectly safe."

If not illegal in the state of Texas.

"The woman helping you in the kitchen didn't want it. You insisted she take it." He frowned as if this had just occurred to him. "Should the nectar be given to a pregnant woman?"

Mercy's smile went stiff as she pinned it in place. "Anna has had a difficult pregnancy. She doesn't much like anything right now. But there's no reason to be concerned. We've birthed nearly twenty babies here in the past year, all of whom came from mothers who loved the nectar. The children are perfectly healthy and fine. I think as a society, we've become paranoid. Humans gave birth for tens of thousands of years without half so many 'rules' as we have today."

He nodded as if he were a typical guy who'd never given babies much thought, rather than a protective brother who knew a lot about pregnancy because his sisters had given him nieces and nephews galore.

No doubt about it; Mercy was fuck-all crazy.

"So who will I meet tonight? What will I learn?"

Mercy threaded her arm through his and drew closer, pressing her breasts against his ribs. Since this seemed to be a favorite trick of hers, it must work on most poor saps. The nearer she came, the more Josiah wanted a shower. At least she'd glued herself to the side sans his weapon.

"You're a bit early, so why don't we take a walk until First Enlightenment begins."

He looked back to see people scurrying around the open space.

All the new victims and their suitcases were gone, shuffled to who knew where. Everyone looked as if they had a purpose. At least a quarter of the women were visibly pregnant. Half the men carried semi-automatic rifles. Everyone wore dull, almost automaton expressions that weirded Josiah out.

"Great. I'm eager to learn more."

"Since you're interested in our nectar, let's start in the green-house."

Moments later, she led him in via a side door. Several scents assaulted him at once, mostly rich earth and fertilizer hanging in the humid air. Greenery covered every inch of the space, stretching for nearly half a football field. How much "nectar" did this group need? Were they getting stoned every day?

"Who tends all these plants?"

She smiled and gave him a flirtatious smile. "I do, along with my green warriors. That's what the people who tend the crops call themselves. I oversee teams of workers who make sure everything is properly planted and rotated, that the soil is rested as need be, that they harvest when everything is ready . . . We're an efficient operation. Same is true of the outside crops we grow in the spring and summer, things like corn, tomatoes, carrots, okra, onion, peppers . . . I think we're nearly poised to keep the whole county in vegetables, if need be."

"Got something against grocery stores?"

Her laughter trilled in the air. "Heavens, no. We use them for what we can't make or grow. We simply feel it's our right and our responsibility to grow our own sustenance. Besides the nectar and the vegetables, we have chickens on the other side of the property that give us dozens of eggs every day. We have cows and some lovely ladies who milk them regularly, then make the best butter and cheese. We raise and slaughter our own pork and beef." She shrugged. "Our way of life strikes people as a bit old-fashioned. I'm sometimes asked questions like yours or why we don't simply rely on food delivery services. But the foundation of Enlightenment Fields' beliefs is that the food chain as it exists or society as we know it now will collapse in the near future, and then what?"

Interesting philosophical question, but this cult must have some conviction about what event would kick off the catastrophic degradation of culture and prosperity.

"Hmm. Why would it change? Gas shortage? Magnetic poles reversing? Government coup? Society can recover from those."

Mercy paused. Her puzzled expression told him none of those situations had ever crossed her mind. His prepper pal had talked about all of those eventualities, so Enlightenment Fields must have a whole different doomsday scenario.

"I suppose, eventually. But how will people eat before order is restored?" She walked slowly through the greenhouse, checking on a hanging group of salvia, then bending to push a group of mushrooms deeper into the cool shade under a table. When she stood again, she sent him a speculative stare. "Do you know what the global population is today? What it was in 1900? What it's projected to be by the start of the next century?"

Okay, those questions were out of left field. "Can't say I've ever paid much attention."

"Ah." She sent him a superior expression, brow raised as she took his arm and led him out of the greenhouse. "Well, let me, um . . . enlighten you."

She smiled at her little pun. Josiah managed not to roll his eyes.

"I'm all ears."

Sunset closed around them. Vivid oranges and pinks cast a warm glow on Mercy's delicate face. She would have been beautiful—if she weren't so fucking crazy.

"In 1900, the world's population was one-point-six-five billion people. By 1960, it was three billion. Fast-forward to the year 2000, and globally we had over six billion mouths to feed. By 2025 we'll have eight billion. Come 2100, this planet will support over eleven billion people."

"Haven't birthrates been declining for decades?"

"Sure. But ask yourself, is our current way of life sustainable for that many people? We already have homelessness, joblessness, poverty, and starvation. Most of the population growth in the decades ahead is expected to happen in low-income countries—places that already can't keep all their healthy citizens alive. Add to that mix all the technology we enjoy and that will continue to develop. It's wonderful . . . until it begins replacing jobs."

"I see your point," he murmured, watching people head toward the barn-church, some carrying folding chairs. Others hauled stacks of pillows. Women held what looked like old-fashioned kerosene lamps. Behind them, a dozen men carted buckets of steaming water.

On the other side of the property's open expanse was a detached garage of sorts. Every light in the place had been turned on. Four strapping teenage boys soaped down a red car under the supervision of one glowering man. Mercy's flashy Mercedes? Josiah couldn't see well enough to tell. The big man admonished the kids about future joyriding as they scrubbed the grill, the tires, the undercarriage. Why bother when the car would have to roll miles down a dirt road before ever hitting pavement? To erase the evidence of Mrs. McIntyre's murder?

Beside him, Mercy stopped and gripped his chin, focusing him on her once more. "Do you understand what I'm saying?"

"I think so." He grasped Mercy's elevator pitch. It was the rest of the Chosen and the behaviors they continually exhibited that made no sense. "You think the world is overpopulated."

"Sooner than we think, we'll have millions of people capable of being productive but no longer needed in the workforce. But they'll still require food for themselves, their partners, and their offspring. Where will the money come from? Where will they find nourishment? Imag-

ine this scenario repeating itself over and over in nearly all industrialized nations where we barely grow our own food anymore. Scarcity
will drive costs up to a point where the majority of the people may no
longer be able to afford to buy the food they need on a day-to-day
basis. What happens when we have a population not eating an ade-
quate number of calories per day but that has absolutely no knowledge
of how to feed themselves and their families?"

"Chaos." If her scenario came true. If no nations banded together
to realize this coming problem well before it hit. If nothing was done
to improve the human condition before it was too late.

"Exactly. Possibly even civil war. Governments might use food
and clean water to control the population. It might also lead to geno-
cide or another rise of feudalism." She shook her head as if those pos-
sibilities troubled her. "The goal of everyone at Enlightenment Fields
is to be prepared for the future, since some scientists think it's possible
the world is already overpopulated and our conditions will deteriorate
fast."

Maybe, but since there was still a McDonald's and a Starbucks on
every corner, that wasn't a problem in most industrialized countries.
Burundi, Sudan, Ethiopia, Haiti, and others weren't so fortunate. Was
she trying to say that those countries' food insecurities could soon
plague the whole world and cause mass starvation? The planet was
capable of sustaining people . . . if resources were allocated properly.
But in a political climate where populations could be controlled by
the food they most needed to live?

"That's a grim picture."

"Adam saw abject poverty during his travels in India and Nepal. It
affected him deeply. The starving children hurt him most. After some
research, he also ventured to the severely stricken parts of Africa. He
was already concerned about global overpopulation, but after seeing
some of the heartbreakingly hungry people, he was motivated to start
a movement that sought to be self-sustaining, of those who could learn
to live off the land, even if that meant embracing a bygone way of life.

We enjoy electricity and running water and all the modern conveniences today. But we are capable of living a much simpler existence. We have prohibited utility companies from building cell towers on our land. We have one Internet connection so we can communicate with the outside world that's too shortsighted to grasp why we won't conform to their way of life. They call us freaks, say we live in a cult." She sighed sadly. "We tune them out. They simply don't understand."

Interesting theories. There was a lot of truth in her global population statistics, the troubles less developed countries had in feeding their citizens, the fact that some governments had used food and clean water to manipulate their people. It wasn't completely out of the realm of possibility. But civilization would have to break down completely before any of this came to pass on a global scale. On the other hand, given the right circumstances, scarcity in food and water could make all of that a reality quickly.

He frowned in thought, relieved when she began to stroll toward the church in the distance. "You have a lot of expectant mothers on the ranch. If overpopulation is a problem, why are so many women here pregnant?"

She smiled his way. "That is an excellent, observant question. We'll have more time to talk about that after we've welcomed our new Chosen into the fold."

When they entered the church, the place was packed. Every pew was crammed full of people. Others had brought in folding chairs and crowded the outer aisles. More had tossed pillows at the feet of the front row and were sitting expectantly, ready to watch the ceremony.

Mercy nodded at various people as she led him up the aisle. She sent some smiles, held out a hand or two to others. But she never stopped her trek to the front and never released her grip on his arm.

They sat in a seat reserved for them at the very front. Mercy settled between two men, who both cast curious gazes his way. One, a big brute, had shorn blond hair and a host of visible combat scars, along with a severe scowl. The other looked well dressed and perfectly groomed. His dark hair and beard framed cunning blue eyes as he sized Josiah up.

"These are my brothers, Marcus"—she pointed to the mean-looking one—"and Michael." She gestured to Mr. Suave.

Both nodded his way. He returned their silent acknowledgment, feeling as if he'd been surrounded by a pack of wolves.

Were these two her biological brothers? Josiah's guess was no. They looked nothing alike. And Marcus glared at her as if he was none too happy that she seemed cozy beside another man.

Inside the church, music suddenly began playing—more of the disturbing, hyperhappy tunes Mercy had recorded. This was a reverent song about acceptance and love and living off the land, which all sounded great on the surface. And she had decent explanations for everything happening on the ranch. But his crazy meter was still pinging at full peal.

At the front, behind the altar, a dozen and a half people walked in single file, wearing head-to-toe flowing robes in white. Four strapping men hefted in a giant wooden tub and set it on what could only be termed a stage. Another cluster carried in those steaming buckets he'd seen earlier and poured them into the tub. Some ladies came behind them with trays of cloudy liquid in mason jars and began passing them out to each of the new converts.

Josiah watched and tried not to shake his head. So the powers that be in this freaky-ass place intended to have everyone tripping before they dunked the new victims like they were undergoing some imitation baptism. Then what?

He didn't have to wait long to find out. Through a door at the back of the church another figure walked in. Instinctively, a tremor rolled through Josiah.

Adam Coleman.

He had shaggy salt-and-pepper hair, sported a short-shorn beard, and wore glasses that made him look almost intellectual. He dressed simply in black jeans and a matching vest with a stark white shirt.

Plain black boots rounded out the look. He wore no jewelry, had no tattoos, just a focused expression. When the man's gaze fell on Josiah, the maniacal spark in his dark eyes jolted him to his toes.

"Good evening, brothers and sisters. As you know, it's a joyous experience when we add to the Enlightenment Fields flock of followers. All of these believers share our worries about the coming collapse and have agreed to dedicate themselves to a brighter, simpler future here. They have shed the worldly chains that have bound them to a futile existence. They have given us their vow to uphold our values and to help us grow the community according to our loving, organized plan. Drink, my children, of the nectar that will give you your first spiritual rapture."

He paused and watched as the new inductees downed their liquid. The brainwashed believers all clapped as if it were a truly momentous occasion. Josiah pretended rapt fascination as he mentally took apart everything Coleman had spewed. Basically, someone had convinced these incoming Chosen that the sky was falling, so they had surrendered all their worldly goods—and all ways to communicate with the outside world—to the cult. In return, Coleman expected total obedience and . . . what else?

The guy said a few more words about the end of the world and how Enlightenment Fields would weather the storm because they were prepared and united. Their solidarity would keep them strong, blah, blah, blah. Their beliefs would fill them with joy and all that bullshit.

Josiah sent a sidelong glance at Mercy. She smiled happily. Jesus, she was eating this shit up.

Then the windbag began to introduce the newcomers one by one. Most were in their early to midtwenties, with a few closer to thirty. One woman arrived with a daughter who looked maybe three. Another couple held hands, looking excited to embark on their next adventure. One big, well-muscled man looked closer to forty than the others. He remained silent and stoic as Coleman described him as an oil-rig worker from Houston who'd had enough of the difficulties and strife in the outside world. He'd think the guy was looking for a hand-out if he didn't look as if he'd already put in years of hard labor.

Beside him, Marcus eyed the burly recruit with a sharply assessing stare. Then he glanced Coleman's way with a little tilt of his chin. The big man, now looking woozy from his "trip," was dunked into the water and hustled to the left side of the stage.

Next was a slight blonde, definitely in her early twenties. She looked soft and doe-eyed. Josiah read the earmarks. Compliant, beyond submissive, and looking for a savior. An easy target for these scum.

She emerged from the tub dripping wet, and it wasn't lost on Josiah that all these robes were basically transparent when wet. Michael looked the woman up and down, then gave their leader an almost imperceptible nod. Coleman acknowledged him by separating the female from the others and setting her stage right.

Soon, Josiah noticed a pattern. Coleman would look to the trio of his most coveted "children" at the front as another new Chosen was introduced. One of them would make a move—Mercy often held up a tiny field flower he hadn't noticed pressed in her palm—then the inductee in question would be either shuffled left or right, or clustered into the center. At the end of the silent sorting process, three distinct groups had formed. At the left stood four men, all of whom looked rough-hewn and capable of hard work, along with two curvaceous females. On the right, five young females huddled beside one man who had been an ER nurse in his previous life. In the center, a motley collection of men and women, along with the lone child, milled in the small space. Several had indicated they enjoyed gardening.

As the service ended, the Chosen in the audience drank of the nectar—except Marcus, Michael, and Mercy. Then Coleman dismissed everyone for a night of frolic, food, and dance on the lawn. The new Chosen would join them soon.

The flock rushed out the doors, eager to begin their feast under the moon. Mercy trailed her "brothers" as she led Josiah toward Coleman.

Marcus claimed the group on the left, inspecting them with a dispassionate stare before he acknowledged their leader. "Thank you, sire."

Coleman nodded. "Teach, guide, and prepare them, as is your duty and your right." Then he turned to Michael, who eyed the cluster of females with a lascivious once-over. "You as well."

"Of course. I take my mission very seriously."

"That you do." The older man smiled slyly as if they shared some inside joke, then reached for the sweet little blonde shivering near his side, her paper-thin robe plastered to her perky tits. "On second thought, I've spoken to this one. She's in need of additional guidance before she'll be ready to join the flock."

Michael ground his teeth, looking pissed off, but he gave Coleman a tight nod. "As you wish, sire."

Oh, of course the prettiest one needed "special counseling" from the group's skeevy leader. Josiah wasn't even surprised.

"I trust your duties to the others will keep you occupied for some time?" Coleman asked.

"Of course." Michael seemed loath to admit that.

Josiah felt fairly sure that, aside from the inductees, everyone understood this conversation way better than him.

"Off with you two, then." Coleman waved Marcus and Michael away, then settled the stoned blonde into the nearest pew.

As the others left with their followers, Josiah leaned over to Mercy. "What's going on?"

"Marcus trains a segment of the flock to defend us in case the collapse happens and we are beset by those who would steal our food. Michael takes in those who can help the Chosen, like the male nurse. Or those who can assist with our goals in . . . other ways."

Other ways? Probably providing a receptacle for his wandering dick. That was the vibe Josiah got. Damn, these people were creepy as fuck . . . "And the rest of the new folks?"

"They'll join the green warriors, tending the crops, inside and out. You see, everyone has a role here."

"They do, sweet Mercy." Coleman put a hand on her shoulder.

It wasn't gentle, and if Josiah hadn't been paying attention, he would have missed her stiffen.

"As I was explaining, sire."

Coleman didn't look terribly moved by her show of deference. "You have another as yet unfulfilled duty as prime sister of the Chosen."

"That's why I've brought Josiah to meet you. For your approval, sire."

He paused, sensing this sudden, unexpected development could be dangerous. He'd hoped not to come under their leader's scrutiny before he was ready—and without backup.

"Welcome. Are you thinking of joining my following? Has Mercy told you of my teachings and our vision of the future?"

"Earlier this evening, yes. I'm giving every word she said proper thought."

"Excellent. If Mercy is already introducing you to me, she's eager for you to join our fold and perhaps play a special role in Enlightenment Fields. Ask her plenty of questions. I suggest you stay the night to aid your decision," Coleman said, but it didn't sound much like a suggestion. "I'll be here to provide any other insight in the morning. Come, little dove. Michael says you're pure of body?" At the woman's wide-eyed nod, he turned a smile on her that was full of fake benevolence. "And pure of heart as well. You'll make a lovely addition here, and I'll make certain you feel welcome."

Josiah wanted to warn the woman . . . but he couldn't, not without blowing everything. And if she was under the group's thrall this much, would she even believe him?

When Coleman helped the dazed inductee to her feet and escorted her out the door, toward a large dwelling in the distance, Mercy watched with a stilted smile. "Shall we?"

Not like Josiah had a choice if he wanted to figure out what the fuck was happening here. But he had some mighty ugly suspicions . . .

As soon as Mercy settled her new followers in a communal barracks, she led him outside. The smell of roasting meat and corn hung in the chilly air. A bonfire roared under the moonlight. Dancing ensued. More spiked liquid made the rounds.

They both grabbed a plate of succulent food, then sat on tree stumps at the edge of the festivities. Josiah was almost afraid to eat, wondering what they might have laced all the grub with. But when Mercy forked in delicate bites, he hoped nothing was too worrisome and cautiously nibbled.

"Thank you for coming. It means more to me than you know." She sent him a sidelong stare that was part shy, part flirtatious.

"Thank you for inviting me." What the fuck else could he say?

"You have questions."

"A million."

"If you'll take a leap of faith and join us, I'll answer them all." She set her plate at her feet and grabbed his hand. "I want that so badly. More than anything."

"Why? You barely know me."

Mercy took a long time in answering. She bit her lip and said, "I was chosen as prime sister almost a year ago. It comes with certain . . . duties. They're not something I can complete alone, and all this time I've been looking for the right someone to embark on this task with, to share in both the burden and the joy. No one I've come across has possessed the right qualities. This requires someone intelligent and open-minded, someone I can talk to, someone I don't mind being beside. Someone I believe capable of loyalty and devotion."

Josiah tried not to blink in astonished horror. What the hell was she about to propose, some sort of culty marriage?

DEVOTED TO LOVE   179

"I'm listening."

She took a deep breath and squeezed his hand. "Our sire's vision is of four prime siblings he hand-selected as the primary ancestors of the next generation of Chosen who will grow up in our joyous way of life and truly understand what it means to live off the earth and share its bounties. You've seen all the women expecting babies, commented even. Marcus and Michael have done their duty by Enlightenment Fields many times over. Adam has even helped. They'll persuade some of tonight's new Chosen as well. And as you can see, we're still seeking one more someone special enough to complete our circle of forefathers and foremothers. To our sire's displeasure, I haven't embraced my duties, though I've had permission for months." Mercy pressed her lips together. "He's been disappointed with my hesitation. But when you came, that began to ease. Now, I'm excited and I'm really hoping you'll agree to join us. It would mean so much."

Josiah froze. Though Mercy continued to dance around the truth, he hoped like hell she didn't mean what he feared she did. "Why?"

"Because if Adam approves, you'll be the first to breed me."

CHAPTER 11

The following morning, Josiah rolled over in the bed. Oh, shit. Mercy was still beside him and he had one thought in mind: That was the first time he'd ever spent the whole night next to a woman he absolutely never, ever wanted to have sex with. He'd forced himself to stay at Enlightenment Fields and look interested enough to be considering her wackdoodle proposition. But holy shit, breed her? He didn't care how much of an honor it supposedly was to be asked to impregnate the only existing prime sister. He refused to touch Mercy and he would never leave any child of his here to be used, manipulated, and exploited.

The whole night had been unnerving and uncomfortable. Before bed, Mercy had approached him on bare feet, locking stares with him, and whispered that she'd ached for him to end her years-long chastity and plant his seed inside her the moment she had laid eyes on him. All he had to do was say yes to Enlightenment Fields. Because he was an outsider, they wouldn't be allowed to touch until he did.

That was fine by him. Even if that wasn't the case, the answer would be a raving "fuck no."

Telling her he'd have to think about her offer, he had pretended to drop off to sleep. Once Mercy found slumber, he managed to get a text out to Zy telling his fellow operative not to expect him until morning and to keep Maggie at home, calm, and safe. His buddy had replied that safe was no problem. Calm . . . not so much.

Grimacing, he'd powered down his phone to preserve his battery, stared at the ceiling, and tried to figure out the cult's endgame. What did Adam Coleman want out of this gig? Zero-cost labor? Tax-free money? A never-ending variety of pussy? All of the above, he supposed. Plus, he got to exercise his need for power, since he clearly called all the shots, including who completed what tasks and who had sex with whom. He commanded his followers at will, exercising his whim. They would do or say whatever he demanded. Josiah bet he got off on that.

Sick fuck.

The rest of the night, he'd dozed all night with one eye open, far too aware of Mercy cuddled up to him in a sheer, pale nightgown. Thoughts of Maggie haunted him.

Dawn was probably twenty minutes away when he rose. He heard rattling downstairs. As soon as he left a vacancy on the mattress, Mercy rolled to the middle, one hand seeming to reach for him.

Time to leave this place. He wished like hell he didn't have to come back . . . but he knew better. This mess was far from over.

He slipped downstairs, peeking into the spare room across from the bathroom that doubled as a greenhouse on the first floor. The sealed wooden crates that had been in here last time were gone—except one. It had cracked and split, rendering it unliftable without breaking. And what do you know? Inside sat a collection of a half-dozen AR-15s all in a neat little row.

Cursing under his breath, Josiah snapped a pic on his phone, then slipped out, tiptoed past two women in the kitchen brewing up more of that fucked-up nectar, and headed outside. After last night's shindig, everyone should be sleeping off their hallucinogenic trip so he could make a clean getaway. Instead, the whole community was gathered around seven people dressed in black robes who shed their shoes and hugged their fellow cultists goodbye. Someone sobbed nearby. A glance beside him proved a grown man was crying.

Josiah stepped closer for a better look, then found a woman, barely more than a teenager, staring in stark sadness, tears pouring down her mottled cheeks. "Are you all right? What's happening?"

"Last Light." She pressed her hands to her chest. "It's always so sad, but today . . ."

What the hell did that mean?

"I don't understand."

"They're leaving us. And we'll miss them."

Seven people had finally found a lick of sense and had decided to blow this festering loony bin of depravity? Good for them.

"Where are they going?" He had a truck. He could take them far away from here . . . after he and Deputy Preston had a chat with them and discerned whatever information they could.

"To the other side," she sobbed.

He froze. Did she mean they were going off to their deaths? "Of what?"

"Life. It was so hard letting my mother go. But she chose this. Her productive time is at an end. She's become a drain on the community's resources. They all have. So after last night's First Enlightenment, she volunteered for Last Light."

She'd *elected* to die? "Productive how?"

"She has a degenerative back condition, so she can't work the fields anymore. And at her age, her body can no longer breed. Since she can't contribute meaningfully to our community, she chose to leave on honorable terms. I understand. But I'm so sad. Her youngest daughter is only four. Mary is so confused. I'll have to raise her." She dropped a hand to her stomach. "While raising my own. But Michael will help me. He always helps me."

Josiah nearly puked. He'd bet Michael helped a whole bunch of women around here—right onto their backs. He seemed more like a lothario than a spiritual leader. Of course Coleman and Marcus had apparently done their fair share of seed spreading, too.

All these followers were absolutely fucking crazy.

"So . . . they walk into the sunrise and what?"

"We don't know. It's a mystery. But the sire assures us they cross to the other side in peace and love."

He watched as each of the huddled figures in black robes took a bottle of something that looked darker and cloudier than the nectar they'd served last night.

"What's that they're drinking?"

"Tranquility potion. My mom said that once she volunteered for Last Light, she was given the recipe for a potion that would deliver her to the other side in serenity and slumber. She made it early this morning, and now . . ."

So they were taught how to poison themselves? And these people did it willingly?

Music began then, this tune meant to be a moving tribute to those Chosen who had taken the "honorable" path. The melody was a mournful if reverent wail. Josiah tried not to shake his head as the seven who had volunteered for Last Light drank every drop of the liquid while the sun finally crested above the horizon. Then they began to walk toward the fiery orb.

Holy fuck. Ritualized suicide?

Josiah couldn't help these seven people by watching them walk toward their eternal slumber. He might not be able to help them at all, but he'd damn well try.

Whirling around, he turned and dashed back to his truck, getting the hell out of there pronto. His thoughts raced.

In the past, he'd volunteered for nearly every mission at EM Security—the more dangerous the better. After Whitney, he'd had nothing to lose, and the adrenaline had been a welcome rush. Now . . . he worried. Of course, with Maggie's safety on the line, quitting was impossible. He had to press on.

But for the first time in longer than he wanted to admit, he worried that he might not make it out of this mission alive. And he could think of only one reason he truly gave a shit: Maggie.

―――――――――

Maggie had a morning routine. Today, she'd abandoned it and instead found herself wringing her hands as she paced the front porch and watched for Josiah to drive up the dirt road. As the sun began to inch up the sky, dread bit into her belly. No one had heard from him since last night. Her texts had gone undelivered. Zyron and Trees didn't seem at all concerned. They just kept telling her that Josiah was smart and strong and he always managed to work himself out of any situation he got in.

That didn't reassure her. The loons at Enlightenment Fields had probably killed both Mr. Haney and Mrs. McIntyre—pillars of the local community. Would they hesitate to do away with an outsider if he stood in their way?

A late-night call to Deputy Preston had been fruitless. He had been up to his eyeballs in her first-grade teacher's senseless death and the growing fear among those in Comfort. Everyone wanted to know why their little town was no longer sleepy and what Deputy Preston intended to do about it. But what could he do without proof?

She'd also called Dixie for the inside scoop, but her friend hadn't been on duty and she hadn't answered her cell phone. Maggie understood the woman worked weird hours and had to sleep whenever the opportunity rose. But none of that was helping her find out what had happened to Josiah.

Half the night, she'd been doing a mental deep dive to find out why it mattered to her. Maggie didn't like the answers.

"Morning."

The sounds of footsteps behind her hadn't really registered until the familiar voice called out in greeting.

"Morning, Sawyer." She spared him the merest glance before turning her attention back to the long drive from the main road.

She sensed more than saw him come closer. "I know you don't

think this is any of my business, Maggie. But Josiah isn't good for you."

"Leave it alone."

"I'm not giving up on you. We had something real good. I really thought we could work everything out. But you've been standoffish since Davis left. And you totally forgot about me once Mr. I'm-Former-CIA showed up."

Maggie sighed at Sawyer's snide sarcasm as she faced him. "You and I were never going to work. What we had . . . I needed it at the time, but I don't see us working out long term."

Because she didn't have the kind of feelings for him that she had for Josiah. When she was with Sawyer, she didn't feel like her heart was free-falling toward love. She wasn't downright eager to be near him in every way. She didn't miss him like the devil or tingle when she thought about his kiss. She definitely wouldn't care if he'd spent all night elsewhere. Josiah, on the other hand . . . Sure she was worried about his safety, but she was also mad enough to spit nails.

"Don't say that. I can't forget you." He clasped her shoulders in his tight grip. "I can't stop thinking about you. I can't stop wanting you."

Maggie wriggled free and turned away. "You have to."

Sawyer chased. "Aww, don't be that way, darlin'. I get that Josiah is a shiny new toy but . . . he found someone else."

She whirled at his words, her heart stopping. "What?"

"He was gone all night. What did you think he was doing?"

"To take care of a personal errand," she hedged. Sawyer didn't need to know about Josiah's investigation.

"More like to do Mercy over at Enlightenment Fields." And Sawyer looked happy to impart that news. "He spent the night with her. You didn't know? What a bastard. But I guess I shouldn't be surprised a guy like him wouldn't bother to tell you before he hopped in someone else's sack."

Betrayal Maggie didn't want to feel stabbed her deep. "You don't know that's what happened."

"Actually, I do. A ranch hand who works outside Boerne is a friend of mine. He was invited out there last night, same as Josiah. He saw your boy toy follow Mercy into her house, watched the two figures through her bedroom window. The lights went out . . . and Josiah didn't come out until just before sunup."

She didn't want to believe it. Sawyer had every reason to lie to her. "Bullshit."

"Ask him yourself." Sawyer tipped his head toward the road and Josiah's truck rumbling over the dirt, toward the ranch. "I won't even say 'I told you so.' And I'm always here to console you, darlin', in whatever way you need."

Whistling, he walked away with a confidence that made her grit her teeth. Maggie ignored him. Whatever Josiah had done last night didn't matter.

Too bad she was terrible at lying to herself.

Maggie tried to look casual as she ambled to the front porch while Josiah climbed out of his dusty truck. He looked tired, guarded. Closed. Guilty?

"Hey." She crossed her arms over her chest and stupidly hoped he'd kiss her, tell her nothing had happened last night, that he'd missed her.

Instead, he barely glanced her way. "Morning. You seen Trees and Zy? I need to talk to them."

To brag to his buddies about last night's conquest? "Around. Find out what's going on out at Enlightenment Fields?"

"Not now." He didn't bother to meet her gaze, just scanned the yard. "I need to find the guys."

Then he walked past her, toward the house, without another word.

She shouldn't follow him. Maggie knew it. They weren't in a relationship. Hell, she didn't want one. That logic didn't keep her from wrapping her hand around his steely arm and stopping him. "Last I checked, it was my ranch you were trying to save. And my bed you just crawled out of. So what the hell is going on?"

"I'll find you when I can and explain. But this argument you want to have . . . I don't have time."

He jerked away and slammed into the house, leaving Maggie standing on the porch dumbfounded, her chest tight and aching.

To her right, Sawyer shook his head as if he pitied her. Then he tipped his hat and wandered toward the south pasture.

Damn it.

She had a choice to make. Cut her losses and forget Josiah existed—could she even manage that?—or march into the house and demand she be included in his discussions about her ranch.

Screw standing here like a damsel in distress. He didn't have time for her? Ha! She'd make sure he *made* time. Then she'd tell him to kiss her ass. There were plenty of other guys in the world; she didn't need Josiah Grant.

But she sure wanted him.

Damn it.

Maggie plowed her way through the door and into the house. She didn't hear anyone talking. Josiah wasn't in the kitchen. Zyron and Trees weren't hanging out in the family room. She frowned until she heard muffled voices from behind her papa's study door.

Were they huddled in there having man meetings that "the little woman" didn't need to hear? Oh, if that was what he thought, he had another think coming . . .

Mr. Former-CIA didn't know this house the way she did. He had no idea that, between the thin wall and the central vents in her grandparents' bathroom, she could hear every word spoken in the study. Every. Single. One. Clearly, too.

Tiptoeing to her grandmother's vanity, Maggie leaned against the counter and listened. Since this affected her more than anyone, she did so without remorse.

"Are you shitting me?" Zyron asked. "Does that mean what I think it does?"

"Yeah. On my way back here, I did a drive-by and tried to spot anyone . . . Nothing. After that, I called Preston to let him know. He had no idea about any of this. Unfortunately, he's stuck in Boerne at the county courthouse testifying about another case. He tried to call Sheriff Wayne. The man didn't answer. Preston says he's probably fishing. By the time either of them surfaces, it will be too late."

"We'll search instead," Trees chimed in. "But you can't come."

"I know. If anyone from Enlightenment Fields caught me snooping—"

"It would blow everything," Zyron agreed. "Trees and I will go. We'll see who or what we can find."

Maggie found herself pressing closer, trying to understand. What the devil was going on?

"Be careful. And for fuck's sake, don't let Maggie in on any of this. She'd go marching over there, full of demands and vinegar and . . ."

"That would be bad. And it would blow your cover totally."

"Exactly. And I don't want her anywhere near those people. For her own good."

So he was trying to keep her safe. That was part of his job. But she wasn't helpless or stupid. She knew things about this town and these people that he didn't. She could be an asset.

"Absolutely. So . . . that's what happened this morning. What happened last night?" Zyron questioned.

"It will have to wait until you get back. But long story short? In the hopes I'll join their merry band of weirdos, Mercy spent all night plastered against me in her bed and granted me the privilege of breeding her."

Maggie's jaw dropped. Did he say *breeding*?

"Are you fucking kidding me? She wants you to get her pregnant?"

"Yep. As soon as possible."

"Dude—"

"I know. But we have to unpack all this later. You're wasting time now."

After some mumbling and grumbling, Zyron and Trees both checked their weapons, grabbed their shoes and car keys, then dashed out the front door. The room—hell, the house—was suddenly silent.

That was when Maggie made her move.

It didn't take long to find Josiah. He stood brooding in the kitchen, nursing a mug of coffee and staring out the window overlooking the side yard and porch swing.

"You have time for me yet? I'm thinking you might have time for me now that you're not busy with your boys. But I get it. Pals before gals and all that shit."

He sighed. "Maggie, I'm not blowing you off. I had to talk to my fellow operators about something time sensitive. They're acting on it now. I checked that duty off my list. What do you need?"

"Information. All of this affects me, my family, my house, my—"

"Not this. What I shared with Zy and Trees has nothing to do with you."

And he clearly had no intention of telling her. His hard expression told her that.

"You're keeping secrets from me," she accused.

"I'm protecting you."

"I didn't ask you to."

"Your sister and brother-in-law did."

"Gee, after spending a bunch of time with your penis inside my vagina, I thought you might have a little more allegiance to me. But I guess I'm just the girl you fucked a few times and now you're on to greener pastures. Whatever."

She turned her back on him. This was exactly why she never got attached to people. Other than her sister and her grandparents, everyone ultimately let her down. Every damn time. Like now.

Suddenly, he curled a steely arm around her waist and settled his lips against her ear. It took everything inside her not to melt at his touch. Instead, she bucked like a bronc. "Let me go."

He released her immediately. "Maggie, don't do this."

"What? Call it like I see it?"

"Put distance between us."

Was he serious? "Oh, you already did that. Congratulations on bagging Mercy. Was she good in bed?"

With a growl, Josiah spun her around to face him. "What makes you think I had sex with Mercy?"

Maggie wasn't about to tell him she could overhear his conversations in the study. First, she might need that sneaky little trick again. Second, she refused to give him any more reason to think she cared. But the shitty reality was that she did. And knowing what he'd done with that woman last night was killing her.

"The rumor mill around here works fast. A friend of a friend let me know you went upstairs with her last night, into her room, and didn't come out until nearly sunrise. I don't think you two were playing tiddlywinks."

"We talked and we slept. Just slept. And I only did it to try to get information to keep you and your ranch safe so—"

"Oh, of course you only shared a bed with the hot brunette for *my* benefit. You didn't enjoy it at all." She rolled her eyes. "How stupid do you think I am?"

"I don't think you're stupid. I think you're stubborn and you're not listening. I won't deny that she seems to like me for some reason. Why shouldn't I play along to see what information she'll give me?"

"I get it now. You suckered information out of her with your dick— and probably that talented tongue, too—because you were so worried about my safety. I'm sure you didn't feel a thing."

Josiah clenched his fists and gritted his teeth. "You have got to be the most stubborn, sarcastic, hardheaded, temperamental . . ."

"Don't stop there." She cocked her hand on her hip. "Tell me what you really think. Of course, all that you accused me of is still better than being secretive, dismissive, backbiting, and—"

He didn't let her finish her sentence, simply lifted her as if she weighed nothing, jerked her against his body, and covered her lips with his, plunging his fingers into her hair at the same moment he plunged his tongue into her mouth. He took possession of her—total, utter, undeniable. Maggie tried to fight. She tried not to notice his musky, woodsy scent. She tried not to succumb to the skill of his mouth. She tried not to wrap her legs around his middle and feel his erection prodding her exactly where she wanted it.

She failed miserably.

Why did this man undo her? Why did she let him? Why did she lose her starch every time he kissed her? Why couldn't she walk away from him with the same ease she'd walked away from every other man?

Josiah set her backside on the kitchen table at the same time he lifted his lips. He pressed his forehead to hers and stepped between her thighs, which had spread unconsciously for him. He was breathing heavily. "You make me crazy, baby."

Yeah? Same for her, only double. Not for anything would she admit that.

"I'll tell you something I shouldn't. Normally, if the job required it, I would have had sex with Mercy. She's crazy, but she's not hard to look at, and if sex makes her lips looser, that's a win. But last night, when some horizontal action seemed possible . . . my answer was a big no." He sighed. "I lay awake for a while after she curled herself up to my side. I had to let her because I can't let on that I have no interest in joining her or Enlightenment Fields. I tried to think about everything I'd seen, ways I could prove they're into dangerous and illegal shit so I could end this farce. I tried to consider all my next moves, how to play this scenario for the best possible outcome. But all I could fucking think about was you."

Maggie's heart skipped a handful of beats. She couldn't bite back her curiosity. "Why?"

"Damned if I know. I'd like to say it's my professional concern. These are dangerous people, and you're my responsibility to keep safe. But I'm not into bullshitting myself. I'm in unfamiliar territory here, so I don't know what this is between us. But I know what it isn't. Casual. Passing. Easily forgotten."

She blinked up at him, her heart in her throat. Against him, she trembled. Mostly because he was right.

"You look as scared as I feel. And I'm not shocked at all. I don't have any interest in trying a relationship again, and you don't commit. We'd be kidding ourselves, right? I keep telling myself that. And yet . . . last night when I couldn't stop thinking about you, one thought circled in my head: I have a bad feeling I'm falling in love with you. And if that's the case, baby, we're both fucked. Because I won't let you walk away from me. I won't let you go."

Her heart stopped altogether. "L-love?"

"It's a real possibility. I'm telling you this because you'll probably do one of two things. Either you'll run away from me far and fast in the next thirty seconds, which will tell me I'm wasting my time, energy, and emotions—and hopefully will keep me from becoming utterly and irrevocably lovesick over you. Or you'll realize that I'm worth taking a chance on and stop pulling away every fucking time you get the screwed-up notion that I've somehow stabbed you in the back or left you." He shrugged. "Regardless of which path you take, I'm further ahead than I would be if I said nothing and let this play out over the next couple of weeks. Then once you, your family, and your ranch are safe, you'd most likely dump my ass and crush my heart in the end."

Maggie gaped. Her heartbeat thundered and her thoughts raced. He might be in love with her? He wasn't the first man to say that. Hell, one boy had written a poem to her beauty. Granted, it had been his class assignment and they had been in seventh grade, but still . . . The guy she'd given her virginity to because he was hot and rumor said he was good in bed had pursued her for months after they'd done the deed. He'd only quit when his family moved away. Two years ago, a man she'd met in a community college class and dated a few times had actually started talking marriage. She'd easily dismissed them all because they weren't serious.

Determination was written all over Josiah's face. He meant every word he said.

"Oh, dear lord."

"Does that mean I should fuck the fuck off? Or . . . that you might be falling for me, too?"

She didn't know how to answer him. That wasn't totally true. She knew what her heart wanted to say. But he'd spent last night in another woman's bed. He was keeping secrets from her. Did she dare tell him that she—gulp—had feelings for him, too? If she didn't, he'd probably walk away. Then, wouldn't she always wonder what might have been?

Maggie swallowed. After a lifetime of breaking hearts, she was actually considering giving this man the power to break hers.

That scared the hell out of her.

"Don't fuck off, okay?"

He let out a breath that seemed to leach the tension from his shoulders. "So you might be falling for me?"

Wasn't it obvious? She wouldn't have given two shits where he spent last night if she weren't. But that didn't mean she wanted to spell her feelings out for him. He was a man. Did he really need the reassurance?

Maybe he did. After all, she wasn't the only one who'd been hurt in the past.

She closed her eyes, terrified by what she was about to admit. "I-I might be."

His grip on her tightened. "Put your arms around my neck, baby."

Maggie did. "Why?"

"I'm going to take you upstairs, lay you out, strip you down, and worship you. Got anything to say about that?"

By now, she'd usually pulled back and figured out a dozen ways to protect her heart. In this moment, Maggie couldn't. She needed Josiah too badly. "Hurry."

CHAPTER 12

Josiah's head reeled. Magnolia West might be in love with him. She certainly kissed him like she was.

The responsible part of his brain told him he should be far more focused on the seven people who had whipped up their own poison and ingested it before trekking toward the sun less than an hour ago. He'd tried like hell, but when he'd been unable to find them and Kane Preston had been in no position to help, he'd enlisted Zy and Trees. His gut told him it was too late to save those people who had sacrificed themselves for Enlightenment Fields' crazy ideals, and he'd have to call EM Security Management soon to give them the scoop and follow up about potential FBI involvement. Hell, if Enlightenment Fields had provided the poison or demanded that their followers kill themselves, the feds would definitely get involved. But Coleman was smarter than that. If the crate of AR-15s had been illegally converted into automatics or Josiah had proof that this wacky cult was stockpiling any weapon prohibited by law, he'd drag the ATF into this fray. But the cult hadn't and he didn't, so he could do precious little now.

Except focus on the woman he couldn't seem to forget.

As he carried Maggie up the stairs, her legs wrapped around his waist, and headed toward the bedroom they'd shared for the last handful of crazy days, Josiah breathed her in. God, she even smelled sexy and sassy. Everything about her should have him whipping out the caution tape and wrapping it around his heart. But she made doing anything except craving her every moment of every day impossible.

"Are we doing something stupid?" Maggie panted as she tore her lips from his.

Josiah dropped her on the bed, in a cloud of thick quilts and soft sheets, and hovered above her, staring into her eyes, so green and uncertain. "Probably. But that's not stopping me."

"Me, either."

"Have you ever been in love?"

"No." She didn't even have to think about her answer.

Honestly, some part of him wondered if he ever had been, either. Whitney's betrayal had hurt him. But in hindsight, it had infuriated him a shitload more. He suspected she'd wounded his pride far more than she'd bruised his heart.

"Because you never let anyone close."

"Never." She hesitated, frowned. "Don't make me regret this . . ."

Her soft threat punched him in the chest. Maggie was all but admitting that the feelings she had for him gave him the power to hurt her. The realization humbled him.

"Never. Give me your mouth."

He closed his eyes and dipped his head. Maggie met him halfway, lips parted, heart open. Thrill chased through his bloodstream as he possessed and partook of her.

God, he could lose himself in her all day and still want more of her tonight.

Softly, slowly, he caressed her pillowy lips, cupped her face, and brushed her downy cheek with his thumb. "I don't know how what I'm feeling is possible. A week ago, I didn't know you existed."

A little furrow wrinkled her brow. "When we were growing up, Granna always told my sister and me that love was something we'd fall into as quick as the snap of a finger—as least it happened that way for her and Papa. It's commitment that takes time, compromise, patience, dedication, and hard work."

"Your grandmother is a wise woman. So why have you resisted falling? Afraid of those things?"

"No. 'Love' made my mother do stupid things, like try drugs, get pregnant at sixteen . . ."

"Abandon her daughters as toddlers."

Maggie swallowed as if the whole conversation pained her. "That. Yeah. I never wanted her version of love. And if commitment took that much effort, why bother? Sex always worked just fine."

Is that what she told herself? It made sense, he supposed. She couldn't get hurt again if she didn't allow herself to be vulnerable.

"Because there's more to life than sex."

"You might be right."

She hadn't outright refuted him, so Josiah called that a victory. Maggie needed to feel valued. Since her mother had run out on her when she'd been far too young to process why, she'd felt betrayed. Hurt. Abandoned. If he wanted something with her that lasted longer than this mission, he would have to figure out how to take all that away. She would have to believe in every corner of her heart that he would always be there for her.

How the hell was he supposed to do that when the job often sent him away from home and had him out of pocket for days, sometimes weeks at a time?

"You and I have a lot to talk about, Maggie," he murmured as he kissed her cheek, let his lips drift down her neck to her shoulder. He pulled her baggy gray sweatshirt off her shoulder—and froze. "You're not wearing a bra."

The sly grin she tossed his way seemed like classic Maggie. "You want to talk about that? Okay, but I can only imagine the diatribe you'll go on once you figure out I'm not wearing panties, either."

Though he suspected she was trying to distract him from meaningful conversation, instant lust jolted Josiah's system. "You're not?"

She sent him a teasing giggle as he wrestled the sweatshirt from her torso and worked the stretchy yoga pants down her legs, tossing both garments aside. Staring down at her, he sat back on his heels with a groan. Maggie hadn't been lying; she was naked as the day she'd been born. The morning sun slanted through the windows, turning her skin golden. Holy shit.

He'd seen at least a hundred naked women. Why did this one take his breath away?

"Clearly, you're not."

Her grin widened. "Nope."

"I swear you're perfect. All I can think about is tasting every inch of you."

"I thought you said there was more to life than sex."

"But I think the sex will be even better because it matters. Because we care. We should test that theory."

As he cupped her breast and teased her nipple with his thumb, she shivered. "Totally."

That was all the encouragement Josiah needed.

He grabbed the back of his shirt in his fist, yanked it over his head, then lobbed it to the far side of the room. The moment he did, Maggie sat up and put her hands on him, palms brushing his chest, fingers curling around his shoulders. She skimmed her lips across his pectorals before she pressed her breasts to his bare skin.

Josiah shuddered and shoved his fingers through her tresses, tugging until she met his gaze. "I think I already know the answer, but I look forward to proving my theory true."

Bending, he took her mouth in a soft kiss of possession, delving deep. He held her close, stroked her back. Maggie fit against him perfectly. Was it possible her skin was even softer than he remembered? Or was he just bewitched by her that much more?

Time ceased to have meaning. The world faded away as he laid Maggie back on the frilly bed once again, covered her mouth, and fitted himself against her curves. He let his lips taste their way up her neck. He nipped at her lobe. He laved her shoulder. Every time, she met him with a touch or kiss of her own that inflamed him more.

Sure, whenever he was with her, he wanted to take her, be one with her. This . . . was different. Today, he wanted to claim her—and not just temporarily. The intensity of his need fueled an urgency he'd never experienced. Maybe it was being away from her last night and being forced to lie beside Mercy. Josiah didn't know, but he felt compelled to make Maggie belong totally to him.

The longer he kissed her, the sweeter her lips tasted. He'd swear they were coated with honey, dipped in pure sugar. The bounty of her body was stretched out under him, and those addictive lips drove him to feast everywhere.

Josiah kissed his way down to her breasts, lingering on the swells. He dragged his tongue across her nipples before closing his lips around the distended tips and sucking them deep. His reward was the bowing of her back and sweet whimpers escaping her lips. She filled his hands as completely as the sounds of her pleasure filled his ears.

Back and forth, he shifted his focus between one tender bud and the other until they swelled. Then he caressed his fingers down her torso, to her folds. She was engorged here, too. Soaking wet. Josiah groaned, eager to arouse her until she burned. Until she surrendered every bit of her will, her body, and her heart to him.

As usual, Maggie surprised him with plans of her own.

She jackknifed and sat up, then gave him a little shove, forcing him onto his back.

"What are you doing, baby?"

"You're always unraveling me. I want to do the same to you."

"You want to touch me?" He couldn't keep the grin off his face. "You find me irresistible?"

"Maybe. And maybe I just want you to feel the torment you heap on me."

More the former than the latter, but she didn't give Josiah any other warning before she bent to him and licked his nipple, nipped her way across his chest and down his abdomen. Then she attacked his zipper until she was breathing on the head of his cock, her exhalations warm puffs on the most sensitive skin of his body. He stiffened at the shock of desire that hit his system. Then he melted into the mattress.

Goddamn, this woman got to him.

When she pressed the barest of butterfly kisses to his abdomen, around his protruding cock, everything inside him clenched and burned. And he knew his theory had been right. Sex had always been enjoyable. One of the greatest experiences in life, in fact. But this, the teasing brushes of fingertips, the worshipping touches of their lips? He'd never felt anything more perfect. If he'd had any doubt this woman was meant to be his, it was dissolving fast.

"Maggie . . ." He hated not being in control as much as he loved it. He never knew what she'd do next. After spending the last three years with girls all too willing to say "yes, Sir" and never provide an ounce of challenge, she was the elixir that made him feel so fucking alive.

"Josiah . . ." she taunted as she skated her tongue over the thin line of hair that led straight to his aching cock.

"Don't toy with me."

"The way you toy with me?" A little smile danced at the corners of her mouth. "You like it."

He couldn't exactly deny that, not when he was harder than he could ever remember being, and she could see the effect she had on him with her own two eyes.

Apparently, Maggie wasn't content to restrict herself to visual confirmation. No, she had to wrap her hands around his erection, squeeze, and force a long, low groan from him.

"I do. But I'll definitely be paying you back."

As she bent to him, mischief danced in her eyes. But it was tempered by something he'd never seen her bestow on him: affection. She wasn't hiding how she felt behind bluster, sarcasm, or one-liners. And the way her eyes glittered with something hot and needy as she worked her hands up and down his shaft completely jacked with his self-restraint.

"I'm looking forward to it," she vowed as she took him in her mouth.

The moment she wrapped her lips around him, drew him deeper, then began to suck her way up to the head, he was utterly done. There would be no hiding how completely he wanted Magnolia West.

His fingers slid into the silk of her hair as the moment swept him up. Her lips enveloped his length. She exhaled against his skin. He let loose a gravelly moan. He had a feeling that the months—hell, the decades—in front of him with Maggie would be an adventure. Yeah, they had to work out the details. They didn't reside in the same state. They lived totally different lives. But if Cutter and Shealyn, an operative and a TV star from opposite ends of the country, could make it work, then there was no reason he and Maggie couldn't do the same.

"Oh, baby. Damn. That's so fucking good."

She didn't answer, simply groaned around his sensitized flesh, her lips teasing their way up again before they tormented him on their way back down.

"You taste like man." She laved the crest before she slipped it in her mouth and drew on it until her cheeks went hollow and he thought he might explode. "And salt. Your musk hits my nose, and I want to spend a year down here cataloging every trace of that scent. You wouldn't mind that, right?"

"No," he blurted once she dragged him back into her mouth with a powerful pull. Then his brain flickered to life and he realized what he'd said. "Wait, yes. I mind. I want inside you."

"Eventually," she promised. "I seem to remember someone who doesn't relent from touching me until he gives me lots and lots of orgasms. I should make the same demand. It only seems fair."

"If you do, I'm only going to insist on more from you," he threatened in a low growl.

"Promise?"

The vixen had played him. She'd wrapped herself around him,

dug under his skin, turned him inside out at the same time she'd scrambled his brain and wormed her way into his heart. He didn't mind bending to make her happy, but he'd be damned if he'd let her undo him without giving as good as he got.

"Baby, I won't get up from this bed until I've made you beg for—" Nope, he would not say Mercy. He would not even think about that whack-job right now.

"Your leniency? Your forgiveness?" Her teasing smile wished him good luck with that.

"No. You'll be torn between begging for more and begging me to stop." While she grappled for a reply, he took control back from her, rolling her back to the mattress and covering her squirming body with his. "And I can't promise which one I'll give you."

In his arms, she shivered. She might surprise and poke him. She might say she didn't like when he commanded her. But he knew how to get to her. Right now, she felt more comfortable showing her affection between the sheets than she did when she looked into his eyes. He'd change that someday. This morning, he'd make sure she knew he was knocking at the door of her heart and he intended to bang away at whatever resistance remained until she let him in.

Josiah didn't give her a chance to say anything. He was done talking, taunting, teasing, or otherwise wasting time on anything except the toe-curling pleasure that bound them together.

He bent and kissed her, nudging her lips open before he swept deep. Maggie wrapped her arms around him and clung. Their breaths mingled as he crushed her mouth beneath his and tasted her sweetness. Her hint of tart chased it, balancing her flavor to perfection.

Josiah didn't break their connection as he eased to her side and skimmed his palm down her abdomen, straight between her restless thighs. The second his fingers dipped between them, she opened and welcomed his touch.

He definitely intended to savor that—just before he took her in every way a man could take a woman.

While he nipped at her lip, he thumbed her clit, rubbing her in slow circles, watching raptly as she tossed her head back and cried out his name. Then he slipped his fingers inside her, gratified when he glided in easily and felt her clench around him.

"I'm going to work my cock right here," he promised against her ear. "Every inch of me is going inside you. You're going to take me and come for me, aren't you?"

"Uh-huh." She bobbed her head as she lifted her hips for his touch.

He withdrew and circled her clit again until she bucked and clenched the sheets, until her heels dug into the mattress and she let loose another unintelligible sound of need that burned his blood.

When she was on the edge again, he pulled back, relishing her whimper and the way she reached out to draw him close. Maggie might have trouble allowing herself to become attached, but the moment she gave herself over to the pleasure they shared, she was at her most open. She didn't fight him then, simply surrendered. Well, mostly. Josiah had a hunch he could use a shortcut to cajole her into giving those hidden parts of herself she held back.

Dragging his fingers back through her slick valley, he traced his way down, circling where he'd never touched her before. Had anyone else?

"And here." He pressed against her rosette, slipping one drenched digit inside her as he worked his way down her body. "I'm going to work my way deep inside you here, too."

Maggie's eyes flew open. She tensed. Her breathing picked up speed. But she didn't say no.

"Josiah . . ."

He understood her unspoken question. Was he serious? Would he really do that? Could it possibly feel good?

"Yes, baby. I want to take you. Everywhere. In every way."

Without waiting a beat, he licked his way down the flat expanse of her stomach, nipping at her hip bone, while he pressed a second finger into her backside. She rewarded him with something between a grunt and a groan.

"Ever had a man touch you here?"

She couldn't find words, merely shook her head.

"Do my fingers penetrating you somewhere 'forbidden' give you pleasure?"

At his words, she bit her lip and clenched, tightening on him. Slowly, purposefully, he invaded even deeper, to the hilt, until he couldn't press inside her any more.

With a cry, she nodded frantically.

He smiled as he worked his body down, planting his face between her legs and taking a long, lingering lick of her most sensitive button. "If you think that feels good, you're going to come apart when I get my cock inside you."

She gave a strangled cry that morphed into a growl as he swirled his tongue around her clit one more time. He stayed, lingered, savored. In less than a handful of minutes, she went taut, gasped, then flew apart in his arms.

Seeing her in rapture undid him. Her eyes closed. She tossed her head back. Her cheeks flushed. Her wail rose between them as her body writhed and glowed. Magnolia West was stunning. Okay, he might be biased, but no other woman affected him this deeply.

"Gorgeous," he muttered against her skin as he crawled back up her body.

She was still panting and limp when he covered her lips again and drew her closer, losing himself in their connection. She seemed to do the same. When he finally lifted his head, she sighed and cuddled against him like a contented kitten. The silent show of trust thrilled and stunned him. Maggie had never been the sort to linger or nestle against him or in any way want to prolong their closeness. She'd always been about the next orgasm or she'd been eager to put distance between them.

In Josiah's estimation, this was a big win. But he was greedy; he wanted more.

He wanted all of her.

Curling up beside Maggie, Josiah peppered her face with soft kisses. "You okay?"

She gave a lazy stretch, then exhaled every bit of starch from her body and peered at him with a loopy smile. "I'm great. You do terrible and wonderful things to me, Mr. Grant. I should make you stop."

The way she bantered and teased was adorable. He'd always taken sex seriously, but with her playing seemed second nature. And so perfect. "All you have to do is say 'stop' or 'no.' 'Please don't do that' would work. So would 'get the hell away from me.' If I hear any of those, I'll back right off, baby."

She cocked her head, seeming to consider his words. "Somehow, once you start touching me, most of my vocabulary disappears. Stringing a whole sentence together seems impossible. And then you say sexy, filthy things to me that rob me of all ability to think, and I find myself giving in to you in ways I shouldn't."

"So it's all my fault?"

"Totally," she assured, tongue firmly planted in cheek.

Josiah laughed. Responsibility and the outside world waited for them, he knew. Zy and Trees would be back in an hour or two, and he'd have to shift focus to whatever they found on Enlightenment Fields' back forty. They'd have to plan and figure out some way to keep Maggie safe. When he was with her, it was easy to get lost in the bliss between them and hard to imagine that someone might want to snuff out her bright light for a piece of land. But if he wanted a shared tomorrow with her, he had to end this threat. The rest of Comfort had rolled over and played dead, allowing Coleman, Mercy, and their fellow crazies to do whatever they pleased. That stopped now.

"Well, I guess I need to see what other dirty, debauching acts I can seduce you with. Besides, I promised you more orgasms and I swore I'd make you beg, so . . ." He gave her a mock sigh. "I should get busy."

Maggie reached down to squeeze his turgid cock. "I'm sure it has nothing to do with how hard you are."

He gritted his teeth to hold in a groan. "Nothing at all. But to be on the safe side, don't do that anymore."

When he nudged her hand aside and broke her grip, she tsked. "So all this dirtiness is one-sided?"

"Basically. At least today." He stood at the side of the bed and shucked his unzipped pants, reaching into the pocket for a condom. "Get on your hands and knees."

"Why?" She froze. "Josiah, you're not really going to . . ."

"Have anal sex with you? Yeah. That's the plan."

Maggie gathered her arms to her knees. "I've never . . . What if it hurts?"

Josiah bent to kiss her. "I know, and it definitely shouldn't. That's often an issue when someone doesn't know what they're doing."

She got even quieter. "And you do."

"Baby, I've had more than my fair share of sex. I was hardly a monk before you."

"Me, too, but . . ."

"This is different. I get it." He shrugged. "Look, we don't have to. I'm certainly not going to make you. But before you decide, can I tell you why I think this is important?"

"Okay."

"First, you're going to enjoy the hell out of it. The sensations from anal penetration are different, as you just saw. And you respond. My fingers were enough to send you soaring. Right?"

She looked reluctant to admit the obvious. "I guess."

"It was a 'hell, yes,' baby. The next step will feel even better. Which leads me to my second reason: I want you to trust what I say to you, that I know how to give you pleasure, that I will take care of you, that you can give me parts of yourself you've never given anyone else and you'll be okay."

"I don't know if I'm ready for all that."

"But what happens if you don't try?"

"And not having anal sex with you damages whatever is happening between us?" she said skeptically. "Is that it?"

"Don't twist my words. I'm not saying I'll care about you less if I don't put my cock in your ass. I'm saying that if you don't start trying to believe that I'll put you first and give you what I think you need, I don't know where that leaves us. What I'm asking you for today is a symbol. If you have another suggestion, I'm open to that. But I know how absolutely fucking intimate this act can be. I know it can connect two people. Will you try? Are you willing to see what it does for us? If you don't like it, I'll stop. Simple as that."

Maggie bit her lip. Apprehension tightened her face. "I don't know."

"Then let's talk this out. What are you afraid of? Pain?"

"No."

Her answer worried him. If she wasn't concerned it would hurt, she could only fear one other thing . . .

"You're afraid of letting me closer."

She clenched her fists and retreated across the bed. "Is that a surprise? The person who gave birth to me dumped me off on my grandparents' porch for twenty fucking years. And she never came back. My sister found *her*. We were so unimportant that she just forgot we existed. Granted, she's tried to make it up since but . . . Now here you are. You've been in Comfort for four days and you've already decided you want every part of me. Dude, you're leaving. I'm staying. So maybe some things are better left alone."

Her fears and insecurities were howling, and he needed to muzzle them fast. "I can't speak for your mother since I've never met her. But I know me and what I'm feeling. I've been holding back and trying not to scare you off, but I'll lay it all out there if you need me to be vulnerable first. I'm not falling in love with you, baby. I'm already there. I don't know why or how. I just know that's the truth, and it's not changing. The logistics of where we live don't worry me; that's easy. Reaching you here"—he pointed to her heart—"is my first and foremost concern. Your mother may have left you, and for that I'm so damn sorry. But *I* didn't do that to you. And I won't. That's my promise to you. So can you meet me halfway? Can you try?"

Tears welled in her eyes. "I hate it when you make me cry."

Because he was getting to her, he'd bet. "This isn't the first time?"

"Wanna gloat about it?"

Ignoring the fact that she always got prickly when he got close, Josiah pressed a kiss to her forehead. "No, just worried about you. Wanting to understand how I can make you feel better."

"Why?" She tossed her hands in the air. "Even when I'm intentionally being a bitch, you care about me. How am I supposed to avoid making a fool of myself over you if you don't stop being so perfect?"

Tears splashed down her cheeks, and Josiah couldn't stand to see her hurt. "Okay. I won't press you anymore today."

Maggie sighed as more tears fell down her cheeks. Then she rose up on her knees and launched herself against him, her expression grim but accepting. "But you're right, and it would be better if I just stopped saying no."

Was she serious? He stared into her eyes, looking for answers. "You're sure?"

She simply nodded.

Because he'd been willing to relent, she was willing to entrust him with her body . . . and maybe her heart?

His heart flipped over. "Oh, baby . . ."

Josiah couldn't stop himself from pressing a tender kiss to her lips. Maggie opened to him with a soft acceptance he'd never felt from her. She'd always kept everything between them either casual or contentious or something else that prevented him from getting too close. Finally, she'd taken down her defenses.

"I promise you won't regret this," he whispered. "You won't regret us."

After another kiss, Josiah positioned Maggie on her hands and knees at the edge of the bed. He rolled on his condom and kissed the small of her back.

"What should I do?" Her voice was almost a squeak.

"I'll tell you when we get there. Right now, just relax. Just feel me."

Then he eased his way inside her sex, gratified to feel her slick and welcoming. Her flesh closed around him as if she'd been desperate to feel a part of him inside some part of her. Josiah threw his head back and let loose a long groan.

For once, she didn't have a taunt or a snappy comeback. Instead, she gripped the quilt in her fists, sucked in a sob, and arched to take more of him. He was awed by how vulnerable to him she was allowing herself to be. She wasn't hiding. She wasn't pretending that tears weren't running down her cheeks. He'd been inside her many times; for the first time he truly felt her soul.

"Magnolia . . ." Josiah urged her upright, guiding her onto her knees, then he pressed his chest to her back and wrapped his arms around her.

He hugged her as he filled her. He drove her higher as he gave her his love. He worshipped her as he slid his fingers to her most sensitive spot and drove her to another gasping climax.

When she sagged toward the mattress again, he positioned her, then withdrew from her slickness and nudged her back entrance with his crest. "This is simple, baby. Arch your back for me. Think about bearing down and opening up. I'll do the rest."

She hesitated, so he petted her hip, kissed her left cheek, and waited until she finally did as he'd asked. "Perfect. So, so pretty, baby. I'll make you feel good. Worshipped. I promise."

But now that the moment was here, tension took hold of her again. She was nervous. Scared. "Don't get in your head. Let go and give yourself to me. Trust me. I'll be here."

Dragging in a shaking breath, Maggie finally nodded and bowed her head. She surrendered.

Josiah held her like something precious as he slowly pushed inside her. He met a little resistance, and she whimpered. "Shh. Arch a little more. It'll be fine. It'll be good."

Maggie lifted her hips a fraction more. The bow in her back was a thing of beauty.

He watched as he slipped past her tight ring and slid inside her completely.

"Oh . . . Josiah."

Her words thrilled him because he heard surprise and desire. What he didn't hear was pain.

"I'm here, baby. I'm inside you. It feels so good."

"Yes." She eased back onto him, seeking even deeper penetration.

She was the kind of woman who wanted to be touched and explored, petted and used and thoroughly loved. If she let him, he would be happy to give her that every day for the rest of her life.

He just had to keep them all alive long enough.

Shoving that thought aside, he pulled back slowly, nearly withdrawing from her. She keened out in protest before he gave in and slipped back inside her velvety passage.

Now that he was less focused on making sure Maggie wasn't frightened or pained, he could concentrate on the feel of her around him. Hot, tight, forbidden, all his—she was everything he'd imagined. Everything he craved. And her response, moving with him as she made those arousing little noises in the back of her throat, was more than he'd dared to imagine. Jesus, she was going to burn him alive.

"That's it. That's my baby . . ." he crooned.

She responded, reaching back for him, fingertips grazing his thigh as she turned to look at him over her shoulder. Her eyes were damp and bright and wide. They burned with desire. Best of all, they held no reservation. She was utterly open. Totally his in this moment. His heart roared as he filled her again.

Josiah settled in to give her all the pleasure she'd never imagined, hoping like hell this act would cement them as one.

Together, they rose, panting breaths, cries that turned hoarse, damp skin, and racing hearts. While their bodies were fused, they melded, their desires and their devotion merging. Fuck, he was so lost inside her, so dizzy with needing her. He'd never felt closer to another human being in his life. As he gripped her tightly, reveling in the rousing wail of her climax, Josiah emptied inside her, giving himself completely to her.

On paper, falling for Magnolia West wasn't a good bet, but he was no more capable of not loving her than he was of not breathing. All he could hope was that he could ensnare her as deeply as she'd hooked him. He wanted forever with her. The question was, did he have a prayer of convincing her to take the biggest chance of all on him?

CHAPTER 13

As Maggie slipped off the sensible wedges that coordinated with the sedate black dress she'd worn to Mr. Haney's funeral, Josiah slipped behind her and wrapped his arm around her waist, dropping a kiss on her neck. Damn, he looked fine in his dark suit. Granted, she'd seen him wear it the night of her sister's wedding, but somehow he looked even sexier today.

Probably because she was ridiculously in love with him. After yesterday, how could she possibly resist? He'd taken her in a way she'd never expected or sought. Somehow, he'd made the act beautiful, meaningful. When they'd finally left the bedroom sated and freshly showered, Maggie felt sure she was glowing. Zyron and Trees had obviously noticed, too, since they'd both stared at her hand joined with Josiah's. Neither seemed thrilled, but she hadn't cared. She'd been floating on a cloud of happiness—or she had been until Trees asked to speak with Josiah alone.

Then reality had come crashing down. Enlightenment Fields. The murders. Mercy asking him to breed her. And whatever else these guys might be hiding from her, probably thinking it was for her own good. She'd gone to the kitchen to make everyone lunch. By the time she'd served a quick tomato bisque and piping-hot grilled cheese sandwiches, their conversation was over. Trees looked defeated. Zyron looked confused. Josiah wore his frustration all over his face. She'd asked him later what was going on, but he'd refused to say a word.

"You okay?" he asked as she stepped out of her wedges.

"Yeah. Thanks for going with me to the service. You didn't have to. You didn't know Mr. Haney."

"It worked out well. I got to be near you. Zy and Trees watched the ranch. Besides, if Enlightenment Fields had spies there, they think I attended the funeral of an old family friend."

"True. If not for that, Sawyer and I could have handled it but—"

"No. Even if you leaving the ranch wasn't dangerous right now, I wouldn't send you anywhere alone with him." Josiah's face darkened. "I don't like the way he looks at you."

That made her crack a smile. "Jealous?"

"Yes, but I'm more concerned that he hasn't given up on you. I don't trust him."

"I'm not interested in Sawyer."

"I doubt that matters to him, baby."

Maggie sighed. Josiah probably wasn't wrong. "You're a tad over-protective, you know that? But . . . I don't hate it."

"Protecting you is my job." He cupped her face and forced her gaze to his. "I love you."

Those three words made her heart catch. She wasn't ready to say them, but she felt the answering pang in her chest and rose up on her tiptoes to reply with a soft, lingering kiss until he lifted away.

"I'm going to step into your grandfather's study and have a quick chat with my boss. I'll be out in a few."

"Sure. I'll be around."

As he walked away, she wrestled with herself. Sneak into her grandparents' bathroom and eavesdrop so she could understand what the hell had all the guys on edge or trust that he would take care of her?

The ringing of the home phone in the kitchen decided for her. She rushed to the device and lifted the receiver from the wall. "Hello?"

"Mags?"

She smiled. "Hi, Granna. How's California?"

"Oh, my goodness. Why didn't you tell me it's a zoo? I don't think I've ever seen this many people in the same place at once."

Maggie laughed. Granna loved the shopping in San Antonio but hated the sheer number of people. LA was far bigger and more crowded, smog and cars everywhere. It was probably a shock to her small-town grandmother.

"But isn't the view from Shealyn's living room something?"

"It is," her grandmother conceded. "Of course, your grandfather doesn't like heights. He says if he looks over the canyon too much he gets sick. And then he worries about possible earthquakes . . . If we have one, this house will go sliding down the side of the mountain and—"

"What have you two done for fun so far?" Maggie cut in. If she let them go on, nothing good would happen.

"Mr. Santiago loaned us a driver for the week. So nice of him. His family is unusual, but what lovely people. Anyway, we went to the beach yesterday. That water is cold!"

"I know! I wasn't expecting that, either."

"And since we were out that direction, we visited the J. Paul Getty Museum. We drove up and down Pacific Coast Highway. Good lord, they have traffic at all hours of the day and night. We've eaten at a couple of really nice restaurants."

"Has it been romantic?"

Granna cleared her throat. "Don't you mind that, young lady. How are you?"

"Well, Josiah, Sawyer, and I just came home from Ben Haney's funeral. It was sad, but most of the town turned out. Even Sheriff Wayne stopped fishing long enough to put in an appearance. Though I didn't see Dixie." And that had surprised her. Not that her high school acquaintance had been really close to Mr. Haney, but the woman never missed the biggest doings around usually sleepy Comfort. Maggie hoped she was okay. "Afterward, everyone gathered at the diner and chatted."

"I wonder what will happen to his land."

"We all speculated about that. Apparently, he didn't have a will."
Maggie shook his head. "Once the county has verified that he died
without any heirs, I suspect they'll auction it off. But the rumor is Enlightenment Fields is already offering to make a healthy donation to
the county."

Her grandmother made a sound of disapproval. "And no one in
Kendall County can pay more for it than those crazy land grabbers.
Lord, we'll be surrounded."

Maggie had already thought of that. Josiah was grimly aware,
too. She didn't want to worry her grandparents, so she remained mute.
But she was terrified for their safety. If those whack-jobs had truly
killed Haney and Mrs. McIntyre—no one else she could think of had
motive—then what would stop them from offing another two elderly
people?

"Let's not talk about that now. Tell me what else—"

"No. You tell me why you didn't call me when someone ran down
Mildred McIntyre in the street in broad daylight."

Damn it. Who had spilled the news to Granna? "Because there's
nothing you can do. Since her body is evidence in a crime, the police
and the coroner haven't released it yet. Her family hasn't determined
when or where they'll have her funeral or if they're going to simply
cremate her and take her to Oregon with them. If you were here, all
you could do is wring your hands."

And be in danger.

"I can't believe it. Willa Mae told me when I called in a prescrip-
tion I forgot to refill before I left. She said she heard the news from
Dixie, who was in the market the other morning picking up some gro-
ceries."

Maggie wasn't surprised, and it wasn't as if Dixie had divulged
anything that everyone around town wasn't already talking about. In a
town as small as Comfort, everyone knew everything in the blink of
an eye. In fact, right now half the town might well be wagging about
the fact Josiah had stood so close to her at the funeral . . .

"I'm sorry. I know you two were close."

"The sheriff have any idea who killed her? From what I heard, it wasn't an accident."

"I talked to Deputy Preston." Or she'd tried to. He'd been infuriatingly tight-lipped. "He didn't mention any suspects."

But Maggie couldn't stop wondering what would happen next to that house Mrs. McIntyre had rented and the land it sat on. Her daughter and son-in-law had bought it years ago. She had insisted on paying rent. But her husband was long gone. Her kids were all grown, married, and moved away. Surely none of them would have any interest in the property. So it would likely be for sale soon, too. Even though the house was at the far end of town, Maggie could just guess who would buy it.

Gripping the phone, she took a few steadying breaths. She couldn't admit to Granna how scared she was. The woman would run home and try to soothe her with homemade cookies and hugs—as she'd done most of Maggie's life. They had taken her and Shealyn in at an age when they should have been thinking about a quieter future. Her grandparents had probably saved their lives.

Maggie intended to return the favor.

"I'll let you know as soon as something changes," Maggie lied. "Until then, you and Papa have to do amazing things while you're in California. Go to Disneyland for me and tell me every detail so I can live vicariously. And go to Catalina. I didn't get to go there and I hear it's beautiful. There's one of those creepy wax museums out there, too. And—"

"That sounds like a lot of going and doing to me. We'll see what your grandfather feels like. In the meantime, tell me how you're faring with Josiah. He seems fairly smitten with you. Any chance that's mutual?"

The question took Maggie off guard. Granna didn't often discuss feelings so directly. She was still from a generation that valued privacy and believed in "polite conversation." Why had she chosen now to ask? "I . . . I'm really afraid it might be. Granna, he stood beside me at the funeral and never let me any farther than two feet away. He must have asked twenty times if I was okay, if I needed to talk, if he could help me in some way."

The only thing that had confused her was that he'd never once held her hand or touched her. Because he'd known tongues would wag? Or because he worried it would get back to Enlightenment Fields? Both reasons were valid, but she'd still missed his touch.

"That's what men in love do, support their women. Ah, Maggie . . ." Granna sighed. "Sounds like you're in love with him, too. Have you told him?"

"No." She was still afraid.

It sounded stupid. A broken heart wasn't the worst thing that could happen to someone, yet she feared it almost more than physical pain or death. Probably because the others were unknowns. But she'd learned early in life what heartache felt like and she'd do almost anything to avoid more.

"Stop letting the past hold you back, sweet girl. If you don't open up and give him your love in return, you won't give him any choice except to leave you. If he's the one, you can't let him slip through your fingers."

"I'm trying, but . . . How did you know you could trust Papa?"

She could almost hear her grandmother smile. "When we were in the fourth grade, Martin Turnsby stole some of the Halloween candy I'd stashed in my desk while we were out for recess. I knew it was him. That crabby old Mrs. Selby wouldn't listen when I told her, said I shouldn't be eating candy for lunch anyway. But your papa confronted Turnsby, who was bigger than him. I don't know what he said or did, but he made that boy cry and confess. And I got my candy back. He promised me on that day that if I'd marry him when we grew up, he'd always stand up for me. I told him I would. The day he turned eighteen, he asked my parents for my hand. I'd just turned seventeen, but they said yes and signed the paperwork. We were married three days after I graduated. I've never regretted it."

They had such a beautiful love story. Maggie was envious. "But Papa is pretty much the best man in the world. Guys today . . ."

Granna huffed. "Men have always been men. They might not behave as respectfully as they used to, but deep down, some are better than others. That's always been true. For all you know, Josiah might not be the man you want him to be; no one can guarantee that he's perfect for you. But what if he is? And you lose him because you're too afraid to believe?"

She was right. Maggie knew she had to let go of this fear. "Thanks, Granna."

"You're welcome, sweet girl. I know you can't change overnight, but think about what I've said."

"Believe me, I am."

They chatted a bit more about their respective plans and things around the ranch before they hung up. Thoughts racing, she wandered to her room, changed into a comfy pair of sweats and a loose T-shirt, then meandered back to the kitchen to start dinner. Once food was in the oven, she'd sneak back to her computer and work on the book she'd promised her agent would be done by the end of the month.

Fat chance with everything going on. Maggie had looked for little pockets of time to plug away at the project, but the cozy, clever small-town whodunit just seemed too close to home right now, and with Josiah barging his way into her body—and her heart—she hadn't been able to concentrate.

She'd barely pulled the refrigerator door open when Josiah emerged from her grandfather's study, looking solemn and tense. His gaze sought hers immediately. Everything inside her went tense when he swallowed and seemed to grapple with his words.

"Maggie, baby . . . We need to talk."

Josiah did not want to do this. He'd give anything not to sit Maggie down so he could scare the hell out of her. Everything he was about to do would distract her from opening up so she could learn to trust him. It could seriously slow down all the fucking progress he needed to make with her ASAP. Because his gut told him this shit with Enlightenment Fields would come to a head soon. Once it did—and if everyone made it out alive—he'd have to be solid with her if he wanted to convince her to share the future with him. If not, EM Security Management would call him back to Louisiana, and he'd go on another job. She would resume her life here in Comfort. Where would that leave them?

Over.

"What's going on?" Her voice shook.

Yeah, she sensed this was going to be heavy.

Zy and Trees exited the room behind him and melted away. Of course they didn't want to be around for what was sure to upset her. Or maybe they were giving him and Maggie privacy because they knew she'd need comfort and reassurance.

Josiah held out his hand. "Let's go upstairs."

She glanced at the open refrigerator, then shut it before putting her palm in his. "Okay."

He was still trying to untangle his thoughts when they reached the corner bedroom they'd been sharing and he shut the door behind them. A few minutes ago, he had shucked his coat and tie. Instinctively, he toed off his shoes and unbuttoned his shirt.

Maggie went wide-eyed. "You scared the hell out of me instead of just saying you want sex?"

"No. I'm undressing so I can hold you against me, skin to skin, while we talk."

She resisted. "I listen way better when you're not touching me."

"Maybe so. But I feel a lot steadier when I've got my hands on you."

That made her melt. "Oh. You need me to—"

"Be naked. Yes." Then he said something he rarely did as a Dom. "Please."

Without being told why, she trusted the gravity in his tone. "Okay."

Thankfully, Maggie didn't waste time. The baggy shirt and sweats came off, and she dropped them into a heap on the floor. By then, he'd shucked his pants and tossed them onto a nearby chair. His underwear stayed right where he dropped them. She ditched her bra, draping it on the nearby doorknob.

Then she came to him, beautiful, bare, and with concern all over her face. She'd compromised to make him happy, and it occurred to him that she might have dated a lot, even slept around, but she'd done it because she'd been crying out for connection. Until him, everyone had wanted her body, but no one had given her what she needed. He was trying like hell, and glad to see that she trusted him enough to want to give back. As Josiah wrapped his arms around her and pressed her warm flesh to his, it was enough—at least for now.

"Thank you, baby. Lie with me."

Again, she hesitated, but only for a second or two. Then she nodded and let him lead her to the bed.

Once they'd settled under the blankets, he pressed his palm to the small of her back, keeping her as close as two people could be, and let out a deep breath. "I need to tell you what's going on. I've kept it from you for as long as I dared but . . . things aren't looking good. You need to know what we're up against if we're going to survive."

"There's more going on than you've told me?"

"Yeah. I have to go back to Enlightenment Fields because—"

"Does this have anything to do with Mercy asking you to 'breed' her?" She pressed her lips together. "I overheard that."

"Yeah. I won't ask how." He sighed. "This motherfucking shit has gotten so ugly. Of all the things I wanted to tell you, that was last. God, when you heard that you must have been totally confused. And furious."

Yet she hadn't confronted him or accused. Maybe she was willing to trust him after all . . .

"A little. I know you said that you hadn't touched her and didn't want to. But why would she ask you to get her pregnant?"

"It's going to take a lot of explaining. Bear with me." When she nodded, he dove in. "You know I've been going out there. I went first to insist they leave your family alone. When that opened a can of worms, I went out there again on Tuesday, pretending interest in joining. On both trips, I've picked up information that's made me worry like hell about what these people are capable of."

"Murder."

"I think that's the least of it, but it's what worries me most right now. Your grandparents—"

"Are their next targets. I figured that out."

He nodded solemnly. "And here's the unvarnished truth: I don't think I can change that, not in the twelve days until they're scheduled to come home. I'll keep trying, but all my efforts to turn this investigation in our favor are netting zilch. My boss has some resources with the FBI, and I was hoping they'd sweep in and take over. So far, they've been totally silent. I don't think they're going to come through."

"So they're just going to let people in this town keep dying?"

"If I had to guess, they don't have much on Enlightenment Fields and nothing that's happened looks too big for local law enforcement to handle."

"Sheriff Wayne is never around, and Kane Preston can't do everything by himself."

"I know. And I wish I had better news. But the wheels of justice never turn easily or fast. I know that sounds cliché. Unfortunately, it's true."

"Is there anything else we can do?"

"I've been trying. The last time I was at that wacky compound, I saw a man chastising some teenagers for taking a car out on a joyride.

He was making them wash the grill, tires, and undercarriage really carefully, which I thought was odd since they live at the end of a long dirt road. I shared that with Deputy Preston, who tried to get a search warrant in conjunction with Mildred McIntyre's hit-and-run. The judge decided there was insufficient evidence to warrant a search of the car or the property. I hate it but he's probably right. It would probably have been ruled inadmissible in court."

Maggie clung to his shoulders, searching his face . . . looking for answers. "Are we out of moves?"

"Not entirely, but now we've come to the tough ones. If you could persuade your grandparents to stay gone another couple of weeks, maybe—"

"I'm going to be hard-pressed to keep them there for another twelve days. Mildred McIntyre was one of Granna's dearest friends. As soon as they announce that woman's funeral and if it takes place in Comfort, I have no doubt they'll come home. So far, they aren't fans of California. They've never much liked being away from home anyway."

"You have to keep talking to them, baby. Convince them to stay. I don't want to scare the hell out of them, but I'll tell them they're in danger if it will keep them away."

"It won't. My papa will come racing back like some knight on a white horse and try to save everyone. He's in decent shape for a guy his age, but sometimes he's got so much macho running through his veins he's convinced he's as badass as he was at thirty."

Josiah grunted in frustration. "Then I don't know what to do. Would they go someplace else? If I got a plane to take them to Hawaii or the Mexican Riviera or . . . anywhere, would they take it?"

"Maybe I could persuade them to visit my mother in Costa Rica. Maybe. But I doubt it."

"Could your sister help?"

"If I call her on her honeymoon and tell her to convince Granna and Papa to travel to a foreign country at a moment's notice, she'll be awfully suspicious. Probably enough to come home. What is your boss telling Cutter?"

"Nothing. That was the agreement. Real life will kick them in the teeth soon enough. We all want them to have this well-deserved time together."

"You're right."

"Talk to your grandparents. See if you can appeal to their sense of adventure. Try to persuade them to visit your mother. That's all you can do. Anything else you can think to sweeten the pot for them, tell me. I'll move mountains if I have to."

Her face softened. She hadn't said she loved him yet, but she sure as hell looked at him as if she did. Josiah hung on to that.

"I know." She cupped his face. "You're amazing at your job."

"Baby, this is personal. We both know you'll lose your grandparents someday. That's the way life is. People are born and they eventually die. But they've got a lot of life left in them, and you need them still."

"I do. And I'm terrified for them."

"My goal is to help them stay around until they're ready to go." But that wasn't the only issue.

Josiah tangled his fingers in her hair and tugged gently, positioning her lips just under his. Then he gave her a lingering kiss, pressing himself against her as if the closer he gathered her, the more he could keep her safe and protected. It was an illusion, but he closed his eyes and melted into her warm skin, audibly drank in her exhalations. His heart torqued with fear. Goddamn it, one wrong move with this woman and everything could end in heartache.

"I'm terrified for you, too. If something happens to them, you and your sister will own the land. Since she's going to be in LA indefinitely, she might sell. They must know you won't and . . ."

Maggie closed her eyes. "They'll come after me. I-I hadn't really thought about it until just now. I've been focused on my grandparents.

But I see your point. Shealyn would never sell. They don't know that, but I do."

"Would you consider leaving here?"

He'd known what her answer would be, but he was still frustrated as hell when she shook her head. "I can't. I could never leave my grand-parents alone out here."

"You can't keep them safe."

"I can't abandon them, either, not when the situation is so danger-ous. I have to stay. And if something were to happen to them, God forbid, the day-to-day running of the ranch would fall to me. I couldn't dishonor them and all my papa's family by letting the ranch go to that crazy cult scum."

"If you fight them, I don't think you can win," he argued, gripping her more tightly.

"Maybe not, but my grandparents have done *everything* for me from the moment they took me in. I have to try."

Frustration raked Josiah's nerves. He understood and respected her decision at the same time he wanted to throttle her for it. But he couldn't simply leave Maggie to her chosen fate. He could not aban-don her. Not only would it crush her heart, she might literally die.

Fuck.

He needed to make more phone calls.

"What are you going to do about Mercy and her . . . offer? I know she's pretty."

"Sure. She's pretty if you like crazy. There's no way I'd ever touch her, much less go out of my way to plant a baby in her belly, especially for some demented doomsday scenario that, God willing, will never happen."

"Yeah." Maggie relaxed a bit in his arms.

Had she actually been worried that he desired Mercy?

"Hey, you're the one I want. You're the one I love. Nothing is going to change that. Is there a chance I'll have to go back there and play

along, see what other information I can gather? Yeah. It's my last resort. I didn't slam shut the door on that possibility, just in case."

"Don't do it." She gripped him as if she were afraid for him.

"I won't . . . unless I have to." He rolled her to her back and reached
into the nightstand for a condom. "In the meantime, why don't you be
a good girl and let me do dirty, lascivious things to your luscious
body."

When he skated his lips down her neck and circled kisses around
her breasts, her breath caught. "You're trying to distract me."

"I'm trying to make us both feel good." *While we still can.*

Thankfully, Maggie let him.

After an hour and five of her loudest orgasms later, Josiah felt
wrung out and limp. All he wanted to do was curl up next to her in
bed, shut the world out, and spend the night beside her. He'd listen to
her heartbeat, match the rhythm of her breaths, inhale the postsex
scent of her he couldn't seem to get enough of.

Instead, he forced himself to roll away from her as she slept,
grabbed his pants from the floor, and fished in his pocket for his mobile as he strode into the hall, softly snicking the bedroom door shut
behind him. Pacing, he flipped through the contacts and paused over
his oldest sister's name. Since she lived outside Boston and was an
hour ahead of him, Dana was probably already getting ready for bed.
But he needed a voice of reason. He was formulating a plan, but he
needed someone to check his sanity before he pressed on.

She answered on the third ring. "What's up, little brother. I thought
you were on assignment."

"I am. Um . . ." Where to start? "Things are twenty kinds of fucked
up here. People are dying. Before you ask, yes. I'm okay right now."

Dana laughed. "When you preface the conversation like that, of
course I'm going to ask, shit-for-brains."

"Funny you call me that . . . In the middle of danger, I did something you'll probably think is stupid." He sighed. "I fell in love."

"Seriously? For real this time?"

He froze. "What do you mean 'this time'?"

"Um . . . I don't think you want me to tell you what I really thought about Whitney or your feelings for her."

"Actually, I do. Whit and I had a fast courtship . . . kind of like the one I'm having with Maggie. Some of the similarities are weirding me out. I've been a little gun-shy anyway."

"Are you having another extreme case of lust? Think carefully before you answer. I couldn't fault you for that with Whitney. She was gorgeous."

Outside, sure. Inside? She'd been a selfish bitch, more than happy to ditch him the day of their wedding for one of his friends with a bigger bank account and a job that kept him in town more often.

"She was, and so is Maggie. Look, it's my fault the relationship with Whitney went that far. I made excuses for her because I kept hoping she'd mature into someone she wasn't. I was the dumbass who wanted to marry her thinking she'd change. She's always going to be the sort of person who puts herself first."

"Yep. I heard she married some guy named Trevor a few months back."

Josiah had heard that gossip, too. "I hope she actually loves him and that they're happy together."

"Me, too. She announced last week on Facebook that she's pregnant."

Once upon a time, the knowledge would have bothered him. Now, he didn't feel a damn thing. "Good for her."

Dana laughed softly. "I'm just glad you're not her husband and baby daddy."

"Me, too."

"So tell me about Maggie."

"She's a million things. If I tell you she was a pageant girl, you'll get the wrong idea, but she was Miss Kendall County for three years. She grew up on a ranch in small-town Texas. Oh, Shealyn West is her sister."

"The TV star? Holy shit! I love her. She seems so sweet. Have you met her? Talked to her?"

"I was at her wedding a week ago. I even danced with her. She is sweet."

"Wow, so her sister must be, too."

"In very different ways. I tried to fight my feelings for Maggie but . . . it didn't work out too well."

Unlike Whitney, Mags was the kind of girl willing to sacrifice herself to keep her loved ones safe and happy. His ex would have wished them the best, packed her bags, and driven away, then cried the loudest at their funeral.

"How long have you known her?"

Josiah sighed. "A week. And I know how it sounds—"

"Sketchy? It does. But you're obviously serious if you're calling me to talk about her."

"Yeah. You think I never really loved Whit?"

"Honestly? No. Do you think you're truly in love with Maggie?"

"Didn't I just say that?"

"Let me put the question this way: The day Whitney dumped you, you didn't try to talk to her. You just drove your truck like a bat out of hell to that skeevy bar by the highway and proceeded to get shitfaced and demand the manager play sad, someone-done-you-wrong songs. Then for the next month, you stopped speaking to all of your friends who'd known about your fiancée's betrayal, which I get. But you also stopped speaking to the ones who hadn't. That was your pride barking, little brother. You spent the next two weeks destroying a punching bag with your fists. Then you went back to work and volunteered for every crazy-ass, utterly dangerous assignment you could find. We all worried like hell about you."

"I know." That made him feel more than vaguely guilty. "I'm sorry."

"So the question I have is, if Maggie left you tomorrow, what would be the most likely reason and what would you do about it?"

And that was why he'd called Dana. She always knew how to cut through the bullshit and get to what was real. Josiah wished he'd been in the frame of mind to listen before he'd proposed to Whitney.

"At this point, I think she'd only leave me for two reasons: One, if I left her first. If you know anything about Shealyn, you know their mom was a drug addict who abandoned them as kids."

"I'd heard that. It's really true?"

"Yeah. Or two, Maggie would leave if I scared her. She has trouble believing that people will love her enough to truly be there for her. And if for some reason she actually walked out on me . . ." It didn't take Josiah long to come to a conclusion. "I'd wait for her. I'd coax her. I'd be patient. I'd tell her every day I love her until she believed it."

Dana gave him a little sniffle. "That's a beautiful answer."

"If you repeat it to your husband or any of my other brothers-in-law, I'll deny saying it."

She laughed. "All right, macho man. We'll keep it between us, but . . . yeah. You sound like you're in love. I can't wait to meet her. Mom will squeal in delight when you bring a new girlfriend home."

Josiah had something more serious in mind, and if he could pull it off, his mom—hell, his whole family—might get the chance to fall in love with her, too.

CHAPTER 14

The following Monday dawned with the roll of thunder and the drizzle of gray rain so close to freezing, Maggie wondered if she'd ever get warm. She bundled up in her warmest sweatpants and fuzzy slippers, along with a tank, a long-sleeved tee, and a hoodie, but she still shivered.

On the other hand, she wasn't convinced the chill caused all her trembling. Fear surged through her veins.

Since their discussion Thursday night, Josiah had been quiet, almost contemplative. Oh, he still held her close, touched her often to let her know that she was cared for and safe. But sometimes his mind drifted elsewhere. She'd pressed him, but he'd simply given her a too-charming smile and assured her all was well.

Maggie wasn't buying it.

Yesterday, she'd called her grandparents. They hadn't been able to talk long, since they'd reluctantly decided to spend the day at Disneyland. Granna had promised to call later that evening. Maggie was antsy. Even odder, Josiah had insisted that he talk to her papa as soon as possible. He wouldn't say why. She wondered what that meant and was frustrated at suddenly being left out again. Yes, probably for her "own good" or whatever, but what plans did he have that he wanted to hide from her?

"A vehicle I don't recognize is coming up the drive," Zyron shouted as he slammed his way into the house from the side yard.

Maggie frowned. She wasn't expecting visitors. Maybe Dixie was dropping in since Maggie had left her a couple of messages? Or the deputy had decided to divulge some helpful information?

But when she darted to the family room and glanced out the front window, she didn't recognize the flashy red vehicle bouncing up the old dirt road. It was small, sporty, and too light for this terrain—not practical for conditions in a Texas ranching community.

"Shit," Josiah murmured behind her.

She frowned. "What? I have no idea who that is."

"I can't tell you who's driving, but I'm almost positive I saw that car last time I was at Enlightenment Fields."

Maggie's heart sank to her stomach. Were they coming back to put the screws to her family again? Had they devised some new way to try to force her to sell?

"Your truck is out front." Trees grimaced in Josiah's direction.

It was. Damn it.

When she turned to glance at Josiah, he was compartmentalizing his panic and doing his best to problem-solve. Funny how she'd already learned to read some of his expressions so quickly. Yet sometimes he was still a mystery . . .

"Maybe you should drive away and make up some bullshit excuse about why you stopped by to 'visit' the Wests?" Trees suggested.

"Or stay and hide and hope like hell they don't realize that's your truck?" Zyron added.

Josiah swore under his breath. "Both options suck. This could get dangerous fast."

"We'll be here," Trees assured.

Zyron withdrew his weapon and checked the magazine before shoving it back into his concealed holster. "And we'll be ready."

"I know. But I only have one choice. I can't leave Maggie."

She marched into her papa's study and came back out with his big-ass shotgun from the gun safe. "I'll be fine. I'm no damsel in distress."

Josiah shook his head. "I'll examine later why the sight of you all badass and weaponed up turns me on. But if there's potential trouble, I'm not going anywhere, Maggie."

Uncharacteristically, Trees swore.

"What's the plan?" Zyron demanded. "They're parking now. We have less than a minute to decide."

"Fuck." Josiah raked a hand through his shorn dark hair. "Okay. I'll step around the corner and listen in. They won't see me in the kitchen. You two are visiting or looking for jobs or . . . fill in the blank. Maggie, if they ask, your grandparents are out for the day. Be non-committal. Put that shotgun somewhere within reach but not in plain sight. That's the best we can do."

Maggie nodded. Zyron and Trees obviously didn't like it but didn't argue.

As Josiah made himself scarce, Trees whistled long and low. "Wow, who's the gorgeous brunette?"

Afraid she already knew the answer, Maggie glanced out the front window and looked at the driver. "Mercy."

The woman who had asked Josiah to join his life with hers at En-lightenment Farms and create more lives together. Maggie was hard-pressed not to claw this chick's eyes out.

"Shit." Josiah cursed from the kitchen. "Who's she with?"

"I don't know. Some tall, lumbering guy and an average-sized man with a mean face."

"The big one is probably Newt. He's devoted to Mercy from what I hear. He'll do anything for her. Watch out."

The sound of car doors slamming, muted only by the walls, told them their time was up. Maggie propped the shotgun up behind the sofa and gripped her phone, just in case. She knew damn well that if she called 911, it might take twenty minutes or more before law enforcement made an appearance . . . but maybe Mercy didn't know that.

In front of her, Trees sat with seeming casualness on the left side of the sofa, but she felt his tension. Zyron seemingly swallowed down his pinging energy and took the recliner on her right. It might not be obvious at a glance, but they were flanking her, and she appreciated it.

Maggie counted down the seconds until she heard a light but insistent knock. Zyron rose, but she stopped him with a shake of her head. "I have to do this. They'll be suspicious if I don't."

He gritted his teeth but nodded, seeing her point.

As he seated himself once more, she unlocked the door. Her hands shook as she turned the knob. As soon as she opened up, the trio filled her line of vision—a beauty and two brutes who looked quite capable of violence. "Hi. Mercy, right? Can I help you?"

"I'm Mercy, yes. Hello, Maggie. We popped by for a neighborly visit and to ask you a question. It will only take a few minutes of your time."

She would have loved to tell them they weren't welcome and slam the door in their face. If she did, Maggie feared that would make them openly hostile much faster. If she played this cat-and-mouse game, found some way to placate them, it would buy some time to consider other options.

"Come in."

"Thank you." Mercy smiled as she stepped over the threshold. The two men followed, eyeing Zyron and Trees.

Maggie suspected the giant and the thug were carrying guns under their winter coats.

With that thought, she wandered back behind the sofa with the shotgun resting an inch from her fingers. "What can I do for you?"

"This is Newt." Mercy gestured to the big bearded guy with the flat expression—unless his gaze fell on Mercy. Then he lit up as if she were his world. "And this is Randy. They're both members of my extended family at Enlightenment Fields. And your friends?"

"Trees. And Zyron." She pointed to each. "They're friends of friends, staying over for a few days while they're on a road trip." The lie rolled off her tongue.

Mercy smiled as if she either didn't care or didn't believe Maggie. "We came by, hoping to speak to your grandparents. Would that be possible?"

"I'm afraid not," she said with a shake of her head. "They're down the road a spell right now. If you need something, I can relay the information."

"Our offer to purchase the ranch still stands. We're dedicated to expanding, and are eager to incorporate your grandparents' property with the land we've already acquired."

"They're aware, and the offer was generous. They simply aren't interested in selling. I'm the sixth generation to live on this land. I intend to keep it that way and to raise my kids here, spoil my grandkids here someday, too. So I'm afraid—"

"I appreciate your family's traditions and sentiment, but I don't think you understand," Mercy cut in. "We're willing to go to most any length for this property. We've been patient, but I'm afraid our family is growing too rapidly to wait much longer. We're producing valuable crops and we need more land to harvest. You're a young woman—and with a famous sister. Why not move out west and experience some of that glitz and glamour yourself? A beautiful woman like you could get discovered and have the kind of future most women only dream of."

What a manipulative piece of crap. Sadly, Maggie bet people fell for that stuff all the time. "Are you interested in leaving your land and your family, Mercy?"

"Well . . . no. I've only lived here a bit less than two years. But I've traveled all over the country. You've been in Comfort your whole life. Certainly, you want to see more, get out and truly live?"

"I think life is what you want to make it. All the people and scenery I love are here."

Mercy's smile tightened. "Think of your grandparents. They're getting on in years. Can they continue to keep up with a spread of this size with just you, a foreman, and a few hands? Your grandfather still oversees the breeding and the branding and other very physical activities. He can't do that forever. I mean, you never know when something tragic could happen. Look at Mrs. McIntyre. Out walking her dog, and then . . . just gone."

That filled Maggie with bubbling fury. "She was murdered. So was Mr. Haney. Surely you're not suggesting that you and your 'family' would resort to violence to have my land?"

Mercy's laugh was totally fake. "Goodness, no. I'm simply stating a fact. Most of the folks in Comfort, including your grandparents, aren't young anymore. The majority of the next generation has already moved away for more education and opportunity, a brighter future. No one would blame you for doing the same. As you know, we're prepared to be financially generous. But we need your answer in the next ten days."

"We've already given one. Thank you, but no."

Somehow, Mercy's smile managed to look even tighter. "I meant a different answer. We'll need that in ten days."

"You could wait ten decades and we wouldn't change our minds. This is our land. You can't force us off it."

The slender brunette cleared her throat. "I'd like you to consider all the good we do for this county—"

"As do the Wests. We have been integral members of this community since 1868."

The pretty brunette huffed. "I suggest you reconsider. Or I fear you'll very much regret your decision."

Because Enlightenment Fields would kill them? That seemed to be the intimation. "Are you threatening me?"

"I would never threaten." She did her best to sound completely shocked.

Maggie was calling bullshit. They might not mention violence, but they certainly had no problem carrying it out. "Well, that's good to hear. It wouldn't be very neighborly of you. The Wests have had friends here for decades. The town wouldn't cotton to that."

"I'm simply pointing out that your grandparents should be allowed to slow down in their twilight years and retire someplace with less upkeep. And you might flourish somewhere you can spread your wings and fly. And since Enlightenment Fields is expanding, we could help one another."

"I've heard your spiel. The answer is the same. No."

Mercy's entire body tensed. "I insist you reconsider. It would be best for everyone."

Suddenly, Trees stood and sent the woman a narrow-eyed glare Maggie would not have thought possible from the quiet loner. "She gave you her answer. I think it's best if you go."

Newt apparently didn't like the menace in Trees's expression. He stepped protectively in front of Mercy, nearly eclipsing her, and growled. "Back off."

Zyron rose to his feet, flanking the cultists. "Things are getting heated. It's time for you to leave."

Mercy pressed her lips into a flat line. "Don't forget what I said."

Maggie refused to acknowledge her veiled threat.

With a little huff, the woman turned away in her vastly impractical dress and flounced out the door. The two goons followed her. Randy was last to leave, swiveling and seemingly adjusting his coat, revealing the semiautomatic on his hip.

Fear struck. Yes, she had a shotgun. But would she really be able to use it on a human being? She'd always imagined if she was in a case of shoot-or-be-shot that she could. But she'd rather not find out the hard way.

Beside her, Zyron wasn't playing at all. He pulled his firearm from somewhere behind him and let it dangle beside his thigh. "You and the Wests should simply agree to disagree. It would be best if you understood that you're no longer welcome here."

As she headed to the red convertible, Mercy stiffened. Then she tilted her head and studied Josiah's vehicle with a long, lingering stare. Maggie's heart stopped.

"That truck belongs to Josiah Grant. You know him?" The consternation on her face appeared instantly, her expression as mercurial as a spoiled child's. "Is he here?"

Thank goodness Enlightenment Fields paid the locals very little mind or Mercy would already know that Josiah had been here for days. And she might guess that Maggie knew him in the biblical sense.

While Maggie would love to toss that information in Mercy's face, she didn't dare. "He and I—"

"Have all been trying to get his truck fixed," Trees cut in. "We all have. It broke down nearly a week ago, and the Wests happened on him along the side of the road and towed the damn thing here. As soon as some parts come in, his ride will be good as new."

"I see." Her frown turned into a smug smile, as if that explained why she hadn't seen or heard from Josiah in almost a week. "Well, tell him to come see me once his truck is running again. I've missed him."

The woman's breathy voice, coupled with an expression that made her look like a cat in heat, crawled on Maggie's last nerve. She couldn't bring herself to answer.

"We'll be sure to tell him," Trees promised.

"Thank you." Mercy suddenly looked like the picture of civility again . . . until her gaze fell on Maggie. "In case you're wondering or you have any designs, he's mine. If you touch him, we're going to have a problem."

Oh, we already have a problem. "Goodbye."

The minute she slammed the door behind the creepy trio and locked it, they backed out and drove down the lane. Maggie let out a pent-up breath. But not for a second did she think she'd seen the last of Enlightenment Fields.

Josiah emerged from the kitchen and came around the corner, to her side. "Holy shit. You okay?"

Maggie relaxed when she felt his arms around her. In this moment, her world was right. "Fine."

"You get all that, brother?" Zyron asked.

"Hard to miss their buckets full of crazy. But they obviously mean business."

"And they will resort to violence again." Trees nodded in agreement. "They all but told us that."

"Their threats weren't very veiled," Josiah said.

"What do we do?" She tried not to panic, but having those three on her property, coupled with Mercy wanting her claws in Josiah, put Maggie on edge. "The next time they talk to us, they obviously won't be using words."

"I'm working on a plan. Give me another day or two. I think we have that long."

But probably not much more.

Maggie was glad her grandparents weren't here, but for the first time since coming to live at the ranch, she didn't feel safe.

Two days later, Josiah wasn't terribly shocked when a taxi pulled in front of the ranch and Glenda and Jim West climbed out. Yeah, he'd figured the conversation he'd had over the phone with the older man on Monday night had rattled a few nerves. As much as Josiah had insisted the couple stay in California, Jim was a man's man. He would always do as he damn well pleased and feel it was his responsibility to protect those around him, especially his woman and grandkids.

As Josiah ducked out the front door, the bright January chill and the old man's scowl greeted him. "Hi, Jim, Glenda," He bowed his head to the older woman, then turned back to Maggie's grandfather. "You shouldn't have come home."

"It's my land and my granddaughter you're messing with."

"With all due respect, I have only the best, most honest intentions when it comes to both, as I did my best to explain on the phone."

"As soon as I get in and get Glenda settled, you and I are going to have a sit-down."

"I welcome that, sir."

"You say that now, but I don't think—"

"At least get in the warm house before you start arguing, Jim. Good lord . . ." Glenda tsked and shook her head.

"Yes, dear."

Despite the grim situation, Josiah resisted a smile. Jim didn't bend for much, but he'd do almost anything to make his wife happy.

"Let me help with those bags." Josiah took a makeup case from Glenda and tucked it under his arm, then lifted the two suitcases the driver unloaded near the porch.

"Granna? Papa?" Maggie met them in the foyer, looking stunned. "W-what are you doing here? You weren't supposed to be home until Sunday."

"The weather out west was lovely, but I've had enough of California to last me," her grandmother said as she shut the door on the January chill. "When we told the Santiagos we'd decided to find a commercial flight back to Texas, they said they wouldn't mind returning home early, especially since Javier and Xander have an unexpected meeting in D.C. on Friday. So they flew us to San Antonio before heading on to Louisiana."

"Then we found the least smelly cab we could to bring us the rest of the way. Cost me a hundred and twenty dollars, plus tip!" he grumbled.

Maggie turned to Josiah with a wide-eyed stare that silently asked him what they should do now. Good question.

"I hear Mildred's funeral is Friday morning?" Glenda asked.

"Ten A.M. at the cemetery." Maggie nodded. "Lunch afterward at her house. Her kids are hosting. The viewing is at Schaetter tomorrow evening at seven. Her family will be going back to Oregon on Sunday."

"What will her daughter and son-in-law do with the land? Mildred told me once that Cora said when she moved away that she'd never move back, but that land has been in the family for nearly a hundred years." Glenda looked worried.

Jim scowled. "Don't like the idea of it going to Enlightenment Fields."

"I have no doubt the group is planning to make them an offer. They paid us a visit two days ago to remind us they intend to own most of the county, including this spread." Josiah leveled a serious glance at Maggie's grandfather.

The older man's scowl deepened. "Let's have that talk now."

"Happy to, sir."

"Oh, dear . . ." Glenda looked nervous.

Jim patted her shoulder and kissed her forehead. "Don't you worry, honey. We'll work everything out. You and Maggie have a nice catch-up and talk about dinner tonight. I'll let Josiah fill me in on what we missed before I speak with Sawyer. Everything's fine."

The women drifted toward the kitchen. Josiah watched Maggie go with a lingering stare. Except during the orgasms he'd cajoled her into, she'd been on edge since Enlightenment Fields' visit. She was still distracted, worried. He had to find some way to put an end to this mess so he could figure out, once and for all, where he stood with her.

Locking the front door behind them, Josiah headed through the house with the suitcases. The rest of the place was already secure; he'd seen to that. As soon as he dropped the luggage in the master bedroom, he headed back to the study to find Jim sitting behind his big, rough-hewn desk with a grim expression.

Without being told, Josiah shut the study door and sat across from the older man. "I won't bullshit you. It's not good."

"Boy, I can read a map. I know we're surrounded. I know what those people want. I'll be goddamned if I'm going to sell out."

"Maggie feels the same. My fellow operatives, Zyron and Trees, are working with me on this. We're doing our best, but I fear this matter is bigger than we can handle. We're trying to get the feds involved, to no avail so far. I have reason to believe the cult is up to their eyeballs in all kinds of criminal activity—illegal narcotics, weapons stockpiling, violating child labor laws, assisted suicide . . ."

"And murder." Jim leaned forward. "Don't look surprised I figured that out. Ben Haney didn't fall on a pitchfork, and Mildred McIntyre didn't run herself over with a car. I knew exactly why you and Maggie suggested that Glenda and I visit California. I tried to keep her there longer, but that stubborn woman wouldn't hear of staying. Now we have to think of an alternate plan."

"I don't suppose she'd go out of town again?"

"Not until after Mildred's service."

"Does she know or understand the safety concerns?"

"I tried to be honest without scaring her to death. I think she has this notion that nearly four hundred acres of buffer between us and them will keep the family safe." Jim shook his head. "What I can't understand is where would these cultists come up with the nearly eight million dollars it would take to buy me out?"

Josiah gaped. He'd known the spread was large, but the value of the land staggered him. The Wests were sitting on a fortune, but the man asked a valid question. "I don't know. Sure, they're fleecing the newcomers of all their worldly goods, but they've already purchased much of the county and they have a lot of mouths to feed. I suspect they take donations from outsiders happily. After a little research, I found out they were granted 501(c)(3) tax-exempt status. I don't know how; I never heard mention of religion while I was there, just general spirituality. Maybe that's enough? Not my area of expertise."

"Mine, either."

"I'll call my bosses back in Louisiana and see if we can get someone at the IRS poking into that. We might be able to cripple them financially."

The older man banged a fist on his desk. "Even so, will that be fast enough to help us or will it really stop them for good? They want this land, they know Glenda and I stand in their way, and they've killed before."

Those facts were unavoidable. "You're right. Maggie stands in their way, too. And I have to admit, I'm as worried about her as you are about your wife."

Jim leaned in with a frown. "You still think you're in love with her?"

"No, sir. I know I am. Like I said on the phone the other night, I want to marry her and I want your blessing."

He huffed. "You've known her . . . what? Ten days."

"Eleven, actually." Josiah shrugged. "Doesn't change the fact you've raised an extraordinary woman who's managed to wrap herself around my heart. I understand she needs love, affection, and a gentle but firm hand. If I can persuade her to say yes, she'll be the center of my world. That's a promise."

"And you'll take her off to Louisiana. She'll come home on holidays until Glenda and I kick off. Then Shealyn will have her glamorous life with Cutter in California. Maggie will be entrenched five hundred miles away. What will happen to this land?" He shook his head. "No. What she needs is a local boy."

"With all due respect, she's already ripped through all of them. Not one of them can hold her. I will."

"You think you're strong enough?" Jim challenged.

"I have no doubt. You met anyone else able to do a better job?"

Jim avoided the question, probably because he didn't like the answer. "What about her feelings for you?"

"She hasn't said the words yet, but she's almost there. Another few days, maybe a week . . . Look, I know you're concerned about the land, especially with everything going on, but Maggie's future simply might not be here."

Jim sat back in his chair, steepling his fingers. "If you think that, you don't know Maggie. I want that girl happy. God knows she deserves it after her rough start in life. Would you be willing to settle out this way?"

And do what? He knew next to nothing about ranching. Maybe there were firms in San Antonio who could use his expertise . . . Shit, everything was happening so fast. He had to make life-affecting decisions he'd had zero time to think through. Normally, he'd take a spell to ruminate about the challenges, then do his best to come up with workable solutions. But his personal and professional worlds had never collided like this. How the hell could he decide the rest of his life while worrying about the safety of everyone around him?

"I could look into it. As I sit here now, I can't promise you more without exploring my options."

The older man tapped his thumb on his desk. "I like you. I suspect you understand Maggie's mind better than most of her former beaus. You might even have the will to hold her. Like you, I guess I have some thinking to do."

It wasn't the answer Josiah had been looking for, but Jim wasn't refusing to give his blessing. It was progress.

"Understood, sir. Could I possibly suggest you and your wife think somewhere else—I'm sure Hawaii would be nice this time of year. Maybe you could leave right after Mrs. McIntyre's funeral?"

"Glenda will resist. Neither of us likes being away from the comforts of home, but I think it's time I put my foot down." The older man cracked a smile. "Like Maggie, my wife can be . . . interesting to manage. And once upon a time, I was convinced I was the only man who could do the job. Still am. I'll talk to her."

"It would ease Maggie's mind to have y'all somewhere safe. If you could convince Glenda to vacation for another couple of weeks . . ."

It wasn't a perfect solution by any means. But Josiah had to hope that somehow something would break—he'd get proof of Enlightenment Fields' wrongdoing or he'd get federal help. Something that would bring this situation to a head. None of them could continue this way indefinitely.

The big rancher nodded and stood. "I guess I'd better start catching up around here and preparing to go away again so that—"

The loud crack of a gun, something high-powered, resounded outside and echoed through the house. It had been fired from a long distance; Josiah knew the sound. He jumped to his feet, dread hitting as he heard shouts outside. He was halfway to the patio door before pandemonium erupted. Then he heard a bellowing cry for help, followed by a shrill, distinctly female scream of fear.

His heart stopped.

"Who got shot?" Jim demanded behind him.

So the other man understood that violence had come.

As Josiah shoved his way outside, he dashed across the yard, toward Maggie bent over a prone figure. Cowboys clustered around her, including Sawyer. They offered their help, their shirts—whatever she needed. Others tried to coax her to safety.

Fuck, someone had clearly been hit by the bullet.

Frantically, Maggie pressed down on the supine victim. From a distance, he heard her wrenching sobs. He ran faster.

Finally, a pair of boots beside her shifted left, and Josiah got a glimpse of the shooter's target.

"Glenda!" Jim suddenly moved like a man half his age to reach his fallen wife's side.

Josiah turned and shoved the man back. "Get in the house."

"That's my wife—"

"And an active shooter who probably wants both of you dead. I'll see to this. You can't help her if you take a bullet, too."

He hoped like hell common sense prevailed. He had to get Maggie to cover now. She'd be another good target, and this guy wasn't done. Josiah could feel danger hanging in the air.

With his blood screaming and his lungs burning, he ran and plucked her from the dirt, into his arms. She screamed in protest, kicking and clawing as panic and adrenaline raced through her veins. Carrying her to safety was like hauling a sack of angry cats as he dragged her toward the house.

Then he heard the report of the rifle again.

Josiah hit the ground, covering Maggie's body with his own. A fraction of a second later, a bullet whizzed over his head.

Manual bolt-action rifle. Definitely at a distance, maybe half a mile or more, to the southwest. But this guy had already hit a target once and come close a second time. He was really fucking good, and they couldn't take more chances.

"Let me go. That's my grandmother," Maggie shrieked.

"It'll be you next if you don't get in the damn house. Call an ambulance and comfort your grandfather. I'll see to Glenda."

"But—"

"While you argue, your grandmother is bleeding, and the shooter is setting up for his next shot. Listen, goddamn it!"

Finally, he got her to the relative safety of the porch. Under the overhang, the bricks of the house would shelter them—at least for a few moments.

He shoved her against the wall. "Do you understand what I'm saying?"

"Yes, but . . ." Tears stained her cheeks. She pointed to her grandmother, her whole body shaking.

Josiah understood. Maggie wasn't trained for dangerous situations. She'd probably never been on the receiving end of live fire in her life.

It was typical for people to react without thinking, for their instincts to be less than logical. It said a lot that her first thought was to protect the woman who had raised her, not to protect herself.

"I'll do everything I can. Go! And stay away from windows."

Maggie bit back a sob as she tore into the house. He didn't want to leave her alone and upset, but he had to help Glenda West. Since he'd had medical field training, he would probably be her best chance to survive—if it wasn't already too late.

CHAPTER 15

Maggie paced the waiting room at the hospital in San Antonio. The entire evening had been somewhere between a nightmare and a blur. Her grandmother had been shot. On their ranch. And she was clinging to life. Maggie knew precisely who to blame. Terror would probably set in soon enough. Right now, she was angrier than she'd ever been in her life.

"Come here, baby."

Josiah's quiet demand filtered through her ears and penetrated her brain. Though she'd never liked being told what to do, his voice steadied her because he was coming from a place of concern, not control.

Funny, she had never believed herself capable of real trust. Today, he'd proven she could trust him in virtually any situation. He hadn't wanted to move Granna while injured, but getting her to safety had come first, and he'd risked his own life to do it.

Her heart had been in her throat as she'd watched him lift Granna gently and bring her to the dining room. Once there, Josiah had done his best to curb the profuse bleeding. It had seemed like interminable minutes before Neil had arrived with the ambulance. He and another EMT had struggled to stabilize her grandmother as she'd gone into what Josiah called hypovolemic shock from loss of blood. They'd nearly lost Granna, but Neil had quickly called Life Flight when her blood pressure fell dangerously low, her heart rate skyrocketed, and the bleeding couldn't be stemmed.

While Maggie and her grandfather had been grappling with the sudden, terrible new reality, Josiah had stepped in and arranged for Papa to ride in the helicopter with Granna. Then Josiah had hustled her into his truck and they'd raced to San Antonio. Despite his clothes being covered in blood, he'd expressed zero regard for his own comfort.

On that harrowing, panic-filled trek to reach Granna, Maggie had come to another realization. She'd always believed herself too removed from the people around her to genuinely be attached. Clearly, she'd been fooling herself. If she lost her grandmother, it would utterly devastate her. She'd have a hole in her life she'd never be able to fill.

The same was true of Josiah. She wasn't possibly falling in love with the man; she was already there.

So thankful for his calming presence, she made her way to him on the uncomfortable industrial orange sofa.

He took her hand and gently pulled her into his lap, seemingly unconcerned that her grandfather looked on. "You wearing out the tile isn't going to make your grandmother's surgery go faster or be any more successful."

"I know. But it's hard to just sit and . . ."

Josiah nodded, cutting a stare over to her grandfather. Maggie snapped out of her stupor and looked at Papa. If she was shocked, the poor man was devastated. He'd spent the last forty-five years loving his wife, living with her, working the land with her, through the tribulations of their only daughter's descent into addiction and the joys of watching their oldest granddaughter reach fame. They'd stuck together no matter what. For the first time, Maggie realized that without Granna, Papa would fall apart. And rather than being terrified by the idea of needing or loving someone that much, Maggie ached to open herself to that kind of abiding, never-ceasing devotion.

She mouthed her thanks to Josiah, then turned to her grandfather, settling on the sofa between the two men. "Papa, do you want some water? Coffee? Food?"

"Nothing, thanks. What do you think is taking so long?"

"The bullet missed her heart but penetrated her chest cavity. There are a lot of organs and arteries in there," Josiah pointed out, maintaining low, rational tones. "Repairing that will take time. I'm grateful we could get her to a hospital with a level-one trauma unit so quickly. If there's hope, they'll make it a reality."

"It's been four hours. The dread . . ."

Maggie threw her arms around her grandfather and gripped tight while she did her best to hold herself together. He didn't need her falling apart, but tears stung her eyes, closed up her throat. Only Josiah dropping his steadying touch on her thigh and his quiet, confident words kept her sane.

"Look at it this way: If they'd been unable to recover your wife from the shock, stem the bleeding, and get new blood in her system, she wouldn't have made it this long, and you'd already know the outcome. As terrible as it is, no news is good news for now."

Papa scrubbed a hand down his face, looking as if his world were about to end. "I'm trying to tell myself that."

In that moment, Maggie also realized how much strength she'd taken from her grandfather over the years. He'd been her pillar, her sense of security. He'd never been anything other than stalwart—the very backbone of their family. But for the first time, he needed her strength. She refused to let him down.

With a glance, Josiah promised that she could draw from him for help and support.

Mostly likely, she would need it. Her existence had become hell with the single pull of a trigger, proving just how fragile life really could be. Yet for that moment, Maggie actually felt blessed. Her mother had walked away from her as a toddler. Her father, whoever he was, had never stepped forward to claim his daughter. She'd always felt more or less like an orphan and allowed the corresponding anger and self-pity to erect walls around her heart. Yes, she'd lost out on years of interaction with her biological parents. But she'd been so damn lucky the day her mother had chosen drugs over her daughters because that allowed Maggie to be raised by the two most wonderful, loving people God could have put in her path. She wished like hell she'd spent more years appreciating what she had instead of lamenting what she didn't.

"We have to pray that everything will be all right, Papa. No matter what, we'll have each other. I love you, and that will never change."

Not in a single one of her twenty-three years had she ever seen her papa cry. But his sharp green eyes now swam with tears. He sniffed and blinked, doing his manly best to hold them back. "I love you, too, sweet girl."

Josiah gave her his silent approval with an affectionate squeeze of her knee and a kiss to her crown. Maggie felt the love flowing around her. For once, she didn't fight the ties. Instead, she let them hold her, grateful for the strength they granted her.

Suddenly, Maggie heard the clearing of someone's throat. She started, heart tight in her chest, hoping she'd see a competent doctor in scrubs with a smile of success. Instead, Kane Preston stood in front of them, looking grim.

"Evening, folks. I came as soon as I finished looking for clues in what I suspect was the shooter's nest. Other than to tell you that he cleared out fast, covered his tracks well, and was probably shooting an MK 15, I don't know anything."

Papa trembled as he pressed a kiss to her forehead. "I think I could use a cup of coffee after all. Would you mind getting me one, Mags?"

She'd do anything for her grandfather, but she didn't want to miss a possible update from Granna's medical team. Nor did she want to be out of the loop on Preston's investigation.

Swiveling around, she glanced Josiah's way. He took hold of her hand and brushed a gentle thumb over her knuckles. A silent apology.

"I'll text you if we hear anything from the doctor. Right now, the three of us need to talk about the crime freely without scaring the hell out of you."

Their overprotectiveness sparked her temper. "I already know that Enlightenment Fields tried to kill my grandmother. Facts won't send me into a screaming hissy."

"You're right," he agreed. "But our time to make decisions is limited. I think your grandfather would speak more freely if he didn't feel that he had to protect you at the same time."

Papa gave her a sheepish nod.

Maggie didn't like it, but he was old-fashioned and he had too much on his plate for her to keep arguing. "All right. I'll be back. Coffee for anyone else?"

Josiah and Deputy Preston both said yes, so off she went, trying to block out the mental pictures of her grandmother pale and still and bleeding . . .

In her pocket, her phone buzzed. She pulled it free, wondering if it was Josiah. A glance at the display told her she'd received a text from Dixie.

How's your grandmother?

Of course Dixie had heard the news. She'd probably been working the 911 dispatch desk when the call had come in.

Still in surgery. We're waiting for information.

I'm so sorry. Keep me posted.

Will do.

Gossip is flying through town. What do you want me to say?

Because people would ask Dixie. They always did.

Nothing until we know something. Right now, she's touch and go.

Kk. Sending prayers and hugs!

Maggie pocketed the phone again, her brain circling. Of course an event as monumental as a near-death shooting would heat up the grapevine in Comfort. She hated the thought of gossip about something so life-or-death. But the town tended to be close-knit. Besides the lurid curiosity of some, most of the town's citizens would be concerned. They'd want to offer their support, whether that was vigils at the hospital or batches of homemade cookies. And they'd want to understand.

All that was great, and Maggie appreciated the town's efforts . . . but it bothered her that all their neighbors would know about Granna's condition before Shealyn would. Call her sister and ruin her honeymoon? Wait until she had some information to tell? Or hold off altogether until she and Cutter returned to LA in five days?

She was still deciding when she grabbed the coffee and returned to the waiting room.

As she distributed the disposable cups filled with steaming java, the men drank gratefully without a word. Deputy Preston looked somewhere between concerned and pissed off. He hated Enlightenment Fields and it showed. Papa looked resigned. Maggie had no idea what that expression was about but it worried her, especially when she glanced at Josiah. The resolution there stopped her in her tracks. He was up to something. No, he intended to fight for something.

When he lowered his cup and leveled a glittering gray stare her way, Maggie had a feeling the something he intended to fight for would affect her.

Another half hour slid by without a word from the surgical team. Preston's phone dinged ten times before he swore, then excused himself because Willa Mae had a bobcat in her backyard, scaring the horses and making her house cats hiss. Despite the grim situation, Josiah smiled. The man had an interesting job.

"I have to go. Update me when you've got news?" Kane asked.

Josiah nodded. "Will do."

With a nod, the deputy was gone. Jim excused himself for the bathroom and a walk down the hall. Maggie shared a lingering hug with the older man once more before he left. Josiah was so proud of how much the little hellion had opened her heart today. It would have been so simple to raise those walls against everyone and try not to feel the pain or potential loss of her grandmother. But she'd done exactly the opposite, and he loved her all the more for it.

"What conversation did I miss while I fetched coffee?" she asked once her papa had disappeared.

"We'll talk about it later."

In all honesty, she'd missed a lot, but now wasn't the time. Two conversations, both less than ten minutes. If he followed through, they would change his entire life. Now he had to find the right moment to put his plans in motion.

She sighed impatiently. "I'm not stupid. I put up with that old-fashioned sexist shit because my grandfather is from a different generation and I'm not going to change him, so I make allowances. But I'm not putting up with that from you. What do y'all think you decided without me?"

Josiah sighed. From the beginning, he'd realized that Maggie wouldn't be easily managed. She wasn't looking to a man for direction and she wouldn't be swayed by a commanding voice unless she damn well wanted to be. Why was it that one of her most inconvenient traits was also one of her sexiest?

"I called my boss back in Lafayette. We discussed possible next moves. There's still no movement from the FBI. Logan will check again and he's hoping the shooter situation will make them get off the pot . . . but there's no guarantee."

Josiah didn't want to mention that, as a backup, he might have to go back to Mercy, hat in hand, and tell her he was ready to be the next inductee to Enlightenment Fields—and the first stud in her creepy breeding program. Better to drop that bomb on Maggie only if he had to.

She shook her head in disbelief. "People are suffering."

"But we have no proof. And as awful as your grandmother's shooting is, it's not a federal offense."

"So we have no recourse?"

"Not at the moment." When Maggie started winding herself up again, Josiah gathered her in his arms. "Keep it together, baby. Let's focus on sending your grandmother all the healing vibes we can. Once she's out of surgery and hopefully out of danger, then we'll start figuring everything else out."

"I know. But I don't want you going back to Enlightenment Fields and even talking to that Mercy woman. She's a nut job. She's dangerous."

Josiah didn't disagree with Maggie's assessment. "I'd rather not, but . . ."

He'd do it for the family's safety if he had to. It wasn't just his job anymore; they were his responsibility, especially after his conversation with Jim a few minutes ago.

She didn't look placated. "The idea makes me crazy. Whoever shot my grandmother would probably have shot my grandfather if you hadn't stopped him from running across the yard."

"That's my guess."

"The same way he tried to shoot me."

He should have known she'd put two and two together. "Yep."

"I don't know how we stop these people and make this situation end. There's got to be something . . ."

"I'm working on ideas. Let me——"

"Mr. West?" A forty-something Hispanic man in scrubs approached.

They both stood, and Josiah shook his head. "No. Friend of the family."

"I'm Glenda West's granddaughter, Maggie."

The doctor grimaced. "She's stable. I can only release medical details to James West."

Josiah glanced down the hall just in time to see Jim heading back. When he caught sight of the doctor, he sprinted down the hall.

"Is my wife all right?" the older man demanded, scanning the man's badge. "Dr. . . . . Hernandez."

With a glance, the doctor asked if Jim minded discussing Glenda's medical condition in front of others. When the older man nodded impatiently, the doctor carried on. "She's out of surgery. You've got yourself a fighter. Your wife lost a lot of blood, but once we were able to extract the bullet and repair the nick in her carotid artery, she bounced back. She stabilized well after we stitched her up. We've given her four pints of blood, and she's doing much better. She's in recovery now. You should be able to see her in less than an hour, but she's still in critical condition, so one at a time."

Relief crashed through Josiah. God willing, Glenda would be all right and Maggie's world would remain filled with the people she loved a little longer.

"Thank you, Doctor. What's her long-term prognosis?" Jim asked.

"We'd like to keep her a few days, monitor her blood pressure, her reaction to medication, make sure infection doesn't set in. If all goes well, then tentatively you should be able to take her home Saturday. But we'll be taking this day by day. In fact, hour by hour for the first twenty-four. So if you haven't rested or eaten, you should plan on doing that after you've visited with her. We'll monitor her through the night and let you know if there's any change."

Tears fell down Maggie's cheeks as she clutched her grandfather. He clung to her in relief. Behind her, Josiah gripped her slender shoulders in silent support and kissed the top of her head.

"Whoever gave her the first-response medical care while waiting for the ambulance probably saved her life."

With that, the doctor left, promising to send a nurse over to let them know when they could visit.

Jim broke away from his granddaughter and faced Josiah. "Thank you. For all you've done. Glenda wouldn't have made it if you hadn't acted quickly and—"

"Maggie was already trying to stop her blood loss when I reached your wife's side."

"But you got her to safety, helped arrange her transportation.

You've tried your best to save my land and now my family. I don't know how to repay you."

"It's not necessary. You've already given me the only thing I want." He shifted his stare over to Maggie.

The older man patted him on the back. "And happily."

Then he kissed Maggie on the forehead, a proud, beaming smile stretching across his face.

"Okay." She crossed her arms over her chest. "We're not talking about Granna anymore. What did you two decide without me?"

Josiah didn't answer. It wasn't the right place or time, damn it. Jim merely cleared his throat. "Is anyone else starving? If we've got an hour before we can visit Glenda, I think we should eat."

Maggie tapped her dainty foot on the tile, not swayed in the least. "I'm good for now."

"Well, I'm going to grab a bite before the cafeteria closes."

And that left Josiah very few choices. He could either try to put Maggie off, let her stew while they choked down industrial food one step above an MRE, or he could take her aside and do his best to persuade her to his way of thinking.

"Why don't you do that? Maggie and I can find us some rooms for the night at a nearby hotel. Sounds like we'll be staying in the city for a few days. Then we'll grab some takeout and head back here. By then, it should be time for her to visit Glenda, provided your wife's health and energy hold out."

"Perfect. Um . . ." He frowned. "Mags, we should tell Shealyn something."

"Now that we have something to tell her, probably so."

"We'll handle that, Jim." Josiah took Maggie's hand. "Let's get out of here and call your sister. You and I will talk soon. I promise."

Only slightly placated, she nodded, kissing her grandfather on the cheek and promising to be back as soon as possible.

Josiah's gut tangled in knots as he took Maggie's hand in his and led her toward his truck. The next hour could decide the rest of his life. Dear god, don't let him screw this up.

"Do you want me to tell Cutter what's going on so he can break it gently to Shealyn?" he offered.

Maggie shook her head. "It would be easier, but my sister will be beside herself. The news should come from me."

"All right. I'll ask for some recommendations for nearby hotels and fast food while you chat with her. What time is it in Maui?"

"About one in the afternoon." Maggie looked nervous and frustrated. "I don't want her to cut her honeymoon short when there's literally nothing she can do here except worry."

And there was his girl, being a good sister this time, showing her concern for her loved ones. She might not open her heart often, but when she did, she did so utterly.

"Then tell her that, baby. I'll talk to Cutter if that will help, too. Just know I'm here for you in any way you need."

She clutched his hand. "Thank you. I couldn't have handled today without you."

"You could have. I believe that. But if I made this terrible crap easier to bear, then I'm happy."

"Why are you so perfect?" She frowned as if he was a puzzle she was determined to figure out.

"I'm not, baby. But I love you and I'll do whatever it takes to keep you and your family safe. Remember that."

Maggie nodded, then pulled her phone from her pocket. He gave her a little privacy and headed over to an information desk a few feet away. After some conversation and some helpful advice, Josiah knew where to go. Still, he held back, letting Maggie finish her conversation with her sister. Well, he tried to. Once the tears started flowing again, he couldn't stand to see his girl in distress and closed the distance between them, enclosing her in his arms.

She leaned into him and tried to hold back her sobs. "No. Don't come home. There's absolutely nothing you can do. I didn't want to ruin your honeymoon. But—" She sighed. "You coming to sit at the hospital won't make Granna better any faster. We have everything under— Yes, Papa is holding up fine."

"Baby, why don't you ask Shealyn to let me talk to Cutter?"

A few exchanges later, Josiah heard the fellow operative's voice. "What the hell is going on?"

"Nothing we can't handle. Maggie has been through a lot today. I know Shealyn is probably upset."

"Probably? My wife is crying." And Cutter sounded pissed off.

"Maggie is, too." Josiah didn't mean to, but he heard the warning in his own voice.

Crap, Cutter wasn't even giving Maggie a hard time, and still Josiah felt the need to protect her. He took a deep breath and paced down the hall a spell. Maggie was wound up and she didn't need to hear an argument. Unfortunately, he wasn't as centered as he should be. If he didn't get calm quickly, he'd be worthless to everyone.

"Of course she is," Cutter murmured. "Shealyn is already packing her suitcase. She wants to come home and support her grandfather and sister."

"Please tell her we've got this. I said I'd handle it. It's my responsibility."

"They aren't your family."

"If I play this right, they will be."

It took Cutter less than two seconds to figure out Josiah's intentionally oblique comeback. "You . . . and Maggie?"

"Yep."

"For more than a night?"

"Definitely."

"You're in love with her?"

"One hundred percent, brother."

"Are you planning to ask her to marry you?"

Josiah peered over his shoulder to see Maggie on a metal bench, dabbing at her eyes with a tissue she'd likely procured from the nurses' station at the other end of the hall. "Tonight."

"Holy shit, that's fast."

"Hmm." What else could he say? They didn't have time to wait.

"You sure you want to do that?"

"As I recall, you and Shealyn fell in love in less than two weeks," he reminded quietly. "Are *you* sure?"

"Point taken."

"He's proposing to my sister?" Shealyn demanded in the background. "Oh, god. Does he know that she's always said she's not the marrying type?"

"Tell your wife I'm aware of Maggie's . . . quirks. We're working things out. I need to go. She's exhausted and she needs a meal. If Shealyn wants to help, tell her to call her grandfather. We'll check in tomorrow."

"Keep me posted!" Shealyn shouted beside her husband.

"You got that?" Cutter asked wryly.

"Will do. Keep her in Hawaii. It's for her safety. Y'all try to have a good afternoon in paradise."

"We'll, um . . . think of something."

With a chuckle, Josiah disconnected the call and returned to Maggie's side. "You okay, baby?"

"I feel like I've suddenly run into a brick wall. One minute, I was fine and then . . ."

"The adrenaline wore off and exhaustion set in. You need to eat and you need to rest."

"And we need to talk. Don't think I've forgotten that you're up to something."

"No, ma'am. I know you too well to think it slipped your mind."

With a little smile, he led her to the truck in the attached parking garage. It didn't take long to find the nearby hotel and procure a couple of rooms, then grab some take-out Mexican. After calories and caffeine—and having to put Maggie off ten times—they returned to the hospital and Maggie was allowed five minutes with her grandmother, who managed to squeeze her granddaughter's hand once before falling asleep again.

Maggie emerged from Glenda's room in tears, a mixture that was both happy and sad. Then they all trekked to their respective hotel rooms, which were thankfully located across the hall from each other.

"Let's plan to return by eight tomorrow morning," Jim said. "Hopefully, she'll be stepped down from the ICU by then and the doctor will come around with an update on Glenda's condition."

After Maggie agreed and hugged the old man again, she headed into their room. Jim gave him an encouraging smile and a thumbs-up. Yeah, he hoped all went well. This was hardly the ideal circumstances in which to be proposing, but Josiah wanted Maggie, and Jim had driven a hard bargain for his consent and blessing.

His granddaughter needed a protector. Jim required a security net. So Maggie could not return to Comfort single.

Josiah mentally buckled up. Things were about to get interesting.

"You okay, baby?" he asked as he followed her into the room. When he flipped on the bedside lamp, he found her staring blankly at the wall. "Can I get you anything?"

Slowly, she shook her head. "The old me wouldn't have wanted comfort from anyone. Maybe my sister, but . . ."

He eased onto the bed beside her and wrapped an arm around her shoulders, bringing her close. "I already know you're tough, but you can lean on me."

"I don't even know why I want to so badly. It's not going to change the fact that my grandmother was shot today and could have died. And the second we step foot on the ranch again, someone could try to murder my grandfather."

"Yes." Josiah wasn't going to refute her when he couldn't.

"I don't know how we put a stop to this violence. I don't even know how they figured out my grandparents were home. They'd been there for ten whole minutes. Has someone been watching us this whole time?"

"Hard to say. That's a possibility." So was the fact they might have a mole living on the ranch. Josiah would love to say that he had his suspicions, but the truth was, he just didn't like Sawyer—for a hundred reasons—most of which had more to do with jealousy than any real reason to suspect the asshole.

"How do we make sure Enlightenment Fields doesn't target them anymore?"

This wasn't exactly the opening he'd been hoping for, but it might be the most effective one he got. "Earlier today, I was going to suggest to your grandfather that he sign over the ranch—temporarily—to someone else. Cutter, for instance. After that, we could circulate the news about the transfer of property all over Kendall County. I'd planned to take another visit out to Enlightenment Fields and make sure they knew, too."

"No." Maggie shook her head. "I mean, yes, sign the land over to someone else. That makes sense, and Cutter is a good choice. But you can't go back out there. Seriously, they're beyond dangerous. You don't know what else they might be capable of. And if they've started watching the ranch, they know now that you've been staying there."

"Good point. The thing is . . . Cutter isn't here for Jim to sign the land over to. But I am."

She gaped. "He's willing to give it to you? Right now? Just, like, snap his fingers and magically you own all the land that's been in his family for generations? He barely knows you."

"But he knows what I'm made of. He trusts me, like I think you trust me. Don't you, baby?"

Maggie hesitated. "If you'd asked me a few days ago, I would have told you I didn't trust anyone. But you have been beyond amazing today. It scares the hell out of me to admit that I'd trust you with my life, but I do."

"I know. And I admire you for facing your fears, especially during a time like this. I won't let you down." He took her hand. "I love you."

Even in the dim light of the room he could see her blush. But she didn't return the sentiment, damn it. Josiah tried not to be disheartened. After everything that had happened today, Maggie was overwrought.

"Your grandfather had one condition before he'd sign the ranch over to me. And I wholeheartedly agreed to it, just like I'm hoping you will."

She frowned, clearly puzzled. "What's that?"

Josiah took a deep breath. Here went nothing . . . "Marry me."

CHAPTER 16

Maggie wrenched away from Josiah, her jaw dropping in shock. "You're marrying me for the land? Did you and my grandfather do some old-fashioned bartering, like I'll give you half a dozen goats for six hundred acres and a wife?" When Josiah reached for her again, she leapt away. "Don't touch me until you've explained this shit."

"I'm marrying you for you. I asked Jim for your hand before they left California because I knew you'd never say yes without your grandparents' blessing. Today, he finally gave me their approval."

That decision couldn't have been easy. It spoke volumes about the lengths her grandfather was willing to go to keep his wife safe. But Maggie still had a hundred questions. "What else did he want out of this bargain? How do you two see this working?"

Josiah scrubbed a hand through his hair, then shrugged off his blood-crusted shirt with a tired sigh. She stared at his bare torso and tried not to lose her train of thought. "Legally, the land will belong solely to you and me until the situation is resolved. We'll tell everyone in Comfort, including Enlightenment Fields, that Jim and Glenda have decided to retire, your sister doesn't want the ranch, and the transfer of ownership is permanent. That keeps your grandparents safe, as well as ensures that your sister and Cutter never become prey. When we've untangled this shit and the danger has passed, we'll sign the acreage back over."

"Just like that, you'll return it?" Did he understand what he was saying?

"Jim told me what the land is worth, but I would never take what belongs to your family."

He wouldn't; Maggie could clearly see that. "So . . . let me make sure I understand. The transfer of land is temporary. The marriage, too? Will that be dissolved once this crazy cult is no longer an issue?"

Not that Maggie was insisting they get hitched now, but she wasn't thrilled about speaking vows that were a farce. After the fiasco with Davis, she knew what she wanted—and what she didn't. By god, she intended to get married once and once only.

"No. The marriage will be binding and lasting, baby. You're going to be my wife for the rest of your life, and I'll relish taking care of you. I'm going to do everything in my power to make you love me back."

She tried not to be moved by his words or the sentiment behind his gesture. He was heaping all kinds of risk onto his own back to help her and her family, all while giving her his heart. After the day she'd had, it was hard not to be moved and harder still to fight back tears. But she couldn't overlook one obvious, glaring issue. "This scheme makes me a huge target. When Papa realizes that, he'll back out."

"We've already thought of that and worked through it."

"Meaning?"

"I love you, and I want the opportunity to make you happy. Jim wants his wife safe and to keep the land in the family. Your grandmother would like to see you happily settled. You and I marrying accomplishes all of these goals."

"What about the danger? How do you expect to work around that?"

"God, you're stubborn." Josiah gritted out with a shake of his head. "We'll marry this weekend, probably here at the hospital. Once your grandmother is released, you and your family will stay in San Antonio, very quietly rent a house so she can recover comfortably. I'll go back to the ranch, hang out with Zy and Trees until we've wrapped up Enlightenment Fields. Then, we'll sign the land back to your grandparents, and you and I will start our future together."

"Are you crazy? The most obvious way to 'wrap up Enlightenment Fields' is to cozy up to Mercy by agreeing to her disgusting scheme and . . ." She shook her head. "No. It's ridiculous. It might even be suicide. I don't want you anywhere near that woman, putting your life in jeopardy."

"Maggie, baby . . ."

"Don't 'Maggie, baby' me. What about what I want? No one consulted me or asked my feelings."

"I'm consulting you now. I can't force you to marry me. I'm asking. And once the danger is over, we'll live as man and wife togeth—"

"I hate this plan." She crossed her arms over her chest. "No."

He approached on soft footfalls, shoulders loose, full of swagger, his gray gaze suddenly full of seduction. "C'mon, baby. I want to put a ring on your finger. I want to make you my queen. I want to love you forever."

Why did he have to say things that, under any other circumstances, would make her giddy? "That's not true. You want to tuck me away in a safe place while you put yourself in peril."

"No, I want to live my life with you." He nuzzled her neck in a way he knew drove her completely insane. "The danger is temporary. You and I? We're real and lasting. Give us a chance."

Despite her exhaustion and shock, Maggie was sorely tempted.

Less than two weeks ago, she would have sworn she'd never again entertain the notion of getting married. Now . . . she could picture the two of them taking over the ranch someday, showing their sons and daughters the spread, watching them participate in 4-H, attending the Harvest Moon celebration every October and the Hot Air Balloon Festival in nearby Fredericksburg in late December. They'd teach their children to ride, care for the animals, and respect the old ways while embracing the new.

Of course that meant Josiah had to survive Enlightenment Fields' worst. It meant she was supposed to wait an hour away while he returned to the killing fields of Comfort, putting himself out there as bait while wearing a giant bull's-eye on his back.

"Your plan sucks. If you want to marry me, we're negotiating a better bargain."

"Yeah?" He breathed against the column of her neck, making her shiver once more. "What do you want, baby?"

Against her will, she squirmed against the rise of need. "Stop trying to distract me."

"Who says that's what I'm doing?" He gripped her hips and pulled her closer. "I've just missed you, and you smell good. I want to touch you, show you how much I love you."

"You want to ply me with orgasms, make me lose my mind, and hope I'll give in to your silly plan." And honestly, if she didn't put some distance between them, she might actually agree in a fog of desire.

"Is it working?" He nipped at her ear.

She pushed at his chest. "No. I have conditions of my own. They're nonnegotiable."

"I'm listening." The sneaky bastard reached for the button of his jeans and flicked it open. A moment later, he lowered his zipper with a hiss.

Against her better judgment, Maggie dropped her gaze to his fly. Damn it, she couldn't see more than shadows and the hint of his erection. It had only been twenty-four hours since Josiah had climbed into bed beside her and made her scream his name in ecstasy for half the night. It felt like twenty-three hours too long. This day had been hellish, and while she would have loved to sink into his touch and let him take the world away for a while, the stakes were too high to let herself be derailed.

In the snap of a finger, she peeled her T-shirt off over her head and unclasped her bra, satisfied when his eyes bulged and his body went taut. "First, you're not going to control me with sex. I'm wise to you, and two can play that game."

"I just want to make you feel good," he assured with smooth tones as his palm glided up her waist, to the heavy fall of her breasts before he cupped her and thumbed her nipples.

Maggie bit back a moan as she wrapped her fingers around his stiff shaft and gave him a squeeze. "I want to keep what's between us in bed honest and real. No games. You use sex to manipulate me and it's a definite no from me to your proposal." For good measure, she brushed her thumb over the sensitive head, thinly covered by his boxers. "Are we on the same page?"

He swallowed, clearly shoving down a curse. "Yes."

"Good."

"That won't stop me from wanting to bend you to my will in bed. I'm a Dom, baby."

The man had a point. "You want to coax me into blindfolds or ropes or something else I've never tried, we can negotiate. If you try to use sex to exert your control over me outside the bedroom, I'm not going to take it well."

When she stroked him again, grip firm, a groan tore from his chest as he nodded. "All right."

"I'm glad to see you can be reasonable."

"Always." A sensual groan tore from his chest. "You have to stop doing that or I won't be able to finish this conversation."

The second she eased up, he brushed his lips over hers, then bent, lifted her nipple to his mouth, and curled his tongue around the bud, drawing it deep.

Maggie hissed and held on to him against the dizzying rush of desire. "Now you're messing with me."

"I'm touching you," he whispered against the sensitive tip. "Because I want to. Because I want *you*. Not because I want you to do anything right now except enjoy this."

Against her will, his words and his fingers both caressed her somewhere deep. Maggie's eyes slid shut as she tipped her head back and drank in the sensations.

The man knew how to get to her. From the first moment he'd touched her, he had seemed to understand her body in a way no man had. He'd had the patience and the intuition to learn exactly how to undo her. He'd plied her with pleasure until she'd had no choice but to give herself—body and soul—to him. For the first time in her life, her heart had followed.

Maggie didn't blame him for wanting to protect her. She understood, just like she understood her grandfather doing whatever he had to in order to make sure he didn't lose his wife. Love could make a man do seemingly crazy things.

Funny that she didn't question the fact that Josiah loved her. Their relationship had been fast, heated, full of contention and danger and a whole bunch of drama she'd never expected. But that didn't make the feelings they shared any less real or lasting.

"I will. But first, you need to stop distracting me," she chided, dragging her lips over his hard, wide shoulder. "We're not done negotiating."

"What do you want? We can't get married at the ranch. It's too dangerous."

As much as she wanted to argue with him, he was right. What would stop someone from Enlightenment Fields from heading to the edge of their property and setting up for a kill shot as she or Josiah—or worse, her grandparents—walked to the barn? Nothing. Sure, she wished she could get married in the same place that her sister, her grandparents, and Papa's parents before them had officially joined hands and hearts. But that wasn't a deal-breaker. They could renew their vows at home as soon as possible. Right now was about keeping everyone alive.

"Agreed. But as soon as we're married, you and I will both be returning to the ranch to deal with Enlightenment Fields. Together."

Josiah stiffened and backed away. "No. Absolutely not."

"That's my condition. Take it or leave it."

He released her, gritting his teeth. "You know you can't get married in the barn but you insist on living there when an entire cult is trying to kill you?"

"You want to protect me. I get that. But you have to understand that I want to protect my family. They shot my grandmother—the closest thing I have to a real mom. I want my grandparents to be able to return to their ranch safely and live there happily for as long as they wish. If I'm not there, will Enlightenment Fields really make a move?" She cocked a hand on her hip. "Realistically, what does killing you alone get them? They'll still have to contend with me. I'll still have to return to Comfort to take care of the issue, this time without you. And if you die on the property, that will cast a giant shadow of suspicion over Enlightenment Fields. The bullet that hit Granna might be written off as a hunter's shot gone astray, but if it happens again . . . No one will buy that story twice. And if they resort to offing you on the property, too, law enforcement will start digging deeper, especially after everything else that's gone down in town lately. They'll start finding facts those cultists would rather keep buried. So I don't think they'll risk making a move unless they can solve the whole 'problem.' They're too smart not to understand they're only going to get one chance. And it had better not look like foul play."

"Exactly. If we're together, we're only making ourselves an easier target for them."

"If we're apart, this will drag out and it will be more dangerous. You think they won't find me in San Antonio? Hell, I could go to Paris—France, not Texas—and they'd still hunt me down. We stand or fall together. Safety in numbers and all that—especially with Zyron and Trees at the ranch. If you want me to marry you, that's the deal." She crossed her arms over her chest. "I'm not budging."

A scowl thundered over his face. "Goddamn it, woman. I'm trying to keep you out of this mess."

"Too late. I'm already in deep," she pointed out. "See reason. In Adam Coleman's shoes, you wouldn't so much as twitch unless you knew damn well that you could eliminate every single stumbling block to acquiring the property. Otherwise, the heat would be too hot and their years of work could come crashing down. So we give them a seemingly good target and be as prepared as possible."

"I don't know if I can handle this if you're in danger. Believe me, I'd love to have you by my side but . . ." He shook his head. "But I don't know how I'd function with the terror and struggle your grandfather has endured today. I've always had respect for him, but now it's mad. He's made of fucking steel. I already love you more than I could have fathomed, but how would I live with this tragedy? He's loved her through decades, kids, ups and downs. How is he coping tonight? I don't even know."

Tears pricked Maggie's eyes. Just when she wanted to be really angry with Josiah, he had to say something wonderful. She swallowed a lump of emotion and tried to slow the mad racing of her heart. But she couldn't deny the truth anymore. "I love you, too."

With a groan, he grabbed her and rolled her to the bed. "Really? I feel like I've waited forever to hear those words."

"Really."

"If it weren't for your grandmother's shooting and the need to keep the ranch safe, would you marry me? Would you say yes right now?"

Maggie didn't even have to think. "Yes."

"Baby . . ." He bent to her, his lips covering hers.

They melted together. The impersonal hotel room with its industrial carpet and starched sheets fell away. Only the two of them existed as the rest of their clothes disappeared. His lips traveled her body, exploring. A brush along her collarbones, a lingering graze over the swell of her breasts, a nip at her shoulder. Maggie absorbed him in return. That musky scent she knew so well, the feel of his arms so strong around her, made her feel secure. He enveloped her, surrounded her. With only a kiss, he filled every space inside her, especially her heart.

Josiah Grant had come into her life in a whirlwind of desire and danger, but she already knew he wasn't going to blow back out. She was meant to be with this man. In fact, she couldn't imagine her life without him anymore. She'd dated enough to know exactly how she felt and why he was different from all the others. Long ago, she'd resigned herself to never loving deeply enough to justify getting married. But now . . . she'd love to be Mrs. Grant. Love to share a future with him. Sure, they had a lot to work through. Where they'd live, what life would look like, how many kids they'd want . . .

First, they had to figure out how to stay alive.

They made love like they both knew there might not be a tomorrow. He worshipped her with his hands and mouth, with every touch, every look, every silent promise of forever. She answered, opening herself up to give him every part of her body and her heart as she'd never done with another man. The room might have been dark, but she swore they basked in a glow of love and devotion, backlit by the fireworks of a passion that surpassed anything she'd ever felt. Josiah was *it* for her.

In the back of her mind, a voice of caution tried to raise its head. *What if he's not everything you think? What if he's duping you? What if he leaves you, too?* Maggie shoved the doubts aside. She'd rather endure a broken heart than half-ass their relationship. If he left her . . . well, that was on him. She'd know that she had given them her all.

With her reservations on mute, she answered his every touch, lips mapping his body, learning again where he was hair-roughened and where he was hard-bodied. She drank in his reactions and loved seeing how much she affected him. For the first time in her life, she wasn't getting off on her ability to turn a man inside out. Right now, she simply marveled at how connected she felt to Josiah. They were one. She swore she could hear his thoughts and understood the language of both his joy and desire, even though they didn't speak a word.

Together, they were unstoppable. She had to believe that.

They sprawled across the room's king-size bed, rolling and entwined, exchanging hearts, needs, and promises for the future. He wrung from her body the sort of pleasure that made her gasp and scream, yes. But he also made her cry with the joy of being this close to the man she could probably live without . . . but didn't want to.

Josiah scrambled to find a condom, then joined her on the bed again, eyes serious, face solemn. "I look forward to the day we don't want to protect against pregnancy."

For the first time, she did, too. "We'll make beautiful babies."

He smiled and smoothed the hair back from her face. "We will if they look like their mama."

His words lit her up from the inside. "You're pretty handsome yourself. If our boys take after you, they'll be heartbreakers."

His face turned. "I'm worried."

"I am, too. But like everything else for the rest of our lives, we need to do this together."

Josiah frowned, worry knitting his brows. "My parents, who have been married for thirty-eight years, say that's what marriage is about."

"My grandparents say the same. They're clearly doing something right. We'll get through this together . . . or not at all."

He held her tighter, his gray eyes suspiciously damp as he pressed a kiss to her forehead. "I love you, Maggie."

"Will you show me how much if I promise to show you back?"

His face softened. "Always."

They shared a night full of passion, understanding, and connection. When they fell into an exhausted heap of arms and legs and curled up together in the wee hours of the morning, Maggie knew there was no turning back. Either they would take down Enlightenment Fields and spend the rest of their lives together forever—or they'd die trying.

CHAPTER 17

The next few days were a flurry of activity. Friday morning, Maggie visited Granna, who had been released from the ICU. Josiah was by her side when they told her grandmother they planned to get married. She sent them a loopy, ear-to-ear grin before drifting off to sleep again. Then Maggie and Josiah had obtained a marriage license and found matching wedding bands. Zyron was kind enough to deliver her grandmother's wedding dress from the ranch, which had been heirloomed and stored away years ago. With a last-minute nip and tuck from a local tailor, Maggie had something lovely to wear for her nuptials. Josiah found a ready-to-wear tuxedo rental in his size. Then he called his family, who were thrilled about their wedding . . . but disheartened to get an impossible forty-eight hours' notice before the big event.

The call to his bosses at EM Security didn't go quite as well. Maggie didn't hear the whole conversation, but the fact that Josiah had blown right past the no-no of mixing business and pleasure—granted, she wasn't exactly a client—and straight to putting his life on the line by getting married and refusing more backup didn't set too well with the brothers who owned the business. Through the closed door, she heard Logan's shout, Joaquin's rapid-fire questions, and Hunter's deadly calm logic. Josiah refused to be swayed. His bosses could come to the wedding or not. As for his future at EM, they would talk about that after Enlightenment Fields had been crushed. And if he was dead . . . well, there was nothing to say.

Maggie tried to shove that worry away.

Sunday finally rolled around. From Maui, Shealyn and Cutter had connected to San Antonio through Los Angeles. They looked exhausted after flying nearly twenty hours across five time zones, but her sister refused to miss her wedding. Neither she nor Cutter were thrilled with this plan and had argued vociferously. But Maggie and Josiah hadn't budged. It was as if their night together, wrapped in one another's arms in that impersonal hotel room, had forged their bond into unbreakable steel.

As sunset approached, Shealyn hugged her in the single-stall ladies' bathroom across from the hospital chapel, wearing a pretty off-the-rack cocktail dress they'd managed to find at a nearby department store. "You ready?"

Maggie nodded, despite all her concerns about their safety. "Beyond. I want to marry this man."

Her sister's face softened. "He's ridiculously eager to marry you, too. I'm not surprised he loves you, Mags. I'm shocked by how much you love him. I see it all over your face every time you look at him."

She blushed. "I know. I never saw it coming . . . I thought you were crazy when you fell for Cutter so fast, but I get it now. It just happened. I braced against it. I fought it. I told myself I didn't need or want it."

"And in the end, none of that matters. What's that saying?" her sister asked. "The heart wants what it wants. Lots of people think I'm crazy to have married a 'nobody.' Cutter can't promote the album I signed on for long before *Hot Southern Nights* ended. He can't bring me more readers for the book I'm writing about my experiences on the tumultuous set of the show and the loss of Tower. He won't get me more viewers for the movies I'm negotiating to film. But he can support me and he can love me with his whole heart. At the end of the day, there's nothing I want more." A cloud of concern passed over Shealyn's golden features. "I don't like you putting yourself in danger, though."

"I'm at peace with it. I need to do this. Granna and Papa have given me everything my whole life, even when I behaved less than gratefully."

"If Granna weren't on so many pain meds and she heard this scheme, she'd bless you out."

Maggie smiled fondly. "I know. But she doesn't need this now. She needs to get better. I need to get married. We need to put all this behind us."

"Cutter and I—"

"Have been through enough. Let me do something for once. You and our grandparents have always looked after me, but I'm a woman now. I love and appreciate what y'all have done, but Josiah and I, we've got this."

Shealyn clearly fought tears as she brought Maggie in for a hug. "Just . . . stay safe. I want to be able to hug you when this is all over."

"I will. Now don't you make me cry and ruin my makeup," Maggie protested with a sniffle.

"You look beautiful." Shealyn pressed a tissue to her nose. "Somehow, Granna's dress is so . . . you."

"Despite it coming from a totally different era, it is." The delicate cream-colored lace wrapped around her slender throat and fell in soft ruffles to the tips of her toes. Gathered gypsy sleeves and simple lines accentuated her slender waist. It was modest and classic and somehow exactly what she would have chosen to forever tie herself to the man she loved.

"I'm proud of you, you know. I've worried about you," Shealyn admitted. "When I went to California, I prayed I wasn't leaving you at the worst time, when you were at your most vulnerable. But you've bloomed."

"You and the grandparents had a lot to do with that."

"Maybe. But I think Josiah had a lot to do with it, too."

"He did."

"So no texting your groom to break things off, then diving into your wedding cake and champagne with me this time?"

"Nope. I don't even know what this cake tastes like—and I don't care. We couldn't bring booze into the chapel, so we'll bring some to the hotel tonight and have a toast of our own. Honestly, I don't care that we don't have any hoopla." Well, that wasn't totally true. "I mean, in my heart of hearts, I wish we were getting married in the barn back home with our friends and family around us."

"I know."

"But . . ." Maggie forced a bright smile. "If all turns out well, we'll renew our vows in the barn and have a great big bash with everyone as soon as it's safe."

Shealyn hugged her. "I wouldn't miss it for the world."

"My phone is tucked into my Spanx since I don't have anywhere else to put it." Maggie grimaced. "Can you find yours and tell me how much longer I have to wait?"

Her sister fished hers out with a laugh. "Fifteen minutes. You're actually ready early. For the girl who was even late to her own birth, this is shocking. That's how I know you're eager."

"Stop messing with me, will you?" Maggie pressed a hand to her stomach. "Lord, I'm so nervous. Will you find me something carbonated before I throw up? Then give Josiah this gift from me?" She reached into her bag to pull out a gift wrapped in elegant silver foil paper and a delicate white bow. "Tell him to open it when he's alone."

Maggie blushed just wondering what he'd think of her unconventional gift.

"Sure. I saw a vending machine at the other end of the hall. Be back in five minutes. It will give me a chance to sneak a peek at my husband in a suit." She winked. "And I'll make sure Granna is doing okay."

"Thanks." She squeezed Shealyn's hands. "Thank you for everything."

Her older sister brought her in for a hug. "I love you. You know that."

"I love you, too." Words she'd never returned to her sister, and that made Maggie feel vaguely ashamed.

But today was about looking forward, not looking back. She couldn't change yesterday; she could only do her best to shape tomorrow by being the most loving woman, sister, granddaughter, and wife possible.

"Mom is sorry she couldn't get here quickly enough."

"I know. We talked." Maggie had heard the heartbreak in her mother's voice and now understood that she truly mattered to the woman who had birthed her. They had even shared a long, honest talk about the past where they'd begun to patch up Maggie's hurts. "It's okay. Really. Her traveling here from rural Costa Rica in less than forty-eight hours would require her to defy physics. She promised to visit in the spring. I think it will be good for all of us."

Shealyn squeezed Maggie's hands again, then withdrew a manila envelope from her bag. "I almost forgot. I picked the papers up from the attorney this morning. This outlines the transfer of property and all the conditions, along with what happens to the land should the worst befall you two." Her sister teared up again.

Maggie soothed her with a squeeze to her shoulders, then put the papers in her tote. "Hey, let's not think about that. Today is for happiness."

The peril would come soon enough, she had no doubt.

"You're right. Papa looked them over. He and Granna will sign them after the ceremony. It's exactly the way you and Josiah asked the conditions to be laid out."

"Thanks. I really don't want to know how much you had to pay that lawyer to draw up the papers this quickly."

"It's not important." Her sister waved her away. "What matters is that he came highly recommended and it's done. Unless I can talk you out of this?"

Maggie shook her head. "It's sweet that everyone wants to protect me. But we've been over this. I need to make sure the threat to our family ends. I was standing two feet from Granna when the bullet struck her and . . . I refuse to walk away now and leave this undone."

Shealyn swallowed back more tears. "All right, then. I'll give your gift to Josiah and be back in five or less. Papa will be waiting at the back of the chapel to walk you down the aisle. Then . . . the next time we talk, you'll be a married woman."

"Who would have thunk it?"

"Honestly, not me. Ever."

"Me, either. Now I wouldn't want it any other way. I don't know why I'm so nervous."

"Wedding jitters. I understand, believe me. Let me get you a soda and hand this gift to your enthusiastic groom. Then . . . let's get you hitched!"

The sisters shared one last hug, then Shealyn slipped out of the little bathroom.

Trying to ignore the rolling of her stomach, Maggie turned to the mirror and fixed a face-framing curl; double-checked her loose, up-swept bun; then tucked her bag into the little corner where the hospital's chaplain had assured her it would be safe for the duration of the ten-minute ceremony. From the bathroom counter, she picked up her simple bouquet of cabbage roses in pristine white and shell pink, tossed with sprigs of greenery and tied together with twined ribbons.

She took a steadying breath. Time for the future.

As Maggie let herself out of the little green-tiled space, she drifted into the hall and waited for her sister's return. The chapel was right across the hall, double doors closed. Behind them lay everyone she loved, waiting to see her tie her future to Josiah's. Her heart swelled so much she swore it would burst from her chest.

In fifteen minutes, she would be Mrs. Maggie Grant. And instead of scaring her, the knowledge that Josiah would be by her side, that they would love and cherish each other forever, filled her with sudden zen.

She was more than ready.

From her left, the pounding of footsteps down the industrial hall-way snagged her attention. She turned to find Sawyer barreling her way.

"What are you doing here?" She hoped he hadn't come to start an argument or trouble.

"I was looking everywhere for you. You have to come with me. Josiah, your sister, you grandfather . . . They're all leaving."

"Leaving?" She frowned. "Why? The ceremony is about to start. I don't—"

"The ranch is on fire. The fire department has been trying to stop the blaze for almost two hours, but you know the land has been bone dry lately. The damn wind picked up this morning. We're trying to save everything we can. The animals are safe but . . ."

Icy horror doused her, and she wanted to ask a hundred questions but they didn't have time. "Oh, my god. Okay. So everyone else has already left?"

That didn't make sense to her.

"We have to act fast, and I told everyone I'd bring you with me. There's no time to lose."

Maggie shoved aside her sadness that today wouldn't be her wed-ding day after all and focused on the situation. "Why didn't you call from the ranch?"

"I tried." He raked a hand through his hair. "Your grandparents don't have cell phones and you didn't answer yours."

She couldn't exactly get to her phone right now, not with it tucked into her shapewear.

"All right. I need a minute." She had to grab her bag, text Josiah, decide on a plan.

"We don't have a minute, Mags. If you drag your feet, there will be nothing left to come home to."

Fucking Enlightenment Fields. They had to be responsible for this. They thought nothing of burning her home and all her memories to the ground. And how much would this hurt Granna and Papa? They'd endured so much lately . . .

"Fine. Thirty seconds," she hedged.

Sawyer approached her, shaking his head adamantly. "Now, god-damn it."

Then he grabbed her in a harsh grip with one hand and pressed a needle into her arm with the other. Maggie gasped and tried to scream . . . but her world went black.

Josiah stood at the front of the little chapel, the chaplain by his side, and tugged at his rented tuxedo tie. Despite the fact it was January, the air conditioning blew a cool draft over his face. It didn't help; he was still sweating.

Not in a million years did he think he'd ever face the altar again.

After Whitney, he'd sworn off love and marriage and promises of forever. He had vowed to steer clear of relationships, disappointment, and heartache. All it had taken to break his pledge was for Maggie to explode into his life in a blast of blond hair, sass, and sex appeal. She and her guarded heart had won him over without even trying. And now he stood in front of her family, with his own watching via Face-Time, eager for his bride to walk down the admittedly short aisle so they could promise to share the rest of their lives, in good times and bad, for richer or poorer, in sickness and in health, forsaking all others until death parted them.

At that thought, Josiah began to sweat more. But he wasn't moving from this spot, not until Maggie was his wife.

To his left, Cutter glanced at his watch. Hunter Edgington shifted in his hard plastic chair, then turned to Joaquin, whose big frame looked packed into the small seat as his hazel eyes scanned the sterile room they'd tried to liven up with a profusion of flowers. Logan looked anxious, too. Unsettled. The same feeling that had been plaguing Josiah for the last fifteen minutes. He'd written it off as pre-wedding jitters.

Now, he was rethinking his assumption.

"I'm going to go check on Shealyn and Maggie. They should have been ready by now." Cutter stood and exited the chapel.

Getting ready for a wedding, even one as rushed as this, wasn't an easy process. He knew that. Still, anxiety clawed him. He kept hearing the *tick-tick-tick* in his head that often nagged him during high-stress missions.

"That would be great."

"You doing okay?" his mom asked from the phone.

He pasted on a smile to put her at ease. He knew how terrible she felt that unavoidable responsibilities kept her and his dad at home today. "I'm doing great. Just a little delay. We'll get started shortly."

His mom looked teary-eyed as she nodded. "You look so handsome. Maggie is a lucky woman. I can't wait to meet her."

"You'll love her."

"Since she swept you off your feet, I'm already in awe," his sister Dana chimed in.

Josiah forced a chuckle. "Maggie is definitely something."

It still shocked him how quickly he'd fallen in love with her. Barely two weeks ago, Logan had dropped her name just before Shealyn and Cutter's nuptials, and Josiah had asked who the hell she was. Now, he couldn't imagine his life without her.

Damn it, she needed to finish whatever primping she was doing and hurry into the chapel so he could make her his for good.

Two minutes later, Cutter shoved the door open, carrying a bouquet. Tension filled his face. "I can't find either of them. Just Maggie's bouquet."

Josiah's heart stopped. Two thoughts pelted his brain at once, both totally horrifying. Either he'd been stood up at the altar again or Enlightenment Fields had somehow gotten their hands on Maggie.

"Be right back, Mom," he said into the phone, then dashed down the aisle, acutely aware of everyone watching him.

He remembered this feeling all too well. The déjà vu wasn't pleasant.

No, no, no . . . This couldn't be happening again. Maggie wouldn't have left him. Right? But if she hadn't, the alternative was far worse. If Enlightenment Fields had Maggie, he had no doubt what would happen. The group had proven repeatedly they were capable of murder.

A cold sweat chilled Josiah as he rushed into the bathroom across the hall and found Maggie's tote abandoned on the floor, stuffed full of the legal documents they'd planned to sign after the ceremony, her everyday clothes, and a variety of cosmetics and hair implements. What he didn't see was her phone.

He turned and found Cutter right behind him, wearing a scowl. "Anything?"

"Can you call Maggie?" His phone was on the tripod in the chapel.

"I don't have her number." Suddenly, Cutter's head whipped around toward Shealyn as she glided down the hall, carrying a can of lemon-lime soda and a cup of ice. "Sweetheart, where's your sister?"

"I left her here maybe ten or fifteen minutes ago. She said she was feeling a little queasy. She was nervous as all get-out and asked for a soda. I fetched her one. It took a bit because I made the mistake of dashing into the cafeteria for ice. I ran into three people who recognized me." Shealyn frowned, looking around in confusion. "She didn't say anything about going anywhere."

Josiah's worry deepened. Maggie hadn't needed to go somewhere to find a bathroom or to visit her grandmother. She hadn't gone herself in search of food or drink.

Either she'd left of her own free will or she'd been taken.

"Call her phone," Josiah demanded.

After a shaky nod, the glamorous star pulled her cell phone out of a clutch tucked under her arm and hit the speakerphone. Then ringing filled the small bathroom. Once, twice, three times . . .

"She's not answering," Shealyn remarked unnecessarily when Maggie's voicemail kicked in.

If she'd left him at the altar, the least she could do was answer the damn phone and explain. She knew Whit suddenly, inexplicably breaking up with him had nearly crushed him. Surely, Maggie wouldn't do that to him, too.

"This makes no sense," Shealyn went on. "She was excited. She even asked me to give you a gift." She withdrew a little silver box. "You're supposed to look at this when you're alone."

Maybe so, but he wasn't waiting. If this gave him any clue about where her head was at . . .

Josiah tugged at the white ribbon and tore into the foiled wrapping paper. He lifted the lid on the small box beneath and found a note.

For your eyes only. On our wedding day.
I love you and I can't wait for us to share everything.

He shoved the note in his pocket. Beneath lay a series of photos Maggie had taken of herself and framed for him. They weren't nudes, but they were damn close. Definitely provocative. Definitely vulnerable. Definitely stills he would treasure once she became his wife.

Josiah stared, angling the photos so no one else could see. Thankfully, the others backed away, as if they knew he needed a moment with whatever Maggie had wrapped in the box. As he stared, he struggled to breathe.

Would she really have left him?

Logically, the answer was yes. Whitney had proven that any woman could leave any man without a moment's notice. If there had been signs that their relationship was doomed, he hadn't seen them until the day that woman walked out. And Maggie had a track record of calling off a wedding the day of the big event.

On the other hand, running off without a word didn't seem like Maggie's style. She was the sort of girl who would fight, not hide. Hell, she'd even texted Davis to break off their nuptials the morning of the ceremony and she hadn't loved the guy. Josiah couldn't help but think she'd at least give him the same courtesy.

"When did Maggie ask you to give this to me?"

"Less than fifteen minutes ago."

For him, that cinched it. "She didn't leave me."

"Heavens, no," Shealyn agreed. "She was excited to marry you."

"She loves me. She told me."

Shealyn smiled. "I know. And Maggie never shares her heart like that."

Which was exactly why Josiah knew he couldn't get mired in his past and look at Maggie through Whitney's lens. He had to have faith and believe in her—in them.

"Then where would she have gone? Maybe the better question is, who would have taken her?"

Pounding footsteps down the hall had Josiah's gaze zipping in that direction. Hunter came running with a security guard in tow. Logan and Joaquin were maybe ten seconds behind.

"The guard saw an unconscious blonde in a wedding dress being carried out by a guy in jeans, a western shirt, and boots less than ten minutes ago. When he asked questions, the guy carrying her said the bride had had an anxiety attack and was sleeping off meds. He thought it was suspicious."

Joaquin nodded, his big chest rising and falling. "We found the hospital's security station and fast-talked our way into a still."

Logan whipped out a paper with the grainy image. There was no mistaking the guy's identity. "Sawyer."

"You know him?" Hunter asked.

"My grandparents' foreman." Shealyn frowned. "He and Maggie had a brief fling during her engagement to Davis. It's been over for a while."

"Except he's had a rough time taking no for an answer."

Shealyn's jaw dropped. "You think he'd . . . kidnap her?"

"Clearly, he did." Cutter motioned to the photo.

"Why?"

Possible atrocities lay unspoken in the small circle. Everyone blinked through a terrible silence, and a thousand worries swamped Josiah. He didn't know if Sawyer was capable of rape or murder or . . . god forbid, if he was in league with Enlightenment Fields. He simply knew he had to find Maggie.

Before it was too late.

"We have to go. Split up. Find her. Now," Josiah barked.

"I'll call the FBI again," Logan offered. "Might not net anything, but if Maggie's disappearance is linked to that wacky cult, they should know."

"Joaquin and I can work on the traffic cameras in the area, see if we can pinpoint what direction he took her, while we try to keep your grandparents calm," Hunter said.

"Shealyn and I will head back to the ranch." Cutter grabbed his wife's hand.

"It's dangerous," Josiah reminded.

"I don't care." Shealyn teared up. "She's my little sister. Someone has her and . . . Oh, god. I need to do whatever I have to. We have to find her."

"Okay." Josiah nodded. "I'll head to Enlightenment Fields."

Despite the gapes and gasps, no one protested. They all knew it needed to be done.

"I don't think you should go in alone," Joaquin pointed out. "I'll leave Hunter here and go with you."

"This might be suicide, and your wife is pregnant. Bailey needs you. Besides, I left suddenly over ten days ago. I'll have to sweet-talk my way back in. If I bring someone, they're bound to get suspicious."

"Those fuckers are lethal," Logan pointed out. "If you walk into Enlightenment Fields and Maggie isn't there . . . will you be able to get out alive? Maybe you should rethink this."

"I can't." He shook his head. "Honestly, I don't think Sawyer is smart or determined enough to have suddenly decided to take Maggie from me. He's had weeks. We were falling for each other under his nose and he did nothing. Oh, he got in my face a few times, but he half-heartedly tried to convince Maggie of his feelings. Mostly, he tossed shade in my direction, then slinked away when we both shut him down. So why would he suddenly do something illegal? Most likely because someone put him up to it. I've been thinking lately that Enlightenment Fields had a mole on the inside, and Sawyer seemed the most likely candidate. I had no proof, though. When he did nothing more than flap his jaws, I didn't give a shit about him. But this just got real. I'm going to grab my phone and get the hell out of here. If I don't come back, you all have my paperwork." Wills and life insurance were necessary in their line of work. "You know what to do."

Hunter nodded. "We'll take care of you. We'll call if we get anything. Do the same when you can."

Josiah nodded. "If you find Maggie, and I don't make it out of Enlightenment Fields alive, tell her I love her."

CHAPTER 18

After ditching his tux, Josiah quickly culled through his belongings. The hospital had a strict 30.06 and 30.07, which disallowed fire-arms on the premises, so Zy had brought Josiah his Kershaw retract-able serrated knife. After tying it around his thigh, he left the hospital, flying down the highway toward Comfort and the isolated dirt road leading to the hell of Enlightenment Fields.

His mind raced. If fucking Sawyer was the mole, when had he turned? What had they given the asshole? Had Coleman lured him with the promise of power? Had Mercy pledged him her pussy? Either or both might apply. What would induce Sawyer to turn on Maggie, whom he'd once claimed to have feelings for?

With a scowl, Josiah drove faster.

Going in alone was probably stupid as hell, but he didn't see a way around it. He'd told his parents and sisters that he loved them before ending the video call at the chapel. He hoped that wouldn't be the last time he spoke to them, but he'd do whatever it took to save Maggie.

In the past, he'd volunteered for plenty of dangerous missions deemed suicidal. The difference between then and now? In the past, he hadn't cared if he died. Now, he couldn't get to Enlightenment Fields fast enough because he finally had something—someone—he gave a shit about. He had a reason to live.

He had Maggie.

He'd just turned down the lane to the cult's ranch when his phone buzzed. Josiah answered with a swipe of his thumb. "Cutter. What have you got?"

"A shitstorm. Sawyer is definitely gone from the ranch. Took all his gear, too. Couple of the hands say he left a letter of resignation and bugged out early this morning. Zy says Sawyer confronted him when he headed to San Antonio with the wedding dress on Friday. Then Mercy and her goons stopped by again yesterday morning. Sawyer intercepted them first. Trees and Zy chased them off the property, but they both suspect something happened after that because Sawyer has been acting weird ever since."

Fuck. "So he probably took Maggie to Enlightenment Fields."

"That's the most likely scenario." The ranch's home phone began to ring in the background, and Cutter snarled out a curse. "No, sweetheart. Don't. I'll get it. If it's your grandparents, you can talk to them. Hang on," he told Josiah.

A garbled thud, footsteps, some muted voices, and a few long minutes later, Cutter snatched up the phone. "Sawyer just called, the smug son of a bitch. He definitely took Maggie to Enlightenment Fields."

Josiah's blood turned to ice. "Did he say what they wanted with her? The land?"

"Yep. Jim and Glenda are supposed to sign it over to him. In exchange, Coleman will give them five million."

So the transaction looked legit, not like extortion. "And then they'll release Maggie?"

"In one breath, Sawyer said that was the bargain. But in the next, he boasted that he'd give her everything she could ever want and that she'd never leave him."

"He's fucking delusional, too. She already got him out of her system. And she's never going to want anything to do with the group responsible for her grandmother's attempted murder."

"No shit. Listen. Enlightenment Fields is too big and probably too well armed. You can't go in alone."

"Too late. I'm almost there." He wasn't turning back now, not when he knew Maggie was less than half a mile away. "This can't wait."

But with a ranch the size of Enlightenment Fields, how would he find Maggie? And with armed thugs roaming all over the property, how would he get her out?

His brain was still racing, and Josiah saw at least a hundred flaws in his plan, but he wasn't leaving Maggie there, alone and terrified. He'd figure some way to get her out.

When he pulled up in his usual spot behind the greenhouse and stopped the truck, Mercy approached in her typical white-lace-and-innocence dress. Artless soft brown curls framed her delicate face. Everything about her looked gentle and harmless—except her vengeful scowl and the trio of armed goons surrounding her.

Surreptitiously, he pocketed his phone as he did the same with the keys to his truck, then he stepped from the vehicle, doing his best to look somewhere between surprised and alarmed by his hostile welcome. "Hi, Mercy. What's . . . going on here? I know I've been gone for a while. Damn truck broke down. But I don't think that's a reason to shoot me."

At his forced laugh, her rosy lips twisted with contempt. "Let's not play games. I just heard that you've been staying out at the Wests' ranch since before I met you and that you've been having sex with that whore Magnolia the whole time. You were never here for me. You never wanted me. You only wanted to use me to try to shut us down when all we want to do is live and farm in peace."

Dread rolled through Josiah. Sawyer must have filled her in on everything. The asshole had done that . . . why? To get back at him? So he could have Maggie to himself? Because he was a bitter, spiteful bastard who couldn't stand that he hadn't gotten his way? That the woman he lusted after hadn't wanted him?

"What do you want?" he demanded as Mercy's most devoted goon, Newt, patted him down and divested him of his phone and truck keys. Thankfully, the big guy didn't feel between his legs and find his knife.

She took both in hand with a huff. "You're not even going to deny it?"

"Why? The only words you uttered that aren't true are that Maggie is a whore and you want to live in peace. The rest I'll totally own up to. So, let's drop the pretense and negotiate. What do you want? The Wests' land, right? Let Maggie go, and I will persuade Jim and Glenda to deed it to Coleman," he lied.

"How stupid do you think I am? I've been naive, true. I believed you because I wanted to. But I know better now. Maggie stays until the ink is dry on the deed and it says Adam Coleman's name. Then I don't care what happens to her. I hope she disappears forever."

"Wait a minute!" Sawyer shouted, and Josiah whirled to find the former foreman barreling toward them with a puffed-up scowl. "Don't forget the deal. I lived up to my end of it. I brought Maggie to you and I told you the truth about this asshole." Sawyer thumbed in his direction. "When the Wests sign their land over, Coleman is going to make Maggie a prime sister or whatever he calls it, and he promised to reward me. Maggie is supposed to be mine to touch and breed and whatever else I want."

Mercy turned with a cock of her head. She was thinking. Josiah froze. Uh-oh. Didn't Sawyer see that was dangerous? Clearly not because he sent her a challenging glare, as if willing her to refute him.

"You did everything Adam asked," she agreed. "You should get exactly what you deserve."

With a casual wave of her hand at Newt, Mercy gestured to Sawyer. Half a second later, the big goon withdrew a Glock from his waistband and planted a bullet right between Sawyer's eyes. Shock had barely registered on his face before blood splattered and he crumpled to the ground in a heap, very much dead.

Holy shit. Mercy might not be in charge here, but she was clearly willing to engage in violence to forward Coleman's agenda . . . and whenever it suited her.

She sent an angry gape at the bearded cultist who had pulled the trigger, gesturing to the red splatters across her white lace. "Couldn't you have let me step out of the way first? Now I have to clean up."

"I'm very sorry, my sister." Remorse poured from his voice, as well as a longing that didn't sound very brotherly at all.

She gave an exasperated sigh. "Dispose of the body. Sawyer is no longer of any use to us." Mercy turned her shrewd gaze back to Josiah. "Here's the deal. If you want Maggie to live, come with me."

Maggie woke with her wrists tied behind her and her ankles bound. Sleep tried to drag her under again. Her lids weighed a hundred pounds each. Besides the fact her shoulders hurt and her hands tingled, an urgency to get free she couldn't quite place spurred her.

As she focused, she saw the unfamiliar room around her was empty, except for a rickety chair, a small table, and a bottle of chilled water still fresh with condensation. Maggie frowned. Where was she? How had she gotten here? All she remembered was getting ready for her wedding to Josiah and her heart-to-heart with Shealyn as nerves swamped her. Then . . . nothing. No, Sawyer. Oh, god. A fire at the ranch; everything was burning. She had to get home. But if he'd come for her so she could help fight a blaze, why was she tied up wherever here was?

Suddenly, the door opened. Adam Coleman strolled in. Dread plunged in Maggie's stomach. Had Sawyer brought her to Enlightenment Fields? Was he in league with them?

She scrambled as far from Coleman as she could, scooting across the rustic wooden floor.

"Don't fret, dove. I'm not here to hurt you. And frankly, you have nowhere to go." As he sat in the room's lone chair, his lips lifted in a smile that was almost benevolent. "I'm not an unreasonable man. Bring yourself to me and kneel at my feet. I'll untie you. Then we'll come to a workable solution."

Maggie didn't believe it was that simple for a minute. She wanted to spit in his face and tell him to perform a sexual act on himself in words that most ladies from Comfort would never use. But she didn't. If he was going to untie her, she had to play along.

As she worked her way toward him, Coleman didn't make a move to help her. Instead, he watched from the chair he sat in like a throne, his gaze dissecting, face still, as she wormed across the weathered floor. She lost her balance and nearly fell before struggling to her knees again and closing the distance.

When she reached his side, it was all she could do not to spit in his smarmy face.

"Turn," he commanded.

Though it went against her grain to expose her vulnerable side to the man, Maggie complied. After all, what were her more appealing options? He wanted her grandparents' land. She was a bargaining chip. She'd be no use to him dead—at least for now.

With deft fingers, he plucked at the rope around her wrists. As it came loose, her shoulders eased back into place. Blood rushed to her hands. She moaned in relief. When the sensation and dexterity returned to her fingertips, she bent to untie the binds around her ankles.

"Stop. I'll do that. Up with you." Coleman held out his hand to her.

Touching him rolled fear through her, but he assisted her to her feet with a gentle tug. Maggie expected him to bend to her ankles and release her ropes.

"No. On my lap." He plucked her off her feet and settled her onto his thighs.

She held her tongue—for now—as he smoothed his hand up her shin, over her knee, and continued up, lifting her wedding dress as he did with his unwelcome caress. When the lace bunched around her hips, he petted his way back down her exposed skin, palm gliding over her in an unhurried stroke.

"I'd prefer to find a way to make this arrangement amicable."

His tender voice took Maggie off guard. "W-what do you mean?"

"You have something I very much want. I believe we have something you also desire here at Enlightenment Fields." He twined his finger into the binding around her ankles and gave a tug, reminding her of his power before handing her the nearby bottle of water. "Drink."

She took it with a cautious grip and tested the plastic lid. But the seal hadn't been broken.

Maggie lifted the bottle to her lips and filled her dry mouth. "You want my grandparents' land."

"Very much. I deeply regret that some of my Chosen have taken matters into their own hands in ways I disapprove of. I'm a peaceful man, and my movement is about the nonviolent embrace of our better selves as we open our consciousness and become one with the land and each other. I fear, in their zealousness, they've stepped a toe over the line."

"A toe? They killed people!" Maggie screeched, then clamped her mouth shut. She needed his cooperation, not his defensiveness.

He sighed like the long-suffering parent of an errant child. "They exercised our collective values on a society that doesn't understand. Ben Haney's health had deteriorated alarmingly in the previous six months until he took much more from society than he could ever contribute again, so yes, my followers sent him to his next life."

"And you conveniently bought the land from the county."

"I did. What was done was done, after all." Coleman tossed his hands in the air as if the situation were out of his control. "I regret that it was an unpleasant death, but my followers are used to the Chosen recognizing when they're no longer contributing members of society and sacrificing for the greater good. Apparently, Haney resisted . . . and it did not end well for him."

Maggie felt sick. Yes, the drugs lingering in her system weren't helping, but Coleman's words crawled over her skin. He acted as if one's life ending merely because they were older and had earned some rest sounded not only reasonable but mandatory. "What about Mrs. McIntyre? She was still active."

"I understand your confusion. She was far more physically mobile than Ben Haney. Her death was the result of an unfortunate joyride by some youths in our midst. They've been dealt with."

She didn't want to ask how. On the one hand, they were kids and she hoped their punishment hadn't been death. On the other hand, the teens had obviously been taught hate and violence. What kind of adults would they become?

"Maybe, but you're still buying the land she lived on."

"Again, I cannot undo what has been done, and I see no reason not to benefit from an admittedly unfortunate circumstance."

"And I guess my grandmother fell into that same 'unfortunate' category, too."

"I'm afraid Mercy has been both too eager in ensuring that Enlightenment Fields has all the land we require and anxious about Josiah Grant." He tsked. "To say she was displeased to learn the man she'd planned to give her long-preserved chastity to was already involved sexually with you would be a vast understatement. But I understand."

Coleman began to pet her hair, slowly, softly, lingering at her neck, reaching for her skin beneath. It didn't escape Maggie's notice that he still hadn't untied her ankles and wasn't letting her off his lap.

Did this creep think she was going to have sex with him?

"She was jealous?"

"Yes, but I meant to say I understand why Josiah chose you over her. Mercy is lovely and so very devoted. Her heart . . . She means well, but she carries a bitter seed. I've tried to show her light and love, but she seems determined to harbor hate in a dark corner of herself. It guides her when she doesn't get her way." Coleman plucked at the bindings around her ankles again, toying but not untying. "You are vital, vibrant. According to Sawyer, you don't hoard your chastity while you're waiting for 'the one.' And your most fertile years are in front of you. We will shower you in love and welcome you at Enlightenment Fields."

Because she enjoyed sex and had a working uterus? "This isn't the place for me."

Coleman gave her a benign smile she didn't believe for a moment. "As soon as I have your grandparents' land and I've given them five million dollars in compensation, you're free to leave."

"And you won't harm them again?"

"Of course not. That was never my plan. Your fiancé, however . . ." He shrugged as if this, too, were beyond his control. "I fear he won't fare as well. Mercy already lost her temper with Sawyer. He came to an unfortunate end."

She'd *killed* him? Was that what this freak meant?

Maggie paled. No, she hadn't liked Sawyer much lately but she would never have wished this on him. "Josiah has to walk free from this place, alive and unharmed."

"I hope that's possible. I'm not in favor of more violence. But Mercy is quite angry with him, and I fear his usefulness to her may be at an end. Michael and Marcus are protective prime brothers. According to them, they sensed Josiah's ill intentions all along. They'll help her mete out whatever fate for him she has in mind." Coleman gave her another c'est-la-vie flip of his hand. "I don't know what will happen, but I may be able to sway her . . . with the right enticement."

Here came his pitch. Maggie swallowed down bile because she was pretty sure she knew what he wanted. "What?"

He smiled as if he was pleased that she'd walked into his verbal trap. The hand wrapped around her ankle found its way up her leg and under her skirt until he gripped her hip with a surprisingly harsh hand. The other he lifted to clutch a handful of her hair. "Stay here, join the Chosen, call me your sire. Give your hands, back, mind, heart, and womb to me. If you do, I guarantee Josiah will live and walk free."

If she didn't join these delusional outcasts and surrender herself to Coleman in every way, including letting him use her body and plant a baby in her belly, Josiah would die?

Oh, god . . .

As Maggie struggled to breathe, Coleman pried into her gaze.

Even his slightly tinted glasses failed to hide his unrelenting stare and how unsettled it made her feel.

Instead of kissing her lips, Coleman lifted his face and pressed his lips to her forehead. The gesture seemed fatherly . . . except for his erection against her thigh. She barely managed not to shudder in fear.

Finally, he untied her ankles. "I'll be back in an hour to collect your decision. I doubt it will take you that long to decide whether you want to save the man you sought to marry, but joining us is a commitment. I want you to come to me sure of heart."

Then Coleman set her on her feet and rose, making his way out the door. A loud click in the silence told her that he'd locked it behind him. The ensuing silence unnerved her. How the hell was she going to escape? The room had only two windows, both covered in bars that would be impossible to squeeze through.

Maggie tried to think through her panic. There must be ways out of this, right? Her grandparents would have already called the sheriff. He might bury his head in the sand, but Deputy Preston would act. Granted, he was one man, but maybe he could call someone for backup. Texas Rangers? FBI? Or maybe Josiah's peers would rescue them. Somehow, they'd get them both out alive; she had to believe that.

But Maggie couldn't wait on others; she had to act. No one had searched her while she was unconscious, thank goodness. The hard press of her phone still lay under her breasts, hugged to her body by her shapewear.

With shaking hands, she reached beneath the long skirt of her grandmother's wedding dress, under the spandex garment, and finally came away with her cell. One bar. The signal wasn't great, but it would have to be enough.

Maggie didn't have to think twice about whom to call first. She tried Josiah. If Coleman was lying or bluffing, she was going to find some way out of there as fast as possible and never look back.

After she pressed her most recent call, Josiah's number went immediately to voicemail. In Maggie's memory, he'd never turned the device off—unless he was at Enlightenment Fields. Unless he was with Mercy. Unless he physically couldn't answer.

Maggie didn't want to think about all the reasons he was suddenly unreachable.

Fear clawed a deep gash out of her composure. She tried not to think the worst had already happened to the man she loved. Instead, she hung up and willed her shaking fingers to cooperate as she dialed emergency services.

"911. What's your emergency?"

Maggie sagged with relief. She'd know that voice anywhere. "Dixie? You've got to help me."

"Mags, is that you?"

"Yes. Send someone. Send everyone. I'm at Enlightenment Fields. Josiah is, too. Coleman is holding us hostage. I worry Mercy will kill Josiah."

"Be careful. She's dangerous. I don't think she has any limits when it comes to protecting her sire."

"You're right. And I can't take any more of creepy Coleman. He talks as if he intends to tie me to his bed until I get pregnant."

"Oh, my god. Really?"

"Yes. So send help. Hurry!"

"You have to keep calm. Take deep breaths. You're going to be fine," Dixie advised. "Sharing the sire's bed is an honor. Carrying his seed is an even greater one. Congratulations! Don't waste time talking to me. Embrace your future, my friend."

Then the line went dead.

Maggie stared in horror at the device in her hand. What the hell? Dixie was one of *them*?

Dwelling on that wouldn't help her out of this bind, so Maggie tried to dial her sister. Cutter would be with her. He would know what to do.

Before the call connected, Coleman burst into the room with a regretful shake of his head and wrestled the device from her hand. "Magnolia, I'm disappointed. I would rather have started our conscious awakening together with love, not punishment. But you made that choice of your own free will. And you will regret it."

Then he—and her phone—were gone. The door locked behind him again.

One thing rolled over and over in her head: No one was coming to save them.

CHAPTER 19

It shouldn't have come to this. I told you what I wanted. I explained how life would be." Mercy pointed an accusing finger in Josiah's direction. "And you chose that slut. *You* did this."

Duct-taped to a chair, he glared. She seriously believed that, because he hadn't given her what she wanted, it was his fault she'd resorted to force and violence. It was official; she was from Crazytown.

"You're going to kill me because I didn't jump at the chance to give up my existence and breed innocent babies into this freak show with you?"

Her face drew up tight, eyes narrowed. "You shouldn't cross me. Ben Haney learned that the hard way. All I wanted was his land. He was too old and infirm to work it. I was nice. I smiled. I offered him money. I even assured him I'd take care of every acre he'd ever tended. The stubborn fool refused."

"So you shoved a pitchfork through his chest?"

"That got his attention, didn't it? And he finally came around to my way of thinking." The batshit bitch looked smug.

Mercy might have Josiah duct-taped to a chair right now, but she was deluding herself if she thought he couldn't get out of this scrape. He'd been in worse. One small female without a weapon wasn't going to hold him for long—especially since he still had a knife strapped to the inside of his thigh.

Once he got free, he would subdue her and have her begging for forgiveness in seconds. Then he'd find a way to destroy this whole backward-ass place.

But what about Maggie? She was somewhere on this compound. Could she handle Coleman and live through whatever he dished out?

"Still not interested in being your devoted stud," Josiah tossed back.

Fury flared across Mercy's face, mottling her cheeks. She came at him, claws bared, and ripped his shirt open, sinking her nails into his flesh. She yanked down, scratching away skin, drawing blood. The gashes stung like a bitch.

"Maybe I don't want *you* anymore." Though she snarled the words, Mercy straddled his lap and grabbed his face, glaring into his eyes. Her lips hovered breathless inches above his.

"Liar." For whatever reason, she wanted him bad. "If that were true, you wouldn't be rubbing up against me right now. I'll reconsider if you let Maggie go."

"That's up to Adam. She's with him, and I'm sure they're *very* busy." Mercy cocked a suggestive brow his way.

Since there was no way Maggie would voluntarily have sex with Coleman, dread twisted Josiah's chest. He couldn't stand the thought of that asshole touching her against her will. Even the idea of Maggie hurting physically pained him.

"If you want me, I need to see her. I have to be convinced she's alive and that she'll leave here that way."

Mercy cocked her head, obviously weighing her anger against her desire, when a knock interrupted her ruminations. "What?"

Coleman stepped into the barren room, tugging Maggie in behind him. Josiah breathed a sigh of relief. Thank god, she was alive.

Their eyes met. He ignored the aching need to comfort her and cataloged her demeanor instead, assessing the damage so he'd know how painfully to kill Coleman later. But Maggie looked only slightly mussed. Her elegant twist was gone, her hair now rumpled. Dirt smudged her cheek and dusted the hem of her dress. Her wide eyes glittered with fear of the unknown, but not the horror of brutality.

"Why did you bring *her* here?" Mercy screeched.

"She promised cooperation once she saw proof that we have Josiah and—"

"She's seen him." Mercy gave an exasperated huff, then snapped at Maggie. "He's with me. Sire will keep you busy. I plan to do the same with Josiah. Go!"

"Child, we've spoken more than once about your self-serving ways. And your petulance. Already, you've scratched him. Physical abuse is no way to heal your bruised consciousness. It still sobs with the sins of the outside world. And it's certainly no way to treat your fellow human beings. Perhaps I have misjudged your readiness to bring more Chosen into our flock."

"No." She scrambled to approach Coleman. "I'm ready. I've been ready. I've waited, just as you asked. My womb wails for children to help us grow our future."

"Someday . . ." Coleman shook his head regretfully. "But not now, I think. Magnolia can provide the additional land we seek. She's agreed to come to me willingly if I release Josiah. I'll arrange her First Enlightenment tonight. Once she's embraced the purpose of her future under my tutelage, he will be free to go."

Josiah stared at the other man. So Coleman would let him walk once he'd coerced Maggie into joining his cult and spreading her legs? That was what his words said, but his eyes conveyed something else entirely. The Chosen's "sire" understood perfectly that if Josiah ever got free, he would rain down fire and hell the moment anyone touched his woman. Coleman would have to kill him first, and they both knew it.

"What?" Mercy screeched. "You have women everywhere, at least six children on the way, and—"

"Eight," Coleman corrected. "Fate and fertility have blessed us."

"I asked for this one man. Just one." She stabbed a finger in Josiah's direction. "And you plan to let him go so you can have another piece of ass someone else has already tapped?"

"Mind your tongue," he snapped, teeth clenched. "Unlike him, she brings land we need. And you forget, yet again, my teachings if your first concerns are about satisfying your own desires."

Mercy huffed. "Your first concern is always your own desires. Josiah stays with me or I tell everyone they're being used as guinea pigs to test new strains of our nectar of Rapture before you sell it to shady dealers who spread it to unsuspecting people outside our walls."

"I seek neither harm nor profit. I give the Chosen our nectar so they can celebrate their conscious awakening together. As for those outside, it is my hope that, as nectar crosses the lips of the unclean, they will chose to become one with Enlightenment Fields."

"You make your motives sound so pure. But that's *not* why you give nectar to girls like Susannah and Lilah. What did you do with them after they were under the influence?"

"Neither had elected to join of their own free will, but came to us as children with their parents. Both recently entered their fertile years, and I felt they required special attention to fully understand their own conscious awakening."

"Naked?" she challenged. "Overnight in your quarters?"

That ruffled red-faced Coleman even more. "Your insubordination disappoints me deeply. You imply the worst and willfully misunderstand because you're not getting your way."

Mercy jerked free. "Are you forgetting how you took *my* virginity at fourteen? And I'm hardly the only one. Should I tell the Chosen that?"

Josiah was hardly surprised that Coleman was a sick fuck. But beside him, Maggie gasped.

"I awakened your body and spirit, and you made that something dirty." Coleman shook his head and wrapped vise-tight fingers around Mercy's arm. "Come with me. Now!"

As he dragged the shrieking woman from the room and locked the door behind them, Maggie gaped. "Oh, my god . . ."

Josiah didn't waste a moment on surprise. "Come here, baby. Hurry! Unzip my pants."

"What?" She blinked. "We don't have time for *that*."

"I have a knife strapped to my thigh."

Instantly, she attacked the button of his jeans, then yanked down his zipper. The feeling of her hands brushing his cock, coupled with the adrenaline surging through his veins, roused a predictable response.

"Seriously? Now?"

"Can't help it. You've always gotten to me." He lifted from the chair as much as his bindings allowed. "You okay? Has Coleman hurt you at all?"

She shook her head as she shoved his jeans down. "He's said some creepy shit disguised as enlightenment for my soul or whatever. Sounds like it's not the first time. But he hasn't actually touched me. Yet."

"Good. Pull the knife free—gently. It's retractable. You'll have to grip the backside of the blade with the indentations . . . yeah. That's it. Good." He praised her as she managed to extend the blade. His heart chugged as urgency rode him. "Fasten my pants again in case they come back, then work on my hands."

She managed to redress him, then scurried behind the chair to saw at the tape. "Are you okay, other than that bitch's scratches? I'd like to do the same to her face."

"Fine. Use the serrated side of the knife."

"I am. The tape is thick."

"They won't be gone long."

"I know. What should we do next?"

Josiah wished he knew where on the ranch he'd been taken, but Mercy's brute, Newt, had shoved a hood over his head before leading him wherever here was. He didn't know how deep in the compound they were. He didn't know what they'd be up against if they busted their way out. But he knew they had to try.

"I'm winging this one. But if you can work me free, I've seen guns stashed around this place. If we can get a couple, we have a chance. Any idea where we are?"

"In a house. Coleman led me from one location on the property, which looked like an armory or a bunker, to here. They weren't far apart."

An armory or bunker was bound to have weapons. "Could you get me back there if we busted free from this room?"

"Yeah."

God, he wanted to hug her right now, not only because she was keeping calm and could actually help them escape but because he was so fucking relieved to see her in one piece.

"Good. Sawyer is dead. Mercy had him shot."

Maggie nodded, her fine tremor a vibration against the tape. "I know. He got me into this mess, but I didn't wish him dead."

Josiah didn't feel the same. "Almost done?"

"Nearly. The tape is hanging by a thread. I'd be faster, but my palms are sweating and my hands are shaking."

"Adrenaline. It's hard to control when you're not used to having stress hormones chugging through your system. Take a breath and—"

Suddenly, the flick of the lock filled the room. Maggie shoved the hilt of the blade into his hand, acknowledging silently that he'd have a better chance of forcing their way out of the situation, and jumped beside him as Coleman came through the door again, this time alone.

He studied them, gaze bouncing back and forth suspiciously. "Mercy is now in the company of her brother Marcus. He has a knack for dealing with her . . . difficult moods. Since she's being selfish today, she's earned a period of readjustment and reflection."

Josiah didn't want to imagine how Marcus was recalibrating her behavior. The big, scarred brute looked short on conversation and long on violence. But having her out of the way meant fewer obstacles between him and Maggie and their exit.

"So"—Coleman turned to Maggie and extended his hand to her—"Josiah is very much alive. He'll be set free as soon as you've embraced your First Enlightenment and my teachings. Come with me so we may begin."

She shook her head and stepped back. "He goes free first."

"Maggie . . ." Josiah warned, pushing against the tape with his biceps and shoulders.

It wasn't giving.

Fuck. They needed to stay together for this escape plan to work. She needed to have faith, to trust him.

Something she'd struggled with all her life.

"That isn't possible," Coleman insisted. "Once I've had time to develop your enlightenment and you've embraced the cleansing of your consciousness, along with our mission, he'll be set free."

The stubborn set of Maggie's jaw told him she intended to argue. But Mercy's example had already proven what not to do, so instead of demanding she cajoled, walking toward Coleman with swaying hips. Behind his glasses, the cult leader's eyes flared with interest.

Yeah, she had his number.

"I won't be able to concentrate." Maggie trailed a finger up his arm, and as much as it killed Josiah to watch her seduce this asshole, Coleman's focus on her was utterly intent. "Or, you know, relax until Josiah is safe. Do this one thing for me and—"

"He won't understand you choosing to remain here. Nor will the outside world." The shyster gripped her wrist hard enough to make Maggie tense. "Unless he sees your happiness with his own eyes and relates it to others, they'll view it as coercion. We wait to let him go until you're mine."

It was all Josiah could do not to come out of his chair. He flexed against the duct tape again, felt it stretching, straining to hold him. But with his blood flow restricted and his arms half asleep, he couldn't muster his usual strength.

Maggie cast him a quick glance over her shoulder, toward his arms. A silent question.

He sent back a clandestine lift of his head. Yeah, he'd get free. He'd do whatever necessary to keep her safe.

"Let him go now." She nuzzled Coleman's neck, exhaling hot

breaths onto his neck. "Or I'm afraid you'll find me less than cooperative."

Displeasure darkened the con man's face. "Threats are no way to begin your conscious enlightenment. Surrender yourself to a higher cause, an existence bigger than your own." He glared Josiah's way. "Leave your worldly pursuits behind."

Josiah forced back his gag reflex and waited for Maggie to lure Coleman's attention again.

"It'll be much easier to forget about all the worldly things he showed me over the last few weeks if he's not here," she argued again, this time rubbing her cheek against Coleman's, their lips inches apart.

The perverted fuck began breathing hard. Beneath his black jeans and shiny silver belt buckle emblazoned with the cult's symbol, his cock was hard. Not seeing it was impossible since it was mere feet away, in Josiah's line of sight.

Seeing the two of them so close filled him with rage. He gathered his strength again, flexing his shoulders and biceps, and swallowed a grunt as he shoved against the tape.

The bindings finally gave way.

Granted, his legs were still secured to the chair, but he could work with that. He might even be able to make it an advantage.

Coleman gripped Maggie's nape. "You'll find I can be very persuasive."

"So can I." Josiah rose with the chair still strapped to his legs and whirled around, sideswiping Coleman with the metal legs.

As the bastard stumbled, Josiah grabbed his man bun with one hand and yanked. With the other, he dragged the cult leader against his chest and held the blade to his throat. "You're going to let us both out of here. Right now."

"My nature is peace, and I will not fight you."

Maggie sagged in relief. She thought it was over, but he knew better. Assholes like Coleman always had something up their sleeve.

Right on cue, Enlightenment Fields' sire delivered. "I can't say the same for my devout followers. They will not take kindly to your violent threats and they'll shoot. They have trained for such a possibility."

Unfortunately, Josiah believed him. Using Coleman as a human shield wouldn't work. He might be able to protect his front, but his back would be exposed—as would Maggie—with enemies all around them. Time for plan B.

With a snarl, he brought the hilt of his knife down on Coleman's skull with enough force to render him unconscious. As the man crumpled in his grip, Josiah let the scam artist fall. Then he bent and cut away the rest of his own bindings.

Finally, he had his mobility. Along with his training, he had to believe it would be enough to save them. "Help me restrain him to the chair."

Maggie snapped into action, assisting as he lifted Coleman's dead weight with a grunt. "What now?"

"We're surrounded." Josiah tried to remember the layout of the compound, but without knowing where he was, he didn't know what direction to run. "Have you seen anything that would help us get out?"

"We passed a barn. It held a red Mercedes. It's not far . . ."

"That's Mercy's car. I can hot-wire it. But it's a fucking convertible. Even with the top up, driving it out of here makes us awfully vulnerable."

"That's better than not getting out at all."

True. He just didn't know if they'd make it to the property line alive. Hell, would the flock of crazies stop chasing them when they reached civilization? Probably not. He'd put money on them doing anything necessary to maintain their sect and keep their secrets.

"Any idea how far we are from the main greenhouse? My truck is parked behind it."

"It's at least a football field away, probably more."

That gave him a clue. "When you entered the house, did it have a little kitchen on the right and, on the left, a seating area with a big brown sofa, a fireplace, and a braided rug, minus a TV?"

"Yes."

Josiah should have assumed Mercy would bring him to her lair. "Perfect. Did Coleman walk you upstairs or down?"

It had felt like the latter to him, but basements weren't a typical thing with Texas's shifting soil.

"Down. We're in something that looks like a makeshift cellar."

"Okay." Josiah scanned the room for anything he might use to secure the sect's leader to the folding chair, but the room was otherwise empty. He set the knife aside and shrugged off his shirt, ripping the arms from the body of the garment, then shoved one in Maggie's direction. "You start with his hands, secure them together *and* to the back of the chair, but keep it loose for now. We're only getting out of the room because Coleman thinks he's untouchable. The next layer of resistance will know better."

Maggie gave him a shaky nod and did as she was bid while Josiah bent to Coleman's ankles and secured him with a constrictor knot. As he finished, so did his girl. She stepped back to give him space, and Josiah slotted right in, binding Coleman's wrists with the same treatment. Then he ripped away the collar from his shirt and shoved it in the con man's slack mouth.

"Let's go." Josiah grabbed the knife again.

With a shaky nod, she followed, looking back as if she worried Coleman would jump up and pursue her with deadly intent again, like an unkillable villain in a horror movie. But he sat slumped—and very much a mere mortal—in the rickety chair. He'd probably be out another five minutes at most. Josiah hoped like hell they'd found their escape by then.

He turned the knob slowly, unsure if Coleman had left anyone guarding the door. Sure enough, as soon as he stuck his head out, he connected stares with one of the big brutes he'd seen before, who went wide eyed. No gun today, but he was still armed with meaty fists and meanness.

Josiah pounced, using the surprise to his advantage. With an uppercut to the jaw and a twist of the neck, the thug fell, the snap of his bones still ringing between Josiah's ears.

"Oh, my lord . . ." Maggie sounded shocked.

She knew he hadn't been a Boy Scout, but this was probably her first rodeo with death. It was right in her face, and Josiah couldn't do a damn thing to change that. It unsettled the average person. As much as he wanted to spare her, he couldn't now.

Instead, he pressed a finger to her lips. "Shh."

When he bobbed his head toward the top of the stairs, she nodded. Good. She understood that someone would likely try to take them down at every turn.

When he gestured her behind him, she fell in as he rounded a dark corner. Thankfully, no one stood between him and the cellar door.

"You're good at creeping quietly," he murmured as much to calm her as to hear her voice.

"Hell-raising teenage years. I sneaked out a lot."

Despite the shit they were in, he grinned. He could picture Maggie, determined not to miss a football game, party, or cute guy to flirt with.

"Had to get past your grandparents?"

She shook her head. "I think they'd halfway given up on restraining me by then. But my sister . . ."

His grin widened. He could see Shealyn mommying her. Well, as much as Maggie would have let her.

"Stay close," he said as he grabbed the handle of the knife tightly and reached for the doorknob.

Maggie sidled up to him. "Selfishly, I'm relieved to see you, but I didn't want you to risk yourself for me."

He dropped his grip on the knob and turned to her. If things didn't go well, this might be his last chance to hold her.

"I'm always going to come for you." He wrapped his arms around her. "I'm always going to be there for you. I'm always going to do my best to save you."

"But you're risking your life . . ."

"I love you."

The squeak of the door opening behind him jerked Josiah to attention. He whirled and dragged the intruder down the stairs. Before the door clicked shut quietly, shards of light penetrated enough for him to recognize the face. "Hi, Michael. Come to check on your daddy?"

Darkness consumed the cellar again. Josiah could no longer see the other man's face, but he could feel the zealot's malice.

"Sire might be peaceful and believe the best of all humans. I know better." He sensed more than saw Michael crouch in a ready stance. "I learned to fight young, starting with my parents, all the way to my pimps. I've fought my way through life. I can take care of myself. C'mon. Show me what you've got."

Before Josiah could attack, Michael jabbed. Josiah ducked out of the way in time to avoid the blow, but Michael managed to knock the knife from his hand. It clattered across the creaking floor. *Fuck.*

Michael dove for it, but Josiah stopped him with a roundhouse punch toward the henchman's jaw. Michael grunted but proved he was a fighter because instead of connecting with the goon's face, Josiah only punched air.

God, he fucking hated brawling in the dark. Unable to watch his opponents and dissect their weaknesses to use to his advantage, he was forced to listen for Michael's every movement, his telltale heavy breathing—while struggling to control his own.

Behind him, he sensed Maggie. She might be staying out of the way for now, which was where he wanted her, but he worried. Had Michael spotted her when he'd entered? Figured out that he could use her against him?

"I saw through you, you know," Michael taunted. "I tried to tell

Mercy you were a fraud. But her pussy has some sort of fever for you because she wouldn't listen. I can't wait to kill you and throw your carcass at her feet."

Josiah didn't bother with a response. He merely gritted his teeth and edged to the goon's side. If he could get behind Michael and take him down, another snap of the neck . . . and he'd be doing the world a favor.

Suddenly, Michael lunged, not attacking him but shoving him out of the way. His back hit old wood packed over soft earth. Then he heard a female yelp.

Maggie.

He hurtled himself toward the sounds of scuffling and grunts of strife. But again, Maggie surprised him.

"Motherfucker," Michael croaked out in pain.

That tone of voice was universal. "You kicked him in the balls?"

"I got my knee under there and shoved as hard as I could," she confirmed.

"God, I love you even more."

While Michael was doubled over and helpless, Josiah plowed the bastard's face with his fist. He went down with a satisfying thud. But when he checked Coleman's deputy for a weapon, he came up empty. *Damn it.*

Josiah lifted Michael's dead weight, dropped his inert form on the floor at Coleman's feet, then locked the pair of them inside the little room.

When he turned back, Maggie was right there. Josiah dropped a quick, hard kiss on her lips. "You okay?"

"Fine. You? Your hand hurt?"

Least of his problems now. Fuck, she smelled good. He'd love to stay and linger . . . but they had one chance to find freedom or it would be too late.

Luckily, he didn't have to grope around the floor for the knife. As he took a step, he kicked it with the toe of his boot. Josiah felt around the floor until the hilt filled his hand again. "Onward."

"With you."

Yeah, she was. Behind him, beside him, with him in every way. Josiah refused to let her down. They were going to get out of this.

No one greeted them on the other side of the cellar door. He popped his head above the ridge of the trap door in the floor and found a pair of women bustling in the kitchen, windows wide open despite the frigid day, as they concocted more of their homemade hallucinogenic brew.

Thankfully, neither was difficult to subdue. They willingly went down the stairs and into the spartan cellar with Michael and Coleman. One rubbed her distended belly with a wail when she caught sight of the unconscious men. Sad . . . One of them had obviously impregnated her. Instead of looking at this as her chance to escape, they'd brainwashed her—and a score of others—into believing they were helping the world by breeding more followers.

What would happen to these kids?

With a shake of his head, he locked the door behind the quartet. The rest of the house was empty. From top to bottom, Josiah searched for a phone, the weapons he knew they'd once stashed here—something to aid their escape. But fuck if the place wasn't devoid of both electronics and firearms now.

He peeked out windows to get his bearings and plan an escape route. Gun-toting crazies roamed everywhere. Suddenly, they appeared keyed up. Dread gripped Josiah. Something was going on.

A small group approached a shack about fifty yards away and pounded on the door. Moments later, Marcus emerged, shirtless and scowling and tense. He had no idea what Coleman's henchman had been doing with Mercy, but he doubted it was painless or G-rated.

As an agitated Marcus dragged a shirt over his head, Newt shouted. The others ignored him, pointing toward Mercy's place, then tossing their hands in the air. Had they noticed Coleman's prolonged absence?

Suddenly, Marcus's gaze snapped in his direction. Josiah dodged the second-story window, but it was too late. The flock had seen him, and Marcus was a warrior. Michael might have fancied himself a tough guy, but Marcus actually was. He'd fight mean and dirty and to win.

"We have to get out of here," Josiah snapped. "Let's try the back door."

"There are too many people," Maggie objected, voice low. "They're headed this way."

"We have to make a run for my truck." Thankfully, he kept a spare key in a magnetic box in the wheel well.

"Can we make it?"

"We can only try." Josiah took Maggie's hand and led her down the stairs, past the bathroom that doubled as a greenhouse, and sprinted for the back exit.

He'd like their odds a hell of a lot better if he had a fucking gun. The only good news? Dusk was setting in. Once the sun disappeared, their creep to freedom would be easier.

Except Josiah had a feeling this would be over well before the sun fell.

Gripping the knob and feeling his heart pound, he squeezed Maggie's hand. She had to live. For the first time in years, he was desperate to stay alive, too. He wanted to draw breath, thrive, and grow old simply to spend all his days with her.

He damn well would—if they lived through the next three minutes.

After opening the door, he led Maggie outside, into long shadows against the house. As they inched across the back wall, voices neared, roaring with righteousness and demanding blood.

When Josiah reached the corner, he peered around the side of the house. A pair of shooters headed straight toward them. Behind him, Maggie tugged on his shirt. He didn't dare take his eyes off the approaching duo.

"Baby, we've got company coming."

"They're already here." Her voice shook.

Josiah glanced behind him. Sure enough, another pair of cultists had flanked them, vengeance gleaming in their eyes.

Fuck, fuck, fuck. They were surrounded, four goons each with a gun—and likely more on the way—against two with a single knife between them.

Their odds of survival had gone from shitty to virtually impossible.

One of the approaching duo grabbed his arm and tried to twist the knife out of his grip. Josiah held tight, ready to fight. It was their only chance.

Marcus marched up behind the others and sneered his way. "Not so tough now."

Josiah tried reason—something he doubted Marcus could grasp. "You can't kill us. People know we're here."

The big soldier shrugged, then gestured to Maggie. "She has a purpose, and if she's too much for my sire to handle, I'll be happy to tame her. You? Despite what Mercy thinks, you're expendable. Let's go."

As Marcus gripped his arm and gave a mighty jerk, Josiah yanked down, whirled around, and flipped Marcus over his shoulder. When the asshole landed on his back with a thud, Josiah reached protectively for Maggie. "Fuck you. You're never touching her."

She was safe for the moment, but as Marcus cursed about revenge, the other four pointed their weapons in Josiah's face.

Maggie squeezed his hand. These were his last moments, his last heartbeats, his last opportunity to give her his heart and tell her he was so fucking sorry. He could only hope she endured long enough to escape or until the cavalry arrived.

"Waste him," Marcus spat.

An instant later, a shot rang out, surprisingly distant. Josiah heard the whiz of a bullet on his left, inches from his ear. Then a *thwack*. The thug at his side dropped to the dirt, a neat bullet hole through the middle of his forehead. His brains spilled out from a gaping opening in the back.

Help is here! Thank god they'd come with hollow points.

In the pandemonium, shouting ensued. Josiah dropped the knife and trapped it under his foot as he grabbed the dead man's rifle and butted Marcus in the face with the stock. Coleman's second-string grunted and fell, out cold. Josiah didn't spare a second to celebrate. He simply backhanded the last goon on his left with the butt of the rifle, knocking out a few teeth, along with his consciousness.

Instantly, he turned to defend Maggie, but whoever had sniped the first Chosen had also managed to take out a second. Despite having a weapon, the remaining follower looked young and damn scared now that his posse had all dropped.

Maggie took a handgun from the dead guy at her feet and pointed it at the last cultist. "I won't flinch. Put your rifle down or I'll blow your head off."

Josiah couldn't help but swell with pride at her toughness as he raised his own weapon and backed her up. "And if she misses, I won't. Drop it or die."

With a strangled yelp, the kid released the weapon and raised his hands. "D-don't kill me."

"Then sit down. And don't move a muscle."

What they needed to get out of here was more shade and an insurance policy. This guy wouldn't do, but Marcus would.

At a dead guy's belt, Josiah spied a few pairs of zip ties and tossed them Maggie's way. "Secure them. I'll cover you."

Questions ran across her face, but she nodded, giving him her faith. His heart swelled. God, he was proud of her. She had a million reasons not to trust. Hell, she'd barely learned how. But Maggie had buried her doubts, regardless of the overwhelming odds against them, and put her fate in his hands. Once she had given her heart, she hadn't wavered. He wanted that—and her—forever.

Maggie quickly bound the scared kid's wrists first, then turned to Coleman's lieutenant and restrained them tightly just as the ugly asshole began to come around.

Josiah switched weapons with Maggie, then pressed the barrel of the semiautomatic to Marcus's temple as a whole new posse of Chosen closed in like an armed mob.

"Get us out of here," he growled.

Marcus refused to move. "You're outnumbered."

"Yep, but I have no problem splattering your brains everywhere. Your drones are mindless enough to think you're close to a god and will do anything to spare you. So start walking or I start shooting."

Snarling curses of retribution, Marcus marched forward, spurred by Josiah's prodding.

As soon as they reached an open clearing, the members of the flock stood and stared in slack-jawed astonishment. Horror flared across most faces . . . but not all.

One young woman came forward, cradling her swelling belly, and spit on Marcus. "I hope someone rapes you in prison. Then you'll understand."

The vindication on her face was full of stark pain, and Josiah could only imagine what Marcus and the other perverted misogynists in this hellhole had done to the too-trusting women who had joined looking for utopia and found only debasement and pain. She'd give birth in a few months and have to look at her child by a man she despised for the rest of her life.

No one in the group dared anything stupidly brave as Josiah shoved Marcus toward his truck. He sensed some were afraid, others relieved.

Either way, Enlightenment Fields' reign of terror in Kendall County was over.

"No!" The female screech to Josiah's left had him whipping around to the sound. "You ruined everything. Die, you bastard!"

Mercy charged directly at him, a board riddled with long, rusty nails raised. As she ran closer, she aimed straight for his head. If one of those went through his skull, he'd definitely be done.

In a moment, he weighed keeping Marcus subdued versus defending himself against Mercy. Failing to do both would be fatal, but he only had one gun and could only point it at one person at a time.

Decision made, Josiah whirled Marcus to face the brunt of Mercy's attack. Her eyes flared as she realized too late she would strike her "brother." She tried to freeze and redirect, but Josiah gave Marcus one fatal shove.

The board cracked over the top of the bastard's head. He shouted as nails penetrated his head in multiple places. He gurgled. Blood spurted. Mercy gasped, hands plastered in horror over her mouth. But it was too late; Marcus crumpled to the ground. If he wasn't dead yet, he would be soon.

In the same moment, the report of a rifle resounded at Josiah's side. He half expected to feel the burn of a bullet through his flesh or see Maggie fall to a heap. Instead, she recovered from the recoil of the rifle smoking on her shoulder, watching as Mercy sank to her knees and clutched her bleeding shoulder with an incredulous shriek.

"That's for what you did to my grandmother," Maggie bit out.

Hate spewed across the woman's face as she clutched her sticky red wound. "I hate you—both of you! You'll pay for this."

Behind him, a loud crash signaled the coming of large, rumbling vehicles. Josiah whirled to the sound and spotted a pair of armored vehicles coming toward them, both emblazoned with a trio of familiar letters he was so fucking happy to see.

FBI.

A long line of black SUVs poured in after that, followed by a trio of Hummers from the DEA.

Hot damn.

"I don't think so," Josiah tossed back to Mercy. "You're going to find the inside of a cell, and I'm going to help put you there."

Maggie stepped closer to the brunette and leaned into her face. "You can enlighten your consciousness while you rot behind bars. Josiah is mine. We're forgetting this place—and you. Buh-bye, bitch."

CHAPTER 20

Ten weeks later . . .

"This time, I don't even have to ask if you're ready." Shealyn smiled Maggie's way. "You're a beautiful bride."

Wearing her grandmother's freshly dry-cleaned wedding dress, Maggie hugged her older sister, joy brimming in her heart. "I'm beyond ready to marry Josiah. I'm grateful every day to have my rock, my best friend, my everything in my life."

"After all you've been through, you two deserve happiness."

A lot had gone down since that terrifying dusk at Enlightenment Fields. Marcus had died in the ambulance on the way to the hospital. Michael had tried to flee the compound in the middle of the raid. When he'd been cornered, he'd fired on the agents. They'd shot back, killing him on sight. After that, most of the followers had cooperated with the federal agents; some even seemed relieved to have their freedom and admitted they'd been afraid they'd be killed if they walked out.

Adam Coleman had pleaded guilty to multiple counts of manufacture and distribution of a controlled substance, as well as four counts of statutory rape. He was going down for the rest of his life. For her part in the cult's grand scheme of murder and obstruction, Dixie was going to prison, too. Mercy had done her best to wiggle out of the charges filed against her, claiming she hadn't known about the atrocities at the compound. Josiah and some of the former flock had testified otherwise, as well as affirmed that she'd been the one to order Ben Haney's and Sawyer Getty's deaths. As of last week, she'd been sentenced to thirty years.

In some ways, Maggie pitied the woman, but the victim had become the perpetrator. Her past suffering didn't excuse what she'd done.

"And you're getting married in our family barn after all!" her sister said with a squeal.

"I'm so excited. Everything looks so beautiful. It's nice to have the whole family here."

"Mom is thrilled to see you again."

"It's nice to see her, too." In the past few days, Maggie had let go of her remaining resentment toward the woman who had abandoned her as a toddler. Bitterness took too much energy, and she was too full of love for that now. "Mom looks happy, and I'm happy for her."

Shealyn squeezed her hands. "And Josiah's family loves you."

"They're so amazing. I don't know how excited they are that I'm moving him to Texas . . ."

"Well, not that part, but Granna and Papa are thrilled."

"We want to be here for them as they get older and assume responsibility for the ranch."

Her sister raised a brow. "Is Josiah ready for that?"

"Not quite yet, but he'll learn. In the meantime, he'll work occasional jobs for EM Security. It's a good compromise."

"A very good compromise," Shealyn agreed. "I talked to Joaquin for a few minutes earlier. He was so impressed by all the evidence Kane Preston had stockpiled against Coleman, Mercy, and the rest that he and the Edgington brothers have hired the deputy. Once he moves to Louisiana, he'll pick up the slack around their office now that our husbands are gone."

"That's fantastic! So you and Cutter aren't moving to Louisiana anytime soon?"

"I can't. I have contractual obligations and my career is going too well. Cutter is on board with staying in California for a while, but we're buying a place in Sunset. We'll live there when we can. His mom will move in, help us keep up with the place. Sweeney might be getting older, but she's still a bundle of energy. And it's nice that she doesn't have to wait tables anymore."

"Everything is coming together for us. When we were kids, I never imagined finding such a happy ending."

Shealyn smiled. "All we have to do now is get you down the aisle so you can say 'I do.' Papa is waiting at the back of the barn for you."

"Let's do this."

"No need for a soda to quell your queasy stomach and jangling nerves?" Shealyn teased.

"Nope. Cool as a cucumber." She'd been through too much to sweat the small stuff, and she wasn't nervous about pledging her life to the man she loved. "Not a single doubt that Josiah Grant is exactly the man I'm meant to spend my life with."

"He doesn't have any doubts, either. I can see how much he loves you every time he looks your way."

Maggie saw it, too. "That's how Cutter looks at you."

Her sister nodded with an adoring smile. "Any last-minute gifts you're wanting to give your groom before the ceremony this time?"

"No."

She'd already given him a pair of socks today embroidered with the words IN CASE YOU GET COLD FEET, along with their wedding date. The bottle of whiskey she'd found with a label that read YOU'RE GETTING LUCKY TONIGHT XOXO would be good for a giggle later. But besides their love, the best gift of all was one they'd share forever—and would be born come November.

Maggie had learned that nugget yesterday and couldn't wait to tell her husband—because, yes, they were really getting hitched this time!—that he was going to be a father before Thanksgiving.

"I don't want anything delaying this ceremony," she murmured. "I'm ready to make him mine."

She and Shealyn hugged one last time, then left the house, trekking through the gently swaying grass and spring flowers, now blooming in the April sunshine. Maggie didn't waver or shake. She drank in every moment, more than happy to give her whole heart to Josiah forever. No hesitation. No doubts. No fear that he would leave her. No need to protect her heart.

It was his, just as she was.

When she stepped into position at the back of the barn, Papa smiled down proudly and held out his arm. "You look so beautiful. And I'm so pleased you've finally found a man worthy of you."

Maggie teared up. "I don't say it often enough, but I love you, Papa."

Josiah's sisters filed in and made their way down the aisle in their soft green bridesmaids' dresses. Maggie smiled fondly. They were both very sweet, but Dana was a hoot. Maggie got along with her really well.

Then Shealyn took her place as matron of honor, smiling at everyone, especially her handsome husband, as she made her way to the front of the barn.

Then the bridal march cued up, and Papa patted her hand. Together, they headed down the aisle, past so many familiar faces. She gave a special nod to One-Mile. He might not have been the most popular operator at EM Security, but his expert marksmanship the day of Enlightenment Fields' takedown had been the difference between Josiah's life and death. The big sniper acknowledged her with a nod in return.

Then Maggie was gliding toward the man she couldn't wait to spend her future with. Anticipation gripped her chest when she caught sight of Josiah at the altar beside Cutter and his two brothers-in-law, who also served as his groomsmen.

Their eyes met.

You look beautiful, wife, he mouthed.

Tears welled.

I love you, she said back without a sound.

Finally, she reached Josiah, and Papa gave her hand to her future husband. Her heart melted when she and Josiah joined fingers and squeezed tight. He smiled her way. His gray eyes, which could seem like flinty cold steel, shone silver with happiness today.

"Remember the first wedding we attended together?" he whispered.

She grinned. "How could I forget? You seduced me."

"You did the same to me. Aren't you glad now?"

"Beyond. Ready to get hitched?"

"I'm ready to call you Mrs. Grant for the rest of my life. But I'm not eating any more Lucky Charms."

Maggie giggled. "As long as you never stop loving me, I can live with that."

"Baby, I'm going to be by your side and I'll give you all the love you can handle forever. You never have to worry about that."

SHAYLA BLACK is the *New York Times* and *USA Today* bestselling author of more than seventy novels, including the Wicked Lovers series, the More Than Words series, and, with Lexi Blake, the Perfect Gentlemen series. For twenty years, she's written contemporary, erotic, paranormal, and historical romances. Her books have sold millions of copies and have been published in a dozen languages. An only child, Shayla occupied herself with lots of daydreaming, much to the chagrin of her teachers. In college, she found her love for reading and realized that she could have a career publishing the stories spinning in her imagination. Though she graduated with a degree in marketing/advertising and embarked on a stint in corporate America to pay the bills, her heart has always been with her characters. She's thrilled that she's been living her dream as a full-time author for the past ten years.

Shayla currently lives in North Texas with her wonderfully supportive husband, daughter, and two spoiled tabbies. In her "free" time, she enjoys reality TV, reading, and listening to an eclectic blend of music.